The Reading Lessons

CAROLE LANHAM

IMMORTAL INK
PUBLISHING

THE READING LESSONS BY CAROLE LANHAM

The Reading Lessons

A Novel by Carole Lanham

The Reading Lessons by Carole Lanham

Acknowledgments

Geri Buss, Emily Thoroughman, Jeanie Thies, David Rush, and Curt and Karen Hoffmeister for their early attempts to make my work shine; Leslie Brown, Mike Norris, and Jeremiah Sturgill for their patience, dedication, and guidance in the work of smoothing out the lumps; and Shana Raywood for her superb editing, attention to detail, and faith in Hadley and Lucinda. Big thanks as well to my parents, Gary and Jeannette Kralemann, and to the rest of my family and friends whom I owe all. And to Chris, Jake, and Ellie whose creativity and support never fail to make me look better than I really am.

God bless you all!

THE READING LESSONS BY CAROLE LANHAM

For Jake and for Ellie
The most beautiful, amazing, and beloved works of art
that I've ever had a hand in creating.

❧

Always and forever
For Chris
How lucky I am to be learning life's lessons
alongside the one I love.

"There are darknesses in life and there are lights, and you are one of the lights, the light of all lights."
— *Bram Stoker, Dracula*

The Reading Lessons by Carole Lanham

Table of Contents

THE READING LESSONS BY CAROLE LANHAM

Love her, love her, love her! If she favours you, love her. If she wounds you, love her. If she tears your heart to pieces – and as it gets older and stronger, it will tear deeper – love her, love her, love her!

Charles Dickens
Great Expectations

THE READING LESSONS BY CAROLE LANHAM

Part 1:
Hadley

Beattie's Bluff, Mississippi 1920

Five minutes after Dr. Mangrove announced that Hadley Crump was going to die, Lucinda walked into the bedroom stirring a cup of chamomile with her finger and smiling as though it was Christmas. Mama had rushed off to the kitchen to fix up a pair of healing socks for his feet, leaving Hadley all alone. Lucinda bumped the door shut with her hip and poked that tea-stirring finger in his mouth as though she meant to feed him the whole cup one lick at a time.

"I brought you something," she said, and she wasn't talking about tea. Hadley followed her gaze to the little strip of violet paper on the rim of the saucer. He didn't let himself look at it until her daddy called her off to work on funeral plans.

I could hear the churning sound of her tongue as it licked her teeth and lips, and I could feel the hot breath on my neck . . .

About the time Hadley got to the hot breath part, his fingers let loose, and the words loop-the-looped away with all the devilish momentum of a broken promise.

Had he not been dying at that particular moment, Mama would have spotted the purple scrap on the floor and wondered why Lucinda Browning was writing notes to her seventeen-year-old son. Then again, had he not been dying at that particular moment, Hadley would have tucked the violet paper in his pocket and hid it away like he hid all of Lucinda's secrets.

As it was, he waited with onions in his socks, curious to see which would take him first, Lucinda or his festering wound.

Because Hadley was the cook's son and Lucinda Browning was a Browning, she was careful to return later and search for her note under his bed. "Did you read it?" she asked.

Hadley nodded.

Lucinda balled up the words and pitched them in the stove. With a sigh that seemed to say, *Well that's that then*, she ran her teeth around the curve of his ear. "I'll be back after your mama falls asleep."

A few minutes later, Mama returned in her nightgown, but before she had a chance to fall asleep, Hadley asked her to open up the right-hand door on the washstand.

"There's nothing in here, son," she said. "Nothing but your *Whoops Jar.*"

Whoops Jars were a Crump family tradition that dated back to slave times. For every misstep he made on the road of life, a Crump was obliged to put a nail in his jar to remind himself that a single moment of poor judgment could amount to another nail in his own coffin. Hadley came from a long line of mis-steppers.

"Hand me the jar, Mama, and that box of nails, too."

Mama reached for his jar like it might sprout teeth and chomp off a piece of her.

Some Crumps favored jelly glasses. Others liked a soup can. Hadley's jar was a spiced-fish jar with the word WHOOPS painted across the glass in pale blue egg-yolk tempera. Except for the stink of sardines, it was entirely empty.

The nail dropped with a doleful clink, spun twice, and settled in under the "OOPS". Mama wiped her nose on his blanket and cried her ever-loving heart out.

The First Nail:

It started with the advertisement for *Experienced Negro Cook*. Mama had circled another one in that same paper too. That one said:

WANTED — An active girl to do the general housework of a large family, one who can cook, clean plates, and get up fine linen. — No Irish need apply.

Mama preferred to stick to cooking, but she had a lot of skills. She'd also circled:

Hardy souls wanted for hazardous journey. Small wages, bitter cold, long months of complete darkness, safe return doubtful.

That's how desperate Mama was.

Hadley was a boy of nine back then, and this was their second week looking for work. Mama wasn't taking any unnecessary chances. She'd tucked a lucky cat bone into her apron pocket and spit on her lucky penny before dropping it into her lucky shoe. Browning House was their third stop of the day. Mama really needed that penny to work.

Stop Number One shut the door in her face before she even said hello. Stop Number Two was kind enough to offer an abbreviated explanation regarding Mr. Brampton Tripp's ironclad policy against hiring jigaboos with *skunk babies*. After Stop Number Two, Mama told Hadley to quit looking so white.

Stop Number Three turned out to be a man sitting in a zinnia bed fanning himself with the morning edition of the *Beattie's Bluff Dispatch*. His house was by far the most elegant of the stops. The front porch was flanked by six big white columns, the lot of which happened to be serving at that particular moment as the Coliseum for the great Lucinda Augustus—First Empress of Rome. It was there, in the shadows of the Coliseum, that Hadley first locked eyes with Lucinda's bright monkey-flower blue eyes, and oh what a memorable day that was.

Making yourself look more nigger-colored can be a terrible task when only part of your blood knows how. Hadley was doing his level best, but when he spotted the girl with the crown of leafs on her head, he forgot about trying to be anything but his old mixed-up self. Mama gave him a swat and tried to hide him behind her good blue dress.

"Quit staring," she said.

It was typical of her to make such impractical demands. Once the words were spoken, Hadley wanted nothing so much as to stare at that girl. Beads of consternation popped out on his upper lip. His heart got jumpy. His eyes would not stay put. He tried focusing on the man in the zinnias. Failing that, he dipped his toe in a puddle and stirred it around, trying to get up a whirlpool. Finally, he rolled up his sleeves and checked his arms to see if they looked browner in the sun or the shade. To decide, he had to step back and forth several times. The answer was shade. In the end, it was all too much. Before Hadley knew it, he was shooting looks everywhere. Zinnias, girl. Puddle, girl. Girl, girl.

"Quit!" Mama hissed.

Only once before had Hadley ever attempted a feat more difficult than looking away from that girl, and that had been when he tried to lift a Guernsey with his bare hands based on some misinformation given to him by a fellow called Tibbs Deets, who claimed that a milked cow was lighter than air. He couldn't lift the Guernsey any more than he could keep his eyes off the girl.

She sat, knees apart, on a chipped wicker throne with an embroidered sheet knotted over one skinny white shoulder. Three red letters stood out on her front: l.B.m. Hadley particularly admired her curtain-pull belt. Even though he'd never had a single day of schooling, he knew instantly that the girl was an emperor. His daddy had been a *Heart of the World* salesman and, according to Daddy, *Heart of the World* was the most important, comprehensive, and artistically illustrated book of recent times. Thus it happened that Hadley knew more than his fair share about Romans. He'd looked at the pages with swords at least twenty or fifty times and considered himself an expert.

While Mama and Mr. Browning talked about the fundamental joy of a good Jezebel sauce, the girl looked him over and raised her thumb in the air as though a deadly Spatha were poised at his throat, awaiting her decision. Hadley pretended to watch the little Leafwing butterfly that was fluttering around his foot, but secretly he was watching that thumb.

Before Mr. Browning concluded that he might possibly be able to stomach an Experienced Negro Cook with a half-breed son, Mama had to promise him a pot of Hoppin' John so peppery he'd cry for his mother. She also had to agree to work for a nickel less a day. The Empress was not so easily convinced.

Lucinda Augustus looked from Hadley to his mama, then back to Hadley again. With a royal shake of her butter-yellow head, she slowly turned her thumb down.

CR

"I'd like to write a poem about you, Hadley Crump," the girl said. "But the only words I can think of to rhyme with *Hadley* are 'badly' and 'madly,' and those are awfully sordid words for a child."

Hadley looked around, sure that she must be speaking to some other *Hadley Crump*. It was his first day at Browning House, and he'd been told to collect shoes for polishing. There were five doors on the second floor with shoes lined up in front of them. The first door was open, and a row of tap shoes formed a scuffed black border between the hallway and the girl.

At first, Hadley only noticed the shoes, most of which were so small and so tapped out that they could be of no possible use to anyone as tall as Lucinda Browning. He kicked a pint-sized one with a broken buckle across the floor, and that was when she said his name.

17

Mr. Browning had introduced him to her while Mama was looking over the new Glenwood cooking range, but never in a million years did Hadley think that Lucinda Browning would use his name to his face. A funny thing happened inside his stomach when she said it. If he didn't know better, he would have sworn he'd swallowed a whole lit string of *Atta Boys*.

"How about 'gladly'?" he suggested, for there was a book called *A Girl's First Poetry Journal* spread open on her flowered carpet, and it was clear she was a poet.

"You do look like the glad sort." Lucinda Browning smirked in a way that would have got him slapped.

Hadley knew for a fact that she was nine years old, same as him, but her mouth was at least twenty. She stood with one hip against the chimney of her dollhouse, swigging a bottle of *Miss Loody's Muscle Tonic* like the stuff didn't cost six dollars an ounce. The label on the bottle promised *rounder, more shapely calves*. Hadley wouldn't have dreamed of checking.

"Have these washed." She picked up a pair of bloomers off the floor and threw them at his face. "And I better get them back."

Hadley and his mama had worked for a family called Tweeb before coming to Browning House. A Tweeb who came into a room where Hadley was working would freeze in place and wait for him to skat. The Tweeb boys, Penrod and Pomeroy, had a regular talent for standing stiff as a corpse. They never let on that anyone was being made to pick up their dirty things. That was their system at Maple Lawn. The family communicated through Sargent, the head butler, and Mr. Tweeb would sooner starve than ask a lesser servant to bring him a second helping of turnips.

Standing there with Lucinda Browning's underwear on his head, Hadley tingled with self-importance. He breathed her bloomers in and out against his face as she proceeded to recite The Hadley Poem.

The Hadley Poem
There once was a boy named Hadley
Who wanted a girl very badly
She was out of his reach
But he hung on like a leech

Loving her madly and gladly.

At the time, Hadley thought it nuts that he would ever love any girl other than his mama. Even so, those bloomers made his brain swirl to such a degree that he became convinced the poem was some sort of witchy incantation. Lucinda's underwear smelled like Ivory soap and the deep dark depths of a cedar drawer. He liked them so well, he decided he might never take them off his head.

"Worm!" Lucinda growled, yanking them away.

It was all very queer. Lucinda Browning was wearing a look on her face that Hadley found oddly familiar. It was the same look Uncle Pink got just before he scarfed down a plate of fat pullets at the supper table with such blind rapture that he choked to death with a smile on his face.

Seeing how he was only nine, Hadley promptly forgot about those bloomers until some weeks later, when Lucinda whirled around the toy room while he was building up a fire. "Wheeeeeee!" she cried, taking off like a top. Hadley got so transfixed watching her, he singed off half an eyebrow.

"It's hopeless you know," Loomis Sackett informed him when he caught Hadley watching her one day on her swing. Loomis was the lay-about hoeboy who knew everything there was to know and didn't do much of anything at all. He was ten.

"What do you mean?" Hadley asked. With every pump she made, big whiffs of Ivory soap floated past him, and he was too young as yet to believe that anything was ever hopeless.

"Look at your hands," Loomis said. "You'd muss her up good if ever you got too close."

"Could be I might wash 'em," Hadley said, and he spit in his palm to demonstrate his plan.

"Shoot." Loomis laughed. "You can't never get 'em clean enough for a girl like that. Unless she likes things dirty, you ain't ever gonna do nuttin' bigger than peep at her from behind this hedge."

What Hadley and Loomis didn't know back then was that Lucinda liked things dirty.

CR

Browning House was unique in that it was built around the original log cabin home of Parnell T. Browning, a coal miner who struck it big when he married the daughter of a rich Northerner and opened *Browning & Beeson Coal* in 1822. The house had twin parlors, twin staircases, and twin verandas, but at the center of its fancy, polished heart was a little room with mud-daubed walls. From the start, the log-cabin room was Hadley's favorite in the house.

There was something about that dusty, piney smell that made him go off his tiptoes the instant he stepped from the marble tiles onto the puncheon floor. Lucinda complained that the room smelled like Abe Lincoln, and if anyone even said the words *log-cabin room,* she would sneeze three times. Due to his daughter's allergy, Mr. Browning had ordered the two doors to the room kept shut at all times.

Upon finishing the mansion in 1822, Old Parnell T. hung up his felling axe over the chimneypiece and hammered a plaque on the wall that read: NEVER FORGET WHERE YOU COME FROM. Hadley once over-heard Mr. Browning tell the head butler, Mr. Sweet, that he'd pay any man a hundred dollars who could pry that old sign off the wall.

Apparently, it was connected to the logs in such a way that it threatened to tear the place down if you pulled on it too hard.

"Someday," Mr. Browning said, "I plan to put up real walls in here, buy a velvet settee, and turn the place into a Kewpie-doll room for Lucinda. Every girl deserves a room for her Kewpie dolls."

Lucinda possessed a powerful love for Kewpie dolls.

Hadley's second favorite room in the house was the canning closet turned Cook's Quarters that he shared with his mama and nobody else. At Maple Lawn, they'd had to double up with Mumbling Willodean whose feet reeked of spoilt cheese even on bath day. The canning closet smelled like bread-n-butter pickles and cracked black pepper, and they had themselves a parlor stove, two cots, and a washstand to call their own. Better still, Cook's Quarters was located next to the kitchen instead of behind the washhouse like at Maple Lawn, so there was no getting wet on rainy mornings. Yes indeed, the canning closet was brimming with all manner of peppery warm luxury.

Every day, at five a.m., Mama whistled up her redeye gravy in the kitchen, singing songs and stirring the air with a wooden spoon, happy as a lark. Mama said folks liked a Negro cook to sing, so she'd learned as many Negro songs as she could. It was as important to the job as good cooking because people liked waking to a soulful tune:

> Yo daddy ploughs ole massa's corn.
> Yo mammy does the cooking;
> She'll give dinner to her hungry chile,
> When nobody is a looking;
> Don't be ashamed, my chile, I beg,
> Case you was hatched from a bussard's egg,
> My little colored chile.

Mama was a stern woman when it came to most things, but the bubble of mush and the smell of corn cakes browning in the oven brought out her sunny side. For Hadley, those early hours didn't feel like work, what with Mama singing and spinning from pot to pot, her apron pinched up between two fingers like it was a velvet dress. The house creaked awake with the sound of her voice, creating a comforting symphony of honking noses, slamming doors, and muffled groans. Pipes gurgled behind the striped wallpaper, shuttering the spice bottles. Footfalls thumped overhead. Mama ladled food on the shiny blue plates and poured cups of coffee, bellowing out her niggery songs . . .

> *AIN'T BUT ONE TRAIN RUNS THIS TRACK.*
> *IT RUNS TO HEAVEN AND RUNS RIGHT BACK.*
> *SAINT PETER WAITIN' AT THE GATE.*
> *SAYS, "COME ON SINNER, DON'T BE LATE!"*

Mama always said, "The boss'll notice a mouse squashed in a trap before he'll notice us. We're like the furniture, Hadley. If we do things right, we're a nice comfy chair, and nobody thinks a thing about us so long as we stay comfy."

Well, Hadley wasn't so sure about that anymore. He had a notion he was a bit better than an old piece of furniture. Didn't the boss give them a canning closet?

The kitchen belonged to them, too. That is to say, unless Lucinda Browning was throwing a fit. The kitchen was where Hadley came to learn just how apt Lucinda's empress title really was.

Hadley's mama was what you might call an *Ear Reader*. She could tell all sorts of things about a person by the shape or size of their ears. Hadley, for instance, had little ears. According to Mama, little ears indicated benevolence and kindness. Problem was, they were hemmed in at the lobes, and this meant there was every reason to beware. Small hemmed ears could just as easily signify insanity as benevolence. Lucinda Browning had flat ears. Flat ears signified a coarse nature.

When aggravated, the girl would steer her father into the kitchen and let him have it in front of God and everyone. It didn't matter if Hadley was snapping peas two inches away. If you were Lucinda, the kitchen was where you went to have a tantrum. She would stomp her feet and cry and throw roast beef at the wall while Hadley peacefully snapped his peas.

"I want a new blonde Kewpie doll, and I want it now." Watch out if there were uncooked eggs around. Mama made a certain kind of look sometimes that meant *Hide the honeydews!* "It's bad enough I don't have a mama. How can you expect me to live without a blonde kewpie?"

Mr. Browning was in charge of two hundred coalminers at Browning & Beeson Coal, yet he was weak as a noddle when it came to Lucinda's meat-slinging. "Of course we'll get you a Kewpie. Get your hat, and we'll go over to Merkin's right now and buy you as many Kewpies as you like."

Lucinda would pull a hat from behind her back and off they would go.

Sometimes she hauled her daddy into the kitchen to complain about how much he was ignoring her, or how cruel it was for him to plan a business lunch during their Daddy and Daughter Day, or how bored she was eating the same desserts week after week.

Usually though, it was because Lucinda wanted or needed something on the double. Often she wanted or needed something on the double because her mother died when she was a baby. Regardless of the reason, Hadley and Mama learned to clear away the cutlery when they heard Lucinda coming.

One morning, after she exploded a jar of piccalilli in the name of loneliness, Lucinda looked over at Hadley, who was chipping mud off the foot scraper quite contentedly just then, and loudly declared, "I need a pet!"

She'd torn her father away in the middle of breakfast, but still he gave her a sympathetic smile. "Of course you do, sweet pea. What would you like?"

"Something little," she said. She snapped at Hadley with the miniature riding crop she was so fond of snapping for no good reason. "Something cute."

"Like what?" her father asked.

"Something black. No. Something white. Oh never mind, Daddy. I can get him on my own."

CR

Like the Tweebs before them, The Brownings did not communicate directly with the staff. Mr. Browning spoke only to Mr. Sweet, the head butler, and then simply to say things like, "There's gray mold on my berries!" or "My shoots are bleeding entirely too much sap." Being a wine-man, Mr. Browning was all about his berries.

Likewise, Lucinda did not speak to Flavia or Lemon who did the laundry, but she did sometimes speak to Hadley. Once, she asked him to clean dust off her shoes while they were still on her feet. Another time, she got her hat strings knotted in her hair, and Hadley had to unknot them for her.

"Mind you, I'd never let you touch me if it weren't the strictest of emergencies," she told him as he worked to free the hat.

Later, when Hadley attempted to explain to Loomis what a rich girl's hair felt like (a thousand paper cuts burning up your hands), Loomis informed Hadley that he didn't have a lick of horse sense.

"You want too much," Loomis said. "Even her stupid hair hurts you."

Hadley didn't get miffed like he did when Loomis called him *Crumpette,* on account of his small size, or when he gave Hadley a head-butt for eating the last Jelly Jumble. He understood that Loomis was jealous over the fact that sometimes Hadley wasn't the same forgotten shadow all the other servants seemed to be. On those rare occasions when Hadley stepped into the full light of day, a yearning inside him burned worse than a million paper cuts.

Why shouldn't Lucinda Browning be in love with him? Sure, his skin was black, but wasn't it white, too? Hadley came from a long line of folks who didn't mind coloreds. And yes, he worked for Lucinda's daddy. And yes, he was the son of a cook. But he was the son of a *Heart-of-the-World* salesmen, too. Anyway, he was beginning to think that Lucinda didn't mind coloreds so long as they had a little extra something mixed in. When he was untangling her hat strings, she'd stood so close, a blonde hair hopped off her head and found a new home on his sleeve. That night, he'd laid his shirt across the foot of his bed and left it there untouched for a week so as to delay losing that small piece of her. Lucinda never stood close enough to drop hair on Loomis Sackett. She would never have even asked Loomis to untangle her in the first place, because Lucinda Browning didn't know Loomis Sackett was alive. He was just a chair.

"I bet you don't know what the 'm' stands for in those curly letters she always wears on her clothes," Loomis said to Hadley one day.

"Do you?" Hadley asked.

"Shoot no. I'm just a servant, same as you."

The fact that Lucinda's third initial was information denied to them, made that little "m" seem as delicious to Hadley as a pair of girl bloomers.

"I'm gonna find out," Hadley told Loomis. "Just you watch and see. Someday I'm gonna know all about her 'm.'"

If Hadley had possessed the wisdom to tell his mama about these new paper-cut-sharp yearnings of his, Mama would have said that paper-cut-sharp yearnings were the handiwork of the devil. Because it happened that Mama was the finest proverb-quoter in the state of Mississippi, she would have said something like: *The shrewd man perceives evil and hides, while simpletons continue on and suffer the penalty.*

Mama collected proverbs like she collected Hadley's baby teeth, with a flawless memory for where each one had come from, and what had grown up in its place.

But Hadley didn't tell Mama about his yearnings, and the handiwork of the devil was just too sweet to resist.

Could be it was Bath Day that ruined him. There wasn't a soul in Browning House that wasn't cranky and full of dread on Wednesdays when Lucinda took her bath. The worst of tantrums were thrown on Wednesdays. No matter how hard everyone tried, Lucinda's bath water was never quite hot enough. Gaynell, the Upstairs Girl, had her eye blackened one week by a flying bar of Lifebuoy, and Hadley had to be hoisted up on the shoulders of big brown LeJeune in order to retrieve the bath brush that sailed atop a light fixture one grim Wednesday in November. Loomis had a theory that Lucinda Browning was so ice cold that she could chill scalding water with the stir of her toe.

Because of these tantrums, there was a closet in the back hall so entirely devoted to the storing of pots, one had to step lightly when passing by, lest they wake the dead with all the clank and the clatter. On Bath Day, Hadley would take from the teetering stacks and line the kitchen floor with filled pots for the stove. It was a process, like slop chore, and they could almost do it in their sleep. Mama boiled water until the windows began to drip sweat, then Hadley pulled on the calico mitts that hung on a peg beside the burner and began the first of many tricky journeys upstairs.

The record was twelve pots twelve pots!—to heat a bathtub that was piped with hot water. Hadley would carry the steaming water up the back steps, place it outside the bathroom door, and knock once. Gaynell would then retrieve the pot, and Hadley would hear whoops and groans and hollers all the way back to the kitchen.

Most of the time, he was as irritated as everyone else by the process, muttering fantastic insults in his head with each new skin-melting slosh, but there were some things about Bath Day that Hadley never failed to look forward to. Each time he set the pot on the floor outside the bathroom door, for instance, he

25

would tip his heated red face over the water and watch his reflection spread in ring-shaped ripples across the surface, all the while imagining where that water with his face on it was bound to end up.

It was always the same daydream: because he was the one with a brain and his reflection was just a wavy, see-through thing, Hadley would convince his reflection to trade places with him. In this way, he was able to slip past the closed door into the whirling clouds of Lucinda's bathroom and be poured into the tub. Meanwhile, his tricked reflection would have no choice but to go down for more water.

Hadley could think of worse things than heating up Lucinda Browning's ice-cold bones.

In any case, the baths were a part of their lives now and life rolled along, week after week, in much the same way, with Mama sizing up cling peach cans for water-hauling potential and Hadley saving up any long buttercup-colored strands of hair that happen to fall on his person. Tantrums and Kewpies and redeye gravy filled up the years. And then one day, everything changed.

Lucinda was twelve years old when she broke her leg during a rousing performance of the shim-sham. As a result, the shim-sham was, in part, responsible for a world of trouble in the life of young Hadley Crump.

One afternoon, in a moment of boredom, the bed-ridden girl announced that she was going to teach the servant children how to read.

"I shall begin with Hadley Crump," she said.

The following Monday, Hadley was pulled from egg-pickling and stood up half-dressed on a stool in the necessary. Mama scrubbed until he was sore, squeezed him into tight shoes, and sent him off to Lucinda's room, wetting his hair with a licked thumb as he went.

"Be nice to Miss Lucinda," she instructed.

It was funny she said that.

"I already learnt how to read," he told Lucinda, picking at a loose thread on the corner of her blanket. A lesser boy would have faked illiteracy, but Hadley always bumbled lies and anyway, it didn't occur to him to be anything but honest.

By now he'd been at Browning House long enough to develop a taste for Lucinda's snide ways. Loomis called her *Miss Fancy Pants* and *Bratty Patty* and sometimes *The White Tornado*, but Hadley would rather get a slug from Lucinda than a kiss from any other girl.

"She's too tall for a pipsqueak like you," Loomis tried to tell him, at which time Hadley pointed out that he was exactly mouth-high to *The White Tornado's* bosom. "No wonder you can't see straight," Loomis said.

Now the girl wanted to watch him stutter through some baby primer like a complete imbecile. If only he could! "My Mama taught me with her Bible."

"Thank heavens," Lucinda said. "I hate giving lessons."

"What are we gonna do then?" Hadley asked, praying she wouldn't send him away.

"Well," said Lucinda, "if you'll promise to stop looking at me like you're about to pee your britches, I might just let you join my club."

"Club?" Hadley repeated with an unhappy shudder, for he did not know how to play bridge, or quilt, or dance cotillions, and these were the only clubs he could think of.

"It's a secret club. That means you can't tell anyone about it. Understand?"

"Does it have a name?"

"Of course, silly boy. *Readers of Violent Indefensible Lust and Evil.*"

"That's too long to remember," Hadley said.

"*V.I.L.E.* for short, you dummy. Anyway, it's not like we're going to have stationary. Now go and prize up that floorboard over by the window that has my boot on top of it."

Under the floorboard was a little cranny the size of two books. Hadley was five minutes wiggling them out.

"Finally," Lucinda said, snatching the books from his fingers. "I didn't think I was going get my hands on these until my leg improved." She held up one of the books. "Ever read this?"

Curly-Q letters spelled out the words *Anna Karenina*.

Lucinda laughed. "Of course you haven't. No decent woman would let her son look at such a thing."

"Why not?" Hadley asked, scratching at the curls his mama had spit down.

"Read this part here." Lucinda instructed. She tapped one of the pages.

Hadley read in a careful way, trying his best to sound schooled. Having nothing but the Bible to read, he was better with *impenitent* or *Amalekite* or *collop* than he was with non-Christian words.

And as the murderer, with fury, and, as it were, with passion, falls on the body, and drags it, and hacks at it—so he covered her face and shoulders with kisses.

"Filthy, isn't it?" Lucinda sniggered.

"Is it?"

"Yes, you little nimrod. Anna Karenina is a married woman, and she isn't married to the man who is murdering her with kisses. This is disgraceful, Hadley."

"Should I put it back?"

"Not on your life. We're going to read every unsavory word of it, and there's going to be a test, too."

"But I already told you, I read just fine."

Lucinda, perhaps the world's most accomplished sigher, sighed expertly. "Looks like I'll have to teach you a thing or two. We're going to read until Daddy fetches you back to work, then I'm going to let you borrow a book. *The Age of Innocence.* I want you to search through it tonight and find me the naughtiest passage you can come up with. Now hand me *Through the Looking Glass* over there."

Lucinda put *Anna Karenina* inside a book called *Through the Looking Glass, and What Alice Found There.* Then she fit the little monocle she fancied into position over her right eye and began to read to Hadley. Mostly it seemed boring, but he enjoyed the way she said the words as if she was telling him a secret.

When it was time to go, she instructed him to hide *The Age of Innocence* down the front of his trousers until he could put it somewhere safe. This turned out to be an unnecessary and highly awkward precaution since Hadley's mama didn't have any idea that the book was evil. When she caught him looking at it under the covers, she said, "It was nice of Miss Lucinda to let you borrow a book."

Mama thought it impolite to turn down reading lessons from a Browning, even if you were already a reader. She was pleased as a tick on a fat man that Hadley was going to have a real book to look at.

The way she smiled at *The Age of Innocence* tied his guts in a hundred and one knots of guilt, but the story seemed harmless enough. It was two in the morning before Hadley stumbled on something lurid.

The next afternoon he read his naughty passage to Lucinda.

He sat bowed over, his head between his hands, staring at the hearth-rug, and at the tip of the satin shoe that showed under her dress. Suddenly he knelt down and kissed the shoe.

"Hmm," Lucinda said, wrapping her finger with the chain of the tiger tooth necklace her daddy had recently brought her from India. "Where are the forbidden caresses?"

"Archer kissed her *shoe*," Hadley said. "I would never kiss a lady's crummy old shoe. He must really like her a lot to do that."

Lucinda looked at him as if he had two heads. Then she grinned. "Hadley Crump, you dirty boy! For a downstairs domestic, you're really rather brilliant."

Encouraged by his brilliance, Hadley began staying up late, searching for the right thing to bring to Club. His mama gave him a stack of recipe cards that had been stained when the kitchen ceiling sprung a leak. Hadley would fill the cards with the lines he copied for Lucinda.

From the kitchen of:
La Creatura Bella Bianco Vestita-Dante
By Victor Marie Hugo

When he came to himself, he flung himself on the bed, rolling on it and pressing frenzied kisses on the pillow, which still bore the imprint of her head. Here he lay for some minutes, motionless as the dead, then rose, panting, crazed, and fell to beating his head against the wall with the appalling regularity of

29

the stroke of a clock and the resolution of a man determined to break his skull.

It was glorious! Better still, Lucinda wasn't the least afraid to read whole stunning paragraphs on the topic of marital relations. She seemed to enjoy it. If Hadley should have to say something embarrassing like *bust* or *naked,* he would clam up or stutter or say it real soft. Not Lucinda. Once, he whispered the words *long milky thigh* into her ear rather than suffering through the twitchy trial of saying them out loud. But Lucinda didn't balk at thighs or nakedness. Hadley began to think that there was nothing the girl wouldn't say. It became his life's goal to test this theory. He studied her reaction to each dirty word like a scientist studies bacteria. Slang or profane, cuss or sacrilege, Lucinda's boldness was awe-inspiring.

Even after her leg healed, Lucinda allowed Hadley to continue meeting with her under the pretext of reading lessons. It was not unusual that he would find a slip of violet paper on a dirty plate with something Lucinda had copied for him. He came to look forward to Lucinda's notes almost as much as the club meetings.

"You're just another charity," Loomis said of the *lessons.* "When rich people spend time with people like us they call it *civic duty.*"

Hadley wanted to whip out one of Lucinda's notes and read it to Loomis in the worst possible way. Instead, he blurted out something entirely different. "I know what the 'm' stands for."

Loomis gave him a dubious look and picked at a scab on his forehead. "Hell you do."

Hadley had asked Lucinda about her "m" one afternoon while debating a vexing line from their current V.I.L.E. selection in which Gringoire says of Esmeralda; *"She is a salamander, she is a nymph, she is a goddess, she is a bacchante of the Menelean Mount!"*

Hadley thought a *bacchante* must be some sort of ancient flower. "He's saying she's beautiful. Like a flower," Hadley said. Flowers were the most beautiful things in the world, but Lucinda was certain that the *Menelean Mount* was a volcano she'd once read about in a school book.

"Gringoire is enchanted, yes, but it's fiercer than that. *Bacchante* is the fire that rains down from the heavens when the inside of the world erupts. Esmeralda is no flower."

Lucinda wore a bracelet with three gold charms shaped like a small "m", a big "L", and a little "b." Hadley watched them jangle when she touched her hair. Seeing the little "m," he forgot all about *bacchantes* and *Menelean Mounts*. He swept the charm into his palm. "What does this stand for, Lucinda?"

Lucinda took hold of his pointer finger and touched it to the gold letter. She whispered the secret word against his cheek, "Maribel."

Ever since that day, Hadley had been murmuring it to himself. Lucinda *Maribel* Browning—Nymph. Salamander. Igniter of all heavenly fire!

Loomis stared at him expectantly, but Hadley didn't want to share Lucinda's middle name.

At Maple Lawn, he'd once missed dinner for saying Penrod's name by accident. "House boys are not to act familiar with Tweebs," Sargent had scolded.

Lucinda let him hold her charm in the cup of his hand. She breathed Maribel-shaped breaths against his cheek. Somehow, he feared that if Loomis learned what the letter stood for, he would feel that hot tickle of pleasure against his own cheek, and Hadley had no desire to share such pleasures with Loomis, the hoeboy.

"It stands for her middle name," he said.

"Good guess, moron," Loomis snorted.

"It's a secret," Hadley said, his ears heating up. Outside of Lucinda's daddy, he felt sure he was the only one in all of Lucinda's Empire who knew the secret meaning of her "m."

Loomis didn't have a clue. He didn't understand what it was like to sleep with dirty books in your bed. Every night, Hadley nodded off with names like Mr. Thwackum and Hester Prynne still shaping his lips. His ribs were poked by pointy buckram corners, causing him to dream of pitchforks and fingernails. Mornings, he woke with gilt-pocked cheeks, and his torch rolled off across the floor, its dim beam trained on an empty wall. This was his world.

For all his years, Hadley had been plagued by the notion that his life had yet to begin. Everything he'd ever done was just part of a boring prologue. Real life was still a page or two away, but it was coming. He could feel it! Every time he took up one side of a book, and she took up the other--he could feel it.

All that was missing now was some sort proof to validate that he'd arrived. A person with a real life had stuff to show for it. They had clutter they wished they could pitch or burn, but they didn't pitch it, and they didn't burn it because, in the end, it was everything. It meant too much. When a person with a real life passed on, no one else had any use for their junk or even knew what it all meant. If Hadley died, there would be no evidence to show that he'd had a life at all. That was how he knew that he'd not really been born yet.

Slip the loop off the acorn button on Mama's sewing box, and you would find so much proof, whole hours would be lost just sorting through it all. Even the smell spoke of living galore. The felt lining was rubbed thin and stamped with the earthy scents of collected feathers and dried petals and the tang of old coins. It smelled like Mama's pearly hand lotion. It smelled like withered paper.

In a compartment meant for sewing needles was an embroidered handkerchief folded in fourths. A lock of hair, nine baby teeth, and a tarnished silver spoon were wrapped up inside like a present. A pair of gloves occupied a little button drawer, the soft fingers coiled into tight musty fists. And in a bigger drawer that was long and slender and molded to the shape of scissors, there were two pocket bibles, one black and one white, a photograph of Grammy Talitha as a fat tintype baby, and a water-stained brochure for *P. Dewrights Cemetery Plots & Ornamental Urns*. Mama kept a few regular things in the box too, like a chain of safety pins and a spool of white thread, but those were purely disposable. What made Mama drag that old sewing box through the years was a Sunday School medal, a pineapple doily, and a curl of Hadley's hair. Hadley himself had an old tackle box that he tossed junk in, but he it didn't seem like the same thing. A boy didn't keep a squirrel bone for any better reason than the fact that he was a boy.

Things were changing though. Hadley was beginning to gather proof of a life he might soon have. Shortly after the reading lessons began, it became necessary to slash the mattress of his cot. When no one was looking, he stuffed purple notes into the ticking.

During summer vacation, "lesson" time was after lunch. Usually Hadley and Lucinda spent the time reading. On a few occasions, Hadley helped Lucinda practice pinochle so she could join Laura Haney-Wayne's fancy card-playing club. Hadley loved pinochle and was pretty tough to beat. Other days, they stretched out across the grape vine rug on the Log Cabin floor and talked until it was time for Hadley to go back to being a house boy. On these days, Lucinda forgot to be allergic to the simpler things in life.

"Why is your skin that color?" she asked him on one such *talking-instead-of-reading* day. She lay beside him, crossing and uncrossing her ankles, her eyes fixed on his skin. There was a book opened in front of her called *How to Be Plump* but she was still on Page One.

Hadley was consumed with the new oxblood marble he'd won off Loomis that morning.

"Dirt," he said, with regard to his color. He rubbed the marble on his shirt and held it up to the light, examining for defects. It was perfect.

Loomis had named the oxblood the *Bloody Lime* because it was a limeade marble with red swirls. Hadley had been trying to win it for months, but Loomis wasn't often inclined to play for keepsies. The boy had been downright unsporting when Hadley took it from him, shouting *bastardwhoreshit* at the top of his lungs while Hadley twisted it out of his fingers. They exchanged a few punches before Mr. Sweet came stomping out of the house and told them to get back to picking the mealy bugs off of Mr. Browning's vines.

Now that it officially belonged to him, Hadley ran the Bloody Lime around the vines on the rug, pretending his new marble was Barney Oldfield in his amazing Peerless Green Dragon. The Dragon took the curves at full speed, the carpet whorls transformed into the flinty narrows and quicksand washes of the death-defying *Cactus Run* . . .

"What about under the dirt?" Lucinda said. She stretched her arm out next to Hadley's, obliterating his racetrack with her sailor sleeve. "I look like milk, and you look like cocoa, even in the places where your skin isn't smudged."

Hadley shrugged. He didn't think they looked so different except Lucinda was pretty, and he was a boy.

"Daddy says it's because you got a nigger in your wood pile."

"That's funny," Hadley said, reaching under her armpit to retrieve his prize. "I don't even have a wood pile."

"Daddy says you're what people call a mule auto. He's always asking me if I've managed to teach that little mule auto how to read yet."

Hadley had a notion that saying mule auto was a lot like saying *bastardwhoreshit.* "I don't know about that," he told her. "But my fifteen-year-old grandad was a USDA Certified slave."

USDA Certified was what Mama always said.

"You can't have a grandad who's fifteen," Lucinda told him. "I don't think they let you be a grandad unless you're old."

Hadley dropped the Bloody Lime in his pocket. "Well my grandad was fifteen, and he got beat to death just for kissing my grammy."

Lucinda stared at him in such a way, he wished he could take the words back. He was pretty sure his fifteen-year-old grandad was supposed to be a secret. Mama always talked about Winner Purdy in the quietest of whispers. She always called him Winner Purdy or Grandad, never Daddy, and the words came out quiet and shaky every time.

"The only thing I ever saw of Winner Purdy is a stick-cross on Slave Hill and the tears that dripped off Grammy's chin every year on my birthday," Mama had said.

Lucinda's eyes were round as marbles. "That is *sooooo* romantic."

"It is?"

"Your grandmother must have been a princess or a ballerina or something important like that if they killed a slave boy over her."

Hadley nodded. "She was a spinning girl."

Lucinda picked up Hadley's arm and started drawing circles with her fingertip around the bones of his wrist. "I wonder if it tastes any different."

"You can taste me if you want to," he offered.

Lucinda waggled her tongue over his skin, searching for the cleanest part. She settled for a place on the inside of his wrist.

"What do I taste like?" Hadley asked.

She licked his skin. She licked hers. It took several licks to decide. "Poor," she said. "Your skin tastes poor. My skin doesn't."

"Is poor bad?" Hadley wanted to know.

"It's surprising, is what it is," Lucinda said. "Poor tastes a lot better than I thought."

☙

One morning, Hadley fished a note from a puddle of honey that Lucinda left behind with the crusts of her toast. At the time, they were reading *The Adventures of Tom Sawyer*, but the sticky words did not come from the story.

We need a sharp knife, Hadley.

Hadley was thrilled.

That afternoon, he went to Club with a boning knife slid up his sleeve. The fun came to a stand-still, however, when Lucinda took hold of it and told him to stick out his finger. "We're going to make a blood pact, just like Tom and Huck."

In Hadley's opinion, it was enough that Huck said cusses like *by jingoes* and *damn*. "We don't need to spill blood over this, Lucinda."

"That's easy for you to say. You trust me. I, on the other hand, have no faith in you at all. Unless you're willing to make a pact that we'll keep *V.I.L.E.* a secret forever, I'm going to have to ask you to quit the club."

Hadley gnawed on his lower lip. "Them boys used a needle, as I recall."

"Needle-dweedle! We're not such cowards, are we?"

He looked down at his finger. "That knife's real sharp, Lucinda. I cut up a chicken with it yesterday."

Lucinda angled the blade so it sparked in the light. "We wouldn't want a dull knife, would we?"

Hadley thought about this. "Okay, but I'll cut my own self, if you don't mind."

She pressed the knife to his skin. "Oh, but I do mind, Hadley. Now quit your squawking and hold still."

In retrospect, this wasn't the smartest moment for him to call her a *Bossy Bessie*, but Hadley didn't recognize that until *after* she cut him.

"Whoops," Lucinda said. "You're quite a bleeder, aren't you?"

ॐ

Usually the lessons were fun. Hadley particularly liked playing *Great Expectations* and, after they'd finished reading the book, began thinking all his thoughts with an English accent. They'd come up with the game one Monday morning when it was too rainy to work outside, and Mr. Browning suggested they fit in a lesson before the sun came out. Hadley got down on all fours so Lucinda could step on his back and reach down the smelly cardboard box in the hall closet that held her mother's wedding dress. Lucinda put the dress on a giant stuffed bear she called Thomas. Thusly, Thomas, who was far too agreeable for his own good, became crazy Miss Havisham, and his black button eyes commenced to shine with sick fancy. To complete the effect, china plates were gathered, clocks were stopped at twenty to nine, and Lucinda's bedroom was transformed into the ripe, candle-lit ruins of Satis House. *Enough House*, Hadley preferred to call it, and even though the bear plotted against him and Lucinda dealt out cards and insults with equal hard-hearted fervor, Hadley enjoyed playing Pip to her Estella. He understood Pip better than any other character in a book.

Two weeks later, when they took up David Copperfield, Lucinda put the dress away and reset the clocks, and Hadley knew to be nervous again. Insults, he could live with, but he had learned that Lucinda was not above taking things too far. He never knew what to expect next.

The following month, when they read *The Count of Monte Cristo*, she convinced him to drink wool dye in order to prove his dedication to *V.I.L.E.* After that, Hadley puked indigo for a day and a half. After that, he quit the club.

"Oh that's a pity," Lucinda said, wrapping her index finger with the chain of her tiger tooth necklace. "And we were just about to start *Romeo and Juliet*, too."

"I know how that story ends," Hadley scoffed. "You can find yourself another Romeo."

"It was the kissing part I had in mind to try," she said, sighing woefully. "Oh well. I guess Loomis Sackett might be interested if you're not."

"You wouldn't kiss a Negro," Hadley said.

The skin beneath her twisted chain was white as a daisy petal. "At least Loomis Sackett is a *proper* Negro."

Hadley shook his head once, and then twice. "You wouldn't kiss Loomis Sackett."

"I'd rather kiss you."

"You would?" Somehow he began to forget about that indigo puke.

Lucinda shrugged. "It might be fun."

"All right," Hadley said. "But no more poison."

Lucinda didn't kiss him, though. She let him lie next to her on the log-cabin-room sofa/burial vault, but they both had to pretend that they were dead. Even so, Hadley reasoned that holding his breath and lying still next to Lucinda was better than nothing at all.

CR

It occurred to him after a year or two that people must think he was awful dumb. Not once did anyone question what a slow-learner Hadley appeared to be. In all actuality, he read fast. Lucinda called him a *Star Reader* because he could read anything she gave him in no time flat.

"You might have been half-smart if you could of gone to school," she said.

Hadley felt instantly proud and suffered an overwhelming urge to share the truth about their secret club with his mama, who thought it a pure impossibility that someone like Lucinda would ever give a Crump anything more than a charitable reading lesson. Maybe she wouldn't feel the need to sew basil in the hem of her slip for luck, or wear a spider in a walnut shell around her neck, if he told her that Lucinda sometimes shared her butter rum candy sticks with him, her tongue happily gliding along the same golden stripe as his own. "Mm!" Lucinda would say, as if Hadley's licks made the candy taste just that much more butter rummy.

But Hadley knew that he could never speak about Lucinda's club to anyone, least of all his mama. If Hadley told Mama about his habit of reading dirty books with Lucinda, Mama would make him put a coffin nail in his *Whoops Jar*, and Hadley didn't want to do that. Mementos were one thing. Mistakes were another. Mama had four nails in her coffee can already, and she wasn't even old yet. Mama insisted that four nails weren't so bad. Grammy Talitha had an even thirty before her nails buried her.

It was Grammy Talitha who came up with the jar idea in the first place. When Mama was little, Grammy used to sit her on her lap at night and tell her all about her shortcomings.

"I made a lotta mistakes in my life," Grammy confessed, "but there's one mistake I never plan to make; I remember every wrong I ever did."

That part was pretty impressive, especially considering all the nails Grammy had accumulated. There were times in his own life when Mama would say: "Hadley Floyd Crump! How did you get these holes in your trousers?" And even though he'd only just ripped his drawers an hour before, most of the time, Hadley couldn't remember where the holes came from. Grammy, he decided, must have had a wonderful memory on account of being so diligent with her nails.

Mama explained the purpose of the nails to him every year on his birthday. "Remembering your mistakes is the key. If you make a point of remembering, you can sometimes change the bad things into good. Mind you, that can be difficult. Sometimes a person can make changes. Sometimes they can't. Me, I got three different nails in my jar for every time I let myself get rooked by your daddy."

Hadley was five when his mama gave him his own jar. "See how pretty it is, baby? You try and keep that jar empty, if you can, cause that's the simplest way to work it. But if somethin' happens, and one day you do need to put a nail in this jar, the most important thing you can do is learn from your mistake."

At the time, Hadley was so busy playing with his new jar that she had to smack his hand to make him listen up.

"A lot of folks talk about puttin' another nail in their coffin. Well, here's a little secret: sometimes, if you're very very lucky, you might find out that what you thought was a mistake wasn't no mistake at all. That's what happened when I had you. For nine months I walked around cursing myself and frowning at you as you grew inside my belly. Wasn't 'til I saw your sweet little face that I knew the truth of it. You weren't no mistake, Hadley Crump. You were the best thing I ever did." She rattled her dented can. "Funny thing is, after I took out that nail I put in on account of you, I had to take out at least one of them nails I put in on account of your daddy. See what I mean?"

In truth, Hadley didn't see what she meant. He dropped in nails left and right because he thought it was such fun.

"No," Mama said, dumping the whole big batch out in his lap. "It's about avoiding the nails, Hadley. Understand?"

Over the years, he'd tried to put a frog in his jar, a *Beech-Nut* cigar band, and a handful of crab apples. Mama always dumped them out. This was the reason he got the Whoops Jar speech every year on his birthday.

Yes sir, Hadley was certain his mama would say that Lucinda Browning was a nail, but he couldn't think what he could do. Lucinda was more exciting than the mini`e ball slug he'd found in *Rabbit Creek*. She was more exciting than Loomis' deck of French playing cards, too. Shoot. Lucinda was right up with the Bloody Lime. If she cost him a nail, so be it. Truth be told, Hadley liked Lucinda even better than he liked his empty jar.

CR

In those early days, Browning House was tended by twenty coloreds, one mule auto, and a Cajun called LeJeune, whom only the long-deceased Mrs. Browning could understand. It was tended, also, somewhat haphazardly, by one Loomis Sackett.

Loomis Sackett was a special case, and he never let you forget it. His mother had the good fortune to land on her deathbed several months before Mrs. Browning landed on hers, and that was the reason he was so special.

Adelandi Sackett started doing the wash for the Brownings when she was fifteen and plump with child. She had the voice of a songbird, everyone said, and Mrs. Browning liked to open all the windows when the girl was hanging clothes so as to fill the house with her soft sweet music. She also had a beautiful hand-carved backscratcher that was painted orange and had a bright green grasshopper on the handle. Adelandi called it *The Grasshopper,* and when Mrs. Browning was carrying Lucinda, Adelandi would work miracles on her employer's back with that pretty orange stick, humming mysterious lullabies and scratching at scratches long after her workday was done. Loomis showed Hadley *The Grasshopper* once. It was chipped now, and two of the wooden fingers on the end were broken halfway down, but that didn't matter anyway because Loomis said it was bad luck to scratch your back with it. When Loomis was four, his mama caught a blood fluke and passed away after a long drawn-out ordeal, probably because she itched herself with *The Grasshopper.* Loomis went to live with his Aunty Fafa in Blackeytown. Fortunately, Loomis had never needed any back-scratching, and as a result, when his mama was on her deathbed, Mrs. Browning made her a solemn promise that, as long as he might want it, Loomis Beauregard Sackett would have a job at Browning House.

Lucky Loomis, Loomis called himself.

"What if you get an itch someday that's so big, you forget yourself and scratch it anyhow?" Hadley had asked, for that orange stick was a desperate worry to him.

"The day I scratch is the day you're doomed," Loomis told him. "I resist temptation better than you."

Loomis then proceeded to chase Hadley around the yard, the broken fingers of The Grasshopper swiping within an inch of Hadley's shoulder blades. Sometimes, when Hadley made Loomis mad, Loomis threatened to sneak into Hadley's room while he was asleep and scratch his back. Hadley didn't think it was safe for a boy like Loomis to possess something so powerful. Loomis bragged that he was the only one at Browning House who could not be fired.

"A deathbed promise is more binding than glue. Hell, I could itch Mr. Browning's back until he croaked, and lessin' they decide to cart me off to jail, there's nothing nobody could do about it. You can't mess with a deathbed promise. I'm as good as married to this fancy-ass place."

Though Browning House wasn't a proper plantation—it had a block of corn, a kitchen garden, a vineyard, forty hogs, two champion riding horses, and a lazy old cow called Toil-n-Trouble, or Tee Tee, for short. Word had it that when Mrs. Browning was still alive, everything was vastly different. The servant children were chauffeured to school in a coal-box buggy by old stooped-over Cuffy the driver. A better cook made meals for the servants in those days, too. The current cook, Miss Missy, was a kindly little thing, but her hoecake was hard as oak. Those that could remember said that Mrs. Browning was a true saint.

To be sure, she had a saintly look about her in the painting that hung over the mantle in the Rose Bud parlor. There was a portrait of her in the Harlequin parlor too, but by then she was suffering with the dropsy that would eventually kill her, and that portrait was just too sad to look at. The painting in the Rose Bud parlor showed a young woman with coffee-colored eyes that seemed to return Hadley's curious stare. Her dark hair was tied with a pale blue ribbon, and Hadley had discovered that, if he stood with his heels against the far wall, she would look at him and cock her chin in a wondering sort of way.

Every time he found himself in the parlor, Hadley searched the paint strokes for some similarity between Lucinda and her mother, but there wasn't a nose or an eyebrow or a smile that appeared to connect them.

Old Cuffy grinned a big crooked yellow grin anytime he found reason to speak of the late Mrs. Browning. "When Missus looked at you, you felt like more than a driver. You felt like a whole person with feelings and dreams and a life beyond the uniform."

Even though Hadley didn't have a uniform, he thought it would be the best thing in the world to be looked at that way.

After Mrs. Browning died, there was no more school for the servants. Miss Missy replaced the more expensive and more talented Cookie James. The Cajun gave up trying to speak. The rooms filled with more and more things to dust.

One of those things was a big deer head that sometimes hung over the telephone table and sometimes would be loaded into a piano-moving cart and disappear for entire weeks at a time. One afternoon, there was a loud crash in the Log Cabin Room, and everyone ran to see what it was. The deer head had fallen off its hook. It lay in the middle of the grapevine rug, staring at the ceiling. Later, Hadley would be given the job of gluing the top half of the buck's right antler to the bottom half, but in those first few minutes, everyone just stood in a circle around the head waiting for Mr. Browning to say something. Eventually, the man cleared his throat and said, "Daddy's dead." Then he went to his study and closed the door.

Because Hadley and Loomis were the most nimble of the gawkers, it was decided that they should move the head out to the summer kitchen until it could be repaired. Loomis being Loomis, he took up the wall mount, leaving Hadley to hang on by the more precarious chin. With the deer balanced between them, they began maneuvering it out of the house.

"What's this old head got to do with Mr. Browning's daddy?" Hadley asked.

A frizzly tuft of Loomis-hair stuck up between the deer's ears, making it look like a Negro deer. "Shit, Hadley," the Negro deer said. "Ain't you never heard the story 'bout Mr. Browning's daddy and this old buck?"

"Nope."

They paused at the kitchen door. "Watch the nose now," Loomis warned. They angled it this way and that way, grunting as they sought to work the thing through. "You bust so much as a nostril off this head, and Mr. Browning will kick you out on your little ass. Your mama, too. I'll be fine, of course."

"Of course." Hadley took extra care with the nostrils. "So what's the story, then?"

"Mr. Browning's daddy is Parnell T. Jr., and one time, Jr. and Mr. Browning went hunting in Montana together, and that's where they shot this buck."

Once outside, Hadley was forced to walk backwards. Palmetto berries littered the path and it was like walking on marbles. He frowned at the Negro deer. "They?"

"That's right. Both men set their sights on the devil, only one of 'em shot through the heart and the other shot through the ear. Did you happen to get a look at that hole, Crumpette?"

Seeing how the deer's ear had been flapping against his lip all the way to the summer kitchen, Hadley had seen the hole close up.

"Ass and damn!" Loomis said as they hoisted it onto the pickling bench. "Bastard's heavier than it looks."

Loomis was fond of cussing whenever the situation presented itself. He had an impressive gift for making up profane combinations that no one else ever thought to use. Hadley's personal favorite was *nipple-balls.*

"Anyhow," Loomis said. "They both claimed to fire the killing shot, and there was no way of settling the matter on account both men was using 22s. Things got so ugly between them, it was agreed they'd never speak again. It was also agreed they would take turns with the head on alternating months."

Suddenly the buck's disappearance and re-appearance made more sense. "Jr. lives with Mr. Browning's sister in Macon. I guess maybe Mr. Browning thinks it meant something today that the buck fell off the wall."

"It's sad they never patched things up."

"Stupid is what it is. They both get to hang the sumbitch on their wall so what they got to complain about?"

Hadley gazed into the blinkless eyes of the mounted deer. It looked far more dignified now that it didn't have Loomis' hair sprouting up between its ears. "I reckon it's a dissatisfying arrangement for them both. Nobody really wins because neither can feel a sense of ownership. Both men know that, even when it's their turn, the time is comin' when they'll have to give it up again."

Loomis shrugged. "If it was me, I'd rather not have it at all."

Mama peeked around the door just then. "Go on back to the house now, boys. Mr. Browning's daddy passed this morning. There's preparations to be made."

Hadley and Loomis looked at each other across the points of a broken antler. "We have ourselves a winner," Loomis said.

CR

In addition to antler-gluing, Hadley's duties at Browning House had grown to include a vast assortment of odd jobs. Had there been an actual *To Do* list (there wasn't), it would have read something like this:

> a) Check vines for Black Measles, Little-leaf, mildew, cutworms, crown rot, and Grape-berry moths.
> b) Chase off nematodes, beetles, rabbits, and gophers.
> c) Help with the milking, the wringing, and the pumping.
> d) Maintain back boiler and household toilets.
> e) Keep Lucinda Browning amused.

Mostly Hadley preferred "e" over chasing off nematodes, but he had a fondness for garden work. His first spring at Browning House, he added a few *secret* plants to Mr. Browning's zinnia garden. The shed was full of seeds in dust-furred packets, if a boy was willing to poke through dried-up June bugs to get to them. Hadley wanted to see if he could get the old seeds to grow. He had a notion that white dahlias would blend in like a lady's carpet with Mr. Browning's salmon-pink zinnias.

According to the packet, a person was supposed to plant dahlias inside for a few weeks before putting them in the dirt. As this was not a practical option, Hadley took extra care pushing the seeds into the soil, giving each one a spit for luck after it was buried. He swirled the seeds around the frog statue and along the porch. He lined the garden bricks. When snowy blooms the size of dinner plates popped up one summer, Mr. Greenthumb, the ground's man, promptly took credit. In fact, before the dahlias, Mr. Greenthumb was known by his real name, Mr. Parch, but after the dahlias came up, this name no longer seemed fitting. Hadley's experiment was the beginning of a long and satisfying arrangement in which Hadley would sneak in rose mallow or bluebonnets, and Mr. Greenthumb would scratch his head and say, "Why yes, I do have a very good eye for color. Thanks so much for noticing."

It was no surprise to Hadley that his rose mallow should glow rosier than any other rose mallow for miles. He didn't know if everyone else was the same way or not, but he'd always thought in flowers. For as long as he could remember, Hadley saw tiger lily sunsets and morning glory puddles. He poured chrysanthemums in his coffee and drank snapdragon-yellow lemonade. For Mr. Browning's birthday, he watched Mama serve the man zinnia-pink salmon on a shiny white dahlia plate. If you were Hadley Crump, the whole world was bloom-colored, and it smelled like a bouquet, too. Sometimes, when Lucinda read over his shoulder, he couldn't help but notice that her hair smelled like sweet peas. Admittedly, this seemed less magical after he got a look at the perfume bottles in her top dresser drawer, but perfume did not explain why Hadley could smell peach blossoms out of season when he was feeling happy enough.

It was a plain fact that, over the course of his young life, Hadley had developed an uncanny talent for identifying flowers. His daddy didn't leave him with much to remember him by, but he did give Hadley the *Young Folks Cyclopedia of Common Things*, the Plants & Animals volume. Daddy said Plants & Animals was where most folks quit paying. Whenever Hadley came across a new specimen, he would looked it up in his cyclopedia and promptly commit it to memory.

As a result of this obsession, Mama had violets pressed between every folded stocking she owned. Her apron pockets were dusty with crumbled dandelion heads. Daisies withered behind her ears.

"You ought to go into the flower business someday," Mama told him.

Indeed, there was something about the dirty knees of Mr. Greenthumb's gray gardener pants that set Hadley to dreaming. He didn't mind plumbing toilets or milking old Tee Tee, but his head was full of flowers.

CR

As the years rolled on, the books for *V.I.L.E.* grew trickier and trickier. Lucinda told Hadley that his ears turned red whenever he gave her a particularly good recipe card.

"You like that one, don't you?" she'd say. "I bet you wish I'd say such things to you."

To Hadley's way of thinking, Lucinda *was* saying such things to him, and he was pretty sure she knew it, too. She liked to poke fun at his short britches and bad haircuts, but she never asked anyone else to join their club. She never let anyone else borrow her books either—not even the acceptable ones. Not even Dickie Worther-Holmes, whose father owned *Worther-Holmes Homes*, the biggest builder of fine homes this side of the Yazoo.

Dickie Worther-Holmes was eighteen and already had a mustache and his own motor car. He also had a trophy as tall as Hadley engraved with the words: *50-meter Smallbore Free Rifle Champion*. Dickie was a gun man, Lucinda said, and sometimes she let him kiss her. Hadley was jealous, but he was sure Lucinda would let him kiss her, too, if only he could find the right naughty passage.

When Lucinda gave him *Portrait of the Artist as a Young Man,* he was sure that he'd stumbled on the path to her heart. It had prostitutes. It had sin. It had youthful indulgence.

"I've been thinking," Lucinda said. "Perhaps the time has come for V.I.L.E. to have its own holiday. If we keep our eyes open, I bet we could come up with the right thing. A sort of Christmas kind of affair, only without Christ."

"Okay," Hadley said, and they immediately set about to find something that might prove sufficiently wicked.

For a while, they considered *Queen Mab-mas*, but Lucinda wasn't sure she wanted to dedicate a whole day to someone tiny enough to be pulled around by a grey-coated gnat being whipped with a cricket's bone. For reasons having more to do with the sweets they might eat more than anything else, they came close to settling on an occasion to honor Frou-Frou, the dangerous racehorse from Anna Karenina.

"If we had *Frou-Frou Eve*, we could hang Christmas stockings in some secret place and leave lumps of sugar for each other," Lucinda proposed. "I love to eat sugar!"

It wasn't until they read about Stephen's encounter with the mysterious and disgusting word *phoetus* scratched on a desk top in *Portrait of the Artist as a Young Man*, that their holiday choice became clear.

Phoetus Day was to fall every year on the day after Lucinda's birthday so as to help them remember the date. The two vowed to keep it holy by scratching a dirty word somewhere on something annually. Presents were optional. Hadley asked that all gifts be held to something of simple symbolic importance. On the first ever celebration of Phoetus Day, he scratched the word *urinal* on the gutter pipe of the smoke house and made Lucinda a little volcano out of mud.

Lucinda refused to say *what* or *where* or *if* she'd carved anything at all, and she gave him a box wrapped in gold foil paper with a brand new pocket watch inside.

"Don't you like it?" she asked, when she saw the look on his face.

"It's very nice," Hadley said, turning the shiny new watch in his fingers. "But I thought we agreed to keep it simple."

"This is simple, dear. You should have seen the other watches in Mr. Berger's case."

"But I gave you a volcano."

Lucinda patted him on the head. "It's okay. I know you don't have money for anything good." She held the watch up to her ear. "Anyway, that old watch of your father's is about to fall apart. Now you can throw it out."

Hadley didn't bother to tell her that she would have to pry his daddy's watch out of his cold dead hand. It was one of the few things the man ever gave him. Outside of a squirrel bone and a dozen or so purple notes, it was just about the only thing he owned.

"It took me three nights to make that volcano, Lucinda."

She snapped the watch closed. "That's nice, dear, but I had to put up with Cuffy's old stories all the way to the jewelers and back. Have you any idea what that's like?"

Hadley weighed her sacrifice alongside his own. "Thank you," he said.

Three weeks later, he came across the word *stamina* written in miniscule letters on one of the iron ribs of the dining room radiator. Despite the fact that the volcano had mistakenly been tossed out as garbage by Gaynell, the new holiday finally felt official.

The next book on the list was *Tom Jones,* and if *Portrait* was rife with potential, *Tom Jones* was an all-out guarantee. Tom Jones had many lovers, perhaps even his own mother. He was a man driven to desperate lengths by love, and Hadley was sure that Lucinda would be hard-pressed to resist desperate love. Somehow, though, the tale distracted her. When they finished reading of Tom's robust exploits, Lucinda decided that she absolutely *must* have a fur muff like Sophia's in the story. In the heat of summer in Mississippi, Lucinda drove her father to the brink of insanity trying to locate something that would suffice.

"You oughta let the muff idea ago, Lucinda," Hadley urged. "Cuffy said they went shopping store to store today and your daddy looked like a heart attack. What would you use a ratty ball of fur for anyway?"

"Ratty ball of fur? You read the book, Hadley. Sophia's muff had significant spiritual meaning. It took her place when she and Tom were forced to be apart. She put it in his bed, for pity sake. They both kissed it! Don't you remember? I don't care if Daddy has to send to Timbuktu for one, I must have a beautiful white fur muff. It's the most romantic thing I've ever heard of."

Mr. Browning stopped at nothing until a white fur muff was found, and the first minute it was in her hot little hands, Lucinda invited Dickie Worther-Holmes to lunch. While Hadley was struggling to come up with an excuse for why he was setting up a ladder five feet from where they sat, he spied Lucinda rubbing the furry new muff against Dickie Worther-Holmes' strong square jaw. Dickie then told about a white moose he'd shot.

"I could make you ten muffs, if muffs are what you like," he said.

Watching Lucinda rub the muff on Dickie's face, Hadley experienced a nausea that came from someplace too deep inside him to force up mere food or drink. He thought he might puke out his own heart right there on the parlor floor. How could she share that ratty fur muff with anyone except him?

He folded up the ladder, put it away, and took to pacing the back hall, clanking the bath pots in the pot closet with his furious stomps.

"Ball-nipples!" he said. "I'm done with her!"

An hour after, when Mr. Sweet sent him for a lesson, Hadley made up his mind to suggest that Lucinda take on a new *student*. Let her toy with Loomis Sackett or Mr. Greenthumb. He was tired of Lucinda Browning and all her sick games.

When he opened the door, she was sitting on her bed, reading a recipe card. Hadley knew exactly what the card said because it was one of his recipe cards.

From the kitchen of:
Tom Jones
By Henry Fielding

To paint the Looks or Thoughts of either of these Lovers is beyond my Power. . . . And the Misfortune is, that few of my Readers have been enough in Love, to feel by their own Hearts what past at this Time in theirs . . .

Lucinda patted the blanket next to her. "Sit down."

Hadley sat on the edge of the bed.

"Daddy bought me the muff today." She petted it as though it were a cat.

"So I saw."

"I put my name inside it," she said. "Just like Sophia." She showed him the little tag with its crooked blue stitches attached to the pink satin lining.

Hadley had an urge to grab the stupid thing and run with it and throw it in the creek. He wanted to see that pristine fur sopping with mud. He wanted to sink it to the bottom.

"Will you kiss it?" she asked.

"Kiss it?" he said, his brain still swimming with images of her muff dying an early death.

She touched it to his cheek, and Hadley jumped, repelled by the thought of touching something that had been touched by Dickie Worther-Holmes before him. But Lucinda cupped his right cheek with her hand and rubbed the muff against his left. He glared at her even as the fur inched steadily toward his lips.

"Please, Hadley. If you don't kiss it, no one else ever will. It's meant for you and me."

"What about Dickie?"

"Dickie? Why would I share the muff with that ape? I showed it to him, of course. So what? Daddy will be expecting me to show it to the whole wide world after the lengths he went to find it."

Hadley wanted to believe this, but he was having a hard time loving the muff again.

"I like what you wrote," she said, nodding at the recipe card.

"Henry Fielding wrote it. I just copied it."

"I like what you copied. It's pretty."

She rubbed the muff on his face again, and his skin itched with distrust.

"After everyone has seen my beautiful fur muff, do you know what I'm going to do with it?" She tickled him under his chin. "I'm going to save it, Hadley."

"For what?"

"For the right moment."

He brushed the fur away. "What's that mean?"

Lucinda covered his mouth with the muff. "Kiss it, Hadley."

"Then what?" he asked against the fur.

Lucinda shrugged. "I guess you'll have to wait for the right moment and find out."

He eyed her over the snowy puff.

"Wait," she cried, pulling the thing away from his face. "I want to see you do it." She held the muff before him, smiling expectantly.

"You first," he said.

Keeping her eyes on his, she drew it to her lips. The smack that followed was loud and wet. She offered it again.

Fearful it was a trick, Hadley lowered his mouth slowly to the warm white place that glistened with her kiss. Taking a deep breath, he pursed his lips and kissed the dewy spot.

One day, Spitbone the pigman told Hadley about a book so scandalous that his young wife burned it in the dutch when she caught him reading it. Other than Lucinda, Spitbone and his wife were just about the only two readers Hadley even knew. *Dracula* was the name of Spitbone's scandalous book, and the man said there was only one place in town daring enough to sell it—*Pringles Second-Hands*. Hadley made up his mind right then to save his money and buy a copy for Lucinda.

It took a long time. He was sixteen before he could afford the book, and the three dollars Spitbone wanted for walking into Pringles and asking for such a despicable piece of merchandise on Hadley's behalf.

"You watch yourself with that, kid," Spitbone warned when he handed over *Dracula* wrapped in brown paper. "That book'll get you into trouble."

Hadley didn't tell Spitbone, but trouble was exactly what he hoped to get into when he read the book to Lucinda.

At first, she glared at it as if it was a shoe with dog poop stuck to the heel. They were sitting on the floor in the toy room, and Lucinda had been thinking they would read *Ulysses*. *Ulysses* was not even allowed in the country, she said. Lucinda had stolen it from her daddy's desk drawer.

"A monster story?" she grumbled upon seeing Hadley's new purchase. "Does anyone actually fornicate in this book?"

"Worse," Hadley said. "They bite one another."

"What's the fun of that?"

"How about this," he said. "You read me something from *Ulysses,* and I'll read you something from my monster book, then we'll decide which one is more fun."

"All right," she said. "But I'm skeptical."

Lucinda read first, the odd, periodless sentences running into each other in a way that would have been annoying had Lucinda not pantomimed the action for him:

I'd let him see my garters the new ones and make him turn red looking at him seduce him I know what boys feel...

Hadley swallowed. Dang. He could certainly understand the appeal of garters. He just hoped Spitbone knew what he was talking about. As it was a stormy day, he reached over and tugged the curtain pull, casting the room in darkness. He switched on the flashlight he'd brought along for just this purpose, narrowed the beam on the words, and began to read:

I could feel the soft, shivering touch of the lips on the super sensitive skin of my throat, and the hard dents of two sharp teeth, just touching and pausing there. I closed my eyes in languorous ecstasy and waited, waited with beating heart.

When he shone the light on Lucinda's face, she popped her monocle. "Give me that," she said, grabbing the book. "What does it mean?"

"It means this girl with the sharp teeth is about to drink this fellow's blood. And I think he wants her to do it."

"Hadley," she murmured in a shivery voice. "Where did you get this book?"

"*Pringles.* Should I read another passage?"

"No!" she cried. "I might swoon if you do."

"Really?" he asked, hopefully.

"The floorboards aren't safe for a book like this."

Not in all his days had Hadley ever felt so proud of himself.

◌℞

Next meeting, Lucinda confessed that she could hardly read the words, as they left her so breathless. "You'll have to read them to me, Hadley," she said. "Problem is, I'm deathly afraid of what will happen between us if we share such words out loud."

Hadley knew Lucinda might only be teasing. He gulped anyway. To his way of thinking, it was high time one of their wicked books inspired something wicked.

From then on, when it was dark enough, Hadley would read *Dracula* by flashlight. When it wasn't dark enough, he'd speak in a gravely whisper so as to keep the whole thing sinister.

On the day Harker drove his Kukri knife into the Count's throat, Hadley grew so excited, he kissed Lucinda.

For years he'd dreamt of kissing her. He could imagine himself doing it any number of ways, but always, in the end, Lucinda kissed him back. Now that it was real, his lips traveled no further than the slope of her cheek, but Hadley kissed that cheek as though it were a pair of open lips.

Lucinda dried her face on her sleeve.

"I thought you liked this story," he mumbled.

"I've other things in mind for us."

"Like what?" he asked, lightly touching her shoulder.

"Hold your horses. It's only our first time through the book."

That night, Hadley didn't sleep a wink. He couldn't wait to read the book again.

CR

Hadley thought the hunt for the count was the most exciting part of the novel. Lucinda disagreed. She liked to read over and over again about Jonathan Harker's encounter with the vampire brides.

"Do you suppose he likes those women, Hadley?" she asked one afternoon, addressing him as though he were suddenly an expert on the desires of men. "Or is he only afraid of them?"

"Both, I think."

Lucinda fanned her face. "Fear *and* passion? At the same time?"

"And don't forget shame," Hadley said. "If you ask me, Harker doesn't seem very proud of himself for liking those brides."

"No wonder he goes mad."

"No wonder," Hadley agreed. "I'd rather be Quincey."

Quincey P. Morris, a slang-talking American, was Hadley's favorite character in the book.

Lucinda laughed. "Don't be silly. No one runs their teeth languorously over Quincey's skin."

"No, but Quincey has a bowie knife."

53

"Oh, Hadley." She sighed. Quick as that, it was clear that he was no longer any sort of expert. "You are a baby, aren't you? One of these days I'm going to have to show you what's really important."

The next afternoon, Lucinda stroked the back of Hadley's neck while he read, the sharp sickle of a lone fingernail dipping down the collar of his shirt to circle the bump at the top of his spine. For a full hour, he didn't dare move a muscle for fear she'd stop circling. When the last page was done, he closed the book, bent forward, and pressed his lips to the toe of Lucinda's shoe.

Slowly, fearfully, he turned his face and looked up at Lucinda.

"Read it again," she said.

Hadley celebrated his seventeenth birthday with a surprise smooch delivered courtesy of the new upstairs maid, a girl by the highly promising name of Ethel Lewse. Ethel grabbed him from behind while he was fishing Mr. Browning's 14 karat gold money clip out of the toilet bowl. Shortly after Lucinda spied the two of them locking lips on the wet bathroom tiles, she gave Hadley a little parchment card with a private birthday message written inside:

Come to the attic at three a.m. to receive your special gift.

Hadley tip-toed up the butler's stairs at exactly five till three. His plan was to act like a sleep-walker if anyone caught him up and about.

Mama barely moved a muscle when he slipped out of bed. She could be suspicious as a fat turkey invited to Thanksgiving dinner, yet she never worried about Lucinda. Lucinda was a Browning; Hadley, a Crump. What could there possibly be to worry about?

At the end of the hall behind a door with a glass knob was the attic. Moonlight snuck in from a fan-shaped window overhead, striking the knob and scattering tiny bright rays in a dozen different directions.

He made his way with careful, silent steps, expecting a bedroom door to fly open at any second. The staff was not allowed to step silently past bedroom doors at three o'clock in the morning. Hadley could lose his job. He could lose Mama's job, too.

The noises were different than the noises one heard in the kitchen at dawn. Snores blasted out of nowhere. The purposeful tick of the clock in the front hall transformed into the gnish-gnash of ratchet teeth chewing forever on the same black moment without going anywhere. Blocks away, a pack of dogs began to bark indignantly. The knob winked at him from across a vast continent of mattress creaks and phlegmy breathing. By the time he reached it, his palm was too slick to turn the thing.

Panic rose in Hadley's chest. What if instead of finding his heart's desire waiting for him in the attic, he found a note written in flower-dotted letters informing him that he was too witless to be in Lucinda's club? The mere thought of it froze him with indecision. The clock seemed louder. Faster. It was hard to think. Somewhere in the night, a dog tore something into pieces. Hadley used his shirttail to twist the doorknob and prepared himself for disappointment even as he hurried up the stairs.

Indeed, the attic appeared empty. An octagonal beam of white light streamed across the floor. In the beam sat an old velvet lounge like the one Harker described in his journal.

"Lucinda?" he whispered. "Are you here?"

No one spoke.

He ran his hand along the spikes of velvet, stirring up little blooms of dust with his fingers. A ceramic clown with a cracked eye watched him from the top of a paint-chipped wardrobe while a beach umbrella poked at his ankle with its rusted tip. There were stacks of photographs, old sewing patterns, and shiny new hatboxes stacked everywhere. And there were mirrors. Too many mirrors. Mirrors enough to scare you with your own warped reflection.

There was no note.

Hadley checked his daddy's pocket watch. It was a few minutes after three. Maybe Lucinda was having a hard time sneaking down that long hallway? He sat on the lounge and leaned back. What if she'd been caught? What if he was about to be caught, too? He leapt at every little sound, but nothing came of them. He watched the dust motes to see if brides would appear. At some point, his heart rate slowed, and he drifted off to sleep.

He dreamt that Lucinda came to the attic with a boning knife hidden in the folds of her dress. "Time for another pact," she said. "What shall we cut this time? . . . "

When something touched his leg, he jumped awake.

His first thought was that it was the knife. Then he was sure it was Mr. Browning. Then he was sure it was Dracula.

It was Lucinda.

Her hair hung in buttery waves around her face, and her lips were red as red can be. Hadley was about to ask what she put on them to make them so red when he realized she was wearing a nightgown with nothing underneath. She smiled and gave his knee a squeeze. Something was hanging around her neck. It twirled and caught the moon, blinding him and making him squint. Beneath the dreamy trail of her hand, his muscles tensed like two-by-fours.

"Relax," she whispered.

Hadley rubbed his eyes. He couldn't stop staring at Lucinda. She looked so different.

"Don't you like me like this?" she asked.

His thigh tremored beneath her fingers. "I like you," he said. When she touched her mouth to his, Hadley smelled peach blossoms out of season. *This is it,* he thought. *At long last, my life is about to start.*

"You're shaking, Hadley. Are you scared?"

Hadley wasn't scared. He longed to grab Lucinda and pull her down on the lounge with him.

"Such wicked passion," she said, clucking her tongue. "You ought to be ashamed."

Hadley wasn't ashamed either. He would have married Lucinda in an instant, if that was what she wanted. But she only wanted him to want her.

Her hot tongue-tip wiggled up the hill of his Adam's Apple and glided down the other side. "Hadley," she said. "You look good enough to eat."

There was something in those bright blue monkey-flower eyes that did, at last, put the fear of God in Hadley. Quick as that, her necklace arced past his face and tore into his neck. It was the tiger tooth.

Jesus God! he thought. *She gonna kill me for kissing Ethel.*

Lucinda's mouth slid in the blood as she tried to seal the gash with her lips. Before Hadley could fully grasp what was happening, she began to suck.

"What're you doing?" he said, kicking his feet and trying to squirm away. "This isn't how it's supposed to be."

Lucinda sucked harder, as if she knew differently.

In his frantic mind, he saw himself pressing his forehead to her forehead over a beloved book. He felt her fingers running circles around the knobs of his spine. He smelled her flowery skin. Hurting him on his birthday after their first kiss was a betrayal worse than any other he could imagine. It sickened him.

"I know you, Hadley," she said, scrapping his hair up in her fist and drinking more deeply. "You matched me breath for breath when they put their teeth on him."

"That wasn't real, Lucinda."

"It is now." She looked him straight in the eye, her red lips redder than before thanks to the smear of his blood.

"But you're hurting me," he said.

Lucinda smiled. "I know."

When she did it again, a terrible fire branched out beneath his skin, knotting and sluicing like an extra set of veins. That his first taste of pleasure should come amid such exquisite pain confused his every nerve. He bucked away from it. He bucked against it. Fight or give in, these strange veins of pain found new places to rush and surge and flood. Lucinda clamped down on his neck so hard, she sucked him straight through to the other side of hell . . . and that place wasn't hell at all.

It was hell's opposite.

CR

Hadley was in bad shape. No matter how carefully they bandaged his throat, his skin split open if he moved at all.

"I might die," he told her testily. It was the next day and they had gone into the smokehouse so Lucinda could try to stop the bleeding. The darkness smelled of blood and ham. Worse still, Lucinda's nursing was about as gentle as a cat hauling.

"Don't be so dramatic," she said, poking the wound with rough fingers.

"*I'm* dramatic? You know, most people make love differently, Lucinda."

"How would you know? Anyway, we aren't *most* people. Oh Hadley, just thinking about it . . . have you been thinking about it?"

Heck, if he could think about anything else.

A slant of sunlight squeezed in through the door, and Hadley watched Lucinda's tongue flicker along her lip. "All this blood is making me want to do it again."

"We better not," he said, but he leaned forward and kissed the spot her tongue had just wet.

Lucinda peeled back the bandage and ran her teeth up and down his neck. Hadley began to shake. He didn't understand what was happening to him. Lucinda's painful affections made him feel special, but they also made him furious. On the one hand, she was letting him kiss her now and that was very nice. On the other, he'd been bleeding steady for a full day.

This could not be good.

Her mouth sought out his cut and kissed it softly. The spot was so tender with pain, Hadley felt like he might pass out. She need only pull a few sips into her mouth, and he was on his knees, hurling once more into that bright and blinding place on the other side of Hell.

That was how he thought of it, for surely the tortuous heights she brought him to could not be the Pearly Gates. God played no part in such a soul-wrecking act. There could be only one explanation then: Lucinda was sending him to an eviler side of hell. And Hadley realized that he liked it too much to make her stop.

CB

In the following days, his neck failed to heal because neither of them could leave it be. Lucinda said she craved him and Hadley, who had never been craved by anyone, could not help but respond with a mix of dread and ecstasy.

A dizzy sense of confusion rushed through him most all the time, yet he knew that the things they were doing were wrong. At night, when he and Mama knelt down to say their prayers, Hadley always spoke to God with the best of intentions. As Mama mumbled pleas on behalf of the sick and asked forgiveness for things like splattering soup on Mr. Browning's lace cloth, Hadley pressed two sets of white knuckles to his forehead and whispered, "Lord, give me the strength to tell her no when she comes to me tomorrow . . . "

That was typically where things went awry.

He wouldn't notice himself drifting until much later when it was too late to take it back. Somehow, instead of praying for forgiveness, Hadley would start to dream about what might happen tomorrow. Perhaps she would slip him a note when they passed in the hall, his hand instinctively opening behind his back at the moment her hand was there with the note. Their fingers would brush, and his wound would open like a wet mouth. WAIT FOR ME, the note might say, BEHIND THE ROSE BUD CURTAIN . . .

"Amen!" Mama's amens were always the thing that snapped him out of it. "Aren't you done yet, Hadley?" she'd ask.

Done? "Actually, Mama, I think I'm just getting started."

CB

Of course he would have preferred a more conventional romance, but he hesitated to complain. Lucinda looked at him differently now. Her cheeks were always hot and red. Every morning, she tapped her feet under the breakfast table as though her bones wanted out of her skin. "Come here," she'd whisper, pushing her untouched plate away and steering him into the bathroom or behind the garage.

He tried to be good. "We could just kiss," he said one day when she cornered him in the dairy.

"No," Lucinda said. "We can't."

His wound got worse, and he got feverish. When he stood up from his prayers, his head spun. It was hard to push a mower, his legs felt so rubbery. "I don't feel good," he told Lucinda.

But she just ran a finger along his jaw and said, "I'll make you feel better, Hadley."

The joy of being sought by Lucinda Browning was temporary, though. Always and, finally, temporary.

Sure, when she put her lips on his neck, a satisfying heat shimmered all through him, tickling bones he didn't know he had. It was lust, to be sure, but not just lust of the body. It was a lust that made him *dream* and *want* and *need*.

Lucinda was gentle at first. So gentle, he'd be fooled. Her kiss was a rose petal on his throbbing skin. He loved her to death when her kiss was a rose petal.

The sucking made him mad every time.

Nerve endings screamed under her lips. His heart threatened to quit. He'd punch whatever he could punch, even once punching her. When she hurt him, he hated her almost as much as he loved her. When she hurt him, it hurt unbearably. Then, at the worst, most awful moment, the pain would melt, and Hadley would feel indescribable pleasure.

ᥫᥬ

Because of the bandage, he'd been forced to invent a complex lie about how he'd tripped on a pair of garden sheers. Battles were waged on a daily basis owing to the fact that Mama wanted nothing so much as to get a peek at the injury. Hadley couldn't bear to let her look at it. He would've sooner run naked down the middle of the road. It was Mama who finally spoke to

Mr. Browning about his declining health, and Mr. Browning who summoned Dr. Mangrove.

That such a small wound could make him so ill was a mystery that had everyone pacing the halls. The doctor concluded that his failure to rally must stem from the inherited traits of a degenerate lifestyle. "Or maybe it's Spanish Flu," Mangrove said.

By Day Three, Pellagra was being proposed. By Day Eight, the doctor was hopelessly bewildered again. "I've never seen anything like it," he declared. "It's almost as though the boy keeps falling on those garden sheers over and over again."

Dr. Mangrove was more right about that diagnosis than any of the others. Hadley was falling on those garden sheers every single day.

ॐ

He held the jar up to the light and watched the nail spin around the glass walls like a rust-colored cyclone. He'd always imagined that it would take thirty or more nails to seal his fate. Now that the end was near, he found himself regretting that he had only one. He wondered if one nail was enough to do the job right. His only consolation was that Grammy Talitha probably didn't have one nail in her entire jar that was as bad as his. He wished he had something a little better for the job than a scrawny old Putnam Burr-Free Shoeing Nail. He wished he'd asked his mama to get him a railroad spike.

"I've come to relieve you, Miss Crump," Lucinda said, startling Hadley so much he almost dropped his jar. "You go on and get yourself a bite to eat. I'll keep an eye on young Hadley here and fetch you if there's trouble."

Mama must have been too sad to find it odd that Lucinda had spoken to her face-to-face for the first time in eight years, because she just nodded and shuffled away, her shoulders round with worry, her hair turning grey before his eyes.

Doc Mangrove had assured everyone that he would not last the night. Hadley reckoned he might as well get on with it then.

He turned his cheek on the pillow, prepared to die the heady and listless death of an addict.

Lucinda trailed her finger down his bandaged neck, and his blood began to sing. Her hair tickled his skin. Her breath heated his throat. Her heat would be the last thing he would ever know. Hadley was fainting, fading, slipping away.

"Hurry," he said.

A rose petal kiss brushed his ear, and it felt much like love. Lucinda Browning loved *him*. A servant boy. A mule auto. A Crump! Hadley would surely have minded dying more had he not understood that this made him incredibly special.

"No," Lucinda said. "We mustn't do it. I will not let you die."

Didn't she realize that it was too late for that? Beneath his collar of tape and gauze, Hadley's artery throbbed in a whole new way. The blackness closing in around him no longer seemed like a pat on the back for earning the love of a woman that he shouldn't have been able to earn. Rather, it was a slug in the nose, and it was ruining his last moment of life.

"If you don't want me, Lucinda, I think I'd rather be dead."

Lucinda wouldn't glance at Loomis Sackett to save her soul, and yet she swapped spit with Hadley every day now. When she wanted to give someone reading lessons, did she choose Flavia? Or Lemon? "Bring me Hadley Crump," she said. Hadley wasn't like the others. He was different. He was something more. And now, when the end was near as near can be, she didn't want him anymore.

"Of course I want you," she soothed, making him smell peach blossoms again when there wasn't any blossoms to smell. She had that power. The Lord God had done some amazing things with bread loaves and fish, but He had nothing on Lucinda. "You're the only one like me," she said, tucking the blanket under his chin. "You just rest and do as the doctor says. So long as I don't drink any more, you're sure to recover in time."

Hadley was as weak as a noodle. If someone would have stabbed him in earnest with a pair of garden sheers, it would have felt heaps better than the murderous pain vibrating under his skin. He had one toe in the grave, to be sure. Maybe he had his whole foot in the grave. He smiled anyway. "Do you like me then, Lucinda?"

"You know I do."

She was holding something behind her back. Her monkey-flower eyes twinkled with excitement. "I've brought you a new book, my darling. When you're better, we'll read it together. Just like Dracula."

Twisting her monocle into place, she spoke against his ear. "It's called *The Pit and Pendulum* by Edgar Allen Poe."

CR

At the first sign of hope, Cuffy set up a camp cot in the Rose Bud Parlor, and Hadley was moved from the pickling closet. The doctor said a window would provide him with the "healing enjoyment of a fresh and salubrious breeze". Since no one knew that it was actually Lucinda who saved his life, much was made of that salubrious breeze.

After Hadley got a window, things seemed to be headed in the right direction. His color returned. His wound stopped bleeding. He ate a lot of soup. He missed her mouth on his throat so much that he dreamed vampire dreams most every night. The dreams were healthier than the real thing, but one night, the cot squeaked, and someone sat down next to him. Hadley felt her hand in his hair, and he jumped and turned and reached for her.

Just as Jesus raised Lazarus from the dead, Lucinda had raised him. The difference being, Jesus didn't kill Lazarus before he raised him. Hadley was relieved to feel her hands again. He didn't really want her to go back on her word but figured it probably wouldn't kill him if she did it just this once.

"I've missed you, Lucinda," he whispered. "I've missed you so much."

The gas lamp lit with a pop.

Mama sat on the edge of the cot swallowing as though a hundred years of bad mistakes were jammed up in her gullet. "Lucinda?" she mumbled around the mistakes. "Why in hell would Miss Lucinda be crawling into your bed at two o'clock in the morning?"

In the time it took to heave a single trembling breath, Mama's eyes grew big and round as she visibly tallied up all the whispers and notes and reading lessons. She didn't believe that people like the Brownings gave two cents about people like the Crumps. As a matter of fact, Hadley was deadly certain that Mama had never so much as glimpsed the buttercup hair or the teasing smile he saw every time he looked at Lucinda Browning. When Mama looked at Lucinda Browning, she saw eyes that never saw her back, and that was an entirely different thing. It had never occurred to Mama that Lucinda might actually *see* Hadley.

It was beginning to occur to her, though. Dozens of uneasy memories unscrolled behind her eyes like the naughty half of St. Nick's list. She looked at the Whoops Jar on the washstand. "What have you done, Hadley?"

Hadley held his chin proud. "Maybe we're in love," he said.

"Oh honey," she said, tears transforming her eyes into two glassy pools. "I hope you don't believe that."

CR

Mama had all sorts of ideas about who was supposed to love who, and Hadley had been hearing those ideas all his life. Mama rattled them off like other mothers rattled off bedtime stories. Some of her stories even sounded as though you could find them in a real book. *Once upon a time there was a spinning girl who fell in love with the wrong boy . . .* The trouble was that all of Mama's bedtime stories had sad endings, and this did not work out well in a story that was meant to put a child to sleep.

The story she told most was the story of Hadley's father, a smarmy Gothamite with a pencil mustache and a hundred dollar-smile. He was a door-to-door salesman who sold everything from suction sweepers to *Pleasant's Purgative Pellets*. Mama said he'd gummed just about everyone he ever knew.

Not surprisingly, they met at the front door. Mama was putting a pie out to cool. Daddy was pitching *McIlhenny's*. "Blame it on hot sauce," Mama liked to say.

Mama fell for Daddy because he wore nice suits and had very white teeth. He also brought her lots of presents. While it was true that Mama never wanted for purgative pellets or a pocket Bible while Daddy was around, she didn't really care about presents. It was the fact that she'd never gotten any before that really did her in. "Those presents made me think that Slip really loved me," she told Hadley. *Slip* was the name of Hadley's daddy, and Mama said the name fit him like a glove.

Hadley had not seen hide nor hair of Daddy Slip since the man went off to halt the hun in Cantigny, but he remembered his white teeth, too, and he remembered that it was always a happy surprise when Daddy showed up. He'd thunder in with an armful of mix-n-match encyclopedias and a sample jar of *No-Tweeze,* shouting in his big New York City voice, "Where's my little bastard?!"

"What's *bastard* mean, Mama?" Hadley had asked when he was a little boy.

"It means your daddy is too much of a dumb-bell to marry me, that's what it means," Mama said. Mama believed in laying things on the line and was never one to mince words. But Hadley didn't understand about bastards back then. When the Muncy's German Shepard had puppies and Mrs. Muncy said that Hadley could pretend like one was his until somebody bought it, Hadley said, "Where's my little bastard?!" and got a swat on his bottom when he was searching for his puppy. It was Mrs. Muncy who did the swatting, and she told Hadley that *bastard* was a very bad word. At the time, Hadley wondered why Daddy Slip would call him a very bad word. Indeed, it seemed like Daddy's story wouldn't be a good one for children's books at all, what with as much as that man liked saying *bastard.*

Mama never looked so disgusted as she did when she spoke of Daddy. "I was thirty-nine years old when I met him, so I should have knowed better. Truth is, we Crump women have been making the same mistakes with men for about as far back as anyone's memory goes. Before Slip came around, I set out to guard myself against it. I've had a penny in my shoe for so long now, Mister Lincoln's face is permanently worn into the ball of my foot. I had Auntie Lutterloh mix me up a bag of Holy Ghost root so as to give me good luck with men. I wet those little Holy Ghosts with whiskey nine mornings in a row, jest like she said, and I carried them in my right pocket, careful not to let them touch tobacco. But did that save me from the slippery charms of that hot-sauce-hawking fool? No sir, it did not. When you were born and you were a boy, I said, 'Praise the Lord. The curse is lifted!'"

Mama thought a boy would be easier than a girl. A girl, she said, was supposed to have a wedding ring before she had a baby, yet there was nary a woman in their beleaguered line who had ever gotten a ring before *or* after she got her babies.

Ever since Hadley was four or five, he'd been hearing; "It's all on you now, son. You fall in love with the right girl and make sure your babies have a mama *and* a daddy. Understand?"

After Mama found out about Lucinda, she said, "You can't be messing with a girl like Miss Lucinda. You got the hopes and prayers of the Crump bloodlines resting on your shoulders."

The last thing Hadley wanted was the Crump bloodlines resting on his shoulders. Nevertheless, there it was, like a salesman with a stack of Bibles he couldn't unload.

Mama did a lot of snorting when he tried to explain how things were between him and Lucinda. Even her words came out in snorts. "Houseboys do not marry girls like Miss Lucinda." She snorted, shaking her head as if Hadley were dumb as a turd. "I've seen things in my time, honey. There's some rich folks that get it in their head that they want to try a nigger. That ain't love. That's another thing entirely."

"You don't know nothing about it," Hadley insisted. "I *mean* something to her. She cares about me, Mama."

The problem was, Mama didn't understand that the garden shears injury was not really a garden shears injury at all, but rather something much more passionate. Also, Mama had never seen the panicky way in which Lucinda kissed him, as if she might just blow apart into a pile of arms and legs and monkey-flower eyes if she didn't put her lips on him. If Mama saw that, she would know how much Lucinda cared. She would know that Hadley's woodpile had nothing to do with anything. She would know that Hadley was something different than all the other servants.

$\sim$

Over the next few days, Hadley prayed that Mama would notice how often Lucinda stopped in to check on him. Oddly, once she'd promised to quit "craving" his blood, Lucinda never once stopped in to check on him.

As time wore on, Mama gave him looks that got more and more pathetic. Hadley wished he could read her one of the notes as proof of Lucinda's feelings, but that would be a little like having your mother in the same room on the night of your honeymoon.

"She bought me a new book," he bragged desperately, holding up the Edgar Allen Poe story.

Mama crossed her arms. "I don't doubt her interest in you, Hadley. Miss Lucinda has always paid you too much mind. I see that now."

"So quit feeling sorry for me," he said. "You don't know what's between us. Nobody does."

"I know this much: whatever Miss Lucinda does with you in private is going to stay private. If you think you'll ever have more than that, you're sadly mistaken."

Hadley shook his head and shook his head and shook his head. Mama used to say he was throwing a *head tantrum* when he was little, warning that he would rattle his brain to pieces if he didn't get control of his head-shaking. Sometimes, when he was bending over the vines, he could feel little pea-sized chips rolling around inside his skull. "You're wrong, Mama. Lucinda likes me. She told me so herself."

Mama ran her fingers through his curls, combing them like she had a mind to comb them uncurly. "Hadley, there's something I need to tell you."

Whenever Mama had bad news, her skin (which was a shade or two more cocoa-colored than Hadley's) turned green as a Spanish olive. Now she looked at him and smiled sadly and turned green as a Spanish olive. "Miss Lucinda got herself engaged last Sunday to Mr. Worther-Holmes Jr. They intend to marry when he graduates from MC in June."

Hadley closed his eyes. He knew, of course, that Lucinda couldn't run off with the cook's son and expect everyone's blessings. Hadley was content with what Lucinda gave him. After all, it wasn't Dickie's blue blood she craved in the dark hammy corners of the smoke house. And when Lucinda read something dirty in a book, she didn't mold Dickie's hand with her thumbs. She molded Hadley.

"Hadley," Mama said, molding his hand with her thumbs until he yanked it away. "I've been in service all my life. This is just the way these things go."

Hadley didn't believe that she was capable of understanding about Lucinda. He shook his head and felt the crumbs of his brain spin in circles around the inside his head. He sincerely doubted anyone had ever gone as far as he had for a kiss.

CR

Two weeks passed as slowly as molasses before Lucinda finally found the time to pay him a visit. By then, Hadley's color was much improved, but not his disposition. Lucinda didn't seem to notice. She tore open the curtains, filling his sickroom with the harsh light of day.

In the sun, her hair was more buttercup-colored than ever. Hadley's fingers on the blankets splayed like a rake, desperate to rip into those bright buttery strands.

"What do you want?" he asked.

"If you're feeling fit, I think it's time we for us to resume our lessons." She fluttered her fingers in front of his face, blinding him with her diamond. "Have you heard the good news, darling?"

Hadley would have struck her right then, if only he'd been born more like his daddy instead of like his mama. Being like Mama, he just turned green.

Lucinda put the diamond behind her back. "Why are you looking at me like that? It's just a little old wedding is all. It's not like I intend to bite him or anything."

"Didn't it mean anything to you, Lucinda?" he asked, proud of himself for not screaming. Or bawling. "I about died for you, in case you didn't notice."

At Maple Lawn it was a written rule that Hadley must put on Sargeant's big floppy gloves before handling the silverware. At Browning House, Lucinda took his blood into her *mouth*.

She ran her finger over the still-tender wound, and the pain he felt was not limited to his skin. "How can you marry *him*, Lucinda?"

"Did you think I'd marry you? Come on, dear, let's read the new book. It's just your sort of story—full of all sorts of breath-taking torture."

"Get out," he snapped.

"Oh Hadley," she said, touching his face. "Are those tears in your eyes?"

Hadley slapped her hand away.

She couldn't have looked more surprised if she tried. "Nothing has changed, honey. I promise."

"That's true," he said. "You're as heartless as ever."

She stepped back as though he'd really used his fist instead of only thinking about it. "How can you say that? After all we've shared?"

Her heart thumped against the fabric of her dress, and for the first time in a month, Hadley sat up without a lick of trouble. He shoved the book at her and crossed his arms so she couldn't give it back. "It's over, Lucinda. The lessons. The secrets. The tricks. I can't do it anymore."

Lucinda's lip actually trembled. Hadley missed those lips so much that he dug his fingers into the flesh above his elbows, shoveling graves in his skin with his nails. The last time her lips trembled like that, she'd pulled him into a broom closet by the collar of his shirt.

There was barely room for two brooms in that closet, much less two people, which only meant that they had to stand as close as brooms. Over the years, Hadley had felt Lucinda's shoulder against his shoulder, her elbow on his knee, her hair on his nose, and her nose on his neck, but he'd never felt everything altogether at once. That day in the closet, Lucinda pressed him to the wall with every inch of herself and clamped down on his throat so hard, he had to bite on a broom handle in order to keep quiet. Afterward, he'd swept the Rose Bud Parlor with that broom, his palm cupped over the teeth-marks, and his blood trickling in a fiery thread down the inside of his shirt.

During their time in the closet, Hadley had memorized the feel of her, especially her lips. Why should Dickie Worther-Holmes have any right to those lips?

He was still thinking about the broom closet when he caught her by the forearms and jerked her down on the camp cot.

Mostly, Lucinda was a closed-mouth kisser and kissed like she was hiding something behind her teeth that was too good for the likes of Hadley. Hadley had tried a number of times to get in there, but as a rule, Lucinda would promptly switch to sucking on his neck the second his tongue got busy. This time Hadley didn't give her a choice. He got in a few angry thrusts before she stabbed him with her diamond. Hadley pulled away. "Ouch!"

Lucinda smiled.

"Get out," he said, and, by gosh, he meant it. He wished he'd never have to see Lucinda Browning again.

☙

When Mama came with soup later, Hadley could tell that *she* could tell that he'd been weeping like a fool. "It'll be okay," she said.

Hadley slurped his sweet corn soup, determined to move forward. "Would you please find Ethel and tell her I'd like to see her today?"

"Ethel?" Mama said. "You mean that cute little upstairs-girl with the Chesterfield haircut?"

Hadley nodded. Lucinda Browning wasn't the only fish in the sea.

"I'm sorry, dear, but I wouldn't know how to find her. Poor thing got let go two weeks ago."

Hadley inhaled a glob of corn. "They fired her?"

"Kissed the wrong person, I heard," Mama said, closing the curtains with a snap. "You see, Hadley, you're not the only servant in this household to have romantic troubles."

☙

As soon as Hadley was back on his feet, he started looking for new work. "Time I move on," he told his mama.

The sight of Lucinda trying on wedding veils or laboring over sofa swatches with Dickie's mama was enough to make him sick. The situation was getting dire. If Hadley didn't find a new post soon, he would be serving pizzelles to the entire Worther-Holmes clan at the *Night of Incantesimo* engagement party that Dickie's sister, Fancy, was cooking up for the last weekend in May. Fancy was married to a Sicilian and thought everything should be Sicilian.

To make matters worse, Hadley couldn't grab a broom without running into a discomfiting memory. The creak of a door might summon one. The turn of a page. A struck match. In the vineyard, he was plagued by thoughts of the afternoon she crept up behind him, squashing fallen grapes with her bare feet. He didn't know she was there until she drew a wet toe across his toes. "Read to me, Hadley."

In the Log Cabin room, he was reminded of the time he'd taken the tiger tooth away from her and pressed it to the old knife scar on the pad of his finger until a black-red bead appeared. While Mama whipped potatoes on the other side of the door, Hadley rubbed blood across his lips and Lucinda ate it off.

Flowers were particularly dangerous. Flowers made him think of the day she'd taken off his bandage by the Butterfly bush. Ten minutes later, they'd both walked away with a headful of lavender petals that were only slightly less purple than the bite on his skin.

Hadley wondered if his memories were the same as those of other people. His memories were made of grape juice and toes, teeth marks and blood, carved words and carved skin. And she was still leaving him notes.

When are you going to forgive me?

One day, when they were setting up in the dining room for Lucinda's spring meeting of the *Association for Moral and Social Hygiene* club, Lucinda touched his "garden-shears" bump, pressing the place with her nail. For several blood-pounding moments, Hadley surrendered to the gentle pain, unable to squeeze out a single breath. In fact, had Lucinda kept at it much longer, he would have keeled over on the radish roses.

"Don't leave me," she said.

His stomach churned with pain. Now the dining room was ruined too. It was time for him to leave Browning House.

"Why don't you try Muggin's place?" Loomis suggested when they were pitching hay together one morning. "That old coot's got more folks working on his lawn than Mister Wilson has tending to the White House."

Hadley had an interest in doing lawn work and thought this to be a fine idea. That Sunday, he headed to Mr. Arthur P. Muggins' place on *Morning Dew Circle* to talk to the man about a gardening job.

CR

Hadley had often told Lucinda that he should be growing flowers instead of shelling peas. "A house ought to have a garden that suits its personality. I think I would be good at growing gardens with personality."

Lucinda had laughed the first time he said this. "Does Browning House have a personality?" she asked.

"It sure does. It's the coliseum, remember? If I were in charge of the coliseum, I'd plant blood-red hortensia under the windows and grow roses that smell like myrrh."

"Where do you get such fanciful ideas, Hadley?"

"Hell, Lucinda, I was born with ideas."

CR

The house on Morning Dew Circle was the whitest, most painted house Hadley had ever seen. With a personality that was every bit as fussy as the mother-of-pearl jewelry box Mr. Browning bought for Lucinda's bracelet collection, its gardens looked all the more showy against its blinding white walls. Three tiers of Bourbon roses tumbled under the front windows like rubies spilling from a drawer. A gazing ball cast sapphire reflections under a flowering Empress tree. And bright blooms fanned the porch in elaborate patterns edged with paths of pink sand. Every flower in the old man's garden seemed planned down to the last petal. Suddenly Hadley's big ideas felt awfully small. *What am I doing here?* he asked himself. *I don't know how to make a bed of forget-me-knots grow in the shape of a doily.* His only hope was that Mr. Muggins' might need his peas shelled. Before he could make up his mind whether to knock or leave, a Negro boy opened the door and made his mind up for him.

Inside, the place reeked of varnish and calcimine and the walls jumped with the steady crack of hammers hammering wood. A fine plastery powder filmed Hadley's skin. He greeted Muggins with a sneeze.

The old fella was sitting in a wheel chair on the screened porch drinking a mint julep. A book lay open on his knee, the title of which Hadley read upside down: THE BRAWN OF BERNARR MCFADDEN: AN ARRESTING PICTORIAL.

He ain't gonna have need of me, Hadley thought as a parade of strong fellows filed by the porch with bricks stacked on their shoulders.

Mr. Muggins watched his army of workers from behind a pair of big sunglasses. Hadley watched, too. Being new to interviewing, he couldn't think how to begin. Should he make small talk so as to appear friendly: *How's that pictorial going, Mr. Muggins? I hear it's very arresting.* Or was it best to jump straight to the point? *I need to get away from Lucinda Browning, and I'm willing to trim your rose canes with my teeth, if that would work for you?*

The Negro boy swished a fan around the old man's head, and Hadley watched three unnaturally black hairs blow back and forth, back and forth. All the while, he couldn't help but think how delightfully boring it would be to work as a fanner for Mr. Muggins. "I've come to ask if you have any work, sir," Hadley said.

Two murky lenses turned his way and gave him a murky once over.

Hadley cleared his throat. "I've been at Browning House since I was nine. Before that I was with a family in Charlottesville called Tweeb."

Muggins' hair blew up. Muggins' hair blew down. "What do you do for Winslow Browning?" he asked.

Hadley squared his shoulders. "I'm pretty handy, sir." He ticked off his handiness on his fingers. "I know how to work a vegetable garden, fix a toilet, bake a Brown Betty, and I've been told I have a very cajoling way with pigs . . . "

Muggins tapped on Hadley's arm. "Let me see them."

"Sir?"

"Your arms. I'm putting in a gymnasium, and I'm looking for strong arms." Hadley peered into the man's dark glasses and saw nothing in return except his own round eyes. "Have you got strong arms, boy?"

Hadley showed his arms.

Muggins kicked back the last of his julep and swatted the fan-boy away. "When can you start?"

"You mean you're hiring me?"

"I pay a decent wage and offer plenty of opportunities to earn an extra buck. Does that sound like something that would suit you?"

Hadley was afraid to get his hopes up. Could it really be this easy? "That all depends. I'm going to need a place to stay."

Muggins smiled for the first time since Hadley stepped into his bright white house. "Today's your lucky day, son. I keep a dormitory upstairs for my boys."

Hadley was so pleased with himself that he let out a yelp as soon as he was through the front door.

"You gonna work on the gym?" a voice asked from somewhere over Hadley's head.

Hadley shielded his eyes and looked up. A boy about his age stood on a ladder, cleaning out a gutter. He was tall and brown and had the biggest muscles Hadley had ever seen. The boy gestured with the claw of a hammer. "Ole man's aw'right. I made an extra V spot last week just for plumbing his drain."

Hadley felt like someone had just lifted a buggy off his chest. No more watching Lucinda doodle pictures of wedding dresses. No more notes that hurt his heart. It seemed a little strange that the old man wanted a gymnasium, what with being in a wheel chair and all, but that's how rich folks were. They spent money on all sorts of useless stuff. It wasn't gardening, of course, and Hadley wasn't sure how long a job as a laborer was likely to last, but he didn't care. He was pleased as punch to be leaving Browning House behind.

❧

Hadley wrote out his notice three times over before leaving it under the coal-lump paperweight on Mr. Browning's desk. Even Mama couldn't complain. She believed the move would be good for Hadley. In a month's time, Lucinda would be married and moving into one of the fancy modern houses on Treebourne Street built by *Worther-Holmes Homes*. Regardless, she was sure to be making regular appearances with her young husband in tow.

"At Muggins'," Mama said, "you can keep clear of Miss Lucinda forever."

Mr. Sweet came into the kitchen just then and told Hadley that Mr. Browning wished to speak to him in the study.

CR

Hadley had built fires in the study, of course. He'd once earned an afternoon off for repairing the baby toe on the claw foot of Mr. Browning's desk chair after Lucinda had taken the coal paperweight to it because she didn't have a mama. But Hadley had never been in the study when Mr. Browning was in the study.

"Sit," Mr. Sweet said, nodding to a chair. The chair was parked directly across the table from Lucinda, who pulled a long pink twist of taffy from her teeth and smiled a Cheshire smile.

Recently, she had cut and waved her hair, and Hadley didn't care for it. He thought it made her look older. Then again, this was probably not such a bad thing. For one, her hair wouldn't be dancing across Dickie Worther-Holmes' cheek nearly so often as it had danced across his cheek in the good old days. For another, Hadley didn't want to be reminded of the good old days.

Mr. Browning was a tall elegant man with eyes that blinked two or three times as often as normal. He was known around town for his bright yellow *pointed-chin* beard, which he stroked obsessively into the sharpest of triangles whenever he wasn't using his hands for other things. Presently, he sat next to his daughter with his hands folded on top of Hadley's letter. He looked ridiculously big behind the spindly writing table, and

Hadley couldn't help but wonder if this was why the man had chosen such a delicate piece of furniture for his desk. He motioned for Hadley to pull his chair up as if they were about to eat. Somehow, the table made Hadley feel like a runt, even as his employer tripled in size.

Mr. Browning did something then he had never done in a full eight years. He released Mr. Sweet and spoke to Hadley with his own two lips. "I'm baffled," he said, blinking ten times. "And I don't get baffled much. No one has ever resigned their post at Browning House. Retired, yes. On rare occasion, we've been forced to dismiss someone. Usually people die first. Resignations are unheard of. So what's the problem, young man? The pay is fair, so it can't be that. The work is reasonable, and the hours are quite standard. What could possibly be the trouble?" He must have seen Hadley shift in his seat because he added, "You may speak freely, of course."

For the first time in weeks, Hadley wanted to laugh. He even shot a look at Lucinda, hoping she'd get wiggly at the thought that he might actually speak freely. *Well, you see, Mr. Browning, your daughter here has been giving me more than reading lessons for the past few years . . .*

Much as he might like to say the words, he didn't have the nerve. He hardly knew what to say at all. Hadley wished Mr. Sweet were doing the talking instead. "A man can't live with his mother forever," he finally said.

"So this is about living quarters? Is that it?"

"No, sir. It's about doing something on my own."

Mr. Browning patted Hadley's letter as though it wouldn't lay flat. He blinked some more. "All right then. I can appreciate that, son, I surely can." He patted the letter again, though this time it was rather more like a spank. "I have to wonder though—how much do you really know about your new employer?" Triangling his beard into a saber-sharp point, Mr. Browning leaned across his little desk and spoke in the lowest possible voice. "Are you aware of the fact that Arthur Muggins has a reputation for hiring young men, such as yourself, to perform special 'duties' for extra cash?" He sat back in his chair. "If you catch my meaning."

Hadley didn't catch his meaning. "He needs laborers, sir."

Mr. Browning gave Hadley the same agitated sigh that his daughter had been giving him for years. "Let me spell it out for you, boy. Muggins has never married. Muggins will never marry. He is of the sort who enjoys fraternizing with his hired help. His hired help are all young men of color. Boys, to be exact. Do you understand what I'm telling you?"

Hadley's ears warmed.

Mr. Browning smacked the table, rattling ink bottles and tipping over a cup of old feather pens. "Arthur Muggins uses his so-called 'laborers' until they get too old, and then he hires new boys to take their place. If his backyard is any indication, *old* would seem to be about twenty-five. Not a good career move for you, I'm thinking, even if being used in such a way by your employer appeals to you for some odd reason."

Hadley kept quiet by sticking the tip of his tongue under his molars. It was horrifying to realize that Muggins may, in fact, be after a similar arrangement to the one Hadley already had. He thought back to the backyard on Morning Dew Circle. Indeed, the whole house had been over-flowing with young men such as him.

"Don't look so down in the mouth now," Mr. Browning said, re-pointing his beard and smiling cheerily. "I have a solution that I think might serve us all." He laid a hand on Lucinda's shoulder. "Miss Browning wishes to hire you as her gardener for her new home on Treebourne Street."

At first Hadley wasn't sure who Miss Browning was. Then Miss Browning nudged his ankle with her toe.

Hadley scratched at a scab of dirt on his trousers and tried not to hear the rubbery twist of taffy being stretched between her teeth. "I'd like to make my own way, thank you."

"Nonsense, boy. There'll be no peace for you at Muggins, and if you don't work for Muggins, where will you work? I'm sure I don't need to remind you how people feel about half-casts. You might consider yourself what my daddy used to call a *passer,* but, like it or not, your mother is Negro, and you go to the Negro church. Not everyone is as enlightened as we are at Browning House. Most people won't touch a chromey with a ten foot pole, Arthur Muggins' pole notwithstanding."

Hadley watched Lucinda lick pastel goo off her thumb.

"Now then, you want your independence, and I don't blame you. I believe working for my daughter is the perfect compromise. We won't be losing a faithful employee, and you'll have your own work away from your mother."

Lucinda's toes picked that particular moment to begin scissoring up the inside of Hadley's calve. Hadley sat up straight in his chair. "I've already begun packing," he said, as if all his belongings couldn't be thrown in a shoebox in two minutes flat.

Mr. Browning clapped his hands. "Wonderful. We'll move you over with Lucinda when the time comes."

Lucinda's foot made a swift traverse of Hadley's knee, and when he tried to shift away, her toes followed his leg. "I don't think that's a good idea, sir."

Mr. Browning sighed spectacularly. "Why ever not?" Lucinda slid the arch of her foot up Hadley's thigh and pressed her toes firmly between his legs. Hadley inhaled too fast and choked on his spit.

Thanks to Lucinda Browning, Hadley was a man who knew what broom handles tasted like. Even so, he had not been touched so specifically since Lucinda gouged his throat with her tiger tooth. He seriously considered directing Mr. Browning's attention to Lucinda's foot under the table. Lucinda smiled around her taffy, confident that he would never do any such directing. In the meantime, she slid her toes and squeezed her toes and walked her toes until Hadley felt as dizzy as a man wearing a winter suit at a summer picnic. She did it so thoroughly that Hadley wasn't sure he wanted to do anything that would make Lucinda put her foot back in her shoe. It was uncomfortable, truly, but even so, Hadley thought his best revenge might be to let it go on for as long as possible. When he stopped chocking on his spit, he said; "I just don't know, Mr. Browning."

Mr. Browning posed some pretty convincing arguments. He offered more money. More holidays. Bigger quarters. He informed Hadley that several of Muggin's nigs had been found twirling from trees in Moon Woods. Hadley figured Lucinda was working up as much of a sweat as he was, what with all the convincing arguments going on.

"I thought you'd never say yes," she grumbled when they left the study together five long minutes later.

Hadley had made himself wait until he could stand it no longer before agreeing to move in with Lucinda. By then, he hardly heard his own voice saying *okay*. He only knew he'd made Lucinda work hard to sway him.

After Mr. Browning shut the door, Hadley yanked Lucinda around the corner into the Rose Bud parlor. Anyone could have heard him: a gossipy maid, Mr. Browning, or his own mother.

Hadley didn't care. "I want you, Lucinda," he said, pulling her body against his own. "In the normal way this time. No Dracula stuff. No drinking poison to prove it. If you feel like you can't marry me, that's not my fault. I'll work at your fancy new house like I said I would, but if you want to put your toes in my lap while your daddy is staring me dead in the eye, you damned well better do it in private, too. I ain't gonna like watching you with Dickie. Only one thing will make it worth my while." Hadley jabbed a finger at her nose. "That's the real deal, Lucinda, the deal your daddy can't make. Now, what do you say?"

Lucinda's eyes turned wrathfully blue. "Good Lord, Hadley. Who do you think you are?"

Hadley didn't rightly know who he was. He only knew that he aimed to get something out of all this for himself. If Lucinda wanted to play with him, why shouldn't he work out a deal that would give him something in return? "I can't hardly think straight any more, you got me so tied up in knots."

Lucinda lifted the circle that was his arms and took him off like a soiled dress. "Well now, we need to get you thinking straight again, don't we, *Crump*?" She slipped her hand, still sticky with taffy, down the front of his baggy trousers.

One touch was all it took

Lucinda unfolded her handkerchief and wiped her hand with it. "Don't try and give me orders, Hadley. It's ugly and no one likes an ugly boy. I feel sure that old chicken hawk Muggins would back me up on this. There's only one 'deal' dear, and this is it: You play nice, I'll give the orders, and maybe, just maybe, we'll both get what we want."

When she left, he slumped against the rose buds, his knees rubbery as taffy and his heart galloping with a powerful excitement born of fear or joy--he didn't know which. From her permanent place above the mantle, Mrs. Browning stared at him, chin cocked in a wondering sort of way.

∽

On June 1, 1920, Lucinda M. Browning became Mrs. Richard Worth-Holmes Junior and moved into the crown jewel of the new housing track on Treebourne Street, four blocks over from Browning House. The young bride christened her three-story mansion, *Wisteria Walk,* despite its mud lawn and distinct lack of wisteria. "That's why I'm bringing you along. Personality."

As Lucinda's gardener, Hadley's first job was to learn all he could about growing wisteria, a subject on which he was about to become a keen expert. He began his new lessons much like he began his reading lessons: with a book.

From page 222 of *Odessa Sheffield's Helpful Guide to New Gardeners*

Wisteria sinensis: These deciduous vines are huge, aggressive, and likely to cause severe upset if ingested. The wise gardener will commit himself to keeping all growth in careful bounds.

Nail Number Two: The Pendulum

It was the painted figure of Time as he is commonly represented, save that, in lieu of a scythe, he held what, at a casual glance, I supposed to be the pictured image of a huge pendulum, such as we see on antique clocks. There was something, however, in the appearance of this machine which caused me to regard it more attentively. While I gazed directly upward at it, (for its position was immediately over my own,) I fancied that I saw it in motion. In an instant afterwards the fancy was confirmed. Its sweep was brief, and of course slow. I watched it for some minutes, somewhat in fear, but more in wonder.

—"The Pit and the Pendulum" by Edgar Allen Poe

While Browning House was being wired for electricity and looking forward to its first plug-in toaster, banners were popping up all over town declaring war on a way of life that had served the Crump line well for as long as anyone could remember: *Worther-Holmes Homes—Bringing Modernity to the Old South.*

Dickie and Lucinda took these words to heart and began assembling what they called a *fully-mechanized* home. "Thank goodness for Daddy Dick," Lucinda said of her new father-in-law. "He's brought the sophistication of New York City to small town living at long last."

The goal of a *Worther-Holmes Home* was to make families less dependent on the shifty habits of household servants by supplying a host of clever new appliances to do the work in their place. Mechanical servants, the ads were calling them, and just about everyone Hadley knew was afraid of being replaced by one.

Wisteria Walk was staffed to the gills with mechanical servants, the lot of which desperately fascinated Hadley, who nonetheless preferred brooms to the bulky electric sweeper that filled the utility closet. Lucinda's fully-mechanized house had a washing machine for washing clothes, a percolator for brewing coffee, an electric refrigerator to electrically chill all the food, and a vast supply of peculiar-looking flat irons, vibrators, and manglers for the ironing of ones' clothing. This meant that you could cancel the ice man. You could cancel the laundress too because the downstairs maid could do the washing *and* the ironing along with all the cleaning. Because Dickie had a fondness for automobiles, there was no need for a livery man. He preferred to drive himself and did not employ a driver. This, in fact, was to become one of Hadley's duties. He was to learn to drive for the purpose of chaurferring Lucinda around town.

"We've got the vote now, for Pete's sake," Lucinda said. "Women don't have time to keep after a household full of servants."

Times were changing, that much was clear. Lucinda had a tub in her bathroom big enough for six people to swim in. Even the bedrooms were cluttered with mechanical servants. Curling irons. Heating pads. Radio. And the most touted modernization of all—the *ventilation* system. Daddy Dick promised that a *Worther-Holmes Home* would always be the perfect temperature.

"You can sleep naked in any season," Lucinda bragged to all her friends. "Imagine! No more nightgowns or bedclothes to wash. It's the height of luxury and thoroughly practical, too."

In olden times, jobs were plentiful for people like Hadley when newlyweds were setting up house. These days, instead of having a Lemon or a Flavia around, Wisteria Walk had a hand-held iron that heated up at the press of a button. It had a girl called Quindora to press the button, and appliances enough that Tilly, the cook, could feed both the family and the help and still have time to spare. There was no Loomis Sackett, no Cuffy, and no Miss Missy. The natural gossip of maids was replaced by buzzers, motors, and electric doorbells that chimed *ding dong*. Hadley liked to fiddle with circuitry as much as the next man but the place didn't feel quite right. Lights weren't meant to turn on clear across the room by a switch. It was confusing.

Dickie and Lucinda loved everything, though, and they would flip lights on and off a hundred times in a row for the pure joy of doing it. Lucinda searched for new hair styles in magazines so she could use her hair iron, and Dickie was fond of plugging things in. To hear them talk, one would think Wisteria Walk was Heaven on Earth.

"It smells like a waste of money to me," Mama said during her first visit to the house. She stomped into the "turret" room with a shopping bag over her arm, thoroughly unimpressed by the perfect temperature or the lack of shifty servants. "Hadley, Hadley, Hadley," she said, her voice echoing up to the tip top of the breast-shaped dome that was the turret room's crowning glory. "I don't see how you can live with her like this."

"I been doing it for half my days, Mama," Hadley pointed out.

The dome had a big pink nipple in the middle that Lucinda insisted was a wisteria bloom. Hadley was willing to admit that he still had a lot to learn, but it seemed to him that wisteria was not normally so anatomical in shape. He couldn't understand why everyone pretended that the thing on the ceiling was a flower when it was clearly a nipple. Blossom or bosom, he felt doomed for the rest of his life to think of nipples whenever he saw flowers in bloom, and to think of blooms when he saw nipples.

"You're a grown man now," Mama said. "You don't have to live with her anymore. And why in hell is there a nipple on the ceiling?"

"It's a nice house, Mama," Hadley said. And it was. If you could tear yourself away from that ceiling.

"He keeps *guns*," Mama said. "I may not know what a person uses a *heating pad* for, but I know what a gun is for. There's a whole big case of 'em downstairs and another rack in the study."

Hadley thought Dickie's gun collection was a thing of wonder. He'd offered to clean them just to get a closer look. There was a Browning left over from the war, a Springfield for skeet shooting, and a Big Medicine gun that was once the property of President Theodore Roosevelt before Daddy Dick got his hands on it. Hadley's favorite gun of the day was a Maxim mg08 machine gun, and it was a real doozy.

"Dickie is a gun man," Hadley told Mama.

That's how Dickie referred to himself. *I'm a gun man, Crump,* he'd said as Hadley set to work on the Springfield with rod and bore solvent and a gigantic case of excitement. *See that you handle my baby with care or I'll have to put a bullet in you.*

"I don't like it," Mama said. She reached for a Bible quote without missing a beat. "The mouth of the adulteress is a deep pit; he with whom the Lord is angry will fall into it."

Hadley had ignored a great many proverbs over the years, and he was prepared to ignore this one as well. "I wanna show you something, Mama." He took her out to the backyard where a clothesline clipped with lace tablecloths had been tied between two poles.

Mama rapped on the wall under the kitchen window with her umbrella handle. "Place doesn't even have brick walls."

"They're cement," Hadley said.

She kicked a dirt clod. "Where's the lawn?"

"It's being delivered by the U.S. Golf Association on Tuesday. This time next week, you'll be standing on grass as velvety as a golf course."

"For mercy sake," she said. "What's wrong with making the gardener grow the grass?"

Hadley got down on his knees. "Have a look at this, Mama," he said, and he ran his fingers through the only clump of green to be found on all of Treebourne Street. "They're four-leaf clovers, the whole big patch of them." Hadley had spent an hour searching for three leaf clovers one morning to no avail. "Have you ever heard of a whole patch of four-leaf clovers before? Surely that must mean something good?"

"Not necessarily," Mama said, shifting her shopping bag to the opposite arm. "Anything so strange is just as likely to be bad."

"Pick one, Mama. I've got ten pressed in the *Song of Solomon* even as we speak."

"Maybe you ought to read that Bible instead of pressing weeds in it," she suggested.

Hadley tucked one behind her ear. "Come on. You haven't seen where *I* live yet."

The gardener's quarters were a far cry more deluxe than the canning closet Hadley had shared with his mother at Browning House. For the first time in his life, he had "things". He had a bookshelf with three books: *Young Folks Cyclopedia of Common Things*, *America Bible Society Holy Bible*, and *Odessa Sheffield's Helpful Guide to New Gardeners*. He had a night table for his jar. He had a drawer for his Phoetus gifts. He even had his own door to the bathroom. The kitchen had a door to the same bathroom, but he could lock it when he was in there so it felt almost like his own.

Mama tapped her toe on the Serapi rug that had been ordered all the way from Persia. "It's shameful," she said. "No ordinary servant lives this way."

"These quarters are standard in all the Worther-Holmes homes. You ought to find a position with one of the young families, Mama. Sit on that bed. It's like sleeping on a cloud."

What Hadley didn't tell her was that, cloud or no cloud, he almost never slept. He couldn't make peace with all the noise.

Mama dropped her shopping bag on the bed, took out a square of purple flannel, and began to unfold it.

"What's that?" he asked.

"Smartweed." She sprinkled a handful on his blankets. "It clears the head."

Mama had come prepared. She tied a catseye shell to the window sash and placed a bag of lucky legumes under his pillow.

"That should do you for now." There was one last thing in the bottom of the bag. She handed him a box. "Happy homecoming."

The box was too big to be a potion or a bar of lucky soap. "You didn't have to get me a present," he said.

"I didn't get you a present. Quaker Oats give it to me for spending two dollars on oatmeal at the store yesterday."

The box had the words *Little Top Hat* printed in red and black letters across the lid. Inside was a big aluminum head. "It's one of them Jolly Nigger banks that's gotten so popular lately," Mama said. "When you drop a coin in the slot, the eyes wiggle. Try it." She handed him a penny.

Sure enough, when Hadley dropped the penny in, Little Top Hat's eyes wiggled merrily. "Thanks, Mama." He put his new bank on the night table next to his Whoops Jar.

Mama touched the WHOOPS on his jar with a shaky brown finger. "What are you doing here, Hadley?"

ひ

Lucinda's bedroom was above his own, and every night it was always the same: hop hop hop hop hop, until a man wanted to sign himself into the nuthouse. Sticking your fingers in your ears didn't make the hops go away. Neither did humming. He'd tried cotton and he'd tried wrapping his head with a pillow. He'd damned near smothered himself with the pillow. Nothing worked.

At first, Dickie was the hardest to stomach. He sounded like a xylophone, only instead of making music, his notes were an ascending scale of pig-grunts that started low and rose in range. The last key, inevitably, sounded broken. Hadley came to look forward to that last broken key. He liked to think that Lucinda did, too.

Thankfully, Lucinda didn't make such passionate sounds. She laughed a lot. She said things Hadley couldn't understand. One minute, he would be diving under his pillow in an effort not to hear, the next he would be sitting up straight in bed straining to make out the words she was saying. This, in its self, was its own form of insanity. Ultimately, her whispers proved worse than his grunts.

On his tenth night in the new house, Hadley heard three words that planted themselves in his head like a case of schizophrenia. Dickie said: *God, your mouth!*

Hadley was more jealous of those words than all the broken notes put together. He worried that Lucinda was using her mouth to drink Dickie's blood. He got down on his knees next to his big new bed and began to pray out loud. "Dear God, please don't let her do that to anyone but me."

It seemed likely that God would send him straight to hell for making such a sinful request, yet he couldn't help but get down on his knees every night and whisper the same prayer. "Let that be mine alone," he'd pray. "Don't let her drink his blood."

Some mornings, Hadley would pretend to tighten a loose screw just so he could stand on a stool over the breakfast table and squint down the inside of Dickie's shirt collar. Every time he handed Dickie the newspaper, he made the man reach so he could check for bite marks under his sleeve. Eventually, Hadley focused on two things: the rapidness of the xylophone and the controlled sound of Lucinda's voice during an abandoned act of passion. Hadley wanted to give Lucinda something a good deal less rapid. Hadley wanted to make Dickie's wife lose control.

ভ্

Over the course of the first few weeks, Hadley put in a cutting garden and learned to drive Dickie's car. When the turf-breeders brought the new lawn, he made sure the four-leaf clovers didn't get covered over with bent grass. From sun up to sun down, Hadley arranged pavers, prepped soil, and dropped root balls into holes. His muscles got sore, then hard. His skin got red, then brown. He worked his heart out every single day, and he waited. He waited for Lucinda to make good on the deal he thought they'd struck in the Rose Bud Parlor.

It was impractical, of course. This was a woman who, while she slept, soaked her diamond rings in a special bowl to keep them sparkling bright. She ordered stationary and gravy boats and pink tiles for the bathroom floor printed with her new monogram. She kept her husband hopping every night. It seemed unlikely that Hadley's chance would ever come.

Then, one day, during their first official fight as a married couple, Dickie stomped on Lucinda's monocle and told her the gosh damned thing looked ridiculous. "Why don't you get yourself a pair of cheaters like everyone else, LuLu?" Dickie was the only one who got by with calling Lucinda "LuLu".

LuLu told Dickie she would rather die than go around in a pair of old-lady specs. "You'll never catch me wearing eyeglasses like some decrepit, weak-eyed fool," she vowed. "I cannot abide them for any reason, so you may as well save your breath." This left only one solution. From that day on, Lucinda had her gardener read books out loud to her under the nippled ceiling in the turret-shaped tower she named *The Reading Room*.

From the start, The Reading Room was a place to hide things that ought not to be seen. Lucinda had special bookcases made to fit the octagon walls, each shelf built doubly-thick so as to accommodate an inner layer of books and an outer. She said she needed the extra space. Only Hadley knew why Lucinda wanted to stash away certain books from view. The inner-shelf was for books such as *The Adventures of a Luckless Fellow* or *Mischievous Maid Faynie*. The outer was for nobler selections like *Kindred of the Dust*. But even *Maid Faynie*, for all her fooling around, was simply a decoy for the real thing.

It was Hadley who built the window seat with the secret compartment, a space capable of accommodating up to fifty volumes of *V.I.L.E* books at any given time. The lid was designed to open without any outward signs of seams or hinges. To the casual observer, the window seat was just a window seat. Atop the secret door, Lucinda arranged a pair of colorful cushions decorated with petit point scenes from *Aesop's Fables*. The cushion on Lucinda's side of the seat was the *The Rose and the Amaranth,* while Hadley habitually sat on *The Salt Merchant and His Ass.*

"We've come a long way since those loose floorboards, haven't we Hadley?" Lucinda asked as she deposited some new window seat books one day.

Hadley was grateful to be reading again, but he didn't think they'd come far at all. For the most part, he hadn't managed to get too much out of their new arrangement outside of a lot of sleepless nights.

∽

The vibration of the pendulum was at right angles to my length. I saw that the crescent was designed to cross the region of the heart. It would fray the serge of my robe – it would return and repeat its operation – again – and again . . .
   —Edgar Allen Poe

While weeding the flowerbeds one day, Hadley got to talking to Quindora, with whom he'd recently become friendly. Quindora was to wash all the windows on the front of the house before

Daddy Dick showed up for lunch. Daddy Dick, it would seem, was partial to salmon croquettes and spotless windows, for he requested both each day when he dropped in for a visit. Of course, if the windows happened to be up to snuff, he might point out a fouled rug or a dingy-looking drape instead. Lucinda claimed to relish his keen eye and worked hard to please him. From five in the morning until twelve noon, everything in the house got polished twice.

☙

Quindora had more on her mind than cleaning windows and rugs. She hoped to become a dressmaker someday. Hadley, when he wasn't working, would let her pin his sleeves so she could get good at not sticking people. He'd let her measure him, too. In return, she would sing him songs. On the day she was washing the front windows, he requested she sing *There is a Balm in Gilead.*

Everything was going along quite nicely: the sun was shining, the weeds were few, and Quindora's voice trembled with such sweet heartbreak, even the birds shut up and listened. Quindora had no less than fifty braids in her hair and, as she sang, one of them came loose. Hadley watched a calla-colored ribbon sail off over the roof. *If you cannot preach like Peter, if you cannot pray like Paul . . . .* She reached the sponge up to Lucinda's window. *You can tell the love of Jesus and say, "He died for all."* The same second He died for all, the window swung open and Quindora gasped. Hadley dropped his trimmers and flew across the lawn with his arms stretched out, prepared to make a catch. Fortunately, he caught the falling girl in the nick of time.

"Lordie Lord," Quindora said after she was safely in his arms. "I thought you were a goner for sure."

"Me?" Hadley said in a shaky voice. His knees were shaking too. "You're the one that fell."

"Yes, but when I saw you standing under me, I thought I'd squish you dead."

Someone cleared their throat just then and Hadley looked up. A bowlful of wilted rose petals and dirty water hit him in the face.

"It won't do to have your servants making you look a fool," Daddy Dick told his son later that same afternoon. Hadley was repairing the lock on the gun cabinet. Dickie was reading the funny paper. Daddy Dick was reading HOUSES FOR SALE IN MADISON COUNTY.

"What are you talking about, Daddy?" Dickie said.

Daddy Dick snatched *Winnie Winkle* from Dickie's hands and sent it sailing across the room. "Christ in a biscuit! Don't you ever pay attention to what's going on in your own goddamned house?"

Hadley was accustomed to minding his own business and focused on the guns. His favorite of the day was a gold-plated Smith and Wesson.

"What's going on in my own goddamned house, Daddy?"

"It's that shit for brains gardener of yours, you dumb lug."

Hadley bobbled a retainer nut. He was kneeling on the floor by the cabinet, a mere kick in the head away from Dickie's shiny new two-tones.

Daddy Dick lit a Lucky Strike. "He's making a laughing stock of you, Richard."

Hadley closed his eyes and held his breath and waited for Daddy Dick to tell Dickie that his gardener was in love with his wife.

"The way I hear it," Daddy Dick said, "your neighbors caught themselves quite a show this morning."

"What sort of show?" Dickie said.

Hadley opened his eyes.

"A white boy carrying on with a darkie—that sort of show."

Dickie laughed. "My gardener *is* a darkie, Daddy."

"Apparently the Hammermills can't tell that from their doorstep. From far away, he looks as white as you or me."

"Well, he isn't," Dickie said, clacking his two-tones together an inch from Hadley's ear.

"We'll see about that. I'm gonna give him the A&P test."

Dickie snapped his paper and went back to reading.

About then, Tilly, the cook, came bustling in with a tray of sweet tea.

"You there," Daddy Dick said, and he pointed a finger at Hadley like a magic wand, transforming him from invisible to visible in an instant. "I need a grocery sack."

Hadley set aside his tools. Dickie had been so anxious to show his father the Mosin-Nagant he'd purchased the day before, he'd snapped the key off in the lock on the cabinet door. Lucinda's husband broke enough stuff on a weekly basis that Hadley's title should have been *Mister Fix-It*. Of course, he was often *Mister Fetch-It*, too. He went off to the kitchen to fetch a grocery sack with Tilly toddling behind.

"What's he up to?" Hadley whispered when they were through the kitchen door.

Normally, Tilly was congenial enough so long as you let her be the boss. Hadley almost lost his balance when she grabbed his ears and pulled his nose flat against the birthmark on the left side of her face. "Who you been poking, Mister Gardener?"

"Ow!" Hadley said. He tried to jerk away, but she pinched his lobes good and tight.

There wasn't a soul at Wisteria Walk that didn't cower from Tilly's birthmark. The story of its origin had been passed around the place a dozen times since day one. Sometimes people tried to expand on it or make it into something new, but Tilly had a knack for sticking her head into a room whenever the tale was being told. "Don't fluff it up," she would say. The un-fluffed version had it that Tilly's daddy was hung from a pecan tree the day before she was born. Lest the deed should pass unforgotten, Baby Tilly popped from the womb with a leaf print stamped around her eye. It was her duty, Tilly said, to use her leaf-shaped birthmark to stare down anyone who was up to no good. "Don't make me get you with my birf mark," she would threaten. She used her mark on Hadley now. "I can't help you, little man, if you don't tell me who it is."

Birthmark or no, Hadley didn't want to tell Tilly who he really loved so he said, "Quindora."

"The one that sings?"

"That's right. I didn't poke her, though."

She threw his ears away so hard, Hadley stumbled back and knocked a pot of macaroni off the stove. "You don't get it, do you? If you kiss a Negro girl, they gonna call you white every time. And if you kiss a white girl . . . shit. They'll string up you from a tree like they strung up my poor daddy."

"Who does that leave then?" Hadley wanted to know.

"Nobody." She pressed her fingers against her pecan leaf and tapped it menacingly. "You just have to hold it in."

"Hold it in?"

"Ain't no help for it, Mister Gardener. When a white folk looks at you, he sees a boy with skin too pale for Quindora and too nigger-colored to be white."

Hadley turned his hand over and looked at in the harsh electric light. He reckoned you could line up a thousand hands in a row and no two would look the same color. He wondered where white stopped and black started. How many drops of Negro blood did it take to move a fellow all the way over?

Tilly turned his hand back over and slapped a grocery sack in it. "That's just the way it goes for in-betweeners like you."

When Hadley returned to the parlor, Lucinda was there, perched on the arm of Daddy Dick's chair. Daddy Dick told Hadley to stick out his arm. "Turn on some lights, Richard."

Dickie clicked the switch.

Hadley held his arm side-by-side with the grocery sack. "See that, dummy?" Daddy Dick said to his son. "This boy's lighter than an A&P bag. In my book, that makes him too white to kiss niggers."

"Well, I'll be dipped," Dickie said, scratching his head. "I guess you're whiter than I thought, Crump."

"This is a scandal in the making," Daddy Dick said. "If you don't do something about it, the neighbors will never have respect for you."

"Aw, Daddy. I can't tell Crump who he can and cannot spoon."

"Can't you?" Daddy Dick said. "One of them has to go. You can keep the nigger or you can keep the gardener, but you can't keep them both. You don't want more chromeys running around the place, do you?"

Dickie looked at his feet. "Well, shoot, having Quindora around is like having a tailor in the house."

"Fine. You'll keep the girl, then."

93

"No," Dickie said. "I want Crump. Lucinda's fond of him, and he works like a mule. I just wish Quindora could stay, too . . ."

"Well, she can't," Lucinda said, putting her two cents in for the first time since Daddy Dick compared Hadley to a paper sack. "Quit looking so guilty and be a man for once. Anyway, it's Hadley's fault, not yours. He should have kept his hands to himself."

Dickie sank back down in his chair. "I'll speak to her in the morning, I guess."

"Do it now," Lucinda said.

CR

"I've got an idea," Mama said on Sunday after church. "Why don't you invite a girl out to supper? You make enough money for it now."

"Who would I invite?" Hadley wanted to know. "Tilly says I ain't Negro enough for a Negro, and everyone knows what they do to men like me if they even look at a white girl."

Quindora had put on a brave face when she left Wisteria Walk. "This frees me up to go after my real calling," she said. Never the less, Hadley worried that an uppity place like *Betty's Bewitching Glamour Gowns* wouldn't give Quindora a job no matter how good she was at not sticking people. Hadley had been to *Betty's* with Lucinda and everyone was blue-eyed and frilly there, even the dressmakers.

"It ain't right," Hadley said as he watched Quindora knapsack up her things in an old frayed shawl.

"Don't worry, Crump. You jest be careful who you put your arms around out there in the world because peoples can be touchy." She cuffed him under the chin.

"Has something happened?" Mama asked him, snapping him back to the present.

Hadley thought again about the goodbye kiss he'd planted on Quindora's lips.

"What was that for?" Quindora said, touching her mouth in surprise.

A regular lightning bolt of rebellious glee crackled through the black and white parts of him. "If I'm gonna be accused of kissing you, it seems only fair that I get to see what it's like."

"You think next time I could maybe kiss you back?" she asked.

Hadley smiled and did it again. Quindora's part was nice. Afterward, she patted him on the head. "I'll see you in church, little Crump."

Hadley liked thinking about that kiss, but he told his mama, "I don't want to invite anyone to supper." He was mad as the devil at Lucinda for what happened with Quindora, but the truth of the matter was, right or wrong, dumb or stupid, that afternoon in the Rose Bud Parlor was stuck in his head like a tumor. Every time Hadley looked at Lucinda's right hand, he felt the annihilating thrill of those fingers all over again.

"For the love of Mary," Mama said. "She's a USDA certified married woman, Hadley."

Hadley didn't need reminding when it came to that. He wanted a girl of his own, especially at night when he heard Lucinda upstairs with Dickie. He wanted more kisses like the kiss he shared with Quindora, too. And he wanted his skin to be all black or all white and not somewhere in between. But those were just wishes. The sad fact was, Hadley felt permanently damaged. In time, he might learn how to think about other things besides the stroke of those fingers, but there was one thing he'd never get out of his system, and that was the way Lucinda's monkey-flower eyes danced over the face of every servant child in Browning House and picked him out for reading lessons.

Mama shook her head in disgust. "The rich rule over the poor, and the borrower is the slave of the lender," she said.

"What does that even mean, Mama?" Hadley used to pretend like he got all of her stupid proverbs. Now he didn't want to get them.

"It means you need to find yourself someone who will be good to you and stop all this nonsense with Mrs. Worther-Holmes."

Hadley watched Quindora and her twin sister, Velzora, chatting on the church steps. When she waved at him, he waved back, but he didn't speak to her. This *nonsense* with Mrs. Worther-Holmes was all he cared about.

CR

Wisteria was a complicated thing to grow, and yet it never occurred to Hadley that Lucinda might be better off hiring a gardener with some real experience. As with all things, he simply set about teaching himself the proper way to get the job done. So it was that, while looking for a book on the subject of wisteria growing, he stumbled on something much more interesting.

The Meaning of Flowers, it was called, and Hadley was hooked the first second he read that prickly pear meant *I burn* in the language of flowers. Not in all his years, had he ever suspected that flowers had a language all their own. Before he could stop himself, he was looking up all his favorite flowers to see what they meant. He liked the idea that something so simple could convey love, deliver an insult, or offer a word of advice.

Hadley was partial to books that offered some sort of bonus in the back, like an epilogue or a glossary or a photograph of the author. It made him feel as if he was getting extra for his money. At the back of *The Meaning of Flowers* was a special section called *The Secret Names of Flowers*. Hadley laughed when he read that chamomile had the secret name of *From the Loins.*

"Buy the book or move along, kid," Mr. Pringles said after Hadley spent half an hour looking up secret names.

At this point, Hadley decided to use the money Lucinda had given him for a book on wisteria to buy *The Meaning of Flowers* instead. Consequently, he spent the whole walk home concocting a convincing argument for why it was more important to know that spurge had the secret name of *Fat From a Head*, than it was to educate one's self on how to get wisteria to climb where you wanted it to climb. To sweeten the news, he picked Lucinda a bouquet of clover and wild orchids on his way in the door. "In the language of flowers," Hadley told Lucinda, "Orchids symbolize beauty and refinement, and clover is a sign of domestic virtue."

They were white lie flowers, to be sure, but Lucinda liked to think she was refined and elegantly domesticated. She had Tilly put the bouquet in a vase next to her bed, pleased as pie by the wisdom of such a unique book purchase.

What Hadley failed to mention was that clover had the distinctly undomesticated secret name of *Semen of Ares.*

ॐ

At Wisteria Walk, Hadley's days were filled with flowers and his nights with fitful dreams. Sadly, the seeds he planted in the sun turned to poisonous weeds in the dark. On a good day, he might go hours without thinking of Lucinda. There was lots of work to be done, and he liked the hopeful feeling he got raking everything smooth in a new flowerbed. Every time a little green shoot curled up from the earth, Hadley felt like passing out cigars. Then night would come, and all those good feelings would wither to resentment.

After a while, he came to believe that the touch of his head on the pillow was what triggered *it.* He tried going to bed earlier. He tried going to bed later. It mattered not. Eventually, the pillow-trigger theory was disproved when he slept sitting-up one night and the thumping happened the same as always.

This left Hadley with only one theory to work with: Women were nothing but trouble. And not just Lucinda. Sometimes it felt like the whole world was full of women that Hadley couldn't have: colored women, white women, Lucinda Worther-Holmes, and Lucinda Worther-Holmes' rich white friends. There was one woman who appeared oddly agreeable. Her name was Babe Butternut. But Babe Butternut was more trouble than the ones he couldn't have.

Once, when the new kitchen girl was feeling croupie, Hadley was asked to serve lunch to Lucinda and her friends. In some homes, it might be odd to be served stuffed celery by the gardener, but in a house filled with mechanical servants, there aren't many servants available with the hands and legs necessary to perform food-serving jobs. It was more the rule than not that Hadley would be whisked from watering and planting on a regular basis so he might climb on a high stool and reach down a flower vase off a top shelf, or carry in a big box of something or other that Lucinda had ordered from someplace or other, or replace a radio tube. Celery-serving was all in a day's work.

Babe Butternut crunched on a stick of celery and announced to the room that she had a terrible weakness for dominos. She licked her lips when she said the word *dominos*, but Hadley attributed that to cream cheese at first.

The only thing Hadley had ever found fun about dominos was soldiering them up on the Log Cabin Room floor and giving them a tap. He couldn't see Babe Butternut getting down on the floor in her short flapper dress to line up dominos. Anyhow, she didn't strike him as being careful enough for it, the way she was always spilling her *peach dos* all over the place.

"You should go now, Hadley," Lucinda said, taking the tray from him.

Hadley thought Lucinda must want him to get the dominos they kept in the china cabinet drawer so he asked, "Do you want me to set up a card table or do you wanna play on the floor?"

"The floor sounds nice," Babe said.

Everyone giggled.

"Go away, Hadley," Lucinda said, rolling her eyes. "That boy is good as retarded."

Hadley happily departed for the kitchen and found Tilly rolling out a piecrust on the work table. "Hey Tilly, do you know why that giggly Miss Butternut likes dominos so much?"

Tilly whipped a powdery hand across her forehead, streaking it white above the leaf. "Iffin' I know that woman, *you* be the domino she's talking about."

Hadley had been called a lot of things, but he'd never been called a domino.

"Keep clear of that one, 'lil Domino," Tilly said. "She eats boys like you for breg'fest."

It so happened that Hadley was just that hard up, the notion offered some appeal.

Babe Butternut was the only woman he'd ever seen who was taller than Lucinda. Her breasts were like the dome at the top of the Reading Room in that Hadley was always looking up at them. Once, when he was trimming the new privet, Babe Butternut leaned over the bushes so far, his nose touched one of her domes. Another time, she instructed Hadley to dab *peach do* off her lap. He looked up then, too.

"That Babe Butternut sure is an awful pain, isn't she?" Lucinda said, the day after the celery.

"I don't mind her," Hadley said. He was on a ladder changing dead light bulbs. Lucinda was handing him new ones.

"You only say that because she acts like such a Dumb Dora around you. Babe calls herself a modern woman, but she doesn't even bandage her breasts."

"Is that right?" Hadley said.

"Do you think she's pretty?"

Lying was never his best skill, but Hadley knew better than to answer that question with any amount of honestly. "Her face could wither a fence post," he lied.

For a full ten seconds, it sounded like a teakettle was whistling in the other room. "Ewwwwwwww!" Lucinda cried. "I will not have my servants being seduced by the likes of Babe Butternut. If I catch you gawking down her dress again, I'll have you tarred and feathered."

Hadley watched her turn the light bulb round and round in her right hand. "I'm lonely, Lucinda."

"Why Hadley? Haven't I kissed you?"

"Yes."

"Then think on that when you get lonely," Lucinda said, and she set the light bulb down hard enough to crack it.

"That only makes it worse."

"Reading with me used to be enough, as I recall."

"I'm not a kid anymore."

She ran her eyes up and down him as if she was only just now noticing this. "Jesus, Hadley. If Dickie wasn't such a sap, he'd know in a heartbeat what's going on inside that one-track brain of yours." She balled her long, pale fingers into a tight hard fist. "If you want trouble, stick with Babe. She's more dangerous than all my nigger maids combined." Spinning in a tornado of buttercup hair, she stomped from the room.

CR

Inch by –inch—line by –line—with a descent only appreciable at intervals that seemed –ages—down and still down it came!

—Edgar Allen Poe

The Pit and the Pendulum was about a fellow who finds himself sentenced to a dungeon rife with all manner of hideous tortures. There was a pit. There was a pendulum. There was unending misery for the man in the pit strapped beneath the pendulum. In Hadley's opinion, it was an awful story. He particularly detested the part where the prisoner realizes that the pendulum has stopped descending while he's passed out, only to resume again the second he opens his eyes.

"I don't care for this one," Hadley told Lucinda. He held the book shut between his hands as if he could keep its claustrophobic terrors from crossing into his world.

They sat on the window seat facing one another with their knees drawn up between them. Though reading was normally the most he could expect of their time together, Lucinda had slipped the door key in her pocket in a way that stirred to life a hundred butterflies of hope in the hollow of his stomach. Dickie was off to the construction site for the day, and her bare toe tapped against his shoe hard enough to cause a bowl of roses on a nearby table to drop one white petal for each tap.

Whenever he was alone in the Reading Room, Hadley liked to trail his hand from spine to spine around the octagon shelves, allowing the smell of book glue and old paper to fill his starved senses. A single yellowed whiff had the strength to conjure swords, a ship, or trembling fingers loosening pearl buttons. All day long, every time he brushed his fingers under his nose, he'd relive the swords and the buttons. That smell, like the tap of Lucinda's toe, had the power to make him burn for a different life. The Reading Room, with its flower nipple and its mesmerizing scents of must and leather, could be highly disorienting.

"Read it like you're the prisoner," Lucinda said. "You can be so convincing when you want to be."

In the street below, the *Pinkie Bell Dairy Wagon* bumped along behind a lazy clomp of hooves. Ding. Clomp. Ding. Clomp. A petal drifted to the floor.

"I don't want to be the prisoner, Lucinda."

"Come on," she coaxed. "The way you say *vibrations of glittering steel* always makes me want to kiss the life out of you."

Hadley didn't remind her that she hadn't kissed him once since becoming Dickie's wife, a circumstance that was fast becoming his greatest irritation in life.

Lucinda drew his hand away from the book and set to following his veins with the pad of her thumb, working them as if she could re-route the flow of his blood if she rubbed just right. As he locked eyes with her across the bridge of his arm, she pressed his pulse against her mouth and licked a wet heart with her tongue. "Please."

Hadley breathed for the first time in over a minute. He opened the book and began to read.

I now –observed—with what horror it is needless to say— that its nether extremity was formed of a crescent of glittering steel, about a foot in length from horn to horn; the horns upward, and the under edge evidently as keen as that of a razor . . .

Razor was the last word he read before Lucinda sent the book whizzing across the room. This time, she slid his hand up the hem of her dress and molded his fingers around the hot skin on the top of her thigh. "I just love the way you say *glittering steel.*"

He threw her down on the window seat, quick as you please, and climbed on top of her, and fit himself between her legs. Much as Poe's prisoner had groped at the walls of his dark dungeon only to encounter again and again the rag he'd used to mark its circumference, so too Hadley arrived at the same familiar cairn—her mouth.

As he kissed it, a multitude of borrowed sins seemed to slip from buckram and gold gilt, leaping free of hidden shelves. Clandestine desire rattled the closed lid of the window seat. Across the room, the Pit and the Pendulum loosed fresh waves of anguish from the surface of a bent page.

He who has never swooned, is not he who finds strange palaces and wildly familiar faces in coals that glow; is not he who beholds floating in mid-air the sad visions that the many may not view; is not he who ponders over the perfume of some novel flower . . .

Lucinda forced her hand between their lips, wrecking the kiss. "Are you going to rape me?"

"Don't push me away this time," he begged.

The slap stung. "You're out of control," she said, and she slapped him again, this time harder.

It didn't hurt. Not like her teeth. Hadley almost wished she'd do it again. "You feel so good," he whispered, wanting to have her like Alec d'Urbeville had Tess, yet eager as ever to play Jonathon Harker to her vampire kiss.

Lucinda pounded on his shoulders. "Get off me, you filthy piece of trash."

Hadley didn't get off Lucinda. For every bed-creak that echoed in his brain, he moved his hips against hers. For every dirty note that led to nothing and every teasing touch and every teasing kiss, Hadley moved against her. For every time she made him explode in the throes of utterly depthless pain, Hadley moved and moved.

Towers of V.I.L.E. books collapsed beneath them inside the window seat. It was snowing petals on the rug. The Pit and the Pendulum clapped shut. He kissed her neck. He kissed her dress. The dress had little bluebells printed all over it, and Hadley kissed from bluebell to bluebell until he reached the one that came three bluebells beneath her bellybutton. This flower he carefully memorized, learning it first with his chin, then his nose, then his cheek. "Delicious," he said, chewing up the bluebell.

She gripped a handful of his hair. "You pig!" she whispered and she wrapped her legs around him.

"Smells like pigs," Penrod Tweeb once said after Hadley picked up a clean pair of underclothes that had fallen off the line. The Tweebs had liked to use a white woman for the laundry. "It's impractical to wash clothes only to have them handled by dirty hands," Sargent said. He demanded that the underclothes be washed again because Hadley had picked them up.

The flavor of Lucinda's dress was in his *mouth*. He rolled it around his tongue and swallowed. He unbuttoned his trousers . . .

A honk ripped through the air like a gunshot. Someone hollered: "Stop what you're doing this very instant!"

Hadley jumped up and his trousers fell down.

In the drive below, Lucinda's husband leaned on the horn of a brand new 1-16 Sport Phaeton. "Come see what I just bought, Lulu!"

Lucinda's eyes shifted from the automobile out the window to the worn knees of Hadley's union suit. "You cracked the window seat," she said. She wiped her lips with the back of her hand. *The Salt Merchant* was standing on his head on the floor and she tossed it on the broken seat to hide the split in the wood. "I'll be expecting you to make things good as new again, Hadley Crump."

With that, she went off to meet her husband, her bluebells soaked with Hadley's spit.

☘

Afterward, he couldn't calm down no matter what he did. *She wants me too,* he said to himself, re-living that moment a dozen times over when Lucinda wrapped her fingers in his hair and pulled his mouth into the folds of her dress. *If only Dickie hadn't showed up when he did.*

In the following weeks, Hadley had his revenge.

"Will you look at that?" Dickie groaned. "Some son of a bitch scratched my pretty Packard Blue door!"

And the next Monday, "Now how'd that mangy mutt wind up in my God-danged front seat?"

And the following Monday, "That's it! Get the cops, Crump. There's a gall-dern nail in every one of my tires!" Dickie couldn't have looked more distraught if Hadley had taken the table saw he was using and sawed the idiot's nose clean off his face. "I'm going to need you to put new tires on right away."

"Yes sir," Hadley said. "Just as soon as I'm done seeing to your wife's seat."

☙

Hadley spent his day off in the park after church every week with his mama. He'd pick wild flowers while she trailed behind, poking at things with the point of her umbrella and occasionally unearthing items of mystical value. Mercury dimes and buckeyes were pocketed on a regular basis. Dandelion fluff was blown to the east. Once, she dug the penis bone of a raccoon from the mud and declared they'd both soon be rich with good luck. The penis bone went in her pocket, too. Meanwhile, it was not unusual for them to go home with a bouquet a piece of Sundrops to go with the dimes and the penises. Without planning to do it, they'd made a game of it.

Hadley had discovered that the first wild flower he spotted each week always tied in somewhat suspiciously with the Reverend's sermon for that day. If the sermon was called *The Second Coming*, the first flower to pop up on their path was sure to be a Bachelor Button. According to Hadley's book, a Bachelor Button signified anticipation. He'd learned to carry the *Meaning of Flowers* under his arm along with his Bible for convenient consultation. Thus, when three spires of the notoriously fickled Larkspur showed up after *Have You Really Given Your All to the Lord?* Hadley was able to clarify immediately.

"What's the book say about Nasturium?" Mama asked of him on Easter Sunday.

Hadley flipped to the "N"s as if his life depended upon it, which, given the day in question, there was a real chance that it did. "Victory in battle," he said, grinning ear to ear. "Says here they keep the whiteflies and squash bugs away too if you eat 'em." Hadley nibbled on a petal. "Tastes like radish."

The Flower Game was a pleasant pastime that lasted all week long. After Easter Sunday, three cream-colored Nasturiums bent over the lip of a jelly jar on Hadley's windowsill, reminding him to fight the good fight for six days straight. Then they died.

This was all well and good until one Sunday in late July when Pastor Blackmon got it into his head to preach on the perils of adultery.

Asa Blackmon had been thundering from the pulpit at *Rocky Bottom Baptist* since before Hadley was born. He could make you wet your pants with his fist-pounding, forehead smacking style of preaching. He was just that lively. When he warned about the devil, he stomped through the pews passing out thumps on the head. And when he baptized a believer, they often emerged kicking and punching, their lungs half-filled with the sinful nature they'd set out to cleanse away. Nothing was official until all that sin got coughed up once and for all. This sometimes took longer than the baptism its self. Even when he was shaking hands, folks two blocks over at *Morningside Methodist* could hear him belting out good morning. Reverend Blackmon might clout you in the head if he thought that's what you needed, and when it came to his sermons, the man pulled no punches.

"You were squirming like a two year old in there today," Mama said after the *Why Adulterers Must Burn in Hell* sermon.

"I've got a stomach ache," Hadley complained. "I think I'll skip our walk today."

"Oh no you don't," Mama said, hooking him by the arm to keep him from running away. "You can't ditch me that easy. I'm sure your stomach's in a thousand knots after hearing what the Reverend had to say about lusting after another man's wife."

"Don't start, Mama," Hadley said. They had gone a whole month without re-visiting that prickly subject, and Hadley had enjoyed the reprieve. He wished Mama had never gotten wind about Lucinda. Church had a way of bringing on her strong principles, as if they weren't strong enough already. If they were going to argue about Lucinda, it was usually after church.

"I'm so worried about you, Hadley. I can't hardly see which foot my shoe goes on. You look like a USDA-Certified scarecrow. Don't they feed you at Mr. Worther-Holmes' house?"

"When have you ever said that I look like I'm eating well, Mama?"

"Not since you were nine and we moved into *that* house."

Hadley put a hand over his stomach. He really did feel ill. Reverend Blackmon said that even thinking about another

105

man's wife was enough to buy you a one-way ticket straight to hell. Not that this was news. Even so, hearing his fate confirmed by a man of Blackmon's authority seemed to resolve the matter with a more professional level of certainty. "I can't talk to you about this, Mama."

"Just answer one thing for me: how is she treating you these days?"

For the hundredth time, Hadley thought about the afternoon Lucinda put his hand up her dress.

"Oh Lordy Lord," Mama said. "Red ears."

"Huh?"

"Your ears look like pickled beets, honey."

He snorted, slipping on pebbles as he hurried down the bank toward the river. "So what?"

"Your neck's red too," Mama shouted behind him, and Hadley could feel it.

Ever since Lucinda had done what she'd done with that tiger tooth, the scar had become a source of heat too. It was almost like God didn't think it was punishment enough to light up his ears for the sin of listening to things he shouldn't listen to, he had to make Hadley burn for the tiger tooth as well.

"Do you still read with her?"

Hadley didn't want to answer that, but Mama had an annoying way of making him feel like he was still under her thumb. "Got no choice in the matter. She can't see nothing without me."

Naturally, Mama popped off with a proverb: "*My wounds are loathsome and corrupt, because of my foolishness.*"

"Wounds?" Hadley said, rubbing his neck.

"You heard me, boy. Sneaking always takes its toll."

Ever since the incident with the window seat, Hadley had been condemned to read in a rocking chair on the other side of the room while Lucinda stretched on the sofa. Alone. Lucinda said he got stirred up too easy when they sat together. Hadley said if she didn't like it, she should put away the spoon.

Mama tugged on his hot ear. "There are other girls out there."

Hadley assumed this must be true, and yet he couldn't see past the perpetual steam that fogged his world. He only saw

Lucinda. His memories were all of her. He was only just beginning to realize that he didn't simply want her body. Hadley wanted Lucinda's love.

Some nights, he tried to recall what Quindora's lips felt like. He remembered that they were soft and gentle, but the memory felt like something told to him rather than something he had experienced. Everybody knew that *Thou Shalt Not Commit Adultery* was one of the Ten Commandments. Like a character in a *V.I.L.E.* book, Hadley reckoned he was obsessed with Lucinda Worther-Holmes. Listening to her every night in bed with Dickie was almost enough to make him wish that she had killed him with her blood-drinking kisses.

"Here we go," Mama said, yanking a bright blue flower from the weeds. "What's the book have to say about Columbine, I wonder?"

Hadley didn't wonder. Hadley didn't want to know.

Mama took the book from under his armpit and looked it up herself. "Cuckhold," she said, putting the flower in his pocket. "The flowers never lie."

CR

When Hadley shuffled in from his walk, he heard Lucinda splashing in her tub, and his feet stopped short. He'd stood on the other side of her bathroom door for years, willing himself across the threshold on the steamy surface of his dreams— dreams he'd carried to her with his own small hands, step by shaky step, careful not to spill a single hot drop. His fist came to rest against her door now. He wanted in.

"What're you doing?" Dickie asked.

The flowery smell of Cashmere Bouquet leaked from under the door like poison gas. *"The richest, most lasting & refined of all handkerchief soaps"* the box said of Cashemer Bouquet. Dickie caught Hadley mid-sniff.

"I think I'm coming down with something," Hadley said. "I don't feel too good."

Dickie was a big man, to be sure. His fist was the same size as Hadley's head. He was carrying a golf club and a ball and a tee. He nodded toward the kitchen. "Have Tilly whip you up a Meadow Sweet cocktail. That always fixes me."

"I think I'll just go to bed," Hadley said.

Sleeping off his misery, it turns out, was not a real option. After Lucinda finished her bath, the bed above Hadley's ceiling thumped as it had never thumped before.

I shouldn't have come here, Hadley thought. *I don't belong at Wisteria Walk.*

As the ceiling quaked above his head, Hadley dropped a second nail in his jar.

Nail Number Three: Semen of Ares

In its size I had been greatly mistaken. The whole circuit of its walls did not exceed twenty-five yards. For some minutes this fact occasioned me a world of vain trouble; vain indeed -- for what could be of less importance, under the terrible circumstances which environed me, than the mere dimension of my dungeon?

—Edgar Allen Poe

Hadley's official title at Wisteria Walk was *Gardener*, yet his duties included everything under the sun. If the boiler broke, he fixed it. If the toaster quit toasting, he got it toasting again. And if a pipe sprung a leak under the kitchen sink, Hadley fiddled with it until it leaked no more. He had a knack for learning new things easily. Always had.

Mr. Browning once hired a painter to change his rooms from Egg Shell to Ocher, and Hadley had followed the painter around for a week, asking questions and watching him work. At Wisteria Walk, he tried mixing up paint recipes written by an old-timer named Hezekiah Reynolds. Thanks to Hezekiah's colorful advice, Hadley learned how to dramatically enhance the store-bought paints Lucinda ordered by the bucket full. Everyone loved the results, and Hadley enjoyed the special feeling of power this gave him. He had a notion that changing the color of a wall transformed the entire emotion of a room, and he liked the thought of being responsible for something so grand. It was widely held that Lucinda Worth-Holmes' gardener could stir up a perfect *Paris Green*.

And then there were the radios. Dickie suffered from an irresistible urge to purchase any crystal set he chanced to come across. There was a whole big room devoted to the putting together of radios, and by August that room was spread from corner to corner with the guts of a half dozen incomplete sets. Dickie, it seemed, lost interest in radios the minute they were out of the box.

One evening, he caught Hadley stealing a look at his new *Aeriola Jr.* and let him take a crack at putting it together. Unbeknownst to the both of them, this was the beginning of an unexpected and productive partnership. Dickie loved drinking bootleg and talking radios, and Hadley possessed an unstoppable desire to figure things out. Many a night, Dickie would drink bootleg and talk radios while Hadley poured over schematics; teaching himself how to turn Dickie's vast sea of radio parts into little things of wonder.

There was only one drawback. On those occasions when Dickie was particularly ossified, he would throw an arm over Hadley's shoulder, drop his chin against his big chest, and start mumbling personal confessions. "My daddy doesn't like me one little bit. Did you know that?" He'd jab at Hadley's nose like it was a doorbell, and one time his head even slumped against Hadley's shoulder. "You probably think I got it made, don't you, Mr. Crump? You probably envy my abilities with all these fine radios, too."

Dickie had a special talent for burping long and loud whenever he was drinking. As a rule, he belched long and loud between most sentences. "Well, don't envy me, son." Belchhhhhh. "My life stinks." Double belchhhhhhh.

There were many things Hadley wanted in life and also many things he didn't want. First and foremost, Hadley did not want to know Dickie. He would have preferred a middle man like Sargent or Mr. Sweet to control all communication between them, but Dickie didn't believe in such things.

"I'm not wasting good dough just to have someone speak for me," Dickie once said. "I can speak for myself."

According to Lucinda, Dickie might easily have been a movie star. With his Douglas Fairbanks teeth and his Charles Boyer's lips, he attracted women wherever he went, or so

Lucinda claimed. "I'd dress him as a pirate every day, if it were up to me," she said.

Hadley had no idea what Douglas Fairbank's teeth looked like, but this mattered not. When he was drinking, Dickie resembled nothing so much as a basset hound, and basset hounds had always made Hadley feel bad.

One evening, after making the same confession about his father four times in as many weeks, Dickie slung his arm over Hadley's shoulder and said, "I'd rather be you, I think. Would you trade places with me, Crump?"

Hadley was naturally disposed to deplore Dickie Worther-Holmes, and yet, the attention flattered him. "I don't suppose you'd enjoy it as much as you think," he told Dickie. "My daddy don't like me, neither. I ain't seen him in years."

Maybe it was just the whiskey, but those basset hound eyes actually glassed over. "You want a snort of this?" Dickie asked, sloshing *Old Overholt* down Hadley's shirt.

Hadley felt genuinely sorry for Dickie in that moment. He took a big swig from the bottle and proceeded to choke his head off.

Dickie laughed so hard, he almost fell out of his chair. He pointed at the new *Bijouphone* Hadley was building. "You stick to your talents and I'll stick to mine," he declared, and he took a big noisy drink.

ℭ℞

Lucinda didn't like it. "We're not paying the man to build your goddamn radios," she said to Dickie after she heard him laughing it up with Hadley.

"I beg to differ, Lulu. I got nine new noise boxes thanks to him. I could open up a store."

Lucinda rolled her eyes. "Surely we can think of better things for him to do?" she said, and she sent Hadley off to build her a new shoe tree.

Over time, Hadley became the chemist, the plumber, and the carpenter. He was also the painter, the chauffer, and the man to call when keys broke off in locks. Because Lucinda was never satisfied with the efforts of her other servants, she was always finding new things to add to his *to-do* list. One day she took Hadley down to the new *Beattie's Bluff Carnegie Subscription Library* and paid a membership fee so he could borrow books.

At first, Hadley thought this a generous offer and behaved gratefully. He was excited by the thought of exploring a whole big building filled floor-to-ceiling with books. Lucinda was excited too.

The ceremony to dedicate the new library had been the biggest event to hit Madison County in years. A multitude of book-hungry Beattie's Bluffers gathered on the new lawn to sing patriotic airs and watch Lucinda Worther-Holmes, President of the local chapter of the *Lincoln-Lee Legion*, cut the ribbon with a giant pair of gold scissors. A time capsule was placed in the wall behind a rectangle of stone engraved with the words of Francis Bacon: *Reading maketh a full man.*

A cheer went up when the stone was slid back into place, but Lucinda told Hadley later that she didn't approve of the capsule. She said it was filled with the most idiotic collection of putrid junk ever assembled by man. "If the people of the future ever open it up, they'll think we were little better than cavemen playing with acorns and smelly bird feathers."

"Well," said Hadley. "What if there are no more trees in the future? Could be, they might use that little acorn to grow themselves a new one."

"Oh, pish. This is our legacy we're talking about, Hadley. A legacy ought to be something that looks nice, smells nice, and accentuates our modernity."

Hadley and Lucinda didn't see legacies the same way at all.

For him, the library hoopla had spelled extra work. He'd spent an entire afternoon cleaning bunting out of the Delphiniums after the mayor's *Salute to Andrew Carnegie* parade tromped across his flowerbeds.

"Are you sure they'll let me in?" he asked as they approached the front door. Four days after the dedication, shiny specks of blue confetti continued to sparkle the steps. There was a fancy feather hat resting on the bottom in the new lily pond. Hadley liked the doorknob. It was carved in the shape of a frog prince and that much at least felt comforting to him.

Lucinda gave him the once over. "You are looking awfully brown these days," she said.

He ran his fingertip over the points of the doorknob-frog's crown.

"Come on, Hadley. You don't think they'd kick Lucinda Worther-Holmes' servant out for having a suntan, do you?"

Since taking on his new post, Hadley's color had deepened by two or three shades. By comparison, the parts under his clothes were lily white.

"Anyhow, you're with me, aren't you?" Lucinda asked.

"I am?"

"And you're probably cleaner than ninety percent of the people in this town." She sneered at the family reading books on a blanket in the middle of the lawn. Lucinda had made Hadley scrub his hands before they left the house. Twice. "Nothing worse than smudges on new books," she had said.

Hadley looked at his hands now. They were very brown. A person got brown when they worked outside. That shouldn't mean you're too Negro to go into a library.

"Shall we?" Lucinda asked.

Hadley clutched the frog head and gave it a pull, and the door opened with a sacred creak that would have put Rocky Bottom to shame.

"P.U.," Lucinda said. "It stinks like old books in here. I was expecting it to smell new."

As a boy, Hadley had made a trip or two to the Old McClay Courthouse to unload coal for Mr. Browning. The new library reminded him of the courtroom he'd seen there, only instead of a judge's bench, there were three desks behind the wooden rail. Each one had a little brass sign. From left to right they read: HEAD LIBRARIAN, BOOKS CHECKED HERE, SUBSCRIPTIONS * INFORMATION * FINES Behind the desks were enormous shelves of colorful books waiting to be borrowed.

Hadley felt a little like a character in a Jack London novel. It was clear that wild adventure resided within these paneled walls. Like road markers painted on a scrap of board and hammered into the face of the Himalayas, hundreds of journeys waited to unfold a mere step ahead. THIS WAY TO DANGER

AND INTRIGUE, the books seemed to say to him. THRILLING DROP OFF JUST AHEAD! TURN RIGHT FOR LOVE, LEFT FOR MURDER . . .

A week before, while waiting for Lucinda to pack up her punch bowl after a club meeting at the big plantation home of one Mrs. Donetta Wexley, he'd picked up a copy of *The Sea Wolf* from the telephone table. Seven pages swam by in a blink, and all too soon, Lucinda was tapping on his head with a ladle and saying it was time to go.

That same smell that Lucinda would plug her nose against smelled like open water to him. Inhaling deep, Hadley closed his eyes and once again climbed atop the tossing prow of Jack London's rugged *Snark*.

Here are the seas, the winds, and the waves of all the world. Here is ferocious environment. And here is difficult adjustment, the achievement of which is delight to the small quivering vanity that is I . . .

"Snap out of it," Lucinda said. Several chins turned their way. A furious set of eyes looked up over the half-moons of a pair of silver eyeglasses. "Jesus, it's only books," Lucinda grumbled.

Only books? Hadley couldn't believe his ears. This was the girl who invented holidays and sliced into fingers based on the simplest of plot devices. Hell, all a fellow had to do was read about glittering steel outloud, and she would let him throw her down and kiss her. Lucinda could pertend that this was just business as usual, but for him, it was no simple matter to step into a room such as this one. With its annual subscription fees and courtroom solemnity, the *Beattie's Bluff Carnegie Subscription Library* was no place for a Negro houseboy from Millport. And yet, here he was, his dusty shoes sparkling with sea-blue confetti, his skin scrubbed for adventure. Lucinda hadn't brought him to the little colored branch of the library on the nig side of town. She'd brought him to the real library, and it felt to Hadley as if he'd achieved something big.

"Come on," Lucinda said. "Let's get you signed up so you can start borrowing books."

Hadley followed her toward the SUBSCRIPTIONS * INFORMATION * FINES desk. "I won't know where to start," he said, his heart thundering

"I'll handle that," Lucinda assured him.

One of the best moments of his life occurred when the large woman in polka dots behind the desk handed him his own subscription card. Breathless and grinning ear to ear, he stopped to read the card the minute they got outside:

Hadley Crump has been approved to check out books from the colored branch of the Beattie's Bluff Carnegie Subscription Library on Dalton Street.

℘

An entire week passed before Lucinda's intentions became clear. "Go down to the colored branch and fetch these books I've written down for you."

Hadley was dying to check out books, but subscription borrowers were only allowed to check three at a time, and he didn't want to waste his checks on books for Lucinda, delicious though they may be. Hadley had it in his head that he might like to read some *real* books. "The Packard is up to its hubs in gumbo over on Mussacuna Road," he said. "I'm suppose to have it dug out by noon. Wouldn't you rather walk over to the white one yourself?"

"A respectable woman can't borrow these sorts of titles for herself." She waved her list at him. "Come on, darling. If you leave this minute, you can dig out the car, run over to the library, and still have hours to spare."

"What about Jack London?"

"What about him?"

"I was hoping to borrow *The Sea Wolf.*"

"Whatever for? You aren't planning a voyage anytime soon, are you?" She unfolded her list. "Have a look at these titles and tell me you aren't keen to read these books with me."

Hadley had a look and grimaced. *The Work Girls of London, Their Trials and Temptations. Wagner the Wehr-Wolf. Vice and its Victim: or, Phoebe the Peasant's Daughter.*

Lucinda smiled. "I have it on good authority that some undisclosed patron has donated her collection of penny dreadfuls to the Negros."

Hadley put the list in his pocket and went off to dig Dickie's automobile out of the mud. Then he grudgingly took himself over to Dalton Street. But for the work girls of London, this job might otherwise have proven the highlight of his week.

CR

It became a ritual. Dickie, who found reading to be the most poorly thought out invention since women's underwear, had recently put a stern limit on Lucinda's book-spending. "The Reading Room already has enough books to give us a good excuse for owning all those shelves," Dickie said. "If you want a new book, get rid of an old one."

Lucinda responded by calling him *cheap cheap cheap* in a voice loud enough for half of Mississippi to hear.

"This is a just temporary," she assured Hadley. "I'll win this war in the end. Just watch me." Until Lucinda got her victory and was able to start buying books again, Hadley was to visit the library once a week and borrow books for her.

This meant no Jack London. No running his finger down the library's long list of exciting titles and laboring over which three to pick. No real books. Clearly, he was not the wild young upstart he'd imagined himself to be when he first walked through those frog prince doors. He was just a servant doing a job, and he was not, in fact, permitted to use those frog prince doors ever again. Instead, he was to use the one marked COLOREDS that opened the little shotgun house on Dalton Street that had been set aside for Negro borrowers. Lucinda still read books with him, there was that much to be said for Hadley's experience with the library. Somehow, this made checking out naughty books no less painful.

Looking busy was the only way to get through the process. Requested books were retrieved from shelves by the librarian on duty. Hadley had developed a method whereby he would slide the list across the desk and then riffle through his pockets as if he was looking for something important so as to avoid looking anyone in the eye. This was a strategy that served him well until the day the librarian decided to speak to him about his dubious selections.

Even though it was set up in a living room that would fit five times inside the walls of the good library, the colored branch was organized in a similar fashion, with three desks, and three signs, and three ladies behind the desks and signs. Instead of brass, the colored branch signs were index cards folded down the middle to form a little tent so they would stand up.

"*Women in Love*?" asked the librarian behind the BOOKS CHECKED HERE sign, reading the first book title from the list. "Another provocative choice, Mr. Crump."

His ears commenced to blaze as though sunburned. "Excuse me?" Outside of wishing him good morning, the librarian had never said a word to him before.

She tapped a pencil on Lucinda's list. "I've noticed you're very fond of the red books."

Hadley went back to checking for important stuff in his pockets. "Red books?"

"It's a coding system we have. Our director, Abby Bowman, says that we need to carry the red book titles if we wish to be a progressive institute of learning. They're thinking of using it at the big branch, too," she said. "Some folks say it's shameful to have these kinds of books in a library, but I'm with Miss Bowman. I admire the fact that you are unafraid to check out our red books, Mr. Crump."

"They're not for me," Hadley said, pulling a balled-up *Cherry Chase* wrapper from his pocket and examining it as though it were just the thing he most hoped to find.

"I'm sorry?" she said. "You're not Mr. Hadley F. Crump?" She held up Hadley's borrower card.

He wadded the candy wrapper in his fist. "Just get the book for me," he said. "I don't got time for talking."

☙

Hadley cracked the door for the umteenth time only to discover that the little book-checking woman was still behind her desk. He'd already stood around for forty-five minutes waiting for someone else to take her place. It was Wednesday. She should have been sitting on the bench across the street with a flowered napkin on her lap eating a lettuce sandwich like she always did at eleven o'clock on Wednesdays. It was now eleven forty-eight. At twelve o'clock, Hadley was to fetch Tilly from the confectionary. If he left this second, he'd be ten minutes late.

This week, Edith Wharton was on the list. Something called *House of Mirth.* He could only imagine what that nosey little librarian might have to say about Edith Wharton. "Horsefeathers!" he muttered to himself. There was nothing to be done about it. If Lucinda had her heart set on Edith Wharton, he'd have to get it from the nosey woman.

He flung open the COLEREDS door a shade too hard, marched up to the desk, and tossed the list down on her desk. "That's right," he said. "Another red book. It's banned in Boston too, I hear. I want it anyway."

The librarian removed a pencil from between her teeth and smiled. "Miss Bowman says that being banned is just about the best thing that can happen to an author these days." She looked at Lucinda list. "Your Mr. Crump is a very fast reader. I wish he'd come in himself some time. I'd love to hear his thoughts on *The Awakening.*"

Hadley fought the urge to search his pockets. "He liked it very much," he said. "Especially the perverse parts."

That shut her up. She delivered his red book with trembling fingers, and that was the end of that.

❧

Hadley handed her the list.
1) *Memoirs of a Woman of Pleasure.*
2) *Moll Flanders.*
3) *The Mysterious Affair at Styles.*

"Good morning," he said. After the last visit, he'd decided he was done working around the lettuce sandwiches. They were too unreliable.

She started toward the bookshelf but stopped midway. "Could I say something to you, sir?"

No, Hadley thought, but he didn't say it out loud, so naturally she didn't wait for real permission.

"I just want to apologize to you. I think I made you feel bad about picking up the red books for Mr. Crump, and I never meant to do that. Personally, I think it's wonderful, him reading all those books. Sure, he's not bold enough to come get them in person, but still, the man dares to read what he wants to read. I hate all the censorship going on lately. You want to hear something really sad: No one has ever checked out *Moll Flanders* before. You'll be the very first. Well, I mean, Mr. Crump will. *Moll Flanders* has done nothing except sit on the shelf collecting dust for two months now. So bravo, Mr. Crump, wherever you are. I applaud you." She clapped her hands excitedly. Then blushed. "Oh dear. Have I embarrassed you again? Your ears are very red."

"Would you like to go for a walk in the park sometime?" Hadley heard himself say.

"When?"

"This Sunday."

"Okay." She slid her pencil behind her ear. "I'm Flora, by the way. Flora Gibbs."

"Flora? Like a flower?"

"I reckon."

"Pleased to meet you, Miss Gibbs," Hadley said. "I'm Hadley Crump."

The minute he was out the door, he smacked himself in the head with Moll Flanders. "What did I just do?"

Seeing how he'd never had the nerve to peek at her for more than a few seconds at a time, he could hardly even recall what Flora Gibbs looked like. "I'm an idiot," he said. He glanced woefully at the door, wondering if it was too late to wiggle out of the walk in the park.

Frances Bacon's words were over the front door here, same as at the big library only they weren't written in stone. Someone had scratched them with a black pen in the weathered gray paint.

Reading maketh a full man the scratchy handwriting said.

"Horsefeathers," Hadley said. If he'd learned nothing else in his short life, he'd learned it was unwise to spend time with any girl interested in dirty books.

CR

Mama was pleased as all creation to hear that Hadley wanted to cancel their weekly walk so he could walk with Flora Gibbs instead. She kissed the lucky penis bone she kept in her pocket and cried, "Amen!"

"I wouldn't go amening about it just yet, if I were you," Hadley said. "Suppose she asks if I got a white daddy? Colored people always ask if I got a white daddy."

They were on their way to visit a sick parishoner before services. Mama was carrying a loaf of soda bread. Hadley was carrying a pot of beef tea. "I don't see any white daddy hanging around, do you?" Mama said. "You just tell Miss Flora Gibbs that you got a black mama, and that's it. End of story." She broke a bite off the corner of the soda bread and popped it in her mouth. "What's her ears like, Hadley? That ought to tell us if she'll be trouble or not."

"Gosh Mama. I don't know what any part of her is like, much less her ears."

"Well give them a check when you see her, will you? I can't help you otherwise." She pointed to the tumbled down clapboard on the corner of Holy Water Avenue. "Here's Parthula's place. Just set the soup there on the step and go get us a pew. I wouldn't want you catchin' a germ on your big day." She reached into her pocket and rummaged around. "Kiss this before you go," she said, offering the lucky bone. "Just to be on the safe side."

CR

Hadley might never have recognized Flora Gibbs had she not brought along *The Beautiful and the Damned*. He was waiting on the bandstand when a woman in a yellow dress looked at him and waved. She ran up the steps brandishing the book as though it were a trophy. "I thought my boss was gonna paddle me for checking this out on Friday," she said. "Usually I'm not a very fast reader, but look – I'm almost half-way through it." Her face was lit up like a peony.

It was a pretty face, too. Not as noticeably pretty as Lucinda's. Flora Gibb's face was more interesting than that. For one, her eyes were so big it appeared that nothing could possibly hide behind them. And they were the same satin-black as the hair ribbon Mama gave him to use as a bookmark after the Robin feather he used to use blew off in the wind. "To keep your place," she'd said when she laid it in the crook of his Bible.

Definitely bookmark-black.

Whereas Lucinda stood two or three inches taller than Hadley and had curves everywhere a man looked, Flora was nicely short and she was trim as a ballerina. In fact, standing next to Flora Gibbs, Hadley was taller than he'd ever been before.

"Mr. Crump?"

"Hm?" He was looking at her ears. He wanted to memorize their shape for Mama. They looked small and sweet, like two apple slices.

"Have you read it yet?" she asked, waving the book around again.

"Of course."

She smiled up at him. Up! "I was hoping you'd say that, Mr. Crump!"

"If you're going to call me Mr. Crump, I'm going to feel like I need to paint something for you, or chop your firewood."

"Why?"

"Because the only one who calls me by my last name is my employer, and that's what I do. I chop his firewood and paint his stuff."

"All right, Hadley. And I'd like to just be Flora, too, if you don't mind?"

"I don't mind," Hadley said.

"What do you think about a woman reading F. Scott Fitzgerald?"

"Oh I'm used to it," he said as they started to walk toward the river. "The lady I work for likes the red books as much as I do. She was the one who taught me to like them."

"Really? I didn't know ladies read such things." A butterfly fluttered around the crown of Flora's head, attracted by her yellow dress. It was a butterfly he recognized called a Confused

121

Cloudywing, which seemed appropriate since it couldn't decide whether to have a walk on Flora's hair or simply hover over the teeny yellow bow that was tied on the end of her braid.

He said, "You can't tell nobody else about this, but ladies aren't such ladies once you get to know them. I mean, from what I've seen."

Flora smiled. "I like your ears. They're very honest."

He put his hands over his burning ears. He thought she was laughing at him and it made him mad.

Flora said, "I blush easy myself. Probably because I always blurt the wrong thing. It's a regular curse, I'm afraid. I'm real good at blurting and blushing." She touched her peony cheek. "I reckon that's why I said to you what I said to you at the library about checking out the red books. It's just a miracle the head librarian, Miss Hazelwood, didn't fire me on the spot. She said it ain't none of our affair if a fellow wants to read sinful books or not. She advised me to do like she does and make a mental note of folks who read vulgarities then do your best to keep clear of them outside of the library." Flora laughed. Unlike that whisper-soft librarian voice of hers, she had a gigantic laugh. It made Hadley feel like laughing, too.

When they ran out of things to say to each other, he suggested they sit on the bank and read Fitzgerald together. The Cloudywing settled on her sunny sleeve.

Flora blushed all over again. "Goodness, I couldn't read this with you. I'm still working my way up to being open-minded when it comes to literature. I'm gonna need to read a couple red books on my own before I'm ready to read them out loud with somebody else."

Hadley wondered that anyone ever read red books by one's self. He couldn't see the fun in that.

Flora said, "Miss Bowman is thinking of getting *Dracula* for the library. Have you read *Dracula*?"

He could have sworn she was staring at the bright, hot scar that ran along the side of his neck. But no. No one would ever guess the truth about that scar. "I've read it. The man who gave it to me called it a dangerous book."

"Is it dangerous?" she asked, her big eyes bigger than before.

"I'd steer clear of *Dracula* if I was you, Flora. You seem too nice for that book."

"What about you, Hadley? Aren't you nice?"

"Well, I read the red books, don't I?"

She laughed again. "You can't trick me. You're a nice man, it's plain to see. I wouldn't have met you for a walk otherwise."

Being a gardener, Hadley had seen more than his fair share of beauty in his time. He'd watched a calliope sip nectar from a patch of coral bells one morning in his hummingbird garden and discovered a tiny purple feather in one of the bells afterward. He'd become submerged to his ankles once when it rained magnolia blooms and was forced to wade home through a sea of pink and white saucers, kicking up creamy lemon perfume with every step he made. He'd watch the rise of Corn Moons and Snow Moons and Beaver Moons, and he'd touched yellow hair with his bare hands. One time, he'd had occasion to eat a full quarter of an orange all by himself. But he had never experienced anything half so beautiful as Flora's satin eyes. "Have you read any Jack London?" he asked.

"I love Jack London," she said.

Hadley was quickly smitten.

ᙯ

"Babe tells me she saw you in the park yesterday," Lucinda said. "With a girl." Hadley was working in the garden, and Lucinda was checking her windowpanes for streaks to prepare for Daddy Dick's visit. "Is that true?"

Here it comes, Hadley thought. Three pleasant weeks had passed since he and Flora Gibbs had started meeting in the park. The day before, he'd spotted Lucinda's friend by the carousel and felt sure that Lucinda would hear all about Flora.

There wasn't a soul in Madison County that couldn't recognize Babe Butternut at a hundred clips. A swizzle-stick thin creature who smoked cheroots in public and wore her blonde hair short and slicked back with a single curl pasted to each cheek, she was the biggest celebrity around. Local legend had it that, as an infant, her father had been so struck by her beauty, he put her picture on the box of his new cereal, Butternut Puffed. *Even babes like Butternut Puffed.* It was still on the box to this day. The baby on the cereal box wore her curls pasted to her forehead and had yet to take up cheroots, yet there remained an eerie resemblance. Hadley had never forgiven her for caving in to fashion recently and binding her breasts. Fortunately, he'd already planned what he would say when Lucinda asked him about his Sunday walks by the river.

"Mama and I like to go to the park on Sundays."

It wasn't a lie, after all, and Hadley said it steady and clear.

Lucinda licked her finger and wiped a smudge off the window. "Babe says she's young and mousy as can be. Your mama isn't young."

"Well maybe Babe needs to buy herself a pair of spectacles."

"And why is that?"

"So she can see how pretty the young lady is that I meet in the park on Sundays."

Lucinda marched through his bed of Toad Lilies, flattening spotted blossoms under her heels. "If you think you can make me jealous, you're sadly mistaken."

"Good," Hadley said, and he slapped some of the dirt from his trousers at her.

"Lovely," Lucinda said, crushing another hapless flower with her shoe. "Now go down to the library and get me a copy of *Unnatural Bondage*."

She thought she was punishing him, of course, and Hadley didn't even crack a smile. He looked at her like a punished man when, deep down, he was relieved to realize that she had yet to discover that Flora worked at the library.

"Must I?" he complained.

"Yes, you must," Lucinda said.

"Fine," Hadley said, and he took himself off to the library to see Flora Gibbs.

☙

Flora had a fondness for the old carousel on the north side of the park. Every Sunday afternoon, they waited eagerly for the band organ to switch from *Jolly Fellows* to *Blaze Away*, signifying Open Ride time. Open Ride meant anyone could ride.

Flora believed in choosing a different horse for Open Ride every week. She was working her way through the outside ones first. Over the years, she'd been to seven different fun fairs, and she'd seen every spinning jinny to ever pass through town. She declared this one the prettiest of the bunch.

"Not all carousels have horses with glass eyeballs or real horsehair tails," Flora told him. "And anyway, I couldn't ride those other fun-fair merry-go-rounds. We're really lucky they started having Open Ride."

On top of the carousel was a blinking sign that read: *THE AMAZING FLYING WHIRLIGIG!* And under this, in tinier letters: *Recommended by Dr. Herman T. Stokes as an aid in circulating the blood.* Flora said it wasn't every day that something that was fun turned out to be good for you.

On their first visit, Hadley had grabbed the brass ring and won a free ride. Flora had looked so proud, you'd think he'd just cured polio. He'd been getting straw dumped on his head when he grabbed for the ring every Sunday since, but Flora was proud of him for trying.

Every Sunday they would ride the carousel then head down to the river to read *The Sea Wolf* on the blue and white Cake Stand quilt that Flora had made with her Granny Gus. Thanks to Flora, Hadley was having a fine time reading a nice book with a girl for a change. *The Sea Wolf* had Maud Brewster, of course, and a fair share of profanity, but the hero was a gentleman. Lucinda would have hated Hump's gentlemanliness. "Jack London is so good, I don't even miss the romantic stuff," Hadley told Flora one day while they were spreading out the quilt.

"What do you mean? *The Sea Wolf* is brimming with romance. There's nothing more romantic than seeing new places."

Hadley had never thought of it that way before. When Lucinda talked about romance, she was talking about people tearing off each other's clothes. He liked the fired-up sparks he saw in Flora's eyes when she spoke of visiting new places.

"Nothing makes my heart beat faster than taking off for parts unknown," she said.

Parts unknown.

Hadley mouthed the words silently a couple of times to himself and was surprised to discover how exciting they felt.

Somehow, it never occurred to him that he might actually see any parts unknown. He could barely remember Charlottesville anymore, and Millport, where he was born, had been completely erased by the passage of time. But that afternoon, Flora's quilt felt like a flying carpet. For the first time ever, Hadley didn't read the words and picture himself as the hero, Hump. He pictured himself as Hadley Crump enjoying a trip to parts unknown.

🙰

Flora Gibbs was kind, witty, and full of deep thoughts. Hadley was pretty sure he didn't deserve her friendship. He knew he didn't deserve to kiss her, seeing how he spent each and every weekday tensed up with longing in The Reading Room.

The things he read with Lucinda were as good as ever. Lucinda might not want him getting stirred up, but that didn't stop her from giving him scandalous books to read.

> *I felt myself more than mortal, holding this loveliest of creatures in my arms, flying with her as rapidly as the wind, till I lost sight of every other object; and oh, Wilhelm, I vowed at that moment, that a maiden whom I loved, or for whom I felt the slightest attachment, never, never should waltz with any one else but with me, if I went to perdition for it!*

"Do you ever waltz?" Lucinda asked on one such afternoon when Hadley was reading to her about waltzing with a beloved maiden.

"Nope," Hadley said. He held his thumb on *perdition* so as not to forget his place.

"That's a shame," Lucinda said. "I was hoping you could show me the *Twinkle Hesitation*."

"What's the Twinkle Hesitation?"

"A waltz, dummy."

Last week, Lucinda had done some showing of her own, demonstrating for Hadley the pleasures of a *Silly Little Secret Kiss*. Had he only heard about it, Hadley would have imagined that a tongue wiggling around inside his ear would be thoroughly disgusting. Feeling it first hand was an eye-opening experience.

"All right, Hadley, as usual I'll have to try it out on you. This is purely experimental, you understand? I want to show Dickie a dance that'll really bug his eyes."

Hadley shrugged. He didn't like to think about Lucinda dancing with Dickie, but he wasn't opposed to serving as a substitute if it meant touching Lucinda.

"Dickie tangos like George Raft," Lucinda explained, as if Hadley might actually give a fig. "Poppy LaRue over at *The Register* called his moves 'positively licentious' after she caught him in action at the *Banana Club* last weekend. I think I'll start you with something slower though, seeing how you're so green."

Lucinda put a record on the phonograph. It was Franz Lahar's *Waltz Entrancing*, she said. Very romantic, she said. Hadley only cared that he got to hold Lucinda's hand. The stylus rasped across the shellac, and a lusty soprano crackled to life.

Other than the *Silly Little Secret Kiss*, Hadley had not been allowed anywhere near Lucinda since the day he busted the window seat. Holding her close after all this time made him feel like he was about to catch fire.

Lately, he might just as well have been called the Library Book Reader as the gardener, reading had become such a big part of his job. To combat the effects that these library books often had on him, he tried to think of other things when reading about love and sex. He'd put together elaborate lists of possible subjects ahead of time so he would be prepared. Brown stomach worms should be a good thing to think about, he'd tell himself. Or the basic steps involved in unplugging a toilet. As a result, he'd dressed many a rabbit in his mind even as a woman undressed in black print. The naked woman, however, always chased off the dead rabbit without much trouble. The truth of the matter was, being a decent man meant all the world to Hadley when Lucinda wasn't around and nothing at all when she was. On this day, he'd planned to think about bad meat.

Lucinda stepped closer.

At seventeen, Hadley was still shorter than Lucinda, but his nose came up even with her lips. A tip of the head would bring them mouth to mouth.

Lucinda spoke to his nose. "Watch my feet. I'm going to start you off with the *Venetian*."

The woman on the record sounded more like a peeled coyote than a song bird to Hadley. He preferred Marion Harris or Irene Day. They played *Alice Blue Gown* every night on KDKA, and Hadley always stopped what he was doing and listened and maybe even tapped his toe. He was not a fan of Lucinda's operetta. When he bungled the steps, he blamed it on the awful music.

"George Raft, you're not," Lucinda said, but she looked like she was enjoying herself. "One two three. One two three. That's it, honey. Now you be the boy, and I'll be the girl." She put her hand on Hadley's shoulder and tickled him under his collar. "Smile, sweetie. Dancing is supposed to be fun."

Hadley would have taken brain surgery less seriously. Dancing didn't seem at all natural to him, though he could see why folks invented it. What better excuse could a man find to hold a woman in public? Or in private.

"That's fine. Just fine." They moved back and forth across the floor, their fingers locked like two pieces of the same puzzle, and for a few paralyzing moments, Hadley pictured how different things might have been if Lucinda belonged to him.

He could see their house and their garden, their children (all one color or the other), their big shaggy dog (big and shaggy and all one color or the other), and their reading room, which was simple and nice and a good deal less resembling of a breast. And in this other, much improved reading room, there were no hidden shelves or window seats because there was no need to hide the books. It was all for them, and they could read what they wanted when they wanted. Hadley was still a gardener in this imaginary life, but he gardened for someone else. Everything he grew for Lucinda, he grew for the fun of it. Of course, he could never afford to keep her in Kewpie Dolls and maids, but there were those rare occasions, like this one, when they became just a boy and a girl, locking fingers and dancing, and he couldn't believe Lucinda would let Kewpie Dolls come between them.

She would ruin the moment any time now, that was a given. Somehow, it would all be shattered, as though she sensed how good it could be if only nothing else mattered. When he stepped on her foot again, he was sure that would be the end of it. She would get mad and stomp on his toes and call him an idiot. But Lucinda didn't do any of those things. She tipped her head back and laughed like a child. And when he ran her into a shelf and *The Breaking Point* bounced out on the floor, she just said, "Who put that bookcase there?" and kicked the book under the sofa. Still, he knew the moment was coming when she'd lose her cool or Dickie would come home or there would be an apocalypse. Just when he was getting ready to end the suspense and declare waltzing dumb, Lucinda did the *Twinkle Hesitation*.

"The *Twinkle Hesitation* offers the best opportunity to get a feel for your partner," Lucinda said. She slid her hand south along his spine and cupped his rear end with her hand. "Not a whole lot to feel, is there?" she said, but she didn't take her hand away. Rather, she mapped out the region real good. They froze in the center of the floor, locked in a dancing pose.

"Lucinda," he whispered. "Do you ever get the feeling that what's between us is sick?" He expected the words to unleash a world of pain, but Lucinda only held him as though they still danced.

"We aren't your ordinary dime novel lovers. We're a thousand times more daring than that."

"Daring?" Hadley said. It was all he could do to keep from laughing. "You mean because you rub my ass, and I kiss yours? We've never dared make love in all this time. How goddamned daring is that?"

"Some things are more exciting than making love, Hadley. Believe me, it's one of the most boring things I've ever done."

"I gotta think you're doing it wrong."

"And what would you know about lovemaking?"

He dropped her hand. "I have ears, don't I?"

"Lord, I hope so," Lucinda cackled. "It's the only thing about lovemaking that gets my heart racing."

"What's that suppose to mean?"

"Come on, Hadley. You know me. I'd have put you in a room out back and built myself a *Kewpie Doll Parlor* off the kitchen if I thought you'd just sleep through it."

Hadley was used to being surprised by Lucinda, but this took the cake. He shook and shook his head. "You're killing me, Lucinda."

Lucinda laughed. "Am I? Next time you hear me with that big boar of mine, you'll know what I'm thinking. What will you be thinking, Hadley?"

The record spun to an end, gasping as the needle searched for the groove that would make it sing again. Round and round it went, gasping at nothing. "I'll be thinking what I always think: that it should be me up there."

Lucinda took his hand once more and pressed it against her cheek. "Here's something for you to dream about, darling: When I touch him tonight, I'll think about touching you. Will you think about me when you touch your little girl from the park?"

"I don't touch anyone, Lucinda."

She lifted his face between her hands so she could look him in the eye. "Is that the honest truth?"

"Only myself."

She fanned her face with her magnolia pink fingernails. "All right, enough is enough. How does next Monday sound?"

"For what?"

She took the record off. "Dickie leaves for Baton Rouge in the morning. I was thinking of giving Tilly and Tapley the evening free." She shut the cabinet with her hip. "We could be alone."

"Alone?" They were alone now. They'd been alone a thousand times.

"The house will be all ours. For the whole night."

He waited for the walls to come down. He looked at the floor, expecting it to swallow him whole. "I swear to God, Lucinda, I'll jump off the roof if you're making this up."

"Well," she said. "We can't have you killing yourself now, can we? That would cause a scandal." She fingered her hair like she always did, smoothed her dress, and checked her earrings. "I need to run along to my *Duty to Dependent Races* tea, but I want you to remember something: Should you hear any sighing from me up there tonight, you'll know it's because I know you're nearby."

That night, Hadley listened to the noises with new interest. Suddenly they didn't seem so horrible. Suddenly those noises became the most thrilling thing he'd ever *not* been a part of. His heart leapt with every hop. His ears fought to understand every sound. And when Hadley heard Lucinda sigh, Hadley sighed, too.

ℂℛ

On Sunday, Mama informed Hadley that he was looking particularly imbecilic. He'd bought her a peppermint ice cream from the hokey-pokey man, but Mama flat out refused to be distracted.

"It's Mrs. Lucinda, isn't it?" she said, letting her ice cream melt away in a trail of pink drips. "You can try to hide it if you want to, but your mouth wants to smile." She reached out and wiped the traitorous orifice with her paper napkin. "There's only one reason I can think of for you to hide a smile from me, and her name is Mrs. Worther-Holmes."

"Don't ruin it, Mama," Hadley said. "Can't I just be happy?"

"What about that librarian with the apple slice ears?" Ants were gathering at her shoes.

"Eat your ice cream, will you? I paid good money for that."

He remembered a time when they actually had better things to talk about than his sorry excuse for a love life. For a while, they'd toyed with the idea of going into the lavender jelly business together. Mama had been offered twenty dollars for her recipe after the owner of the Burlington Hotel tried it on some lamb at Mr. Browning's dinner table. Mama being Mama, she'd declined to sell her secrets, so Mr. Lizenbee purchased five jars at two dollars apiece and vowed to return for more. Of course, Mr. Browning kept the money since the jelly had been made on his dime, but Mama had it in her head that lavender jelly might make them rich if they could find a way to produce it on the side.

Hadley was to be in charge of growing the flowers. He'd already bought the seeds. Mama put in a request to use the summer kitchen on her day off. She planned to trade mustard pickles for lemons. The company name was settled as well.

After weeks of bickering and scratching their heads, they looked for flowers to inspire them. "What's the book have to say about lavender?"

Hadley ran his finger down the 'L"s. "Larch, Larkspur, Laurel, here it is. Lavender. Lavender was one of the holy herbs used to prepare the essence in the Song of Solomon. In the language of flowers it means love."

"That's it! *Love Jelly.* We'll drop a little bud in every jar to fill each bite with love."

"Sounds kind of dirty, don't you think?" Hadley said.

"I think it's pretty."

Now it seemed like Mama didn't even remember about Love Jelly, and Hadley almost always forgot to bring along his flower book so they could search for deeper meaning on the road of life. Whereas, they used to jump around like lunatics and try to grab a falling leaf in mid-air to protect themselves against catching cold, or spend whole entire mornings arguing about which songs God liked best, the praises or the sorrows (Mama thought the sorrows), the only arguments they had now were about things that were none of Mama's concern.

She said, "I loved a man once who didn't love me. It was lonelier than being alone."

"It's not the same thing," Hadley said. "Lucinda isn't Slip."

In her own strange way, Lucinda loved him, he was about eighty-nine percent sure of that. It was "society's" fault they couldn't be together. Hadley knew this because he often over-heard the radio broadcasts from Pittsburgh that Lucinda listened to during supper. There was one particular fellow at KDKA who used that word all the time, mostly with respect to the *ills* of society, which, it turns out, there were a great many.

Society was eating all the wrong foods, the man on the radio said. They were drinking spirits on the sly. too. Crime was rampant . . . boot-legging, swindling, racketeering. And if you didn't believe the fellow at KDKA, all you had to do was listen to the advertisements to know that this was the gospel truth. Society was losing its hair at an alarming rate. So much so, that some of the world's leading hair experts had been called in to develop an astounding new bald-reducing tonic. Society had warts, too, and itchy skin, and more corns on their feet than ever before. According to the radio, some people were still living in the Dark ages and had yet to purchase a Sunbeam Toaster or the new Silex Automated Juicer. Things were a real mess. And if itchy skin was such a national problem, was it any wonder that true love was not allowed to prevail in today's broken society?

"Lucinda was forced to marry Dickie," Hadley said. "If she could, she'd be with me."

"I don't know, Hadley. You're a handsome boy. I think Miss Lucinda just wants to have her cake and eat it, too."

"You're dripping."

"You should be getting married and starting a life that doesn't involve her. Soon you'll be eighteen. I know you don't believe this, honey, but life flies by so very fast. Before you know it, you'll be an old man."

"Isn't that all the more reason to be with the person you love?"

Mama closed her eyes and a tear leaked out. "It's wrong. Don't you see how wrong it is?"

"I don't care."

The next day was Monday. Hadley couldn't think about anything except that.

ભ

For the first time, Flora's chipper chit-chat wore badly on his nerves. Hadley could hardly take how sweet she was being. He looked around, hoping to find an escape.

A banner had been strung up across the bandstand. APPEARING TODAY: *PEANUT JONES AND THE DIXIE DANDIES – Brought to you by the fine makers of Pall Mall and the Southern Chapter of the Anti-Horse Theft Association.* "Damn!" he muttered. He'd completely forgotten about the concert.

Flora was telling a story about how her father had stumbled across several cases of canned peas that fell off a truck in the middle of their street. "And the good news is, we'll be set for peas until the end of time . . . "

Hadley couldn't listen to another cheery word. "I don't think I should see you anymore," he blurted.

Flora's cheeks lost all their flame and, for one instant, it was like the sun had been snuffed out. "Have I done something wrong?"

"Gosh no. You're the nicest person I've ever met. It's me, Flora." He took a deep breath. "There's this other girl."

Peanut's trombone let out a bleat. "Oh," Flora said.

People were beginning to weave around them as they made their way toward the stage. Flora was carrying her granny's quilt. They had planned to listen to the band together. "I've been trying not to love her, Flora, but I can't seem to let it go. You deserve someone nicer than me. I've always thought as much."

"Don't be silly. You're a nice young man. I'm pleased and proud to know you."

Hadley knew Flora wouldn't feel half so pleased and proud if she knew what he was planning to do with a married woman the next evening.

"No need to look so glum," Flora said. "I'm fine. It's been real fun talking books with you. I've enjoyed every second of it."

"Me too," Hadley said, feeling genuinely sad. Flora was the one he should love. Lucinda was mean and stingy and likely to disappoint him. Flora was not mean and stingy. Flora would never let him down.

She held up the quilt. "I'm gonna go watch Peanut now, okay?"

By then the band was so loud, Hadley was forced to yell in order to be heard. "I reckon we'll still meet up at the library, unless you don't want me coming no more?"

"You better come. The red books would be lonely without you."

She had a good smile, too. Hadley never realized just how good it was until he was walking away from it.

Stumbling against the flow of the crowd, he walked headlong into Babe Butternut and her three show dogs, a manly bunch of Boston Terriers that went by the preposterous names of Ambrosia, Adorabelle, and Apricot. Babe hooked him by the waist of his pants as he plowed through their leashes. "Whoa. Slow down there, honey."

Hadley spun in circles, trying to unleash himself.

"Have you had a lovers tiff, poor dear? Come and sit with me for a while. My girls will cheer you up."

"No thank you, Miss Butternut," he said.

Adorabelle looked particularly insulted and made a grab for his pants. It was a miracle Hadley managed to break free. "I need to go."

At the time, it didn't occur to him that Lucinda was sure to hear about his "lovers tiff". If it had, he might have wondered how such news would affect their night together. As it was, he didn't give it a second thought.

 C3

"I'm sorry, but I couldn't get rid of Tapley no matter how hard I tried."

It was Monday, and Lucinda was giving him the same *what's-a-poor-girl-supposed-to-do* shrug that he got whenever her library list contained any dreadfuls written by Cherry Awntop. "He says he hasn't a place to go and would just as soon work as sit in his room with nothing to do. He's polishing the Conway even as we speak."

"No," Hadley said.

This had been the best day of his life. He'd whistled through it, happy as a lark, untroubled by the bee sting he got first thing, or the rip in his trousers, or the bone in his soup. He'd made the best of the previous night's romp, too, secure in the knowledge that on Monday it would be *his* turn to be alone with Lucinda. "At last. At last. At last," he'd said as he drifted off to sleep.

He threw down the *delicatas* he'd spent half his pay on and buds scattered across the floor. "You can't back out on me, Lucinda. I meant what I said about jumping off the roof."

"You think you can blackmail me into touching you, is that it?"

"Blackmail?" Hadley shook his head and tried not to scream. Or burst into tears. "I love you, Lucinda. Don't pretend you don't know that."

Lucinda folded her arms. "You've never said as much before."

He closed his eyes and tried to remember some small kindness she had shown him, settling on the time she bought an electric fan for his bedroom. All he need do was mention how stuffy it could get when Tilly was cooking, and there was

Lucinda, bringing him a fancy new electric fan. That fan had changed his life, it was such a pleasant thing to have.

When she married Dickie and moved to Wisteria Walk, Lucinda could have brought along Loomis or Lemon or Flavia. Flavia could get stains out of a dress like nobody's business, and Lemon had a secret method for darning three socks in under ten minutes. But Lucinda didn't bring Lemon or Loomis. She brought Hadley and no one else. And she gave him his own electric fan. And she slipped him a piece of Christmas orange in her handkerchief. And she made up a holiday for them to call their own. And she promised him an evening alone with her.

"Please," he said. "Make Tapley go. I need this night with you."

All day, he'd dreamed about how it might go. Maybe they'd share the Coconut Kiss he brought for her. Maybe they'd dance. Pringles had wanted three dollars for a water-spotted copy of *Mary Marie,* and he'd been glad to pay it. He'd bought a record, too. *My Regards Waltz.* Lucinda loved to listen to music, and Hadley loved watching Lucinda listen to music. Sure, he'd thought about touching her, but to court Lucinda's love, this was what he dreamed of more than anything else.

"Make him go," he hollered.

"God love it! Lower your voice. Do you want Tapley to hear?" She steered him out the kitchen door, leading him behind the row of bedclothes pinned on the line.

"I'll embarrass you if I have to," Hadley threatened. "Tapley won't be the only one to hear me."

"Quit it, Hadley. You're acting like a baby."

Hadley's breath sped up like a child set to bawl. "You promised me this night, Lucinda. You said we'd be alone."

"There will be other business trips."

"Uh-uh," he said. An embroidered corner of sheet flapped against his cheek, and he batted it away. "I ain't waiting no more. You can't make me listen to you with Dickie one more night. You think it's fun to push me? Well, you've pushed me to the very edge, Lucinda. There is nowhere else to push." Hadley did some pushing of his own and backed her up against the house.

"What are you doing?" Lucinda said.

"Send Tapley away this instant, otherwise, I'm gonna take you right here. Against this wall."

"You most certainly will not."

"Oh you'd like that, I think. You'd like to slap me and pretend that you can't stand the sight of me. Well, I want it to be nice Lucinda, but that isn't a requirement."

The bedclothes billowed in the breeze. "The neighbors might see," Lucinda whispered.

Hadley stepped closer. "So make him go then."

She stared him in the eye. "No."

"Suit yourself," Hadley said, pushing up her dress. "I warn you though; I don't intend to be as speedy as your husband. I've waited too long for this."

"Promises. Promises," she said.

Hadley grabbed her by the face. "I'm not playing with you. It's gonna be the bedroom or it's gonna be this here wall. You decide. Right now."

Lucinda fingers danced over him as she groped for his buttons. "The wall."

The wall.

It wasn't pretty, and it wasn't speedy, and Lucinda did slap him around a bit. So much so that he was forced to pin her hands above her head. "Why do you taunt me like this, goddamn it?! Can't you just be friendly?"

She craned her neck and licked her lips, thrashing against him as though she wished to break free. "I do it for you. I do! I want you to die when you push inside me." The wall of sheets snapped at his back. "Do you want to die, Hadley?"

He released her hands.

Hadley discovered that making love against a wall did pack a deathblow of sorts in that his whole life with Lucinda passed before him like flipping pages in a book. From childhood until this moment, the days whirred by. There he was on the very first page, scribbling dirty words down on recipe cards, his heart pounding like a mallet. Next page. There he was, stretched out with Lucinda in the attic letting her rip into his skin. Next page. Her foot. Next Page. Her hand. Next page. Her bluebells. Next page. He was about to die . . .

"That's nice. You do that real good."

Hadley couldn't take his eyes off the body under his hands. Lucinda couldn't take her eyes off the Brewster's windows. "Look at me," he said, turning her attention away from the Brewsters. "Look at me when I die."

Lucinda looked at Hadley.

"At last. At last. At last . . . " he sighed, the cement behind her shoulders creating a tattoo on the skin of his palms.

After years of dreaming about being with her, Hadley Crump had Lucinda Worther-Holmes up against the wall behind the clothesline under the kitchen window while Tapley polished the piano bench. And he didn't stop having her until Lucinda struck her fists against his back and gave a spiraling moan some five or more times. "God," she spat, gritting her teeth, the words flying from her like a curse. "You're going to kill me."

The bedclothes whipped. The ground tilted. All colors blurred into one. "I love you," Hadley choked. They sank to the ground, forehead to forehead, smashing clovers under their knees.

"There now," Lucinda said. "Aren't you glad I made you wait?"

❧

"I'm going to need you to drive into Bixby and pick up some sleeping powder," Lucinda told Tapley. It was ten minutes later. Eleven minutes later, she slipped into Hadley's bedroom. "Can you do it again?" she asked.

"On the bed this time," he said. "Take off your dress."

❧

Dickie Worther-Holmes was a decent fellow. Those that didn't want his wife so much might even go so far as to call him *likeable*. It was tough to hate a man whose happiest moment of the day came when he opened the newspaper and turned to Winnie Winkle. Hadley wished Dickie would drive his new Packard off the edge of the Beattie's Bluff on his way home from Baton Rouge

When that didn't happen and the car drove up on Tuesday afternoon unscathed and with Dickie safely inside of it, Hadley took to praying that the chandelier would drop on his head when he walked through the front door.

"It's good to see you, Crump," Dickie said, stepping inside without any incident. His dark eyes actually twinkled, like he was truly glad to see Hadley. Then, calm as you please, he withdrew a pistol from his pocket and pointed it at Hadley's head.

Hadley tried to think what he could say in order to save himself. His eyes darted to Lucinda. Would she really stand there calm as can be and let him be shot down in cold blood? Her monkey-flower eyes locked on the gun.

Seeing how she wasn't compelled to throw herself in front of Hadley and beg for his life, he decided he was on his own and started trying out speeches inside his head:

I'm sorry, Mr. Worther-Holmes, but I couldn't help myself. No. This was not the sort of apology to offer a man who had his finger on a trigger.

It was an accident! Remember that time when Quindora fell? Well it was kind of like that only with laundry instead of a ladder. Hmm. If he had even the smallest amount of skill as a liar, he might be able to do something with that one. But no. He had no skill in that regard.

The truth was the only way to go. *I've been in love with your wife for most of my life . . .*

"Pow," Dickie said. He laughed that big sad-as-hell laugh that he always laughed. Hadley checked himself for bullet holes. "God damn, boy. You're white as a corpse.." Dickie handed him the gun. Hadley was still checking for holes.

It wasn't a real gun, Dickie said. It was a pistol-shaped *Giblin Radioear.*

"It looks real," Hadley said.

"Naw," Dickie said. "Not if you're a gun man " With that, the gun man caught his wife by the waist and gave her a big squeeze, oblivious to the impending peril he faced from the six-armed chandelier overhead.

Hadley stood by, loosening ceiling screws with the brute force of his mind. Holophane shuddered. The bulbs dimmed. As soon as Hadley could get the thing to come crashing down, he

139

planned to push Lucinda clear and turn himself into a hero while at the same time disposing of his enemy.

The screws held, though not for lack of effort.

When the hopping started up that night, Hadley rubbed his temple with the radio pistol, gathered up his bedclothes, and made himself a bed on the bathroom floor.

℈

For all his life, Hadley had wholeheartedly believed that, if he could have Lucinda just once, he would finally be free of the spell. That didn't happen. He only wanted her worse than before. He laughed at himself for thinking he could ever be content with the deal he'd tried to make in the Rose Bud parlor. Hadley had never loved anything so hard as he loved Lucinda. And now he knew that she cared about him, too.

"Oh Hadley," she'd said. "I wish we could do this every night."

The first chance he got, he sent her a note:

From the kitchen of:
When can I touch you again?

Hadley had gotten much more than he'd bargained for. It was torture seeing her black lace Dancelette hanging over the tub. He wanted to kiss under the curls at the back of her neck. Even a sheet on the clothesline had the power to undo him. Lucinda waited three days to respond to his recipe card:

Hold your horses, Hadley.

He'd made love to Lucinda four times the night Dickie was in Baton Rouge. Afterward he could hardly walk, but that didn't stop him from wanting to push Lucinda up against the wall again on Tuesday.

On Friday, Lucinda sent him to the library. "You need to get out of the house, honey bun. You're looking a little unglued." So Hadley went to the library to try and glue himself back together.

"How are you, Flora?" he asked as he slid his list across the desk, same as always.

"I'm good, Mr. Crump. How are you?"

Hadley's heart froze. "Come on, Flora. You ain't gonna start with that Mr. Crump business again, are you?"

Flora rolled her eyes in the direction of the formidable head librarian, Miss Hazelwood. Miss Hazelwood was a nervous little raisin of a woman who was given to kissing her cross necklace every time she glanced at Hadley.

As such, Flora spoke to Hadley out of the corner of her mouth. "There are some *people* who think that you're to be avoided at all cost due to your indelicate reading selections," she said. "We mustn't let on that we're friends."

"Are we friends?" he whispered. The thought elated him.

"Yes, indeed, Mr. Crump," Flora replied in her normal librarian voice. "We are an open-minded institution, after all."

Hadley felt the urge to throw up his hat but refrained on account of Miss Hazelwood, who gave him a dark, somewhat frightened look and hastily pressed her lips to Jesus' green-tarnished crucified body. "I'm so glad to hear that, Miss Gibbs."

She is definitely too good for me, Hadley thought. He tucked his dirty books under his arm and went home to Lucinda.

☙

There were four memories that played over and over again in the theatre of Hadley's over-active mind. They played while he pruned bushes and laid out garden bricks. They played while he spackled and hammered and plumbed. And when he slept, if he was lucky, they played in his dreams.

The first memory took place behind a flapping wall of bedclothes. It was awkward and sloppy and probably his favorite of the four. Spiritually speaking, its significance was immeasurable. Unfortunately, the details of this particular memory were fuzzier than the others. Hadley's brain couldn't quite duplicate the scene without adding things to it. Once, he dreamed they'd ripped down the sheets and tangled themselves up in them. Another time he dreamt that Wisteria Walk collapsed around them like a house of cards. Twice now, he'd added a silvery spray of water from the garden hose.

The second memory was no less urgent, but it was surrounded by softness because of the bed. In Memory Number Two, Hadley got to see Lucinda naked.

There were parts of a woman's body he'd never been able to accurately picture before that. Loomis had a set of French playing cards that showed the top half of the female body real clear, but the bottom was inevitably covered up by a ruffled skirt or a coquettish hand or an ill-placed ostrich feather. As an alternative, Loomis had recommended the *Telfair Academy of Arts and Sciences* in Savannah. According to Loomis, there were dozens of nude paintings and sculptures on display, and anyone at all could look at them. Hadley had never been to Georgia, and therefore, he'd never gotten around to seeing the nudes at the *Telfair Academy of Arts and Sciences.*

"What are you looking at?" Lucinda asked when he stopped touching and started staring.

"Everything," he breathed. "You look like a goddess, Lucinda."

She looked so beautiful, in fact, that he was torn between wanting to touch all that amazing beauty with his own body, and wanting nothing more than to stare at it all night long. The main difference between the first time and the second time was that, the second time, Hadley knew what Lucinda looked like. Knowing this made lovemaking even nicer.

The next memory began with him waking up beside her, which was his wildest, most wonderful dream come true. Daffodil fingers of sunlight inched across her body and Hadley was instantly jealous of anything that got to touch her skin, even sunshine. There were bruises in some places that had been made by his mouth. "Dickie's gonna see me on you," he whispered, secretly hoping they'd be caught.

Lucinda smiled a drowsy smile. "Not in the dark he won't."

"Well, if it was me, I'd have the lights on every second."

"Not Dickie," Lucinda said. "Dickie likes it in the dark." She trailed her fingers over the top of the blanket. "Goodness, darling; haven't you had enough?"

"Never," he said, kissing her in a way that was sure to put more bruises on her bruises.

Lucinda rolled on top of him. "You sure do have a lot of energy, Hadley Crump, I'll say that for you."

"I've been storing it up," he said.

Hadley never knew there were so many different ways to do it—in bed, against a wall, on the floor... He was certain he'd never be able to live without sex again. "If you were my wife," he told Lucinda, "once a night wouldn't be enough. I'd never do anything but look at you and make love to you. That would be my life."

Lucinda then reminded him that she was not his wife.

The fourth memory came to pass a little later, when he was supposed to be getting dressed. Rather than pulling on his pants, he bent Lucinda over the footboard of the bed.

"Jesus, Hadley. I've never been so contorted in all my days. Aren't you getting tired?"

Hadley was whipped to the very bone. Still, he would be happy to kill himself, if she'd allow it, in just this way. "I don't want it to end, Lucinda," he said. Even though his legs wanted to fold up like a stick of gum, he would have made love to Lucinda all day, if only he could have gotten away with it.

It was afterward when Lucinda told him that Dickie had but one position in bed—half-drunk on top of her.

Hadley began to burn with rage. He hammered his fist on the nightstand hard enough to topple a lamp. "He's wasting you!" Hadley said. "If you were mine, I'd love you so well, I swear to God, I'd give you anything."

Lucinda ran her hand over her dress, brushing her bruises with her palm. "You're a real surprise to me."

"Why?"

"Dickie is a man of experience. You've only had books."

Hadley stood the lamp back up. "Well, I'm a fast learner."

Lucinda combed her fingers through her hair. "Yes, you are. You always have been."

"Anyway, you drank my blood. Remember?"

"That's different though." She fixed his collar like a regular wife and rubbed her thumb over the bumps of his scar. "Isn't it?"

A hot delicious pain bubbled up inside his veins. "Yes. And no."

"Do you still think about that, Hadley?" She touched her tongue to the place and gave it a quick lick.

"All the time."

143

"And last night? Will you think about last night like you think about me drinking your blood?"

"I don't guess I'll think about anything else ever again," Hadley said.

And it was true. Those four memories followed him more closely than his shadow.

ов

The following Saturday, Dickie threw a party for Lucinda's eighteenth birthday. The theme was rubies, and everything had to be red. Dickie gave out ten dollar bills to anyone who could come up with a good red idea. All told, the red ideas cost him two hundred bucks, but Dickie proclaimed the results well worth it. Red Christmas lights draped the beams in the *Fireside Room* like a big jeweled necklace. Ruby-colored gallicas were brought in from Landcaster, and ruby-colored tapers were stood up in ruby-colored candlesticks on ruby-colored tablecloths under ruby-colored lanterns. The gallicas were Hadley's red idea.

In keeping with the theme, the food was a smorgasbord of cranberry gelatin, rosy iced pudding, lobsters, salmon, and slabs of rare steak. Sparkle punch was stirred up in a big crystal bowl. Strawberries were held up to a jeweler's loop and inspected for redness before being permitted on a tray. The whole banquet blazed like a police siren.

Lucinda was not normally fond of the *Fireside Room*. With its stone walls, walk-in fireplace, and deer-carved beams, the place had the tendency to make her sneeze. "It's too log-cabiny for my taste," she said once. Indeed, the *Fireside Room* was a man's room. It was also the biggest room in the house. As such, the transformation from leather and taxidermy had to be thorough.

On the morning of the party, a pair of black Fords pulled up in the alley behind the house, courtesy of Dick Worther-Holmes. Four pock-faced lugs in overcoats piled crates of cordials, gin, and Vine-Glo in the hall. Bars were set up around the foyer and in the buffet room. The household staff was divvied into groups of waiters and bartenders. Hadley was assigned to the latter and made to practice his skills by mixing Old Fashioneds for Dickie all afternoon.

At seven o'clock, *Harlan Angel and the Mississippi Boys* were set up by the piano playing cocktail music. Dickie greeted their guests in a white flannel suite with a Chesterfield bobbing between his lips and Old Fashioned number six in hand. Lucinda wore a red dress that made Hadley want to bite through his fist.

Ever since he'd spent the night with her, his nerves had been hopelessly shot. If Dickie so much as passed Lucinda the butter, Hadley's spine went stiff. Maybe it looked like he was fixing a wiggly chair leg, but he was watching them, waiting for their fingertips to brush, or one of their eyes to wink, or their lips to curve with a secret smile. Lurking under car bumpers or behind hedge clippers, Hadley observed every move they made. If Dickie kissed Lucinda, his blood boiled. If Lucinda kissed Dickie, he died.

Mama didn't like the looks of Dickie's ears. Movie star ears, she called them. "Movie star ears might look glamorous," Mama said, "but they hide a violent nature." Villainous ears, was more like it. Dickie used his advantages like he used a rifle, and his aim was dead on. It was hard to compete with a man with good ears. Sometimes it didn't feel fair. Dickie could dance like George Raft and grow a real mustache like it was nothing. His clothes were always pressed. His skin was one set color. And he had money coming out the wazoo. Worst of all, Dickie Worther-Holmes was the sorry cheater who'd come between Hadley and Lucinda, never mind that he was her husband. Hadley saw her first. And so, when Dickie winked at Lucinda one morning over the top of the newspaper, it was all Hadley could do not to plunge his screwdriver into Dickie's movie star ear.

The party only multiplied his suffering by one hundred. All evening long, Hadley watched as Lucinda kissed every man in the room but him. His heart began to hurt so bad, he ducked down behind the bar and had his first-ever shot of bathtub gin. Ten seconds later, he ducked down again and threw up his first-ever shot of bathtub gin in the wastepaper basket. He'd barely rinsed the taste from his mouth when the orchestra began playing *Cuban Moon*. Dickie took Lucinda by the hand and twirled her under the ruby lights. Everyone clapped.

Hadley gave himself strict orders not to look. He wiped up the bar. He watched closely as Babe Butternut retrieved a silver flask that had been lashed around the top of her leg with a necktie. When it was offered, he accepted a drink despite the fact that his stomach was still turning summersaults.

"How is it?" she asked.

"Hot," Hadley said.

And then he looked.

Lucinda was doing the *Twinkle Hesitation* with Dickie.

❧

Hadley spent the rest of the evening mixing up sloppy concoctions that brought about instantaneous sputtering and quailing from anyone remotely sober. As luck would have it, few people were sober. By two in the morning, the only ones with their eyes still open were Hadley and Babe Butternut, who was thumbing through a deck of cards at the end of the bar and smoking her fiftieth cheroot of the night. Even the ever-efficient Tilly sat with her forehead dropped on a dirty red tablecloth, snoring like a door buzzer.

Dickie and a handful of stumbling idiots had wandered out to the front lawn to try out the unicycle with the big red bow that Lucinda got from her *Jolly 17* club. The rest of the bartenders and waiters got to go to bed, but Hadley was to stand by and make Stingers for anyone who survived the cycling, and Tilly might be needed to whip up a sandwich or two.

Hadley tried to concentrate on cleaning up spills while he waited for the endless evening to end, but his mind kept returning to that moment when Lucinda ran her hand down Dickie's backside while they danced the Twinkle Hesitation. Scrubbing at something sticky under a stool, he pictured Dickie's fat head pinned under his mop and set out to mop his way down to China. The only speck of joy he'd felt all night long was the joy he felt when he imagined that Dickie's heart was the lime he cut into little green triangles and gave away piece by piece on the rims of Rum Rickys.

While Hadley mopped and moped, Babe Butternut ground out her stogie in the ashtray he'd just wiped clean and muttered, "Love stinks."

Honestly, Hadley couldn't imagine what a woman like Babe Butternut could possibly have to complain about. He'd noticed her kissing Mr. Houston, from the bank in the middle of the dance floor shortly after the Twinkle Hesitation, and they'd looked fabulously happy together. Then, not an hour later, he'd spotted her behind the hatcheck with her arms around Dickie's Sicilian brother-in-law. They too made for quite an ecstatic pair. And a half hour ago, she'd been smooching it up with that newspaper woman with the big dark red lips. Poppy LaRue. Stinky or not, Hadley didn't know how anyone could ask for more love in one evening than that. Nevertheless, Babe Butternut folded her arms on top of the bar and said, "You look like a man who could use a distraction."

Even though Babe Butternut didn't seem like a choosey soul, he felt unaccountably important. It was rare to come across a rich white woman who would drink after a colored fellow from the same flask. A silver flask with her initials on it, no less.

She smiled crookedly and shuffled her cards. "Have you ever had your future told?"

"Once, when I was five or six. My auntie had a gazing ball, but she said there were too many things still in question for her to say how I'd turn out."

"Well you're grown up now, aren't you? How about I give you a free reading?"

Hadley was tired and still suffering a strong urge to scrub things into oblivion, but she tapped the deck of cards on the bar and said, "I'm especially proficient when it comes to the ways of love."

Hadley didn't doubt this. "What sort of cards are those?"

"Fortune cards." She began to lay them out. He'd seen a deck or two in his time but none this nice. Miss Butternut's cards had gold edges, and the backs were printed with sphinxes and serpents and lotus blossoms.

"See here," she said. "I've put the Life card in the middle and the others around it, like so." She made a rectangle shape of them and added two cards on each side, facing the outer ones

147

the opposite way. "The cards closest to the Life card are the most powerful," she explained. "The secondary cards are minor influences and each card influences two cards from the inner square. Card seventeen is tied into cards fifteen and sixteen . . . "

Hadley yawned. He'd hoped this might prove interesting. There was really only one thing he wished to know: "Do I end up with the one I love or not?"

Babe Butternut pursed her lips in a way that looked riciculously naughty and consulted the deck. Hadley consulted the deck too. There were words written across the top of each card, and he started reading them to himself.

The first one said: A SECRET WISH HAS BEEN GRANTED THAT LIES CLOSE TO YOUR HEART. *Indeed*, thought Hadley. *But what comes next?*

A LOVEABLE, UPRIGHT WOMAN the second card informed him. *Upright?* He skipped to the next one, hoping to see something that made some amount of sense.

NEWS RECEIVED AT NIGHT. *Could mean anything.*

A YOUNG GIRL IS VERY JEALOUS OF YOU. Hadley looked around the place as if he might spot her. Tilly snorted in her sleep and nearly fell off her chair.

BAD HABITS DIE HARD.

Was this some sort of joke?

AN UNSELFISH ACT OF LOVE COULD LEAD TO UNEXPECTED JOY IN THE MIDST OF YOUR PAIN IF YOU ARE WISE ENOUGH TO SEE IT.

Babe Butternut's gaze flicked pensively from card to card. She touched the last one.

THE COURSE IS SET.

Hadley brought his fist down on a slice of lime. "Well?"

She looked at him with her famous cereal box eyes. "These cards are warning of danger."

"What sort of danger?" Hadley said.

"Deception," she whispered. She tapped on the card that mentioned bad habits.. "Lopsided love."

Hadley smiled uneasily. It was just a game, after all. The love he shared with Lucinda was certainly dangerous but lopsided? Anyone who heard the way she said his name when he touched her would understand the depth of what was between them.

"I see desperation," Babe Butternut said. "And lies. And a potential for violence." She began to gather up her cards. The unselfish act went back in the red box, followed by the jealous young girl. "I'm sorry, Crump, but my fortune cards are right more times than they're wrong. You want my opinion? Get out before it comes to spilt blood."

The door to the Fireside Room burst open, and Dickie staggered up to the bar holding his gashed head. "I need some ice," he hollared. "And get me a Stinger on the double. I'm bleeding like a tomato."

Hadley and Babe Butternut looked down at the last card just as Dickie dripped on it. BAD HABITS DIE HARD. "Keep it," she said. "I don't want it anymore."

☙

The day after the party, Hadley was given the job of driving Lucinda over to Browning House for a private birthday celebration with her father.

"We need to talk," he told her when she climbed in the backseat. There were octagons engraved in his forehead from sleeping on the bathroom floor. "I can't stand this anymore."

Lucinda produced a clean piece of purple stationary from her handbag and began writing out birthday thank-you's on her lap. "What do you think, Hadley? Does *peridot* get a capitol *p*? Or a baby one?"

Hadley didn't know peridots from parakeets. "Are you listening to me? I'm about to completely snap, Lucinda."

"I know, dear. I want it, too. Now pipe down, would you? I need to finish my notes."

Hadley had spent most of the night planning out what he wanted to say. "I can't pipe down . . . "

"Shh!"

"Something has got to give . . . "

"Well, that's just swell!" Lucinda said, glaring at him in the rear view mirror. "I just wrote *dangly earring* twice. Could you

149

please hush up until I'm done with this? I'll be happy to listen to every little thing you want to say when I finish up my notes. I want you to hand deliver them for me this afternoon, and I have an even fifty to write."

"When will you be done?"

"Next year unless you shut up." She wadded up her paper and threw it at his head and started over again.

Hadley squeezed the wheel so hard, he about popped the stitches on his driving gloves. With Lucinda, it was always *later.* Later, after we read Dracula again. Or later, after I'm married. Or later, after Dickie goes out of town. It felt like he was always waiting for Lucinda to finish up with something that was more important.

Earlier, he'd put the ball of his foot down on a cellar spider and smashed it to a gluey pulp. Usually, he had an over-abundance of sympathy for all little creatures and would gently transport even the teeniest of specks out to the garden to be set free. But not today. Today, nothing went free.

Over brunch, Mr. Browning gave his daughter an Eisenberg dress clip of Austrian rhinestones and the seal-skin flapper coat she'd been eyeing in the window at Warson's Department Store. While the two of them polished off mimosas, ham and eggs, and a chocolate vinegar cake in the Rosebud Parlor, Hadley was free to visit his mother. Somehow, though, he got distracted on the way to the kitchen.

It had been months since he'd set foot in Browning House, and it seemed certain that someone had moved all the doorknobs down an inch or two and made the ceilings lower. And when did the ceiling in the entry begin to crack? Nothing shone the way it used to. Hadley felt surprisingly sad. He put one hand on his stomach and swallowed hard. The pungent smell of the old-fashioned gaslights was making him queasy. *I've grown spoilt* he thought. *This is a fine old house and I've become too good for it.*

Before his feet had chance to inform his brain what they were doing, he found himself in the place that had once been like a chapel to him, the Log Cabin Room. Here, at least, things felt familiar. It didn't matter where he looked or even if he closed his eyes. In the center of the room, wearing a bright blue bow and tap shoes, a twelve year old version of Lucinda was dancing the *Aunt Jemima Slide* on the coffee table while young

Hadley clapped his head off. The sound of clapping hands echoed still. Under the felling axe, on the far wall, thirteen year old Lucinda was elbowing Hadley and daring him to stick his head in the stove—which he did—while Lucinda clapped *her* head off. And by the window, a fifteen year old Lucinda parted the dark curtains and extracted a loose eyelash from his fifteen year old cheek. "Make a wish and blow."

Hadley ran his fingertip along the dull blade of Parnell T. Browning's dirty felling axe as he listened to phantom sneezes, tapping tap shoes, and the clack of one marble striking another. Lucinda was on the pillows, behind the drapes, and in the whorls of the grapevine carpet. She was tickling his ribs and tussling his hair and scooping up his loose eyelashes. NEVER FORGET WHERE YOU COME FROM the sign over the axe reminded him.

"Hadley?" Lucinda said. At first he thought it was just another memory speaking to him from the past, but the voice proved real. "What's going on? You look like you're losing your marbles."

His finger trembled on the axe. He'd slept in his trousers and there was a playing card in his pocket with Dickie's blood smeared on it. "I want to kill him, Lucinda."

"You wouldn't hurt nobody. That's just crazy talk."

He shook his head. "That dance," he said. "How could you do it with *him*?"

"He's my husband, dear. If you'll recall, I do a lot of things with him. You're just lucky it wasn't worse. In case you didn't notice, Dickie was fried to the hat last night."

"But you don't love him, so why dance with him that way? I'm sure you bug his eyes just plenty being an accommodating wife every night."

All morning, he'd been trying to squeeze that red dress out of his mind. It clung like dumped ketchup to the inside of his skull.

"Who says I don't love Dickie?"

He waved the thought away. "You spent the night with me while he was out of town. I know why you married him."

She crossed her arms. "Why did I marry him?"

"Because your father wanted you to."

151

"Hadley honey, you ought to know by now that I don't do anything I don't want to do." She closed the door and stepped into the Log Cabin Room, sneezing three times like in the good old days. "I love Dickie just fine. You know as well as I do that he's a good man so stop all this nonsense about killing him."

Hadley was still thinking of that old eyelash-wish he'd made all those years ago. He'd blown the thing half way across the room, he was so determined to have his wish come true. His voice croaked when he spoke. "You *love* Dickie?" He collapsed on the sofa as though she'd whacked him with a frying pan. "What about me, Lucinda?"

"Come on, darling. Did you really think I'd throw away a perfectly good husband just because I like fooling around with you?"

He closed his eyes. There was a time when he'd held himself still as death on this sofa, prepared to hold his breath until he expired if Juliet asked him to. "I hoped we were in love," he said.

Lucinda sat on the burial vault and put her hand on his knee. "Listen to me, Hadley; I don't think you know this about yourself, but a girl could look at your face for a long time and never find a single thing to complain about. You've got the gypsy looks of Heathcliff and none of his cruel ways. I dearly like that about you. You're a real go-getter in bed too. Your stamina is like a breath of fresh air. If only you could figure out how to hold your horses when it comes to being alone with me, I think this might work out real nice for the two of us."

Hadley was so fed-up with Lucinda telling him to hold his horses, he could have swallowed a horn toad backwards. "What the hell is *stamina?*" he asked. He'd read the word somewhere before, but he didn't know what it was. He suspected it was something hard and uncomfortable to do.

"Stamina means you got endurance."

"Yeah, that's me. Good 'ole enduring Hadley. I do nothing but hold my horses for you."

Lucinda squeezed his leg. "Enduring as you are, dear, I'm not in love with you. I love Dickie. I would like for you to take me to bed again real soon, but you mustn't get any fancy ideas about that. Lust and love are not the same thing."

"I must be crazy," Hadley said, cradling his head in his hands. "How can I love a woman who sleeps with her servants behind her true love's back?"

"Servant," Lucinda corrected, as if that mattered one diddly bit. "Oh! That reminds me. I've got something for you." She reached into her pocketbook. "Here," she said. "Merry Phoetus, darling."

Hadley had forgotten all about Phoetus Day. "I don't want anything from you that can be wrapped up in a frilly box, Lucinda."

"Just open it, will you?"

Hadley peeled off the paper in angry strips. It was a Tiffany shoehorn with his initials on the handle. "I didn't get you anything," he grunted.

"Not yet you didn't, but I know exactly what I want. Now if we hurry, we'll have a whole half hour before I have to get to my *Upright Citizens for Moral Decency* meeting. Daddy has left for Aunt Arabelle's house so we can lock the door and get cozy right here. Let's not waste time arguing."

"No," Hadley said. To keep strong, he fixed his eyes on that old mounted buck over the telephone table, a prize that brought life-long unhappiness to a father and son despite the fact that they both men got to share it. If you squinted, you could still make out the seam of glue that ringed the right antler. "I'm gonna need the afternoon off," he said, and he stood up.

"Where do you think you're going?" she demanded.

Hadley opened the door. "I have to get out of here."

Her voice followed him from room to room as he made his way through the house. "I'll fire you, Hadley Crump. If you don't stop where you are this instant, I swear to Christ, I'll fire you!"

Hadley didn't stop. He had no idea where he was going. There was only one thought in his head, and this was the fuel that drove him forward: *Lucinda loves Dickie.*

He'd been so certain that Lucinda's marriage was a marriage of convenience. The ideas he'd created in his head had all the makings of a *V.I.L.E.* plot. In fact, in almost every book they'd ever read together, true love was tested, denied, and sometimes crushed to smithereens by the mighty wheels of social injustice, and yet, in the end, some small piece endured. In books, that one small piece was usually enough. It never occurred to Hadley that he was just fitting himself into someone else's love story. His passion for Lucinda, his obsession, it was more than lust. Never mind that there wasn't a man alive who wouldn't find Lucinda appealing, her appeal for him ran deeper. Not because she was nice. She wasn't. He thought about something that Cathy told to Heathcliff: *Whatever our souls are made of, his and mine are the same.*

Lucinda once told him he was the only one like her, and Hadley had believed this with every fiber of his being.

◈

He didn't see the sign that read BOOKS CHECKED HERE blow over and summersault to the floor along with five years' worth of *Good Cooking By The Altar Society of Our Lady of Sorrows* that he knocked out of Miss Hazelwood's arms when he ran into her. He didn't even see Miss Hazelwood. In fact, Hadley didn't fully come back into his body until Flora rushed around from behind her desk, and took him by the elbow, and said, "Are you alright, Mr. Crump?"

"No," Hadley said. "I'm dying."

"Oh," Flora said, touching her heart. "Maybe we should step outside . . . "

Miss Hazelwood was not pleased. Hadley noticed that much even in his state of all-consuming despair. He heard her say something to Flora about staying away from *The Red Book Man.* Flora gave Miss Hazelwood's bony arm a pat. "It'll be okay," she said, and she left the library with The Red Book Man.

"Are you really dying?" she asked Hadley once they were safely out the door.

"She doesn't love me," Hadley blurted. "She never did."

Flora should have smacked him for saying such words to her. He even flinched expectedly, but Flora wasn't one to smack anybody. "I'm sorry," Hadley mumbled. "You're the only friend I have."

He thought of Loomis Sackett and old Spitbone, but he hadn't seen either one of them since Lucinda's wedding. It never occurred to him to look up Loomis, and talking to Mama was out of the question.

"I've been really stupid, Flora. You can't imagine how stupid, and it wouldn't be gentlemanly of me to say much more than that."

"Oh, now," Flora said, in that kindly way she had. "I'm sure it was just a little spat. Everybody quarrels from time to time." She patted his arm in the same consoling way she'd patted Miss Hazelwood.

"Wasn't no quarrel. I just had things wrong, that's all."

"Goodness Hadley, you're breaking my heart, you look so sad." Indeed, she looked quite heartbroken. "I don't get off work until four o'clock, but we could have a cup of coffee if you can wait an hour for me."

"I'll wait," Hadley said. "Thank you." He lurched forward and kissed her on the mouth, then jumped two steps back. "I'm sorry, Flora. I'm real confused right now."

"Wait for me, all right? I can bring you some books to read, if you like?"

"I'm just gonna stand by that tree over there."

"For an hour?"

Hadley nodded. "Go on. I hope Miss Hazelwood didn't see me kiss you. She'll think you're headed down the road of depravity."

"Oh boy," Flora said. "Wouldn't that be something."

℘

The High Point Diner was too cold, too greasy, and too sticky. Hell, the coffee wasn't even a "high point". Mama was old-fashioned and refused to set foot in the place. She believed a woman ought not to be seen in a diner. Hadley regretted bringing Flora. He hadn't planned on needing coffee money when he left the house that morning. *The High Point* was the best he could afford in a pinch. He glanced out the nose-smudged Pullman window. You couldn't see a thing on account of the big pie-slice sign that read: HOT FOOD, CHEAP.

Flora was a good sport though. She warmed up by curling her hands around her coffee cup and pretended not to notice the crumbs of meatloaf left by the last folks.

"You know what would really make me feel better, Flora?" He unfolded his napkin and set his knife on the table between them. "I thought I wanted to gripe about my life, but after standing under that tree for an hour and a half, I'm sick of my pathetic self."

"I'm sorry you had to wait so long," Flora said. "Miss Hazelwood was threatening to march out there and tell you to get your filthy-book-reading soul to church. She might just as well have chained me to the desk for an extra half hour while she made her case against you."

"She's probably right, Flora, but I'm glad you didn't listen."

Flora laughed that big, pretty laugh of hers. "She means no harm. My mama and her were children together, and I think she feels responsible for me. It was her that got me this job."

"See there, I don't know very much about your life, and if it's all the same with you, I'd rather hear something about Flora Gibbs instead of crabbing about what a mess I've made of my life."

"Oh dear," Flora said, sympathetic as ever. "I'm afraid I'm not that interesting."

Hadley gave the knife a spin. When it slowed to a stop, the tip of the blade pointed to Flora's elbow. "Tell me anyway. Tell me all about you." It seemed like he'd learned almost nothing about Flora during those weeks they'd spent down by the river, and he wondered now how he could have been so distracted that he'd failed to find out even the most basic of facts.

"I know how knife-spinning works. I play *Spin-the-Knife* with my Daddy, and you only get to ask one question per spin."

"Really?" Hadley said. "That's a funny rule."

She smiled at Hadley. "I thought I invented that game."

"Nope. It was me, and I think we ought to use my rules."

"The trouble is, there's not that much to tell. I like to talk, you know that. It wears on people's nerves sometimes, but Daddy raised me to be chatty. He thinks shy people are rude. I don't think that's true, mind you. If not for shy folks, who would listen to all of us blabber mouths?"

"You're not a blabber mouth," Hadley said. "And you listen real good, too."

"Listening is as fun as talking, if you ask me. Anyhow, what else? I'm too short, I guess, and I work in a library, and that's really all there is. My mama died four years ago of Diphtheria. My Daddy and I live on Dixon Street in the same house I grew up in."

Hadley tapped his fingers on the table, trying to think what else to ask. "Oh! How old are you? Do you have any hobbies?"

"I'm twenty-one on the eighth of December, and I keep birds and collect spoons."

"Hey, December eighth is my mama's birthday, too!" Hadley exclaimed.

Flora gave the knife an expert flick. This time the blade stopped in front of Hadley. "How old are you?"

"Seventeen." Hadley spun the knife again, cheating so that it did a half circle and stopped. "What do you collect spoons for?" *To stir men up?* he thought to himself.

"I buy them at souvenir shops whenever I go someplace new. I have spoons from Tennessee and Kentucky. I've got one from Florida too, but I haven't been there yet. Miss Hazelwood brought it for me when she went to visit her sister last year. It has a little palm tree on the handle, and you've never seen anything so cute in all your life."

"I'd like to see a spoon with a palm tree on it," Hadley said, thinking that Flora's spoons weren't as bad as they sounded. "What kind of birds do you have?"

"A canary, two love birds, one parakeet, and a maniah."

"Boy, where do you keep them all?"

"Everywhere. The kitchen, the sun porch, and Mr. Peeps stays by my bedroom window. Poor thing's blind as can be, but he's good company for me."

Hadley wiped pickle juice off his arm with a napkin. "I never met anyone who collected spoons before."

Flora set her cup down with a clink. "Well, don't go feeling sorry for me now, Mr. Crump. It might sound like I'm an old maid librarian, but I was almost married once."

"You were? What happened?"

"Countee caught that bad flu four winter's ago. I lost him and my mama one month apart."

"Shoot, Flora, how can you stand it? It's bad enough that the girl I love doesn't love me back. I don't think I could lose my mama, too. Yet you don't seem a bit sorry for yourself."

"We all got heartache inside us, I reckon. But I'm happy, too. I like the library. It's just about my favorite place on earth, and I get paid to be there. How lucky is that? Do you like chopping firewood and painting stuff for people?"

"I don't know. I've always done it so I've never really thought about it. Ain't much to it really."

"That's because you're good at it," she said. "I painted the sun porch last year, and boy was that a disaster. My daddy keeps saying we're gonna have to tear the whole thing down and start all over again, it's such an eye sore."

"I'll paint it for you," Hadley offered. "I'm dumb as dirt when it comes to women, but I'm good with a paint brush."

The waitress sloshed more coffee in their cups and Flora warmed her hands again. "I'll bet your girlfriend is feeling real sorry about your tiff and wants to take it all back. In fact, you can tell her I said not to be so cocky or someone might just steal you away."

"I wish someone would. Anyway, she won't take nothing back. She never does. Either you love a person or you don't. If she don't love me after all these years, I can't think what could possibly change things now."

Hadley had noticed that Flora didn't finger her hair like Lucinda did. One braid was coming loose and her sweater hung crooked off her left shoulder, but Flora Gibbs didn't look like a girl who worried about such things. She smacked the table with her palm. "If you love her, you need to fight for her."

Also, Flora's nails weren't the least bit magnolia-colored. They were ordinary see-through nails, and they were short and clean. They didn't look one bit painful.

Hadley shrugged. "I'm starting to question my definition of love. Maybe what I call love is really hate."

"Don't turn cynical. It makes me so sad when people turn cynical."

"It's too late for that." He thumbed through the gravy-splattered menu. "Would you like a sandwich or a piece of pie,

Flora?" He didn't have much money in his pocket, but dinner seemed like the least he could do.

"Yes I would. I'd like a nice big piece of chess pie, thank you."

Hadley looked at the section marked *Specialty Pies.* "Looks like they only serve apple."

"Chess pie is what I'll be making for us tomorrow evening. If you patch things up with this woman, we'll celebrate. If not, well, at least we can enjoy something tasty. I make mighty good pie."

She gave the knife one last spin and stopped it with the saltshaker so that it landed on Hadley. "Next time we play, it'll be your turn to tell all."

☙

Hadley wandered for hours, passing Wisteria Walk three times before deciding it was safe to assume he'd missed the nightly show upstairs. Lucinda's voice caught him by surprise when he tiptoed in the kitchen door. It had a raspy, beat-up sound to it, as though she'd worn it out with yelling. "Where have you been, Hadley Crump?"

Normally, the only time Lucinda liked cigarettes was when she was getting a Marcel Wave and had to sit still for hours, but loops of smoke hung over her head like words written in the air. IF ONLY the smoke said.

If only his heart didn't hurt so damned much. But it did.

If only Lucinda didn't love Dickie. But she did.

If only Hadley could find a way to be happy with what she gave him. His life was a happy vacation compared with most fellows he knew. Loomis would have told him he ought to be in pig-heaven over the electric fan alone.

"What do you care where I've been, Lucinda?"

"Oh I care, darling. You know I do."

If only Hadley weren't so love-sick, what a high time they might have shared together in the Log Cabin Room today. What difference did it make if she loved him? What would it change if she did?

"You'll be pleased to know that I've decided not to fire you, dear." She tapped her ashes in the sink. "In fact, let's just pretend like today never happened."

"Where's your husband?" Hadley asked.

"Snoring off gin slings in the tub. Everyone's asleep. Except you. Except me." She pitched the cigarette in the dishpan.

How many times now had he imagined them drawing together in this same way in the middle of the night, unable to sleep, unable to breath, unable to keep their hands off each other? Now it was real, and they were alone, and the only thing he could see was the next fifty years of his life spent sneaking around, waiting for his chance, sacrificing everything he cared about in order to spend a few stolen moments with Lucinda.

"This is what we do best," she said as she wrapped her arms around his neck.

"But I don't love you any more, Lucinda."

"Don't be silly, darling. You loved me madly six hours ago. A heart doesn't change so fast as that."

"You ruined it," he said. "I might not have changed my heart as yet but give me a few days."

"Come on, Hadley, let me make it up to you by doing something nice." She tickled him with her hair.

Tell me you love me, he thought. *That's all I need to hear.*

"I'll make you so happy, I swear to God." She took a deep breath.

Just say it.

"Okay Hadley, I'm just going to say it." She took another deep breath. "I'm willing to put my mouth on you." With that, she shoved him in a chair, dropped to her knees, and pushed his legs apart. "I know you want me worse than air."

"I do," he said. Even now, she was everything to him. She was kneeling at his feet! *His* feet. She must love him!

"You'll see, Hadley," she whispered as she opened the top of his trousers. "Some things are better than love."

Hadley couldn't help himself. It was against the law for a man to slap the lady he worked for, but Hadley didn't think about that until after he did it. After he did it, he remembered about that fellow who got locked up for two years just for saying, "I ought to slap you," to a white woman. *ATTALA*

NEGRO DOES THE UNTHINKABLE, the newspaper headline read that day. Well, Hadley had done plenty of unthinkable things with Lucinda over the years, but he'd never slapped her. He wondered what she would say to the police if she called them. *Well you see, Officer, I was just unbuttoning this here nigger's pants when he hauled off and smacked me across the face."*

For a split second, Hadley thought it might be worth two years in the cooler just to hear Lucinda say those words.

But no! Lucinda deserved a slap. "You can't keep me leashed up like this no more. Lord knows, I don't have much pride, but I honestly thought there was something meaningful going on between us." He stood up. "If I didn't love you just a little bit still, I'd have waited another ten minutes to say that."

Lucinda held her cheek with one hand and his pants leg with the other. "Don't ruin things, Hadley. This might not be what you set out to get, but it's better than nothing at all."

"No it's not." He shook his leg free. "I'm done with you, Lucinda." And by God, he meant it. "If you ain't going to fire me or call the police, I reckon I'll go on and plant your flowers same as I always have, but I don't want you to kiss me no more, and I don't want you to touch me. I got no intention of spending the next fifty years sneaking around after you." A geranium splotch in the shape of his hand bloomed on her pale skin, but Hadley couldn't feel bad about that. "I got my own life to lead," he said.

And by God, he meant it.

Nail Number Four: Those Good Peas

Hadley looked around the little house on Dixon Street and realized he'd never been in a house where people weren't paid to keep things clean. It was all he could do not to dust stuff off with his elbow when Flora gave him the tour. Books and magazines stood on top of the icebox and along the windowsills. The wastebasket overflowed with empty cans of Those Good Peas. There were several sacks on the floor that were also filled with Those Good Peas. Outside of two little circles the size of dinner plates, the kitchen table had been entirely devoted to unopened mail. "Watch your head," Flora advised. Hadley narrowly avoided garrotting himself, ducking just in time to miss the jungle of electrical cords winding overhead. Sunflower seeds rolled under the soles of his shoes as he went from room to room, being introduced to the birds.

"Hello there, Mr. Peeps," Hadley said. "Hello Tootsie. Hello Feather Brain." Really, he could barely concentrate on the birds. When Flora wasn't looking, he emptied his glass of lemonade on a poor thirsty ponytail palm in the corner.

On the sun porch, a naked dress dummy was the only thing left standing amid an explosion of sewing fabric. A paint can blocked the entryway with a hardened brush stuck to the lid, its red, twisted bristles making Hadley think of head wounds.

Flora's untidy habits struck him as both discomfiting and spectacular. He couldn't imagine inviting company over with so much junk stacked up everywhere, yet it felt wildly bold. Lucinda's entire house had been crafted to impress. She even chose book titles with an eye for how important they sounded.

With her awful red walls and pea-can towers, Flora didn't appear to give a care. This concept was so new and so strange to Hadley, he might just as well have been dropped on his head in front of the pyramids.

He'd brought a *Dainty Bess* wrapped in Cellucotton that he'd picked for the occasion.

"Did you grow this?" Flora asked as she buried her nose in the ruffly bloom. "I can't imagine growing anything that smells as pretty as this."

"I picked it for you because pink roses mean Thank You in the language of flowers."

"You don't need to thank me."

"I most certainly do. I'd have stepped in front of a truck the other day if you hadn't calmed me down."

"Well, we're even now," she said, and she put the rose in a blue bud vase and stood it on top of a three year old issue of *Opportunity* magazine.

Mr. Gibbs ate a pile of peas and a slice of pie off the same little yellow plate at the cluttered kitchen table. "Flora tells me you paint houses for a living?" he said. He waved his piecrust as he spoke, sending a snowstorm of flakes fluttering down on the mail.

Hadley had been afraid of meeting Flora's father and, sure enough, the man had suspicious eyebrows. He stared at Hadley when he shook his hand like there was something hanging out of his nose. Hadley wondered if Mr. Gibbs was seeing a white man or a Negro standing in his kitchen.

It was a funny thing, what people saw. He'd jumped in the white line at the post office once when the Negro line snaked out the door. Nobody gave him a second look. At church, however, he was always black. Every so often, someone sensed that he didn't belong; a perceptive soul in the form of a nosey five year old would twist around in his seat to stare at Hadley. *How come they let that white boy into church, Mama?* And then there was that nurse who sent him packing when he tried to visit Mr. Jessup, the butcher, after he broke his hip. She was sorry she couldn't let anyone with dark skin in, she said. Mostly Hadley slipped by. The "knowers" were out there, however, and the "knowers" had the power to ruin everything in his life. If Mr. Gibbs was a knower, Hadley would never see Flora again.

They'd probably make him quit the library, too. For a split second, Hadley felt certain that Mr. Gibbs could see he wasn't altogether Negro.

But then the man just smiled and offered Hadley a chair, and his eyebrows looked a lot less distressing.

"Hadley does handy work and gardening for Mr. Worther-Holmes," Flora explained as they ate their pie.

"Junior, actually," Hadley added.

"Fancy people, those Worther-Holmes," Mr. Gibbs said. "I seen their houses around town. Not much character if you ask me, but I guess some people like 'em well enough."

"They do sell a great many, sir."

"How's that pie?"

Hadley smiled at Flora. "I ain't never tasted pie like this before." Mama was the Beethoven of Boston Brown Bread, but she couldn't flute crust half so well as this perfect specimen of piehood on the table in front of him.

"Flora gets her expertise from the Johnson branch of the family," Mr. Gibbs said. "Not everyone masters piecrust, you know. My grandmother's was so hard, we regularly broke forks when we ate it."

Flora wiped her mouth with the corner of her napkin. "If you're done, there's something over here I was hoping to show you." She led him to a wooden rack that hung in the hall by the back door. "Look, it's that palm tree spoon I told you about."

Hadley had never seen such tiny cutlery before.

"Do you wanna hold it?" Flora asked.

"Yes please." He rubbed his finger over the miniature fronds. "Do you ever eat with it?"

"No," Flora said. "It just hangs here on display."

"If I had a little palm tree spoon, I'd eat applesauce with it," Hadley said. There were six spoons in all on Flora's wooden spoon rack. "Have you really been to all these places?"

"All but Florida. I save my money and buy a bus ticket whenever I get up enough for a trip."

"I've never been any farther than Columbus," he told her.

"But Hadley, you must go farther! You must see the world, even if you only travel twenty miles away. Things are different everywhere, but they're the same, too. It's exciting and comforting at the exact same time."

Hadley admired the fire he saw in those bookmark-black eyes. "Maybe I'll save my money and go to Alabama," he said. "There's an azalea that grows by the Cahaba river that you can't find no place else in the world. It's shaped like a funnel and smells like lemons, and I'd dearly like to smell that azelea for myself."

"Do it, Hadley. You'll never regret it."

Flora's father shuffled up behind them, working a mouthful of peas in his jaw. "You saw the porch, I reckon? Kinda makes you want to put a bullet in your head, don't it?"

Hadley thought it peculiar that the man should care so much about Flora's paint-job, given the state of the rest of the house. "I'm off on Sundays, Mr. Gibbs. I could paint your porch for you, if you like?"

"But not red," Mr. Gibbs said. "I don't know what Flora was thinking when she painted it red."

"Daddy likes blue," Flora said.

"Bird egg blue," Mr. Gibbs said. "Could you paint it bird egg blue?"

Hadley stood in the Gibbs's cluttered kitchen tingling from head to toe and feeling like a man with something special to offer for the first time in his life. "I'll mix up some bird-egg blue this week," he promised.

"Say, Flora," Mr. Gibbs said. "If this goes well, maybe we'll have to let him take a crack at Helen."

"Whose Helen?" Hadley asked.

Flora led him to the backyard and pointed to a small building made of quarry rock. "Helen lives *there*?" Hadley asked, his mind instantly flooded with images of a disfigured sister crouching in rags on a cement floor.

"No one lives there. It used to be slave quarters before the war. Daddy stores his buckets and rakes inside, but the place is in real need of repair."

Hadley walked around the perimeter, jiggling and kicking things. He jumped on the back of an over-turned wheelbarrow, and looked at the roof. "The angles at the lintel are rusted through, and the anchorage has come loose. That's not an easy fix."

"You mean, you can't just paint it bird-egg blue and make it all better?" Flora said with a crooked grin.

"I could put together a support of some kind and fix those mortar joints. It's a fine little building otherwise." He patted a yellow stone. "So who is Helen anyway?"

"You're looking at her. Here, give me your hand." She put his palm against the front door, and Hadley could feel the carved letters under his skin.

Helen.

"That word is all we know about this old place. It's referred to as *Old Slave Quarters* on the plot. Dixon Mansion used to stand right over there, but it burned to the ground a long time ago. People started buying little pieces of the land and putting up houses like ours. The man who sold my daddy the property called this place a guesthouse, but we've never had the nerve to put anyone in here. We worry enough about the rakes as it is."

With his affinity for carved words, Hadley felt a warm spot for the old building right off and was instantly compelled to save it. "Imagine if these old walls could talk, Flora. Wonder what'd they'd say?"

"Mayor Applewhite thinks we ought to tear it down. He said it's a disgrace to leave a slave house standing. I disagree. You can't hide important parts of history just because things got sloppy for a while."

"Things are always sloppy, I suspect," Hadley said.

"That's so true. It's kind of like Daddy wanting to knock down a perfectly good sun porch because he doesn't like the color. Shoot, just because a wall is red right now, that don't mean it can't be blue someday. Live and learn, I always say."

"I like the way you think, Flora."

Hadley had never had a finer day. He whistled *Goober Peas* all the way home, wondering if it was possible to visit parts unknown while traveling no further than Dixon Street.

☙

It's a known fact that some spots are more prone to resist change than others. Hadley used vinegar and water on those places where the red wanted to cling and sanded his way through the rest.

"It's a process," he told Flora. "We need to give the surface a good tooth so the new color has something to stick to."

She'd cleared a lot of the junk off the porch and dropped tablecloths over anything that wouldn't budge. The dress dummy had found a new purpose in Mr. Gibbs' bedroom and was now wearing the doughboy uniform he'd worn as a stevedore in St. Nazzaire during the war. Similarly, a re-discovered rocker made for a fourth seat at the dinner table, and displaced reams of fabric pressed against the front windows like so many plaid watchdogs.

Flora tied an apron over her dress and helped Hadley with the scraping.

"What made you choose red anyway?" Hadley asked as he feathered his way through a particularly stubborn drip of old paint.

Flora laughed. "I wanted to try something contrary to my character. Did you never try something contrary to your character?"

"Not on purpose."

"Well I like to do it every now and again. Speaking of contrary things, are there any new developments with the woman you love?"

Most folks would have avoided that subject like the plague but not Flora. Flora would talk about anything.

"Well, I told her I don't love her no more. I guess that's new."

"But that can't be the truth."

"That's just what she said. Still, I figure if I say the words enough, I might get to feeling like I don't love her. Do you know what the Twinkle Hesitation is?"

Flora shook her head.

"Good!"

"What is it?"

"It's this special dance you ought not do with anyone but the person you love. I danced the Twinkle Hesitation with her, and

167

she danced it with someone else. That's the kind of person she is."

"You mean she betrayed you?"

"It's okay. I got plans that don't involve her. As a matter of fact, I'm off to the great state of Alabama just as soon as I get up enough money for a ticket, and I have you to thank for that."

"Didn't it make her sad to hear that you don't want to be in love anymore?"

"I think she is sad, actually. Too bad. She ain't as sad as I am." He stopped sanding the wall. "You make me happy, though."

Flora stopped sanding too. "You ain't thinking of starting up with me, are you?"

"I'd like to, if you'd let me."

Flora's cheeks turned sun porch red. "It ain't healthy. It's too soon. I read *Women's Voices*, you know."

"I know. I seen 'em stacked in the bathroom. And the kitchen. And on the windowsills. You must know all there is to know about being a woman, judging by how many you've read."

"Well," she said, puffing out her cheeks. "I know a thing or two. For instance, I know a person ain't gonna be over love in a week, or even a month. I didn't talk to another fellow for over a year after I lost Countee Burkes."

"Why not? I can't help it if I like you. Why do I have to wait a year?"

"Here's another problem: I'm older than you."

"Are there rules about that, too?"

"There's rules about everything." She poured him a glass of sweet tea from a pitcher on the radiator, but he didn't drink it. "You're the one who invited me over for pie, remember?"

"I know," Flora said, gulping her tea in big, noisy, manly swallows. When the subject wasn't bus trips or spoons, she didn't seem so brave.

"Gosh, Flora, you're standing so close, I could kiss you right now without hardly moving a muscle."

"I know that, too. I like you. I'd like it if you kissed me, and I can't help standing close to you. I'm just saying, it ain't smart. Anyway, you're probably going back to her."

"Oh no I ain't!"

"That's what you think now. Sure shooting, that's what you thought the first time you took me walking in the park. But the heart wants what the heart wants."

"I'm done with her. She hurt me bad. I don't want to feel like that ever again."

"I said that once about birds, too. That was eight birds ago."

"I won't kiss you then," Hadley said. Instead, he let his finger take the place of his mouth on her lips. "I'll prove that I'm done with her first. Okay?"

A smile spread beneath his finger. "Okay," Flora agreed.

CR

The next week seemed to pass as slow as a snail traveling through peanut butter. On Monday, Hadley and Dickie put together a Salt Box Radio in the radio room. In spite of him being done with Lucinda, Hadley still had an urge to wrap a piece of Belken wire around Dickie's neck and pop his head off.

Dickie was oblivious to any such murderous compulsions. He held up the *Morton* salt box and tipped the radio sideways. "Lookee, Crump! It pours."

Dickie, like always, was drunk as Cooter Brown.

Hadley held the drinking against the stupid ingrate, too! Dickie was married to the woman Hadley had spent six long years pursuing, yet the man drank himself into a blind stupor every night. The injustice of it all made Hadley's blood boil. And to add insult to injury, Dickie was constantly breaking radios by accident. When he started fiddling with the AMP on the little four tube that Hadley had recently completed, Hadley moved it out of reach.

Dickie sighed heavily and folded his hands on the table in front of him. "You know Crump, I never did feel good about that whole business with Quindora."

Hadley sighed too. They'd come to his least favorite part of the evening, the part where Dickie spilled his guts about something awkward and/or dull. The only surprise tonight was that Dickie still remembered Quindora's name.

"I had a Quindora of my own. She was called Jewel." He wiped his mouth with the back of his hand. "She was a palmist."

Hadley had no idea what a "palmist" was, but it sounded awfully alluring.

"Jewel was a jewel in every way," Dickie said, squinting like he was looking at something right there in the room with them. Hadley looked around, but there was nothing there. "A jewel among jewels."

Hadley continued working on the radio, reminding himself that he didn't give two cents about Dickie's long lost Jewel. The last time they'd built a radio "together", the man had gone on for a full hour about a dog called Jupitor that Daddy Dick let lose on the other side of town after it was discovered that the mutt was deaf. *"Poor old Jupity Jupe. I dream about him still . . . "*

"It's the damndest thing," Dickie said. I dream about Jewel still."

It occurred to Hadley round about then that, while it might be perfectly true that Lucinda married for love, maybe Dickie didn't. It was no secret that Daddy Dick and Lucinda were as thick as thieves. Their foreheads were perpetually pressed together as they plotted and schemed. Could it be that Lucinda connived her way into Dickie's house? What if Dickie only went along with the marriage like he went along with losing old Jupity Jupe? What if Dickie loved Jewel the Palmist?

Hadley started to get that uneasy feeling that he only ever got when he and Dickie were alone. *No! I won't do it. I won't feel sorry for someone like Dickie Worther-Holmes.* Even if Dickie had been pushed into marrying Lucinda, he'd still gotten himself one hell of a compromise. He was rich and handsome and lived in a big house. He drove the best cars and drank the best scotch. He slept every night with Lucinda. Hadley experienced a momentary sense of relief. Social injustice for a man like Dickie Worther-Holmes still meant that Dickie came out on top. So long as Dickie was on top, Hadley could cling to his sense of resentment like a baby blanket rubbed soft from year after year of needy handling.

"We did a bang up job on the salt box, didn't we, Crump?" Dickie said, nodding at the newest radio. It was typical of Dickie to say "we" when really Hadley built the radio, and Dickie just sat there burping. Hadley turned his chair so he wouldn't have to look at him anymore.

"I hope Quindora did okay for herself."

Hadley clenched his fists under the table. He wished Dickie would just go on and pass out like he sometimes did, but the man was strangely bushy-tailed tonight. "She washes for Mr. Buckley now."

"Washes?" Dickie said, as though Hadley had just informed him that she'd popped up dead in the river. "Now that's a gosh damned shame. That woman had a real way with a needle."

"Yes she did," Hadley agreed. Whenever he pictured Quindora, he saw her with a mouth full of pins, and a yellow tape measurer looped around her neck. "She wanted to make dresses."

Dickie stared at his knuckles. "A gosh damned shame," he said.

ᔓ

On Wednesday, Hadley was engaged in an all-out battle with a bad case of Crown Gall when Lucinda marched into the backyard dressed for the seashore and unfolded a beach chair next to where he was working. She had a book in one hand (*How to Diet Your Hips Off*) and a bottle of Coca-Cola in the other, and it took her a full minute for her to wiggle her behind into a comfortable place on the chair. Not that Hadley noticed. He had his diseased roots to keep him busy.

"You're looking awfully sweaty over there, Mr. Crump," she said.

The fact that Hadley wasn't sweaty in the least until all that wiggling started was certainly typical enough. What wasn't typical was the way he was able to turn his attention elsewhere without any trouble at all. He was, in fact, so fuming mad at himself for putting in an infected plant, he was only dimly aware of Lucinda's new skin-tight tank suit.

"The wisteria is under attack," he told her. "I'm going to have to pull all this out and make a fresh start of it."

He went off to fetch a shovel and didn't return until sunbathing time was over.

Ↄ

All week long, Hadley thought about Flora and wished for an opportunity to visit her at the colored library. He passed it once on his way to J.C. Penney's to pick up curtain rods, but there wasn't time to stop. When Sunday finally rolled around, he went out to the garden shed and mixed up the perfect shade of blue. It was two parts the color of a robin's egg and one part the color of Flora Gibb's dress the last time that he'd seen her. He dipped a brush in the bucket to test it and painted the back of a rock dress-blue. It was just right.

After church, he set off across town with his paint bucket and a big fistful of Johnny Jump-Ups. "Johnny Jump-Ups are a symbol of happy thoughts," he told Flora when he gave her the yellow bouquet.

"Have you been having happy thoughts?" she asked.

"Yes I have. I've been thinking of you all week."

Mr. Gibbs gave the paint a stir with his finger and held it up to the wall. He must have liked the color because he said, "I'm making creamed peas & eggs for lunch. We'd be happy if you'd join us, Mr. Crump." He wiped his finger on his pants and disappeared into the kitchen.

Hadley stared at the first wall. "What message should we put on the wall before we make it blue?" he asked Flora.

"Message?"

Hadley tapped the brush handle against his chin as he carefully considered his blank canvas. "It's sort of a tradition I've started. A few years ago, a painter did some work at Browning House, and he let me do a kitchen wall on my own. At the time, I was mad at a friend of mine for cheating at *Crokinole* so I put something nasty about him on the wall before I painted it. *LOOMIS SACKETT IS A NO GOOD DIRTY ROTTEN CHISLER.*

"I can't tell you how satisfying it was for me, and anyway, it was the gosh awful truth. After that, every time I got peeved at Loomis, all I need do was look at that yellow wall, and I'd have to laugh a little. Of course, I don't live at Browning House no more, but my secret still does. I've got a message at Wisteria

Walk, too." It wasn't polite to say what that message was, though. "Get a brush, Flora. You have to help me with this."

"I thought I was banned from painting?"

"It doesn't have to be neat." Hadley lifted himself up on the balls of his feet and wrote his name as high as he could in concise expert strokes.

Meanwhile, Flora welded her paintbrush like it was a knife. "You sure you trust me with this thing?"

To be on the safe side, Hadley stepped back.

Flora wrote her name in drippy splats about six inches under Hadley's.

Between their names, he squeezed in the word "thinks."

Flora read the wall aloud. "Hadley thinks Flora . . . "

She wrote two letters after her name, dribbling paint on her feet: "**i**" and "**s**".

Hadley began a new word, making these letters bigger and bolder than all the rest. The first he painted was a big blue **"B"**. Flora stood back and watched him work. It was a long word, and Hadley took his time with it. When he was done, he moved clear so she could read the whole big bird-egg blue thing.

"*Beautiful?*" she exclaimed. "Lordy be. No one has ever called me beautiful before."

"Well, if ever you get to doubting it, just look at this here wall. Unless you decide to scrape off the blue, it's gonna be here for all of time like a little reminder. A reminder that there's a fella walking around out there who knows how beautiful you are."

He started to paint the top corner of the wall, but Flora grabbed his arm. "Hold on, Hadley. I want to look at my message a little longer before it becomes a secret."

☙

In the centre yawned the circular pit from whose jaws I had escaped; but it was not the only one in the dungeon...

—The Pit and the Pendulum by Edgar Allen Poe

Hadley was proud of himself. Over the course of two weeks' time, he'd survived rape, incest, and a pact with the devil with an uncommon amount of aplomb. To be on the safe side, though, he didn't congratulate himself until he turned the final page of *The Monk*. It officially became a worthy accomplishment then. Hadley didn't touch Lucinda once.

"I think I'd like to read *The Arrow of Gold* next," he told her, when at long last the temptations of The Monk were past.

Lucinda was predictably abhorred. "Dear God, why? It sounds hideously boring."

"It's very popular, Lucinda. Never mind, I'll read it on my own." *The Arrow of Gold* seemed like just the ticket after two weeks spent in a lurid triangle with a lust-crazed priest and Lucinda's pink fingernails running down his arm.

"Since when do you read books on your own, Hadley?"

"Since tonight, when I start *The Arrow of Gold.*"

Lucinda wiggled in next to him on the window seat. "Will you never forgive me, darling?"

"Sure," Hadley said. "You're forgiven. What's next on the list?"

"*Candide.* I've read ahead, and it's delicious. The chambermaid, Paquette, gives syphilis to a gentleman called Pangloss."

"Nice," Hadley said, half-heartedly, because he really didn't long to read dirty passages with her the way he used to.

Lucinda slapped at an old stain on his knee. "Pangloss is a philosophical man, yet he foolishly forgot the most important rule of all: An aristocrat should never lie down with the lower classes."

Hadley saw no point in remarking on this. He opened *Candide* and began reading it out loud, fully resigned to the torture that lie ahead. He hadn't stopped wanting Lucinda, of course, and he reckoned he never would. In recent weeks, however, he'd gotten better at keeping his feelings to himself. If he wasn't mistaken, she didn't like it so awful much now that he'd learned to hold his horses.

The previous Sunday, she'd snatched up his hands when he came in from Flora's and proceeded to feverishly examine his cuticles. "Whose house have you been painting?" she demanded to know.

"It's my day off, Lucinda. I don't have to tell you nothing."

Lucinda threw his hands away in disgust. "You're a wicked man, Hadley Crump. I hate you!"

It smarted a little, hearing that, but it was just as well. As Hadley fell into Candide, he said a silent prayer that someday he'd build up a strong immunity to dirty books.

❧

"In olden days, the arrival of the painter was cause for big celebration," Hadley explained on Sunday while adding another coat of blue paint.

"I can believe that," Flora said. "Ever since you started painting, Daddy's been celebrating with an old bottle of Guckenheimer's he was saving for a special occasion."

Hadley had strong notions about the effects of paint color on a home. The right shade of color could add spice, bring harmony, or make a man want to put a bullet in his head. The color he used in the sunroom tinted everything from skin to sunlight a soft hydrangea blue.

"I think the walls of a home say a lot about a person," Hadley said. "For instance, choosing red paint for this room announced to everyone what a game young woman you are, Flora. You aren't afraid to try new things, even if they are uncomfortable. Maybe your daddy's reaction to all that red was really more a fearful reaction to your independent nature. Maybe painting the porch blue is his way of trying to go back to a safer time when you were still his little girl."

Hadley's ears got hot when he saw how closely she was listening. "Then again, maybe he just likes blue." He shrugged and laughed at himself. "Sorry, Flora. Gardeners have a lot of time on their hands to think."

"Actually, you might be onto something there. My mama liked everything sunny yellow and that suited her to a T."

Flora sure did look beautiful with hydrangea tinted skin.

"What color are your walls, Hadley?"

"White. White's the safest color for folks like me who are afraid to make a choice."

CR

The subject of color came up again the following Sunday when Hadley and Flora started *Uncle Tom's Cabin.*

Hadley hadn't ventured out in public with Flora since the day they had coffee at the High Point diner. Mama insisted that no one would ever guess his "dual nature," but Hadley listened to the radio every day. Shoot, if Lucinda's maids cleaned half as well as they gossiped, they'd have polished the knobs off the doors long ago. Every time a Negro came to ill, Hadley got an earful one way or another.

"What do you think of people who are part white and part Negro?" he asked Flora. They were sitting side-by-side on the porch swing, holding hands in the place where the folds of her dress bunched up against his pants leg.

Flora was sniffing the chrysanthemum he'd brought from Wisteria Walk. "That's a funny question."

"Well? Do you like them?"

"Let me see, I like myself so I guess I do like them."

Hadley looked closer at Flora's caramel brown skin. It was much darker than his own, but it was pale compared to Tilly's. It was the color of a candy apple when she blushed. "Was your mama a white woman, Flora?"

"No, but her mama was. Does that bother you?"

"Not me, no." Hadley tugged on the rusted links that attached the swing to the roof. There was a grinding sound coming from somewhere and every time they swung forward, the chain objected. "Does it bother you, Flora?"

"My mother had a hard way to go. Someone set her family's house on fire the day they passed the White Drop Rule."

The chain whined as Hadley moved the swing back and forth with his foot. "That's sad."

"Why did you ask me about this?"

Hadley had been dreading this for weeks. He hadn't known Flora long, but he couldn't imagine his life without her. "My daddy is a white man."

"Well then, I see." Flora pressed the flower to her nose and closed her eyes. "I'm disappointed."

Hadley closed his eyes, too. "I should have told you right off. I know that. But . . . "

How could he explain? It wasn't right to put a nice girl like Flora in danger when she didn't even know she was in danger, but he didn't want to lose her.

Flora gave him a little thump. "I will not take *but* for an answer," she growled. "That's what Mr. Langston Hughes always says."

"I'm awfully sorry."

"Did you think I wouldn't like you, is that it?"

"People never look at me the same way once they know the truth. Happens every time."

"Listen to me." She turned him by his chin so they were stuck there face to face. "I'm not disappointed that you've got a white daddy, and I understand why you'd be hesitant to tell people the truth. I'm just disappointed that you couldn't tell that I'd never use something like that to hurt anybody."

"You mean you're not gonna kick me out of your life?" he asked.

"Not for that, Hadley. Never for that."

Hadley wanted to kiss her worse than ever, and yet, now that the cat was out of the bag, he needed to know that she understood the ramifications of what he was telling her. It was one thing to live your life without judgment, another to live in a world that was full of it.

"This is no small thing, Flora. I've had rocks thrown at me, it makes some folks so mad when they see a white Negro walking down their street. There are men out there who would kill me for sitting on this swing with you if they knew about my white side."

Flora nodded bravely. "You're just going to have to learn to trust me. I know real trust takes time to grow, but if you give me a chance, you'll find I'm up to it."

"I know," he said. "You've got apple-slice ears."

Flora touched her ears and blushed.

"My mama believes you can tell all there is to know about a person's character by their ears. Apple-slice ears indicate a trustworthy and upright soul."

177

"So when do I get to meet your mama anyway?" Flora asked.

Hadley ran a finger around the edge of her ear. "Do you want to meet her?"

"Now what do you think? She's the one who made you, isn't she?"

"According to my mama, making babies ain't nothing special in our family. Everyone does it."

Flora held up her chrysanthemum. "What's this mean?"

"Truth," he said.

"I like the sound of that." Flora popped up off the swing so quick, he was sent flying. "Stay put, now. I made us a treat." She slid the flower over her apple-slice ear and ran inside the house.

Hadley had learned that Flora wasn't a girl to carry on about things that couldn't be helped. Her biggest flaw was his saving grace: Flora took to every adventure with a chipper sense of faith.

"Here you go," she said. She handed him the palm tree spoon and a little red bowl of applesauce.

"What's on yours?" Hadley asked, as he slurped the treat off his special spoon. Flora was eating with a little spoon too.

"Davy Crockett."

He turned her hand so he could see it. A wilderness man stood before the silver-plated mountains of Tennessee with applesauce running down his legs. "How's he taste?"

"Yummy. And your palm tree?"

Hadley gleefully popped Florida into his mouth. "It's even better than I thought it would be."

☙

The following week, Hadley invited Flora to go on a picnic and meet his mama. "I could skip First Street Meth if you'd like and go to church with you?" Flora offered.

Hadley tried to picture himself walking into Rocky Bottoms with a girl. He could hear the sound of a hundred asses turning in their seats to look at Flora. Bottomites traditionally spoke their minds in church. Each and every Sunday was a revival. When Edgecomb Nagle brought that creole lady a few weeks after his wife died, there was nearly a riot. As a general rule of thumb, you didn't want to subject a person to the scrutiny of Rocky Bottoms unless you were mating for life.

"I think we best stick to meeting Mama for now."

As it turned out, the Reverend Blackmon chose this particular Sunday to join the Young Men's Bible Study at the park for some spareribs and horseshoes after he finished up preaching. Once the YMBS spotted Hadley with Flora, the jig was up. More than a few horseshoes were thrown off course by the gawking men of the bible group.

Mama gave them the evil eye and shook her finger at Wilkee Brown who was staring worse than all the rest. *"Stop judging that you may not be judged; for with what judgment you are judging, you will be judged; and with the measure that you are measuring out, they will measure out to you."*

Hadley gave Mama the evil eye. "Huh?"

"Matthew 7:1-3."

The study group was picnicking under the pavilion officially known as *The Mami Thomas Pavilion.* Unofficially, it was called *The Negro Tables.* Hadley had spread his tablecloth nearby on the picnic grounds. Everything was going fine with Mama and Flora until Mama decided to take her bread crusts down to the pond for the ducks, and the reverend cornered her near the water.

"You got to forgive all the staring," the reverend said to Mama. "But tensions are running high right now. Didn't young Hadley hear about that nigger over in Doddsville who got hanged for asking a white woman in marriage?"

"Hadley isn't asking anyone in marriage, Reverend Blackmon," Mama said in Hadley's defense. "And Flora isn't white."

"No, but Hadley sure do look white sitting there next to her."

Mama got shamed then, which didn't happen often. When they first met Reverend Blackmon, Hadley was nine years old. They were new to the church, so naturally there were a lot of questions. A lot of sideways looks. Mama didn't tell Hadley until he was almost grown that Reverend Blackmon had pulled her aside that first day and asked her about her white son. They didn't want white people coming to their church, but he said they would accept Hadley, provided his daddy really was out of the picture. Mama promised that he was far out of the picture, and the church graciously decided that Hadley was colored and never brought it up again. Until now.

Hadley was fuming mad. Yes, he had heard about the Doddsville nigger. He'd also heard about a nigger in Russum who got dragged through a cornfield on account of giving someone the wrong change at the hardware store. As far as he was concerned, as long as there was a chance in life that he might get dragged across a cornfield or strung up by his neck, he would just as soon it was over a woman. It was a pity that the YMBS had to show up at the park on this particular day. He and Flora had spent every Sunday in this same spot for weeks and never run into anyone from church.

Mama fidgeted with worry the whole afternoon, but it was clear she liked Flora. The first thing she did was steal a peek at Flora's ring finger. "Well ain't you pretty," Mama said.

Flora was a hit in every way, and not just because she was single. She took a stroll past *The Negro Tables* and said hello to people who would never in a million years say hello back. She brought chess pie and Swiss cheese and a bookmark she'd made for Mama using two of Caesar's yellow feathers. Flora took to Mama like she took to eating applesauce with a Davy Crockett spoon, and Mama couldn't help but take to her, too.

"She's real nice," Mama said when he walked her home after the picnic. "And she gave me six cans of peas, too."

Hadley was so proud of himself for having the good sense to know someone like Flora, it was a wonder his shirt buttons didn't shoot off his puffed chest like bullets.

Mama said, "You be careful you don't muss up things with this one."

"If by *mussing up*, you mean Lucinda, I'm pleased to inform you that I am almost entirely out of love with her."

"It's the 'almost' part that scares me. Do you care about this woman?"

"Can't you tell?"

"You look happier than I've seen you look in a great many years."

"Thank Flora for that, Mama. I do."

But Mama did not intend to be so hasty. "And what does Mrs. Worther-Holmes have to say about all this happiness, I'd love to know?"

"Mrs. Worther-Holmes is keeping me busier than a soldier ant on the Fourth of July, but I don't care. Sundays are all mine."

Mama stopped on the sidewalk in front of Browning House. "I know this much: you and Miss Gibbs would make awfully pretty babies together."

That was Mama for you. Until the Crump Curse was broken and he gave her a baby properly born to a husband and wife, Mama was never gonna shut up about babies.

"Slow down there, Mama," Hadley said. "I ain't even kissed her yet."

 C3

Lucinda was waiting in the front hall when he got home, tapping the corner of a new *To Do* List against her shiny scarlet lips. Hadley was in such a hurry, he didn't notice her red robe.

"It's Sunday," he said when she waved her list at him. "Give it to me tomorrow."

"Sunday Smunday," Lucinda said. The clip-clop of her fur-trimmed mules followed him into the bedroom. "I need your help with something."

"What is it?" He snatched the list and gave it a split-second read. "These things can wait, Lucinda."

"Not number five."

Hadley skipped to number five: *Brainstorm fundraiser.*

"What's that mean?"

"It means that no-good, lazy Martha Truesdale has put me in charge of the charity event for the annual *Daughters of the Confederacy Pie Bake-off & Family Fun Frolic.*"

Sadly, Lucinda's penchant for joining civic organizations had not diminished over the years. Besides *V.I.L.E.*, she belonged to at least five other social clubs.

Hadley had his own things to worry about. He hoped to have Helen back in shape by Flora's birthday. "What's brainstorming have to do with me?"

"I need help," she whined. "Martha says I'm to come up with the best idea anyone's ever heard of, which means a quilt auction is out of question because it's been done to death, and you can forget about Bingo, too. And a dance marathon. And any of the usual mumbo jumbo that everyone does for the poor. Honestly, Hadley, I'm not as clever as everyone thinks."

She ran her hand over her hip, and for the first time, he noticed the robe. It was silky and red and split open down the middle from her waist to her feet. "It could take hours to come up with a suitable solution."

It surely was a nice robe. "I need to be somewhere at one, Lucinda."

"We'll meet at four then. Just you and me." Lucinda stepped closer so that Hadley was forced to come chin-to-cleavage with that red robe. "Between the two of us, I just know something wonderful is bound to come up."

☙

Hadley could tell that something was wrong the minute Flora opened the door. "Oh thank goodness you're here," she said. She grabbed his sleeve and pulled him in the house.

Flora was not easily distressed. "Look," she whispered.

Hadley peeked between the crack in the swinging door that led to the kitchen. Mr. Gibbs was sitting at the kitchen table eating. Things looked perfectly normal.

"He won't stop with the peas," Flora said.

Sure enough. Hadley watched Mr. Gibbs wolf down an entire bowl in about ten seconds with one of Flora's little spoons.

Ever since the applesauce, Flora served everything with her souvenir spoons. "Which spoon is he using?" Hadley asked.

"Does that matter?"

"I was just wondering."

"Mississippi, I think. Look at those cheeks. I swear to God, he's turning green."

Hadley squinted through the crack. Damned if Mr. Gibbs didn't seem to be turning a greyish, brownish, *Those-Good-Peas* green. "Ain't he sick of them by now?"

"I asked him that very question not one hour ago. He said, 'Who am I to be sick of them? Those peas are like pennies from Heaven, Flora.'"

"Pennies from Heaven?!"

"That's what he said."

"Jesus Flora, we have to get your daddy off those peas. I think they're turning his brain to mush."

"What should we do?" she said.

"How many cans are left?"

Flora shuddered at the thought. "Enough to color him green as a turtle. I've been sneaking cans off to the neighbors while he's napping. There are a lot of people who could use some peas, but he's starting to get suspicious. Last night he called me a *pea-thief.*"

Hadley scratched his head. "Say, this gives me an idea. I think I got a plan that might help out everyone involved."

ℭℛ

"You're late," Lucinda said. She was waiting for him in the Reading Room, dressed in the slinky robe.

"I'll make it worth your while, I promise," Hadley told her. He dragged a *Brick's Minced Meat* crate into the middle of the room.

Seeing how Lucinda didn't have the best eyes in the world, looking inside the crate involved the sort of bending over that jiggles all things great and small. "Peas?" she said, when she could focus.

"They're for the poor."

Lucinda felt his forehead. "Are you delirious?"

"A little," he confessed, staring at her robe. "I've been doing some brainstorming like you asked, and I figure there are a lot of folks out there that just might have an extra can or two of food around to lend to a good cause. Why don't you collect cans for your club? You can call your fundraiser PEAS FOR THE POOR. Or better yet, how about PENNIES FROM HEAVEN?"

It had taken Flora all afternoon to convince Mr. Gibbs to part with his good fortune. Luckily, he had a heart for charity.

Lucinda jiggled upright. "You really are delirious. No one collects peas for poor people. I'll be a laughing stock."

"You can do peaches and tomatoes, too."

Lucinda tapped her slipper. "I don't know. It's different, I suppose. Why don't we have some tea and talk things over more?"

Hadley glanced at the robe. "I got another crate in the wagon outside. Where do you want me to put it?"

Lucinda stuck a leg out through the silky slit. "Where do you want put it?"

Hadley laughed, in spite of himself. Only Lucinda would have the nerve to turn a project for poor people into something dirty. He thought about Flora brooding over the greenness of her daddy in the house back on Dixon Street.

"I'll stash it somewhere safe for now, if it's all the same with you."

Lucinda's canned food collection was proclaimed an unprecedented success. There was even talk of instituting an *Annual Daughters of the Confederacy* PENNIES FROM HEAVEN *Can Drive for the Poor*. Better still, Mr. Gibbs was beginning to return to his former ordinary brown self.

☙

Hadley had been scrupulously setting aside money for a bus trip to Alabama, but when Flora's twenty-first birthday rolled around, he decided to use the money to take her to the Salamander Club instead. The Salamander Club was on S. Pearl Street where all the Negro clubs were located, and the place was creating quite a stir. Most of the joints in blackie town were dim, smoky places with no running water, and you had to use an outhouse if you needed to go. Hadley had never visited any of them, but Flora had been to the Swing Inn a few times and also Dizzy's Café. The Salamander Club was a big new place with an elegant atmosphere and strict codes for behavior and dress. People said it was so nice, white folks were showing up with flasks of corn whiskey inside their dinner jackets and money to burn, hoping to get a seat in one of the fabled Pink Booths near the music stage. The Pink Booths were reserved for big tippers, celebrities, and pretty girls hand-picked by the club owner, Virggie Liggins, who strolled about every night looking out for beauties.

Liggins was creating quite a splash, arguing permits with the city and serving Coca-Cola to coloreds when usually only Nehi and Double Cola were allowed. He was hailed for muscling his way past politicians in order to provide the fanciest Negro club anywhere around, and at the same time, he was lambasted for catering to wealthy white patrons. The newspaper said you could recognize him by his pink cigarettes and flashy stickpins.

Flora had heard that Charley Patton and Willie Brown were known to stop in and play their guitars on the spur of the moment, and this was why she brought up the club to Hadley. She said the Salamander was a real nightclub, unlike the little makeshift jukehouses and cafes all around it.

"My friend Marva went last weekend and ate stuffed clams and a fruit cocktail cup with little marshmallows and powdered sugar sprinkled on top. She danced until her feet fell off."

Hadley didn't know Charley Patton from Adam. They listened to operetta and white radio shows at Wisteria Walk. Flora, on the other hand, was more worldly, what with working at a library and reading all those Harlem magazines. When he said he wanted to take her to the Salamander Club for her birthday, she assured him the place was too costly.

"It's far too much money to spend in one night."

"I wouldn't be spending it all on just one night," Hadley said. "I'd be spending it on one perfect night we'll remember as long as we live. It's a bargain when you think of it that way."

As the son of a cook, Hadley knew which fork to use when eating a refined meal. He'd learned all it all—the butter rules, the napkin placement, how to cross your silverware on your plate when you were finished eating. He gave Flora lessons before the big night. Luckily, she was a quick study when it came to utensils.

"I shouldn't be surprised," Hadley said, "what, with all your experience with spoons."

By the time her birthday arrived, the sun porch had been restored to its natural disorder, and Hadley had begun work on

Helen. The structural problems weren't as bad as he'd first thought. He'd fixed the masonry in one day and cleaned out the chimney so Flora's father could have a fire on chilly nights when he got around to building his radios. Mr. Gibbs grumbled like the improvements were a bad thing. He said that Hadley had made the place too nice for the rakes and buckets now and wondered, did Hadley have any ideas about where he ought to put them instead?

The more time Hadley spent repairing Helen, the more attached he got to the old place. The building contained two medium-sized rooms, several nice windows, and a hearth built of good sound quarry rock. Declarations of love had been scratched into the glass on one of the windows. *Conny Barbour & Letty Swann Owctowber 3, 1812. Big Brown loves Matilda 18403. Marry Me Alice! 9/2/46. All right I will 9/3/46. Ginny and Flournoy Nelson 1-1-1901. I love Ampy Anderson June 12 .*

If the mayor had gotten his way, all of this love would have been lost forever. One day, Hadley found a corncob baby stuffed between the hearth rocks. The eyes had just about bled away, but the smile was still good. He stood it on the mantle next to Mr. Gibbs' pruning shears and decided that Flora's father was right. This place was too good for the rakes now.

Using the edge of a penny, he scratched his own declaration into the glass.

⌘

Hadley was permitted to leave work three hours early on Flora's birthday, which, as luck would have it, was also Mama's birthday. In his request, he neglected to mention that it was not his mama's birthday he intended to celebrate.

Flora clapped her hands when he gave her the magnolia. "No one ever gave me flowers until you came into my life."

"Not even Countee Burkes?"

"Countee Burkes wasn't as romantic as you are when it comes to gifts."

"Oh, the magnolia isn't your gift," Hadley said. He pulled out a package from behind his back. "This is your gift."

Flora tore through the paper like she'd never gotten a real present in all her days. "An Alabama spoon? Did you sneak off to Alabama without my knowing about it?"

"Nope. I found it at *Pringles Second Hands*. I know I ain't been to Alabama yet, or you neither, but I think we should go there sometime and smell those lemony azaleas." The rims of his ears fired up like a griddle. "Maybe we could go for our honeymoon?"

"Honeymoon?" Flora said. "Are you drunk?"

"I've been thinking about this real hard, Flora, and I can see it in my mind. I mean, if you can? I can see us together. I can see our life and our kids and our cluttered-up house. We'd be so happy, don't you think? We'd be real good to each other."

Flora ran her thumb over the Alabama spoon. "It wasn't that long ago that you imagined your life with someone else."

"I knew you'd say that, but the fact of the matter is, you need me. I never knowed it was true before, but not everyone has business using a paintbrush on a room. You and your Daddy don't fix anything. You don't even open your mail. I'm good at those things. *Women's Voices* might say otherwise, but I think I'd make you a fine husband, Flora, and I'd be the luckiest man alive to have you."

"Do you love me, Hadley?"

Hadley took her hand and pressed it to his lips. "In a better, more right, and happy way than I ever loved anyone else. I live for Sundays, Flora. You mean everything to me."

"My goodness."

"And your pie is special, too. I meant to mention that right off. And you aren't too short. You're just right." He sucked on his lower lip, trying to think what else he might have forgotten. "Oh yeah . . . what do you think of me, Flora? I was going to ask you that before I asked about Alabama."

It should have seemed risky after what happened with Lucinda, but Flora made him feel safe. She threw her arms around his neck. "I love you, too, you crazy boy. You make me very happy."

"What about my . . . obligation?" A few weeks earlier, Hadley had told Flora about the pressure he was under to produce the first lawful baby in his ill-begotten line. He was giving *trust* a chance at the time, testing to see if she'd be scared off, but Flora was sympathetic as ever.

She rubbed her fiery cheek against his and softly whispered, "I've dreamed of being a mother all my life."

"Do you want to marry me, Flora?"

"Yes. I do."

⊗

It felt like a funny place for them to be, with Hadley in one of Dickie's cast-off jackets, and a long line of fancy cars lined up out front. Hadley had to tip ten dollars just to get a table.

"Look!" Flora said. "It's the Pink Boothes."

Sure enough, circling the shiny black dance floor like a giant set of puffy lips were the notorious pink leather booths they'd heard so much about. Flora wasn't sure, but she thought one of the men holding court in the booths was Fats Waller. Outside of Fats Waller and two young colored women, the Pink Booths were filled to capacity with white girls.

"This menu is bigger than the Declaration of Independence," Flora said. "I'll never make up my mind." But she was smiling. The band was playing *Drifting and Dreaming*. A soft mist of cigarette smoke curled around the room. Everywhere you looked, there were palm trees covered with twinkly lights.

"Well, I'm gonna try *Stormy's Pecan Goose Cassoulet*. Tilly won't fix anything with pecans."

After much consternation, Flora settled on the cassoulet as well. "It's not every day a girl can get her goose cooked so fashionably," she said.

Hadley cleared his throat. "There's something else I been wondering about, Flora."

A pink napkin folded like a fan sat in the center of every white plate in the room. Flora unfolded and refolded the fan, teaching herself how to do it.

"Do you think your Daddy would rent me Helen?"

"I don't know about that," she said. "He's awful set on starting up with radios over there."

"Shoot, with you and all your junk out of the way, Flora, he'll have room to build a Viking ship inside that house."

Flora laughed. "If we moved my birds into Helen, where would we eat? I don't think there's room for birds and a table."

"We'll hang the cages from the ceiling. There's room for that. I don't know what it is about that place, but it feels special to me. I think we'd cheer it up if we lived there, don't you?"

Flora fanned her face with her napkin-fan. "I'd live in a cardboard box with you if you asked."

"You would?"

"Of course. But I like the idea of renting Helen better."

"Now we just have to convince your Daddy." Hadley had made some diagrams to help him visualize where everything might go. "The place needs a stove and a sink. A bathroom would be nice, too, I reckon."

"Daddy's still sore about losing his peas."

"If he lets me move in, I'll grow him all the peas he wants."

Hadley touched Flora's shoe with his shoe under the table. The band started playing *The Love Nest*. "Do you think we should try and dance?"

"Definitely," Flora said. "It's not every day a girl gets to go dancing at the Salamander Club."

Flora was a better dancer than Hadley, but not so good that she lost patience with him. "Ain't it a beautiful song?" she asked.

"It ought to be our song, Flora. If your Daddy rents us Helen, we should call it the Love Nest instead of Helen. It sounds nicer."

In a small room, tea set of blue,
There's the ballroom, dream room for two,
Better than a palace with a gilded dome,
Is the love nest you can call home.

Hadley was so happy, he didn't even notice trouble when it came wiggling up behind him in a low cut dress. "Why don't you teach her the *Twinkle Hesitation*?"

Hadley didn't turn around. He danced them away, as if they might escape, determined to ignore her.

"Hadley?" Flora said, squeezing his fingers and looking at him expectantly. She nodded at the woman behind his shoulder, waiting to be introduced.

Flora was a polite girl, there was no denying that, a kind-hearted girl with a magnolia pinned to the front of her dress and an Alabama spoon tucked away in her pocketbook. She smiled even though she knew full and well that the woman in the red dress was probably the one he danced the Twinkle Hesitation with.

"You must be Flora." Lucinda said, offering her hand. "I'm Mrs. Worther-Holmes."

CR

Flora gave her napkin a murderous snap. They'd returned to their table before the song was done, and she had yet to stop staring at Lucinda who sat in a Pink Booth polishing off crawfish with a loud and drunken Babe Butternut.

"Why didn't you tell me? All this talk of being in love, and not once did you mention that the woman you love is the woman you work for. You *live* in her house, for heaven's sake."

"So what?" Hadley said. "You know how I feel about you. You're the one I love."

Flora rubbed her nose like she was about to cry. "You never said anything about her being married neither."

"Come on, Flora. Don't let this ruin our night."

She picked up her teaspoon and looked at her upside-down self in the shiny silver. "You never said she was white. Or pretty. Or rich."

"I didn't know you wanted the details."

The waiter put down their plates with such a dramatic flourish right then, Hadley thought Flora's mind might return to happier things. He smiled at her hopefully over his goose.

"Does she know you were planning to propose to me tonight?" Flora asked.

Hadley reached for her hand across the table, but Flora moved it into her lap. "It's none of her business," he said. He followed her sad gaze across the room to where Lucinda was laughing it up like she didn't have a care in the world. "She has no say in what I do with my life."

"*A lost lover welds more power than a whip,*" Flora said, quoting from a magazine article she'd read to him called *Ten Sound Reasons for Avoiding a Jilted Man.*

"That's nonsense, Flora."

"Is it? Look at that red dress." Flora bit down on lip. "You aren't really going to marry me, are you?"

"Of course I am," he growled. He smacked the table with his open hand, and the candle fell in his goose.

"*Denial is Passion's unholy bridegroom,*" Flora whispered. "*Their dark marriage is eternal.*"

It was like eating dinner with Mama.

℧

He dropped her off at ten thirty. Without a kiss. It didn't seem right anymore, even though he'd been planning all week to kiss her. Instead, they held hands awkwardly on the front stoop with Flora standing three steps higher, ready to sprint for the door.

"I won't tell anyone about Alabama yet," she said.

"Nothing has changed, Flora."

Flora's eyes were glassed with tears. "You should have told me who she was."

He let loose of her fingers. "It wasn't meant to be a secret. Anyway, I can't undo the past."

"You told me that you loved her, but there's one more thing I'd like to know. Was it . . . just wishful thinking?" She took hold of his necktie then and pulled until he lifted onto the tips of his toes. "I don't think I can bear the idea of you working in that house if you had an extramarital affair with Mrs. Worther-Holmes."

Hearing the word "extramarital" come out of Flora's sweet mouth was enough to make him regret every poor decision he'd ever made. "I'll get a different job," he said.

She stared down at the tie clenched between her fingers.

"Put the spoon up with the others, Flora," he said.

"We'll see." She dropped the tie and turned to go.

"Wait! I didn't get a chance to tell you everything I wanted to say tonight."

Flora paused with her hand on the doorknob. "What else is there?"

"The meaning of magnolias." He turned her back around to face him. "*Happiness in marriage*. We can have that, Flora. Please hang the spoon up on your spoon rack."

She kissed him lightly on the cheek. "I'll think about it."

ॐ

I still quivered in every nerve to think how slight a sinking or slipping of the machinery would precipitate that keen, glistening axe upon my bosom . . .

—Edgar Allen Poe

Hadley expected to find Lucinda waiting in the shadows, ready to hit him with some new bit of monkeyshine meant to keep him by her side. When he found the kitchen empty, he tiptoed into the bedroom and checked behind the curtains, but there was nobody there. He got down on his knees and peeked under the bed. He saw a slipper, a lost comb, and a handful of dust bunnies. He opened the closet door. "A-hah!" he cried when something moved, but it was only a bumped hanger.

With a sigh of relief, he sat on the bed, pulled off his shoes, and chewed himself out for coming up with the bad idea of taking Flora to such a fancy place. He was angry with himself for not coming completely clean about Lucinda, too. He couldn't think why he hadn't. Part of him even thought that he had. Part of him thought that it was bad manners to speak about her as much as he did.

When he was done chewing himself out, he kicked off his trousers and carried his pillow into the bathroom and yanked on the light.

There was a bathtub with a white plastic curtain that nobody except Hadley ever used. He kept his bedclothes there. Tonight, the curtain was ripped off its rings, and the bedclothes were in the middle of the floor. Mrs. Worther-Holmes sat on his sheets, rubbing a blanket against her face in a way that made him more nervous than anything she'd ever done.

"How long have you been sleeping in the bathroom?"

"Goddamn it, Lucinda," he said. "What are you doing here?"

She hugged the blanket against her robe. "All this time, I thought you were *listening*. We had a deal about that, remember? Or is this your way of being faithful to little Miss Flora Gibbs?"

Hadley squatted on the octagon tiles and looked her in the eye. If he didn't know better, he'd think those were real tears dripping down her cheeks. His heart beat with both sympathy and revulsion. "Go to bed, Lucinda."

"I don't want to," she whimpered. "I don't want to go to bed with that big old boar."

Not for the first time, he wondered if she wasn't just a little bit crazy. He was gladder than glad that he'd found a nice girl like Flora to love. "You got no cause to be here, Lucinda. "

She ran a cold hand down his stomach. "What do you want with her? She isn't as pretty as me. Do you think she's as pretty as me?" Her fingers found the waistband of his union suit and yanked so hard, he almost fell off his feet. "You love *me*. You said so."

Hadley got close enough to smell if she'd been drinking, but Lucinda said alcohol gave her dark circles under her eyes, and she rarely touched the stuff. She smelled like she always smelled. Like his daydreams.

"I'm going to marry her," Hadley said. He knew it was a mistake to let such words come out, yet saying them was important. He wanted to see that spoon hung up in Flora's kitchen just as soon as possible. It wasn't right to keep quiet about a happy thing like love. "I can't work for you no more."

There! It was done. Her irises burned so fiery hot, it was like putting your face down on a gas jet, but so be it. *Let her explode*, he thought. *Let her call Dickie down here and tell him what I did to her against the wall of his house. He can just go on and pound me to a nub! At least I was brave enough to tell her . . .*

But Lucinda didn't call Dickie down. Instead, she ran her fingernail along the inside of his thigh, snagging his new "patented for durability" underwear until Hadley smacked her hand away.

"You can't stop me from marrying her, Lucinda."

Lucinda squeezed the tiger tooth in her fist until it punctured the heel of her palm. Red drops splashed on the octagons. "That's where you're wrong, dear."

Part 2:
Nina

From PAGE 3B of the Beattie's Bluff Examiner, June 3, 1932:

FREAK CRASH TUMBLES DICTATOR

Late Thursday afternoon, Mrs. Winchell P. Lovette of Number 9 Tulip Hill Road, lost control of her husband's new Studebaker Dictator, running it into a tree in the 400 block of Archway Boulevard and Treebourne Street. According to witnesses, injuries occurred when Mr. Lovette put his fist through the living room window after being informed of the damage done to the automobile he had saved ten years to buy. Asked how she managed to lose control on such a nice clear day, Mrs. Lovette indicated she had become distracted by a particularly fine display of wisteria growing in a neighborhood lawn. Said Mrs. Winchell P. Lovette of Tulip Hill Road, "When I saw all that wild beauty, my head got to swimming and I drove into a tree."

Nail Number Five:
The Window Seat

Nina first came across the books in the window seat when she was eleven years old. Oh, what a memorable day that was. Thanks to the Timpone cousins' hopeless lack of imagination, she was dragging her way through the world's most *humdrum* game of hide-n-seek ever played when she happened upon the discovery. As all the really worthwhile hiding spots had been squeezed into long ago, she desperately wedged behind the aquarium and butted the library ladder. The ladder toppled sideways, crashed down on the window seat, and made the lid hop up. And what a surprise that was!

Nina and the cousins had hidden in the curtains next to the window seat some five thousand times before, and Nina had once stretched out on top of the window seat and lined up the cushions head to toe across herself, but the Timpones had noticed the lumpiness and immediately jumped on her face, and the mud turtle in her pocket had been smooshed. It was also popular to hide under the table next to the window seat and doodle on the baseboard, as this was the safest of all vandalism. Anyone too big to fit underneath would never have the chance to see the crime. Usually a crayon was used for the job, but some gutsy soul had *eschewed* tradition and scratched the word STRAP with a dime long before Nina came along. In spite of all this poking about, no one had ever discovered that the window seat actually opened.

When Nina bumped the lid with the ladder, she knew she'd stumbled on something significant. She flipped it open, fully expecting to unearth the rotting body of the twin sister she never knew she had, or a suitcase full of stolen money. The books were a disappointment.

Nina couldn't imagine what could possibly be interesting about a collection of books hidden in a room that was crammed floor to ceiling with books. Still, something told her that this was an important discovery, and instead of hiding in the best place in the whole wide world, she locked the door to the Reading Room and hauled the books out on the floor. Sure enough, inside the first volume, Nina came face to *penis* with the most confusing picture she'd ever laid eyes on.

"Hmm," said Nina. She turned the page sideways. She turned it upside down. She snapped the book shut and returned it to the pile. Were there spicy pictures in all the books?

One of the volumes she picked up was called *Lady Chatterly's Lover*, and it had words instead of pictures. Nina fanned the pages, picked one at random, and began to read.

> . . . *as he felt the frenzy of her achieving her own orgasmic satisfaction from his hard, erect passivity, he had a curious sense of pride and satisfaction. 'Ah, how good!' she whispered tremulously.*

No sooner had she gotten to the juiciest part, when Rich Rich jiggled the knob. "No fair locking the door!" he griped, and he proceeded to hammer his fist until the hinges were set to bend.

"Nina's not in here," Nina called, impersonating her mother perfectly.

"Open the dim-damn door, Nina. I found you."

Still impersonating Mother, Nina said, "Richard Luciano Ignazio Timpone! Did I hear you say 'dim-damn'?"

There was silence then, which seemed encouraging, but then Nina had to go and push her luck. "Go and sit on your bed until I bring the hairbrush." The hairbrush being the equivalent of a belt.

"Oh farts," Rich Rich said. "I know it's you, Nina, and I'm gonna go tell the Stinkberry that you locked the door." He clomped away like Paul Revere, shouting his tattletale news.

Whew, Nina thought, *alone at last.*

It didn't take a genius to figure out that *Lady Chatterly's Lover* was nothing like the other books on The Reading Room shelves. Nina was a collector of words, so she was practically a professional when it came to understanding anything that was rare, fancy, or the least bit indecent. It was her habit to pick out two or three new words each week and use them as she saw fit. She printed them in straight columns in her *Fibber McGee and Molly* notebook, keeping careful track of dates, any unusual reactions that might accompany the usage, and the consequences, if relevant. *Piss ant*, for example, was spoken on Oct 1, 1932 so the entry looked like this:

PISS ANT. 10/01/32.
Lifebuoy instead of macaroni for dinner.

Just looking at the words in *Lady Chatterly's Lover* made Nina taste soap. It might be a challenge to find an appropriate situation to make use of the phrase *erect passivity,* but Nina wasn't one to back away from a challenge. She liked *frenzy*, too, and was immediately in a frenzy to use the word *frenzy*.

The next book, *Of Mice and Men,* showed promise as well. For one thing, it used the words *son of a bitch* plain as day, and that had to mean something good.

Luckily, Nina was just about the craftiest girl she knew. She straightened up the pillows on the seat and buried *Lady Chatterly* in the art box that had been left lying in the middle of the floor since the completion of her postage stamp-size rendition of the Lord's Supper several weeks before. She then un-locked the door and stepped behind the curtains.

By the time Rich Rich came back with Miss Dinkleberry, Nina had succeeded in making him look like the little liar he so often was. Rich Rich marched up to the curtains and whipped them back. "You locked the door," he grunted.

"Did not," Nina said.

"Did too!" he shouted.

"That's enough," Miss Dinkleberry said, for she avoided confrontation at all cost, often times to the advantage of her young charges. "How about a nice game of Neck & Neck?" she suggested. "I think we're Hiding-Seeked out."

CR

Due to its delicate content, Nina was forced to read *Lady Chatterly's Lover* by flashlight after everyone else was asleep. Huddled within the daisy-printed cave of her blankets, she pondered the same question night after night: Who put the dirty books in the window seat?

The most obvious guess would be Father, since he was a man, yet Nina couldn't quite believe it of him. Although her father did have a fondness for saying *son of a bitch*, it was almost impossible for Nina to imagine that he'd ever heard of things like *orgasmic satisfaction*. Nina had known him all her life and felt as if she could safely say that he would not be interested in anything so exciting as that. If he'd heard of it, he probably coughed and buried his head in the funnies like he did whenever Rich Rich cussed. Anyway, Nina had never seen Father read anything but the funnies.

No, Father was a gun man, not a book man. Nina had been hunting with him since she was five, and she knew what made him tick. Father was only patient when crouching in buck vine with his finger on a trigger. He liked the speed of a bullet. He liked to eat what he shot, too, but he ate it rare—rare didn't taste better, but he could never hold out for well done. Nina couldn't see her Father having the attention span for *Lady Chatterly's Lover. Nope*, Nina decided. Just because Father liked saying son of a bitch didn't mean he gave a tinker's damn about orgasmic satisfaction.

Nina's favorite answer to the question was Miss Dinkleberry. It would be the most fun if it turned out that their old maid governess was hiding dirty books in secret places around the house. If the books were Miss Dinkleberry's, Nina would have to tell Rich Rich and Guido about it immediately. No one could appreciate the irony of such a development more than her two cousins. It had been her experience though that people who hid things were generally jittery, and she was one hundred percent certain that the Stinkberry had looked just as wooden as ever when Rich Rich found her hiding in the curtains by the window seat. Disappointing as it was, Nina scratched the governess off the suspect list.

That pretty much left Mother.

Yes. The books belonged to Mother, Nina would have staked her life on it. Mother had surely heard of sexual things, otherwise she wouldn't dress the way she did. Or laugh the way she did. Or smile at Neville Pillwater the way she did whenever he came around with new drapery material for her to poke through. Yes, Mother would read these sorts of books and like them, Nina felt certain of it.

The thought of uncovering one of her Mother's secrets made her heart jump track. Surely such naughty information could prove useful? Luckily, Nina was clever and knew to keep the books to herself until the time came when Mother's secret might benefit her in some way

There were some close calls in the years to follow. Ever since Aunt Fancy's Sicilian husband went in the red and jumped off the Bucatunna Creek bridge, she'd been dropping her boys off for weeks at a time, unable to deal with their rambunctious presence during her endless period of mourning. As a result, Nina had been all but permanently saddled with the Timpone cousins for every waking hour of the day. And every sleeping hour, too.

Guido Bertrando Innocenzio Timpone, who was four years younger and a perpetual baby, once knocked Lady Chatterly out of bed when he crawled in during an electrical storm.

Guido had been born with a fear of storms, and Nina cursed herself for not thinking ahead when she heard the first clap of thunder. Guido switched on the light, picked up the book and said, "Whatcha reading under the covers, Neen?"

Nina dearly liked having something on her mother, but she didn't want Guido having something on her. She folded the book against the pearl buttons of her nightgown as the first fat rain drops began to tap at the panes. "I'll confide the truth if you don't tell," she whispered.

Guido lifted her arm and put it over his quaking shoulder, his eyes growing double in size in the flash of lightning that followed. He could be chicken-hearted, but he was a sucker for secrets and kept them surprisingly well, unlike Rich Rich, who was a mere four months younger than Nina and generally rotten to the bone. Once, at Christmas dinner, Rich Rich announced that Nina had written a love letter to one Eugene Starks of her third grade music class, then he proceeded to delight the entire table with snippets of heartfelt verse that had been meant for 'Dearest sanguine-haired Eugene' alone. The whole horrid transgression occurred not so much because Rich Rich had been born with loose lips, but because he knew the effect it would have on Nina, who turned so purple with rage, she flicked maple syrup pie at his big head in front of God and everyone. The pie-flicking resulted in Mother sentencing Nina to her room during the wine toast—which, as Rich Rich knew perfectly well, was their only shot at wine-toasting for the entire year.

Guido was not Rich Rich, however, and vowed to seal his lips up like a tomb, even as he pulled the bed sheet over their heads.

"Well," Nina began, clicking on her flashlight inside the dark sheet-den. "I didn't get my reading done at school on Friday, and if Father gets wind of it, I'll have to read double this weekend for sure."

Guido had been born with the face of Gabriel, but in that precise moment, his Gabrielic face screamed disappointment. Nina smiled and propped the book up on her knees. "Want me to read you some of it?"

"No!" Guido crowed. "I've had enough of school this week.

Nina was nothing if not understanding. "I'll just put it up for now."

Another time, The Stinkberry yelled at Nina for messing up the cushions on the window seat. "You know your Mother insists that you keep away from the books in this room," the old bat said, even though it wasn't a bit fair. Rich Rich had left his disintegrator pistol in the middle of the floor, and there was a big glob of grape jelly on the ship clock that everyone had been ignoring for three days. The room was hardly the museum The Stinkberry made it out to be. Still, Nina reminded herself to be more cautious in the future. After she straightened the cushions, Miss Dinkleberry poked her beak sharp nose around the window seat so suspiciously, Nina almost wet her pants.

The only thing better than reading the dirty window seat books was concocting scenarios in which Nina caught her mother reaching into her *stash*. This had, in fact, become Nina's favorite daydream. She had been born with her father's love of the hunt. She'd made her first bellow's call out of a piece of shoe rubber when she was only a kid of seven. Father bragged that Nina could *shoot skeet to beat the band*. In order to jump shoot Mother, she fancied the idea of a hidden jerk string that set off bells and whistles and exposed the woman to deepest embarrassment when everyone in the household ran to see what all the fuss was about. Other times, she imagined leaving drops of Guido's model glue on the back cover of a book so that, when Mother picked it up, it stuck like a little airplane wing to the palm of her hand. Oh, wouldn't it be funny to watch Mother trying to drive Neville Pillwater into a state of erect passivity with a nasty book stuck on her hand?

For a while, Nina toyed with the idea of telling Rich Rich about her plans. Sneaky as he was, Rich Rich had the necessary skills to come up with something truly inspiring to snare the woman. Getting back at people was just about his favorite pass-time, and he would have appreciated the opportunity to pay his aunt back for what he commonly referred to as the *Kix Cereal Incident*. The *Kix Cereal Incident* came to pass when Mother saw to it that her face all but blotted out his own the day the newspaper came out to photograph him for winning the *Kix Cereal Contest*. Under the big bold headline—*Local Boy Wins Kix Cereal Contest to Name Silver's Son*—there appeared a picture of a beautiful middle-aged woman in a fluffy fox scarf next to one half of a boy's head.

"I will never forgive her for the *Kix Cereal Incident*," Rich Rich vowed.

But, alas, the dirty books were Nina's secret, and she liked it better that way. Rich Rich would have to find his own form of revenge.

☙

On the surface, Nina's mother looked harmless enough, fingering her hair in such a delicate way, people might think butter wouldn't melt in her mouth. She was head of the *Christian Women's League* and the *Afternoon Bridge Girls*, and co-chairperson with Mr. Keaten Powers of the *Madison County Optimist's Club*.

Behind their backs, she said of her fellow optimists, "If not for having Keaton to look at every week, I couldn't abide all that optimism."

Mother had her charities, there was no forgetting that. She managed to work them into at least every other conversation and with such finesse, people never failed to gasp and say,

"What a tireless soldier you are for the needy, dear." To which she would inevitably respond by quoting that corny old quote that hung in Grandpa's house, "Never forget where you come from, I always say."

Of course, Mother came from one of Beattie's Bluff's finest old mansions. Nina knew because she had slept in Mother's mansion when Mother and Father went to Niagara Falls to rekindle the old fires. No matter how nobly Mother managed to say it, Nina couldn't understand what was humbling about remembering the mansion you came from.

The charities were but a minor grievance in the scheme of things. Rich Rich particularly detested Mother's nightgowns, which he said were enough to make him want to form his own charity; *The Charity for Boys Who Cannot think of Anything But Their Aunt in a Slinky Nightgown*. Guido was too sweet to find flaw with anyone. He liked to point out that Mother's nightgowns made terrific *Ming-the-Merciless* capes.

Mother admitted that she was not the mothering sort. "I do not cuddle," she liked to say. "But I plan a damned fine birthday party." And this was true. When it came to Nina's mother, one had to be content with ponies and clowns and inordinately large cakes covered with icing-roses the size of your head. She was not the parent you went to with a splinter or a torn teddy bear arm, but, if you reminded her that you were soon to turn twelve, she would pull out all the stops. Nina, however, was far too smart a girl to be wooed by fancy birthday parties. She had her own ax to grind with the woman.

It might just as well been called the *Miss Bell Incident* for it was much like *The Kix Cereal Incident* only Nina's incident involved a dance recital instead of a contest. Despite the fact that Nina was the one who danced the cha cha so terrifically, Mother managed to have the whole auditorium crowded around her immediately after the performance. Mother had presented a plaque to the dancing director, Miss Bell, on behalf of the *Beattie's Bluff Sisters for Wholesome Art*, and everyone thought this was so dear of her. Nina remained calm by picturing her mother with the Kamasutra glued to her hand. Mother would not have been in a position to discuss wholesome art, had her hand been weighted with her dirty little secret.

Likewise, when Nina was buying her Turkey Hop dress at *LuLu's Bewitching Glamour Gowns*, the salesgirls would have been too ashamed to go on about how pretty Mother's new hairdo was if one of the window seat books had been conspicuously stuck to her person. And if the men of the *Happy Hunting Club* had any clue how phony she was, they would never have used up important bulletin board space by covering over the photograph of Nina holding twenty-five quail, with the newspaper picture from the *Kix Cereal Incident.*

Never did Nina wish to use the secret more, though, than the night her mother made eyes at Del Wiggins, her slick-haired Turkey Hop date.

"Holy bangtails, Nina! Your mom's a real looker," Del was dumb enough to say after they left for the dance. Delbert was a big reader of detective stories and always spoke hard-boiled. "I just hope I don't dust the old man's bucket, I'm so lit just smelling her," which, in detective-speak, meant that Del was worried he would crash his daddy's car because Mother was a big hussy.

It was the night before her sixteenth birthday, and Nina was in no mood to come in second place to her mother again. "Aw, close your head," she told Del Wiggins, which in Spade-speak meant shut-up.

In reality, she couldn't really blame poor hapless Del. Mother had wiggled up so close for the *Mother/Turkey Hop-Date* picture, she might be pregnant with his child. Anyhow, Nina was used to it, or she tried to be. Disgusting as it was, her mother seemed to have that effect on men. Later, after a long gloomy night of listening to Del bump gums on the subject of her mother's gams, Nina expressed her fury the second she got home.

When she came in at ten o'clock and asked if they could talk, Mother was brushing her hair in her bedroom.

"Of course, dear!" Mother said, taking Nina by the hands and hugging her against her great big silk-entombed busts. "I want to hear all about the dance. Did Delbert kiss you goodnight?"

Nina untangled herself from the busts. "Nope. I'm sure he would have been happy to kiss you though."

"What?" Mother laughed, clearly tickled by the thought. "Don't be a silly-nilly."

"What do you expect, Mother, rubbing up against him the way that you did? The boy was in utter agony all night long."

Mother clapped her hand to her throat. "Now wait a minute, Nina," she said. "Delbert Wiggins is a child. I would never . . . "

"I shouldn't have even went to that stupid old dance," Nina snapped. "It was a total calamity, thanks to you." "Calamity" was Nina's word of the week.

"Well that's a fine way to say thank you," Mother said. "After all the trouble I went to with Viv Wiggins, too. I swear to God, Nina, you are the most ungrateful creature God ever created."

Nina dropped down on the bed. "Do you mean to tell me you arranged for Del to invite me to the dance?"

Mother resumed her brushing. "Damned straight I did. No boy in his right mind would have the gumption to ask out a snotty tomboy like you. They'd be afraid you'd shoot them dead." Mother found it despicable that Nina liked to hunt, probably because it was the one thing Nina did with Father that Mother didn't know how to do.

"I hate you," Nina said, and it was the god-awful truth. With her big blonde hair and her big blue eyes and her big old bosoms hanging out for all to see, the woman was just about unbearable. "I wish I'd never been born."

Mother threw her brush down on the vanity. "Sometimes, Nina darling, I wish the same."

ᘕ

Nina had kept mum about the window seat books for five long years, but the time had come to use her leverage. She wanted revenge on her mother and couldn't think of a better way to achieve this than by exposing the woman as a Bible-reading fraud. Wouldn't the ladies of her charity groups die of shock when they learned what secrets Mother hid in her lovely little Reading Room?

Nina planned to hide in the window seat and, when her mother came to sneak out a book, jump up and scream her head off for all the town to hear. Maybe she would even see to it that some of Mother's dirty books went flying out the window. Nina had noticed that the books in the seat were almost always moved around on Tuesdays. She had also noticed that Mrs. Pearlie Cooper-Carter's temperance group met every second

Tuesday of the month on the lawn next door to make angry signs and eat lunch. Mrs. Pearlie Cooper-Carter was one of the gossipiest women on the street. Thus it came to pass that, on the Tuesday after the Turkey Hop, Nina ditched school, pushed opened the Reading Room windows, and hid in the window seat, praying her mother would think herself alone and feel in a reading-mood.

It was hot and the seat and felt like a casket. Nina couldn't quite stretch out her legs. *Hurry up, Mother*, she silently pleaded, shifting miserably in the coffin-like gloom. Already, she regretted hiding in the seat. It had been at least an hour, and Mother hadn't come in for a single book. The temperance ladies sounded like they were putting up their hammers and getting ready for lunch.

Finally, the Reading Room door squeaked open, and Nina almost jumped out then and there, she was so happy and relieved. But no. That would ruin everything. "Shh . . . " she heard her mother whisper. "The Stinkberry is downstairs."

Nina wasn't sure what surprised her more, discovering that her mother was not alone, or hearing her refer to Miss Dinkleberry by the same name the kids used for their governess. In any case, whoever she was with said nothing in response, but Nina heard other noises. Lip-smacking noises. Breathing noises. Grunts.

Ewww, Nina thought, *she's with Father!*

Nina got so alarmed, she almost upset the stack of books wedged under her ribs. It occurred to her that if she were caught now, she would be the one with egg on her face. She covered her ears and prayed with all her heart that whatever they were doing, it would be over quick.

"Slow down," Mother said--Nina wanted to bawl. "Little Rock is hundreds of miles away. There's no need to rush."

Little Rock? It was then that Nina remembered that her father had left for Little Rock the evening before to attend *The Amazing Buck Stanton Red, White & Blue Auto Rally*. But if Mother wasn't kissing Father, who was she kissing? Neville Pillwater? Del Wiggins? Sucking in her breath, she raised the lid and peeked out in the room.

Holy Spumoni! Nina said to herself, "spumoni" being the new word of the week. *Mother is kissing the gardener!*

This was even better than the dirty books.

He was old, of course. Twenty or thirty or maybe even sixty. He opened doors for them and pulled weeds and drove them around. What else did she know about him? He had a Negro mother who worked for Grandpa Browning. After Rich Rich discovered that Mrs. Crump was actually the mother of *their* Crump, they had taken to calling him Sambo behind his back.

Why is Mother kissing Sambo? she thought.

She was vaguely aware that he was nicer than some, but since when did Mother appreciate folks that were nice? Nina felt entirely sure that her mother got giggly around the draper because he had a dirty smirk and pinched her bottom under the barkcloth. Neville Pillwater was not nice. He was not polite. He was a letch! Then again, listening to Mother finishing up with Crump, he sounded pretty lecherous himself. They were knocking books off the shelves, and it was downright icky the way Mother kept saying, "Yes . . . oh . . . yes . . . oh . . . yes oh!" Nina didn't relax until she heard the sound of books being slid back into place.

"I'm going to need the Mercedes waxed and ready for the *Founder's Day Picnic*, Hadley," Mother said.

Hadley? Was that his last name? His first name? A pet name like Annie Oakley's *Little Sure Shot*? Nina lifted the lid to watch how they said goodbye. Her crafty mind reasoned that this might tell her whether this shocking thing with Crump had ever happened before.

Mother was tugging her dress into place, and Crump was buttoning things. "He's in Jackson again on Thursday," Mother said, like she was telling him which bushes to trim.

Crump kissed her cheek. He was younger than Mother. Or maybe just shorter. "Okay," he said. Like he'd just agreed to get those bushes for her.

All told, Nina spent more than two hours in the window seat before she could make her escape, but it was worth it. Afterward, she had the giddy feeling that her life might never be the same again.

That afternoon, she watched Crump tend a flowerbed from behind the curtains of her bedroom window. There was something strangely violent about the way he went after weeds, beating them silly as though they were dirty thoughts come to ruin his flowery world. But he was gentle, too. At one point, he came across a broken bloom, smelled it, and tucked it in his pocket. After what she'd witnessed earlier, she wondered if perhaps those weeds weren't really more like his conscience, and the dirty thoughts the treasures he carefully saved up in his pocket.

When Rich Rich and Guido came bounding home from school, Crump stood up from his work and said hello. He was nice like that, Nina realized. Rich Rich threw a football right through the petunias he'd been working so hard on, yet Crump laughed and tossed the ball back. After the boys bounded inside for Fig Newtons, Crump grabbed hold of his shirttails and stripped off his shirt.

It was a hot day, and Nina was pretty sure she'd seen him do this a million times before, but it had never struck her as interesting until now. He was a skinny man with slick sweaty skin, and even though he was part Negro, his skin was suntanned to match his missing shirt, coloring him browner in some parts than others. He had the hard arms of a laborer, and she could count his ribs from two stories above. *So that's what Mother likes about him*, Nina thought, suddenly liking it herself. Father was a soft man with a flabby gut who liked martinis too much. Crump would be a reed beside him. And he was filthy, too. Just like Mother's books.

She saw something else of interest as well. There were three distinct marks across his shoulder blades - the same marks she'd seen on another man of theirs called George Vinegar. George Vinegar was old. He'd been working for the Worther-Holmes since he was a slave boy of five. Nina glimpsed his back one time after he got bit on the bellybutton by the Hibbles' bloodhound. Just like old George Vinegar, Crump had whip marks across his back.

The next day was a Tuesday and Tuesdays were piano lesson day at Miss Maple's. The children had been taking lessons for two years, although Rich Rich swore he would quit by June or kill himself. "Hell if I'll spend another summer day cooped up in that hot parlor."

Nina didn't much care either way, but on this particular Tuesday, she was looking forward to her lesson. Crump was the one to drive them every week, and she was anticipating getting a closer look at the man. Her curiosity had multiplied by a thousand during the course of the night as she revisited every memory she had of the gardener.

She dimly recalled that he taught her and the boys how to play a card game called pinochle once. None of them had the patience for it, but Nina had liked all the little terms that went with the game, *like royal marriage* and *bare run* and *make it walk.* She had especially liked the word *pinochle* and had made it one of her words of the week. He taught them some marble games too, and when Rich Rich was eight or nine years old Crump built him a tree house. Mostly though, Nina hadn't paid him much mind over the years.

On Tuesday, he stood by the door of Father's new Phantom 111 limo, a single shock of dark curly hair hanging over one eye, and she wondered that she had ever ignored him before.

"How are you today, Miss Nina?" he asked.

"I'm fine I guess. How are you, Crump?"

It seemed to Nina that there was a dance going on in his eyes, for she had never asked how he was doing before no matter how many times he asked the same question of her.

"I'm quite good, thank you," he replied.

I'll bet you are, Nina thought. *Mother pays you so well . . .*

When he touched her elbow to help her aboard, a flaming arrow of anger shot through her blood. "I can do it myself," she said.

That put him in his place. Wasn't Mother worried that her *servant* would start feeling too important? Someone had to remind him that he was just Sambo the Weed-Picker.

"And how are you today, Mr. Rich?" Crump asked, and then moved his attention to Rich Rich. At fifteen, Rich Rich was desperate to drop a *Rich* and automatically appreciated anyone who left off the second *Rich.*

Once they were settled in the car seat, Nina asked her cousins what they thought of Crump while he brushed wisteria blooms off the windshield.

"He's okay," Rich Rich said. "He's got a mean arm."

"What's so mean about it?" Nina wanted to know. She thought of the mean-looking marks on his back.

"He throws good, dummy," Rich Rich said. He made like he was going to poke her in the eye.

Guido said, "He fixed my Rollfast for me last week. Uncle Dickie ran over the handlebars and said it was wrecked, but Crump got a hammer and hammered the thing up good as new. Aunt Lucinda says he's the handiest man she knows."

"He's handy alright." Nina smirked.

"What are you asking about him for, Neen?" Rich Rich said. "You got a crush on him or something?"

"Shut up, you little monster," she said. "The man's as old as God."

"So what? Del has the hots for Aunt Lucinda, and she's old."

Nina would have let Rich Rich have it right there except Crump slid into the front seat just then. Guido scooted over and took Nina's hand. "He's only teasing, Nina."

Nina barely heard. She caught Crump looking at her in the rear view mirror.

On Wednesday afternoon, Nina accompanied her father to Big Black Lodge to watch Buster Wiggin demonstrate how to carve decoys. Buster Wiggins was the President of *The Happy Hunting Club* and, like most of the other members, he was in the house-selling business, but he was best known for his realistic-looking ducks.

Mother was not a fan of the lodge. She said it smelled of armpits and a waste of time. She supported it for the sheer reason that it got Father out from under foot. Occasionally when she tagged along, Mother sat next to the window holding a perfumed hanky under her nose. The men never got put off by her disdain. They were too appreciative of the way her skirt rode garter-high every time she kicked her toe in boredom. Del Wiggins (son of Buster) recorded the club minutes most months with a thoroughness that made the Bible look like a post card. When he posted the minutes following one of Mother's visits, the single sheet read: "What gams!"

Once, every few years, the members of the *Happy Hunting Club* would discuss replacing the curling screens with glass windows and purchasing a furnace. It was noted that other clubs had Adirondacks on their porches and nice leather club chairs inside their lodges instead of folding ones and hand-me-down lawn furniture.

"We could buy a poker table," Mr. Wiggins suggested every time the subject came round.

But then Mr. Tart would worry that a real table might ruin his luck, and Mr. George would point out that leather was sure to be ruined if they sat on it in their muddy gabardines, and everyone would inevitably agree that more would be lost than gained by fancying up the lodge.

The Happy Hunting Club was started by four brothers who longed for a rugged place where they could hunt, fish, and be dirty. Much as they might enjoy staring at Lucinda Worther-Holmes' gams, they wouldn't like to give up their shabby paradise for anything.

Nina liked it rough herself. Most of the time, it kept Mother away and it kept other women away, too. Outside of Mr. Lusk's wife, Claudine, Nina was the only female who ever came down to the lodge to hunt. The men all brought their sons. Rich Rich had been banned from using the club grounds after he shot a reindeer in the butt. The dastardly deed occurred the previous winter when Blitzen escaped from a nearby Christmas display. The animal was wearing two big red bows and a harness of jingle bells, but Rich Rich evidentially wasn't paying attention. He was too reckless, even for Father, who had a reckless streak himself when it came to driving fast. But as Father put it, "I'd rather go out in a fiery ball of flames than take a bullet in the ass from that nitwit."

Nina fell in love with hunting for two reasons: The first time Father mentioned teaching Nina to shoot, her mother turned *vermilion* with fury and said he was out of his stinking mind if he thought she was going to let him turn their little girl into more of a snot-nosed boy than she already was. This alone made Nina determined, never mind that she was seven. But the biggest reason she fell in love with hunting was the true blue smile her father gave her the first time she nailed a rabbit with her brand new Steven's Single Shot. And because of the frown he gave her when she first blew a shot at a deer. Nina liked the fairness of it all. Father's pride or disappointment reflected the same pride and disappointment the other members gave their boys. On their first real hunt, Nina got the same ritual blood-smearing that all the sons got after their first kill. And on her second real hunt, when she missed the deer, Father cut off her shirt tails and nailed them to the lodge wall to commemorate the miss. Mother was abhorred by such behavior.

"I'll never know how I ended up with a filthy little tomboy," she complained. That Nina danced and played piano was of little consolation. "You're a savage, Nina Worther-Holmes. A vulgar little savage!"

God, how Nina loved to hunt.

On Wednesday evening, the decoy-carving did not hold Nina's attention. She was too busy working out the proper phrasing to keep her father in town on Thursday. The truth seemed largely appealing until Nina actually scripted out the telling of such painful news:

If you leave town tomorrow morning, Mother will make whoopee with the gardener. Again.

The truth was sure to spark his anger, and anger might lead to the both of them going out in a fiery ball of flames on the drive home. As such, Nina considered various lies that might keep her father home. Unfortunately, none seemed drastic enough. Father looked irritated when she tugged on his sleeve halfway through Mr. Wiggins' instructions on band sawing a breast.

"We could both play hooky and go hunting tomorrow," she cheerfully proposed.

Father's eyes were still on the duck. "Will you lookee how realistic that breast looks."

This response tended to rule out the only other option she could think of: subtlety. If Nina were to say, for instance, *Did you ever notice how little gardening actually gets done while you're away?* Father would probably just shrug and say that he didn't care about flowers anyway.

After they got home, she thumbed through the dictionary and wrote down the new words of week in her *Fibber McGee and Molly* notebook:

Fruitless

Impervious

Bollixed

By Thursday, Nina was frantic with the *fruitlessness* of it all. Father was never good at concentrating on more than one thing at a time. His dreamy smile was such that, Nina reckoned, he was more in love with that auto show than he was his cheating wife. Maybe he even felt grateful to Crump for keeping her busy. Still, Nina gave it one more try.

"Don't go, Father."

"Tell LuLu I'll be home by six," he said.

All day at school, she pictured her mother and Crump kissing amid an avalanche of tumbled books. She didn't hear one thing the teacher said. Thanks to the window seat, she could envision the act more clearly than a girl ought to be able to envision such things. She could hear it, too—hear them grunting like pigs under the big white dome that, much like a giant blister, covered Mother's putrid pus of lies.

Oddly, each time Nina re-played the lurid scene in her head, her stomach would begin to tickle when she got to the part where Mother said, "Yes! Oh! Yes! Oh! Yes!" The reaction baffled her, seeing how she'd been revolted when Mother was saying the words for real.

This wasn't the first such instance either. The first time the tickle happened, Crump was holding the umbrella over her head after they left Miss Maple's lessons. Miss Maple had given Crump a whole big *William's Anti-Pain Ointment* tin full of homemade cookies.

"I know how you like my ginger snaps," she'd said, her homely old piano-teacher cheeks blooming like Mother's prize roses. Nina looked from Miss Maple to Crump and wondered if he was keeping company with her, too.

"They are to die for," Crump said, and Nina wished she were old enough to decode adult innuendo. Surely there was more to their exchange than a simple cookie compliment?

Before Nina hid away in the window seat, the man had never seemed like anything much, certainly not the cookie-loving, sigh-inducing poet she saw sweeping women off their feet from Twilight Street to Wisteria Walk. Yet, when she looked at him under that dripping umbrella, her mind returned to those impassioned Reading Room cries, and for the first time, Crump made her stomach tickle. She shivered to think that he could cause a cold-hearted beast like Mother to lose all hold of her senses. Best of all, when she looked at him under the umbrella, he wasn't looking at that gushy twit, Miss Maple. He was looking at her.

"Do you like ginger snaps?" he whispered as he steered her by the elbow toward the Phantom.

"I consider them a fruitless waste of stomach space," Nina said.

"Me too," he confided.

Tickles aside, by the time she arrived home from school on Thursday, Nina wanted to put a bullet in his brain on behalf of her foolish Father.

"How was school, Miss Nina?" he asked as he tossed fertilizer on his jonquils.

"Hideous," she snapped. "How was your day?"

The man didn't have the gall to look up from the manure. "Just fine, thank you."

She pictured him running his manure-blackened hands over Mother's yellow hair, and proceeded to flatten the jonquils on her way in the house.

She was still thinking of Crump's hands when she marched up to her father's closet and chose a shirt with a tag that informed her it was *Made in Hawaii*. Father had recently taken a liking to shirts Made in Hawaii. His favorite had coconut shell buttons and featured at least four colors that had never been invented before. When Father came home at six o'clock, he was livid to find the tails of his beloved *Hibicus Lady* shirt hammered to the front door.

❦

Crump was an ordinary man. Very ordinary. A half-breed with probably no schooling to speak of. He could fix bicycles and grow jonquils. So what? Father had the physique of a prosperous man, and he was heir to a virtual empire. He wouldn't grunt over a woman, nor would he betray his beloved wife the way his wife so carelessly betrayed him. Crump was an adulterer, and he was dirt-poor to boot. He didn't have his own wife and kids as would a respectable man his age. He just snuck around taking what wasn't his, pretending all the while like he was a kind and loyal servant.

Crump was disgusting.

On top of that, any man in love with Mother had to be a shallow pig, Father excluded because he had been too young to know any better when he married her. Where was the imagination in loving a woman like Mother? Outside of herself, the woman had no interests except for reading smutty books, sleeping with servants, and flirting with school boys. She wiggled good, that much was true. She had the prettiest fingernails in the whole wide world. These were her accomplishments.

It was obvious now that Crump was a deceiver. Every shy smile made him just that much more of a hypocrite. Who knew what he was up to all that time when he was acting like gardening and painting and fixing bicycles was the only thing he cared about. She hated him for liking Mother. Nina watched Crump like she would watch a clay bird: with an eye toward picking him off.

Then something happened.

It started with a flower. On Nina's seventeenth birthday, she came down to find a Lily of the Valley waiting on her breakfast plate.

"Tilly?" she asked. "Did you put this flower by my poached egg?"

"No, miss. Weren't me."

"Rich Rich?"

"Are you kidding?"

"What about you, Guido?"

Guido shook his head. "It was probably Crump. Do you know anyone else who likes flowers?"

The Lily of the Valley arched around her egg like one half of a heart. Nina thought about the way his dark eyes snuck a look at her in the rear view mirror. Saw his mischievous smile when he confessed he didn't like Ginger snaps. Remembered the way he hacked up weeds in the flowerbeds until his face was pouring with sweat.

THE READING LESSONS BY CAROLE LANHAM

She found him after breakfast, replacing the hinge Father had recently broken on the front door. "Did you give me this flower, Crump?"

Crump smiled that phony shy smile of his. There was a smudge of grease on his chin. "Everyone should get a flower on their birthday."

Nina dimly recalled other flowers on other birthdays. "Do you mean to tell me that you keep track of our birthdays?"

"Just yours and the boys."

"What about Mother's?"

Crump nodded. "I grew up at Browning House so I know your Mother's birthday, too."

"What did you give her on her birthday?" she asked nastily.

"Hemlock."

"I beg your pardon?"

"Hollyhocks."

Nina shook her head. "You said hemlock."

"I meant hollyhocks." His eyes sparkled like pancake syrup.

"Will you be working at my party tomorrow night?" she asked.

Crump opened and closed the door, testing the new hinge. "I most definitely will."

He needed a haircut. Badly. The way things stood, a person was tempted to drag their fingers through all those big loose curls just to see what they felt like. At that moment, standing there beaming over his new hinge, Crump seemed boyish for a man, yet manish compared to the boys at school.

"Thank you for the Lily of the Valley. It's very nice," Nina said.

He looked surprised to be thanked. Probably because she had never thanked him all those other years, or even paid his flowers much notice at all. He nodded and went back to opening and closing the front door.

Nina took the flower to school that day and twirled the white bells under her nose every chance she got.

Then there was the accident.

The night before Nina's *Moonlight Serenade Birthday Extravaganza*, she and her mother were hanging up little tin foil moons over the bandstand when the whole thing collapsed.

Boards snapped, moons flew, and Nina and her mother crashed through the floor in a hail of curses and screams.

The bandstand in question was *not* of Crump's making. Rich Rich and Guido had hammered the stage together to contribute to the party, and Nina's first thought was that Rich Rich had purposely built it to implode. *I'm going to beat that little monster to death with a broken two by four,* she said to herself.

It happened that the words of this particular week were:

Pungent.

Perilous.

Plot.

Nina had recently adopted a system for word-picking that involved using words that began with the same letter. Next week all her words were going to be B's, and she already had braunsweiger slated for the notebook. So far the Ps were proving remarkably easy to use. She stared at the hole above her head. "Mother?"

"I'm here," Mother answered from somewhere in the rubble.

Quick as that, boards were being slapped away, and two arms reached in, grabbed Nina, and lifted her free of the disaster. Carrying her like a baby, Crump sped through the petunia garden, propped her up against the plum tree, and began peeling off his shirt to use as a bandage. His face was as white as a white man's.

"There's so much blood," he said, and it was only then that Nina noticed that her chin was dripping. "What hurts?" he said.

"Everything," Nina moaned.

Mother let out a peel of dismay, and Crump looked toward the disintegrated stage. "Get her out of that bandstand," he snarled at George Vinegar as he blotted Nina's chin with his shirt. "Your foot looks funny."

"It hurts," Nina said.

George Vinegar stumbled over with Mother and dropped her next to Nina. "Are you all right, Mother?" Nina asked.

"Don't mind me," she snarled at Crump. "I only fell through the god damn bandstand."

Nina's blood streaked his arms. "Get Miss Nina into the kitchen and wash her up," he said to George Vinegar. "I'll get Dr. Mangrove."

Then came the argument.

Nina's ankle had been broken in the fall, and her chin needed stitching, too. Mother got off with some bumps and bruises, though she didn't seem happy about it. In all the chaos, Nina had been brought into Crump's kitchen to be washed off, and afterward, she was put in Crump's bed to wait for the doctor.

The gardener's quarters were next to the petunias and therefore the most convenient. Nina had never set foot inside the place before. Rich Rich had climbed up on the roof last summer on a dare, but Tilly caught him before he could make the most of this, and she made him clean out her grease pots in exchange for keeping quiet about what he'd done. Another time, Nina and Rich Rich boosted Guido up to a window to see what was inside, but the most exciting thing he had to report was that the kitchen had a sink.

For the most part, Nina had ignored the place, much as she'd ignored Crump. George Vinegar dropped her down on the bed and looked around, his old yellow eyes round with curiosity. It occurred to her for the first time that Crump was the only servant to have his own little house. Tilly and Narcissa occupied a room off the kitchen. George Vinegar, Lymas Polk, and Hurd the Turd lived over the garage. Nancy, the housekeeper, went home to her own family every night. Only the gardener warranted a place of his own.

Unfortunately, Crump's house was about as revealing as his face. Nina might have hoped for leopard skin on the bed or a naked woman on a calendar. What she got instead was bright, headache-white everywhere she looked. His bath towel was white and his bedclothes, too. The onions in the white bowl on his white sink were white. The only thing she saw that was not white was a pink bottle of bleach.

George Vinegar said, "He sure do like things white, don't he?"

The plan was for Crump to carry her up to her own bed after the doctor left, but Nina fell asleep and woke up in the middle of the night, still tucked in the gardener's big white bed. Because she was in Crump's bed, Nina was able to hear the argument going on in his kitchen.

" . . . leave me lying there like a damned sack of sugar!" Mother trilled. "For all you knew, I might have been dead."

"I would have thought you'd want me to see to your daughter first," Crump said. "She *was* bleeding, after all."

Nina could hear the clop clop clop of Mother's cork-wedged sandals pacing the kitchen tiles. "You see to her too much. What about me? Just because I'm a grown woman, don't I count? Couldn't I have broken my foot, too? She wasn't the only one bleeding."

"But you're okay. She wasn't."

Nina heard the sound of skin slapping skin.

"Go to hell," Crump muttered, and those three words were so shocking to Nina, they about shocked her half to death. She'd never heard a servant speak that way to anyone, much less their employer. It was a lucky thing that Nina could hear through the walls like they were made of paper. As a matter of fact, this was one of the biggest complaints about *Worther-Holmes* homes. Thin walls. Lately Father had been taking a lot of flak for his thin walls.

"Don't you *ever* ignore me like that again," Mother hissed. "I won't play second fiddle to anyone, not even my daughter. I deserve more from you than that."

"I'm done talking about this," he said, and five seconds later, Nina heard the sound of breaking glass.

"Oh! I'm sorry, Hadley. I'm sorry. Are you all right?"

"No," Crump said.

"Look at all that blood," Mother said.

Nina sat up like a shot, wondering if all this business was about to end in murder.

A chair scuffed across the floor. Shoes crushed glass.

"Get away from me," Crump said.

Nina swung her legs off the side of the bed. What if Mother was killing Crump?

"Like you don't want it, too," Mother jeered.

Nina froze beside the bed. There was something about her mother's tone that reminded Nina of the icky things she'd heard in the window seat.

"Mmmm. That's good. Isn't that good, honey?"

His voice was still angry. "It hurts, Lucinda."

219

"What about this?" she asked, and on the other side of his thin white walls, Crump gasped.

Mother said, "I bet you aren't thinking about little girls now, are you Hadley Crump?"

I can steal him, Nina thought. First there was the flower, then the accident, then the argument. No one had ever picked Nina over her mother. *She's scared I'll take him away from her!*

Nina lay awake in Crump's bed, her head on his pillow, her face in his bedclothes, thinking about how nice it would be to feel his dark curls sliding over her fingers like shiny rings.

There was a glass jar on his windowsill with the word *WHOOPS* painted on it, and inside were three nails and a little woodpecker-shaped spoon carved with the word *Alabama.* On the nightstand was a book. *The Meaning of Flowers.* The flowers were listed in alphabetical order, and Nina thumbed through the pages until she found the L's:

Convallaria maialis Lily of the Valley –
You've made my life complete.

She rattled the jar as she formed her plot—the perfectly pungent and perilous plot to seduce Hadley Crump.

Nail Number Six: A Perfectly Pungent and Perilous Plot

"Would you mind it if I call you Hadley?" she asked.

It was the next morning, and Crump had a gash on his head that severed his left eyebrow directly down the middle. He was carrying Nina upstairs, but he stopped mid-step, and the look he gave her was like the look she got when she asked what happened to his eyebrow.

"I suppose that's up to you, Miss Nina."

Nina had stayed up all night, rubbing the soles of her feet on his white sheets and feeling him in the wrinkles. She prayed that when he rubbed his feet on the sheets, he would feel her in the wrinkles, too.

Crump proceeded up the steps, his arms hooked sturdily beneath her as if she were ten rather than seventeen. She pressed her fingers against his collar, willing him to feel her the way she felt him. She let her thumb brush through the hair on the back of his neck.

"Then I believe I'll call you Hadley, Hadley."

Nina had discovered that most people looked less beautiful the closer you got to their face. Maybe their teeth were more jumbled than they appeared from far away. Maybe they had hair sprouting out of their nose. Crump was *more* beautiful up close. Up close, his lashes were as long as a lady's, and he had perfect teeth that were as straight and white as the shiny tiles that formed his kitchen floor. How could she have missed his beauty for all these years? The maple syrup eyes. The strong arms. The gentle hands that rescued her instead of her mother. Even with a sliced eyebrow, Crump was a beautiful man.

"Thank you, Hadley," she said when he put her on her bed.

It would be hard to remember to call him Hadley, but she felt a bit more even-steven with her mother just saying it out loud. She wanted to say it again and again, so she did.

"Could you open the window, Hadley?" "Bring me my book, Hadley." "Oh Hadley, I'm going to need a glass of water." "Gracious, Hadley, aren't I a pain?" Calling a grown man by his first name felt cozier than a kiss. "I sure hope I didn't hurt your back, Hadley?"

"It's no problem, Miss Nina, but I need to pick up Mr. Rich over at the Buxleys by one, so I need to get going."

Rich Rich? Nina was furious. Until she spotted the vase of Lily of the Valleys waiting on her bed table.

Father wouldn't like it if she married a gardener, and an older man at that. Never mind that he was a sambo. He would probably kill poor Hadley Crump, which wouldn't be hard to do, seeing how the man had let Mother bash him around with barely any fuss. Nina had spotted a sickle-shaped scar on his neck, too, when he was carrying her. She managed to graze it briefly with the ball of her hand and was overwhelmed by the heat she discovered there. And then there were those scars she'd noticed on his back. Nina liked to think his scars were secret doors into his white walls. Just thinking about them, she felt an overwhelming urge to heal him. And to leave her own mark as well.

The best way to get his attention was to have him fix things. Her bedroom light was crooked and *needed* fixing a few days later. Crump set his toolbox down by her bed. He had a sunburned glow about him, and his hair was powdered with whiting.

"How's the ankle today, Miss Nina?"

Unlike Mother, he always remembered that it was her ankle, not her foot, that had been injured in the stage mishap. "Its better, Hadley, thank you for asking."

He laughed when she called him Hadley. Then he got to work. His nimble fingers knew exactly which tools to use. "I heard the party has been put off until you get back on you feet again," he said.

"Oh, I'm not in the mood for a party anymore."

Crump took off his shoes, laid a piece of newsprint on the velvet seat of her vanity chair which he'd pulled up next to the bed, and stepped up on the face of Mrs. Eleanor Brandywine of First Presbyterian who was holding her prize-winning peanut pie proudly aloft on page 12c of The Dispatch. He was not a tall man and was forced to reach in order to get to the light. As he reached, Nina noticed something just below his bellybutton. Another mark of some kind. His trousers sagged, and his shirt rode up just enough that she was able to catch sight of it twisting down the front of his waistband.

"What's this?" she asked, touching the mark.

At first only his skin jumped away. Then all of him jumped, and he kicked over the chair.

"It looks like you've got some sort of picture on your skin," Nina said.

Crump stepped back further still.

I'm bothering him, she thought. His eyes followed the strap of her nightgown as it slid off her shoulder. "What's the matter?" she asked.

His tongue darted over his lips. "Umm. I forgot. I'm supposed to pick up the boys at Miss Maple's."

"They're not done for another hour," Nina said. "I really do need my light."

His hands hung stiffly at his side, screwdriver dangling forgotten in his fingers.

"What do those funny marks mean, Crump? Hadley. Where did you get them?"

He tossed the screwdriver down, hiked up his pants, and tucked in his shirt. "Hurd can finish for you if I don't get back to your light today."

They both knew he wouldn't get back to her light today.

"Does that mean you don't want to tell me?"

He slipped on his shoes. "It's not a thing to talk about with a young girl, Miss Nina."

"I'm seventeen."

The toolbox clattered shut. "Just a child," he said.

"How old are you?"

"Old," he grunted. "Old as your mother."

"Mother is thirty-five."

"Well, there you go. I'll send Hurd up."

He was running away, and Nina couldn't think how to stop him. "What about my bookshelf?"

"What about it?" he asked.

"It's cracked."

He waded up the newspaper and brushed off the velvet cushion on her chair. "I might be able to get to it sometime in September."

"I'll be back to school in September."

"September it is then," he said.

He sounded so damned relieved to be going, Nina could only feel pleased. *He thinks I'm a child, but I'll show him.*

Unfortunately, there was no coaxing him back to her room. Crump told Nina he was sorry, but broken bones made him uneasy.

One week later, when Nina was able to move around on crutches, she made her way downstairs to the window seat to search for something worthwhile to read. It had been horrible knowing that all the really interesting books were downstairs while she was stuck upstairs. She'd just about had her fill of *Little Women* and Alice bumbling through Wonderland. With so many to choose from, it was pure chance she came across a book called *Handiwork of the Gods* in the bottom of the window seat. *Handiwork of the Gods* was authored by Luther Daniel Davies, and her heart skidded to a stop when she realized what the book was about.

Nina always read the first few lines before making her choice, and she'd almost hobbled off with the more attention-grabbing title *The Hard-Boiled Virgin*, when the slender orange book caught her eye. Easing herself down on the floor to have a look, Nina whispered the opening passage out loud:

In Micronesia, people believed that the gods gave them the following message: You should be tattooed so that you become beautiful and so your skin does not shrink with age. The fishes in the water are striped and have lines; therefore, also human beings should have stripes and lines. Everything disappears after

death, only the tattoo continues to exist; it will surpass you. The
human being leaves everything behind on earth, all his
possessions, only the tattooing he takes with him into the grave.

Nina had been spending a lot of time thinking about the picture she'd seen on Crump's skin and had decided that it looked like a letter of the alphabet. Reading the little orange book, the pieces fell into place.

Lordy, Nina thought. *She monogrammed him.*

Until she'd seen the look on her mother's face after the bandstand collapsed, Nina had imagined Crump to be one of many. Now she felt sure he was something much more. Did Neville Pillwater wear Mother's monogram on his fat hairy tummy? Probably not. Probably the most Neville Pillwater ever got was a discount-inspiring flash of knee. If Mother was mad enough to cut Crump up for coming to Nina's aid when she was hurt, how much more insane would the woman be if he fell in love with her?

But there were problems.

Outside of Del Wiggins, Nina had never even stepped out with a boy, much less kissed one. She'd wrenched Clyde Bledsoe's arm out of socket for whistling at her at the lodge once, and she badly regretted this now. Perhaps the boy might have proven useful for something, after all. Lord knows, he wasn't much of a shot. Mother, on the other hand, knew the art of Micronesian tattooing. It seemed highly improbable that Nina could ever find the wherewithal to steal a man who would let himself be marked in a way he would take to the grave.

She returned to the book, hoping it might yield a much-needed tip . . .

Tattoo enhanced the body as an object worthy of
admiration. It marked a boy's entry into manhood and the
beauty of his tattoo attracted women to his manliness, proven
by his ability to endure pain. Parts of the tattoo were covered by
clothing and would only be visible during intimacy . . .

"Hi," he said.

225

Nina slammed the book shut. Crump was standing in the doorway, smiling at her.

"What do you want?" she asked. He'd not been to see her in two weeks.

"I came to do your bookshelf."

"Now?" she stuttered, clumsily shoving the book inside another.

"How have you been?" he asked. "Is your ankle better?"

"It's coming along. How about your eyebrow?"

The wound was a yellow snake of a mark now. "Just a little scar," he said.

Nina began to perspire. Perspiration, she decided, was a sure sign of love. Her imagination had long-since finished the part of the picture he hid inside his pants; the part that ended in twin mountain-like peaks just below his bellybutton. She was sure it was an "M".

But why Mother's middle initial? Why not "L" or even "W". Nina didn't even know what her mother's middle name was. She only knew she wanted her mother to feel the pain of losing Hadley Crump.

"What are you reading?" he asked.

She checked the cover of the book. "*Little Women.*"

"No you're not," he said.

"I am," she argued. She shoved the book in the drawer of her night table. "Why are you looking at me like that?"

"Sometimes you remind me of your mother."

Was this good? Bad? A lie? Definitely a lie. "No one ever thinks I look like my mother."

Mother had pale hair and a girly figure and big blue eyes that made everyone think of sparkling sapphires. Nina had Grandma's plain brown hair and a boy-body. Her eyes were the same color as her hair, and they never made anyone think of anything, much less sparkling sapphires.

"I didn't say you looked like her. I said you remind me of her."

Forgetting her need for crutches, Nina climbed out of bed. "Is that a good thing, Hadley?"

He picked at a loose chip of paint on the door. "Just don't grow up too fast, Miss Nina. My mama used to tell me that, but I didn't listen."

And now you have an M *branded on your body. And someone's been whipping your hide...* "Where are your tools, Hadley Crump?"

He gnawed his lip. "Guess I forgot 'em."

Nina was glad she'd put on the red nightgown. It was the most womanly one in her closet. "Want to check my bookshelf anyway?"

"Sure," he said, stepping forward.

Nina held her breath.

"Oh, I almost forgot," he said. "Your father told me to send you down for supper. Maybe I'll have your shelf fixed by the time you're done."

"Or maybe it'll take all night," Nina said.

He shook his head. "You aren't listening to me, Miss Nina."

She pushed the door shut with her toe. "I can't quit thinking about that picture on your stomach."

His eyes darted to the door. "Hold on now, Nina."

If not for her bum ankle, Nina might have jumped for joy right then and there. "You called me Nina."

He looked rattled. "I'm sorry. Open that door. You're gonna get me fired."

"Why? What are you planning to do?"

"I . . . nothing. It's wrong to talk like this, Miss Nina. For a million reasons, it's just plain wrong."

"Name forty."

He ran a hand through his hair. "You're too nice for this, Miss Nina."

"That's only one."

"That one reason is enough."

Nina took another step toward him. "But you like me, Hadley, I can tell."

Crump stepped back. "I like all you kids. I always have."

"You like me best, I know you do."

They did the step-up/step-back dance again. "Open that door or I'll scream, Miss Nina."

THE READING LESSONS BY CAROLE LANHAM

"Why do you like me best?"

He reached for the knob with a shaky hand, and Nina laughed at him. "Go ahead and run, Hadley. We both know what will happen. One of these days I'm gonna get a better look at that picture of yours."

She touched the scar on his throat with her index finger and pulled away with a start. It was almost too hot to touch.

Hadley

Nail Number Seven:

Darratu

Hadley grabbed hold of the bedposts and closed his eyes. He shivered as her hair brushed the length of his stomach. How many times had he warned himself to be strong? Playing dumb never worked out for him. He'd tried to keep busy with the new White Flower Garden he'd started under the Silverbell tree, but after all these years, Hadley reckoned he was trained to succumb.

"Quiet now," she whispered. "We don't want anyone to hear."

He sunk his teeth into a corner of pink chenille bedspread, biting so hard, his molars nearly cracked. Hadley had been drawn into some crazy things over the years, but this took the cake. If he were caught in her bed, there'd be no explaining it away.

"Open your eyes," she said. "I want you to watch while I do it."

Hadley opened his eyes and sucked the bedspread halfway down his throat. She was kneeling between his legs wearing nothing but a smile.

"Am I beautiful?" she asked.

Her skin was the buttery color of a Francesca rose, the sort that Mama peeled apart and stirred into her Rose Pear soup. Hadley spit out the bedspread. "Delectable."

She cupped his cheek and gave him a kiss that was soothing and nice, but he was keenly aware that she'd never done anything like this before.

"Are you sure?" he asked.

She stuffed the bedspread back in his mouth. "Trust me."

Hadley's stomach clenched like a fist as she set to work with a maddening precision. It was all he could do to hold onto the bedposts. He spit out the covers. "God damn!" he cried. "That hurts, Lucinda."

She'd given her sewing needle a bath in a teacup of rubbing alcohol, then held it over a flame until the silver blackened and glowed. Next came the ink—a grim concoction of coconut oil and ash that she pricked into his skin a full one hundred and seventy times before the awful thing was done. That she finished up the job with a soft sweet kiss hardly made up for the agony.

"There," she said, as though she'd just given him a most amazing prize. "Now you'll take me to the grave."

Hadley was twenty-two when Lucinda did the tattoo they'd read about in *Handiwork of the Gods*. He was twenty-four when she strangled him while re-inacting *Justine*. Twenty-eight when she used the riding crop on his skin as a follow-up to *Venus Wears Furs*. And thirty when she asked him to punch her in the eye like Cora from *The Postman Always Rings Twice*. He was a thirty-five year old man when Nina put the tip of her finger on his M. The tip of Nina's finger was the worst. Her touch was more painful than needles. Hadley knew he should stay away from the girl, but he couldn't.

There was a long spell when Dickie didn't go out of town, which didn't help matters none. Lucinda was never interested in him when other people were around, and he couldn't get two minutes of her time if Dickie was nearby. Meanwhile, her daughter stepped up her attack.

She cornered him in the Reading Room, of all places, and asked him to read *Arabian Nights* while she sat with her newly healed ankle stretched out on the widow seat, watching his every move in a way that tied his intestines in a thousand knots. It scared him how much she could be like Lucinda.

"You need to find a nice boy and settle down," he told her.

"I've already found one," she said, and, to his horror, she came and knelt at his feet. She would have put her hand on his knee, too, if he hadn't blocked it with his elbow.

"You need to get married and do things right, Miss Nina."

"Why didn't you ever get married?" she asked.

He hated when she called him Hadley. "Wasn't meant to be, I reckon."

"Don't you think I'd make a good wife?"

"Sure," he told her. "A lot of boys are going to fall in love with you."

She frowned at that. "No they won't. No one's ever interested in me after they get a look at Mother."

The way she said it made his skin prickle, like she knew about him and Lucinda. "Let me tell you something, Miss Nina: you're a lot nicer than your mother. Smarter, too. Don't you never forget that."

She put her hand on his knee after all, challenging him with her eyes. "I want you, Hadley."

Bearing such things was like swallowing knives. He stood up. "That ain't never gonna happen, Miss Nina, do you hear me?" Her eyes filled up with tears, but he didn't let that stop him. "And here's something else that's real important: you wait until you're married for that. That's what nice girls do."

"Maybe I don't want to be nice," she hollered so loud, he could already feel how bad it was going to hurt when Dickie broke his nose.

"Please, Miss Nina. Your daddy will call the police if he hears you talking to me like this."

She looked at him with those pretty brown eyes and ran from the room like her heart was breaking. Hadley couldn't stand it. He found an old piece of violet writing paper and scratched down a note.

We have to talk, Lucinda.

"Make it fast," she said as she undid her dress. "He's with Daddy Dick at The Banana Club, but that won't tie him up for long."

Hadley waited until she was down to her slip. "I just want to talk."

She snapped her fingers impatiently. "Hurry, will you? Jesus, Hadley, we don't have all day."

"It's Nina."

She crossed her arms. "Lord have mercy. Sometimes I think you're more obsessed with that girl than you are with me."

"She's trying to seduce me, Lucinda."

He expected shock. Horror even. Anything but the nutty laughter that followed. "Dream on. You're old enough to be her father."

He grabbed her arm. "This isn't a joke, Lucinda. If you were paying one bit of attention, you'd know I'm not dreaming. Heaven knows, she's about as subtle as you are."

Lucinda wrenched her arm free and stepped back into her dress. "What do you expect me to do, Hadley? Tell her the truth?"

"I think the time has come, yes."

That started her laughing again. "What should I say, dear? Hmm? 'You can't have a crush on the gardener because the gardener might be your daddy.' You're the one who's so worried about her tender little god damn feelings all the time. What do you think that would do to her?"

"Set her straight."

Lucinda snorted and rolled her eyes.

"At least, she'd know to keep her hands to herself."

At last, Lucinda looked appropriately queasy. "Jesus, Hadley."

"It's one thing to screw up our own lives. I won't stand for seeing her life ruined too."

"You know perfectly well that she might not even be your daughter."

"She's mine, Lucinda."

"You can't ever know that for sure."

"It doesn't matter. I would love her no less if I found out for certain she was Dickie's. But she ain't Dickie's." He handed her Nina's note. "Read this."

She held it close to her nose and squinted.

Dearest Hadley,

I don't care how old you are or that you have Negro blood. I can see you like me, too. Quit fighting what's between us and give our love a chance.

N

"What does this mean, Hadley? 'I can see you like me, too'. What have you been doing with that girl?"

"I'm doing what I've always done, Lucinda: loving her from afar. She's reading things into it because she wants to, and because she doesn't know who I am. It's wrong. We done a lot of wrong things, but this is the wrongest thing of all."

If he lived a thousand years, he'd never forget the night Lucinda put his hand on her belly and said, "I'm gonna have a baby."

He was seventeen and he'd just asked Flora Gibbs to be his bride. Lucinda was sitting on his bathroom floor. Hadley was in his underwear. "Is it mine, Lucinda?"

Every little thing in the world depended upon her answer, yet Lucinda shrugged. "Maybe. Maybe not."

"Maybe? I'm supposed to give up everything for a maybe?"

"That's up to you, Hadley, but if you quit working for me, I swear to God, you will never know this baby."

Some fellows might have liked the thought of that, but Hadley had the hopes and prayers of the Crump bloodlines resting on his shoulders.

Lucinda started kissing him. Not on the mouth, but any place she could get one in at: his ribs, his knees, his elbows.

I don't care! I'll choose Flora, he decided. *I have to. I said I'd marry her.*

He looked at the round soft swell of Lucinda's belly. It was in there. A child. A child that belonged to him. A Crump.

Lucinda kissed his hand even as he twisted it away from her lips. "I'll stay," he said. "God damn you, I'll stay. But not for you, Lucinda. For the baby . . . " Four times. Dickie was all over Lucinda every night. Hadley had only been with her one night. Four times.

"What do you figure the chances are?" he'd asked her after her stomach got big. He was touching it, and Hadley didn't get to touch it much. In those days, touching the baby became a longing that rivaled the usual longings.

"Unless it comes out looking like a straight-up Negro baby, I guess we'll never know for certain whose it is," Lucinda said.

"Do you want it to be mine?"

She put her hand over the top of his and pressed it to the child growing under her skin. "Regardless of who did it, she's yours and mine." Lucinda always called the baby a girl even before they knew it was Nina. "She's what came of all those years of waiting. Dickie and I didn't make a baby any of those other months, did we? This little angel came along to keep you and me together."

There was many a night when Hadley wished it wasn't true. Then he'd feel bad. He'd hurry up and whisper to the ceiling that separated him from her, "I'm sorry, baby. I'm sorry."

Mama had warned him. Lord, his entire heritage had warned him. "There's a price to be paid if you do things the wrong way." That's what Mama said, but he'd been too young at the time to understand the half of it.

Hadley paid the price every time he was forced to listen to Lucinda making love with Dickie. He watched Dickie put his lips on her stomach and sing *Cheerful Little Earful* at the breakfast table. He listened to Dickie propose names for Hadley's baby like Pumpkin and Georgie. "I knew a girl named Georgie once, and she was a real firecracker." Hell, Hadley was made to build the awful crib that Dickie designed on a wrinkled bar napkin in spite of the fact that it was a silly, drunken-looking piece of nonsense. Painted it scarlet red too, just like Dickie wanted, and who ever heard of a scarlet red baby crib? Oh, he paid all right. When Dickie had Hadley haul the heavy rocking horse he'd had as a boy down from the attic so they could use it for Ritzy (his latest choice of names), Hadley was fed up to his ears. "Leave him, Lucinda. Leave him now!"

It seemed a matter of practicality at this point. If little Ritzy was made to ride that giant clunker of a rocking horse, she'd crack her skull in two.

Lucinda just smiled and shook her head. "Don't be ridiculous."

Hadley said a prayer that Lucinda would give birth to the brownest baby anyone had ever seen.

When it was time for the child to come, Lucinda decided against a midwife. She was a member of a group called the *National Twilight Sleep Association* whose aim it was to create a more perfect motherhood. Instead of doing things at home the regular old way, Dickie took Lucinda to the hospital for a *restful* birth.

While Lucinda rested and gave birth in a twilight sleep, she contracted a terrible infection. A week later, the doctor informed her there would be no more children. Lucinda said this was just as well and named her new whiter-than-white baby "Nina Anna Worther-Holmes".

"The Anna is your part," she told Hadley the first time he held the baby. By then, Nina Anna was a month old. It seemed only right to Hadley that his part should be in the middle. "And look," Lucinda said. "God gave her your sulky eyes."

If the baby's sulky eyes weren't enough to resolve the question, when Hadley opened the shades on the morning of Nina Anna's first birthday, it seemed certain God was out to settle the matter once and for all.

According to *A Treatise on the Theory and Practice of Landscape Gardening*, young wisteria plants could take up to fifteen years to bloom, yet at Wisteria Walk, every white wooden trellis exploded in a celebration of purple-pink that no other birthday gift could match. Nevermind that his affair with wisteria was a love/hate relationship, Hadley had always believed in the secret meaning of flowers. In order to get Wisteria plants to take off, a man was expected to toil relentlessly for years without seeing a single thing bloom. On June 3, 1922, less than three years after Hadley put down roots, the flowers spoke.

Now his Nina Anna was seventeen, and he was scratching his head, trying to come up with a way to get the girl to stop making eyes at him for all the wrong reasons.

"I know how we can put an end to this foolishness," Lucinda brightly declared.

"Thank goodness for that. I'm about at my wit's end."

"It's easy, Hadley. All we have to do is get her to hate you."

Lucinda was serious as a heart attack, which only made her suggestion all the more painful. "Why don't you just beat my brains in with a brick," Hadley said. "That would hurt me a hundred times less."

"Well, I guess you'll have to leave then. I can't tell her you might be her daddy. My whole life would collapse."

"And mine won't if I have to leave her?"

"Don't forget, dear, you'd be leaving me, too. I'm tired of playing second fiddle to that girl."

Now that was funny!

"Nina says the same of you."

"Well, you can't leave us, Hadley, so you got no other choice."

"Yes I do," Hadley said. "I'm gonna find myself a woman."

"What do you mean?"

"If Nina sees I've got a woman, she'll have to leave me alone."

Lucinda was wearing the sort of scowl that foreshadowed broken lamps. "You wouldn't use a woman like that," she said.

"After all I've done in order to be with Nina, do you really think I'd let anything stop me now?"

"Flora Gibbs wouldn't take you back, even if she is an old maid librarian."

"No," Hadley said. "Not Flora. Never mind. I should have thought of this weeks ago. Nina thinks I don't have anyone. She thinks I'm lonely as sin. She's right on both accounts."

"Well!" Lucinda said. "I didn't realize your were such a sorry case, Hadley Crump."

"Well I am," he said.

"How about a parting gift before you move along?"

"I thought you said he'd be back soon?"

"Shut up." For the second time that afternoon, the dress came off. "There's been entirely too much talking going on here today."

༄

"What's going on here?" Dickie demanded.

Lucinda looked like Fanny Hill after a night of selling her virginity on the streets. Her hair was pointing one way and her dress the other. Hadley barely got his trousers up before Dickie, who was known to break all varieties of locks, shattered the lock on the Reading Room door.

"Jesus, Dickie," Lucinda grunted. "There's nobody here but Hadley."

"And why is *he* here?" Dickie wanted to know.

"Why do you think?" Lucinda said. "We were discussing the new floor."

"With the door locked?"

Dickie had graduated from M.U., but that didn't make him bright. Lucinda had been duping the man for a long time now. She said, "Damn it, Hadley, I told you to fix that knob last week. Guido was stuck in here for a half hour on Saturday."

Dickie looked around the room and sniffed. *He's gonna rip my head off,* Hadley thought.

Dickie squinted at Hadley. "Naw," he said, speaking as if he were in the middle of a conversation with himself.

Hadley had long suspected that Dickie's dumbness stemmed from his trusting nature. Dickie trusted that he lived in a world where women like Lucinda would never allow half-breed-gardeners like Hadley to lay a finger on them. If Dickie believed they were discussing flooring with the door locked, this was only because it was easier for him to believe than the notion that his wife would let Hadley touch her.

We could be naked and he'd refuse to think the worst, Hadley thought. But then Dickie cracked his knuckles a mere two inches from Hadley's nose. "Fix the door, Crump. I've got my eye on things, don't think I don't."

It was a warning.

In twenty years they'd never come close to getting caught by Dickie. Tilly, yes. Tilly might not have graduated from M.U., but that didn't make her dim. When Narcissa first started in the kitchen, Tilly said, "Don't you smile at this one now. I jest got her learnt on canning."

"What do you mean?" Hadley said.

"I sees the way she watches you."

"Narcissa?"

"Don't act the fool with me," she said, facing him down with her pecan leaf. "Ain't no body likes *reading* so much as Missus Worther-Holmes. Iffin' she fires Narcissa, I'm gonna start hiding burrs in your trousers to remind you to keep 'em on."

Dickie tucked a wild curl behind Lucinda's ear and stalked out of the Reading Room.

I need a woman, Hadley thought.

A woman would set things right in so many ways, and Hadley was sure he wouldn't be using her. On the contrary, he'd be the most grateful man alive. Lucinda could be jealous as a demon, but this time she would have to go along with it.

Maybe this'll turn out to be a good thing, he thought. *Maybe Dickie won't have to kill me after all.*

That only left the question of who. Who would want him after all these years?

Hadley was thirty-five years old, and he'd hardly kissed anyone other than Lucinda. He hadn't wooed a girl since he was seventeen and things had ended badly that time around. He couldn't so much as think of Flora without breaking out in a rash.

As he ran through the short list of possible dinner dates in his head, Hadley realized that he didn't know any women. To make matters worse, he didn't know the first thing about them. He only knew about Lucinda, and he was pretty sure she didn't represent the gender particularly well. He'd let her carve him up pretty bad over the years, too. Hadley had the body of a man who'd decided long ago that he wasn't going to need it for anything except Lucinda Worther-Holmes. The thought of explaining himself to someone new was enough to make celibacy look like the only alternative to what he already had.

Over the years, he'd developed a rather uneasy relationship with pain. As far as he could figure, something got wrecked in his brain when he let Lucinda drink his blood. The damage was permanent. It was entirely possible he might want things that only Lucinda knew how to give.

Nope. Much as he liked the idea of finding a woman to love, that was completely out of the question. Hadley reckoned he'd best settle for finding someone who would have coffee with him and *look,* to Nina, like a girlfriend.

☙

"Hells bells," Lucinda said the day after Hadley found himself a date. "Just because Nina doesn't know the first thing about men, doesn't mean she's going to buy a femme fatale called Vaseline Jenkins. No one is that dumb."

How she'd found out about the hostess from the *Dinner Bell* was anybody's guess. "What's wrong with her name?" Hadley said. "I think it's pretty."

"Pretty?" At that particular moment, he was trailing Lucinda out the door of Warson's Department, and she came to the sort of grinding halt that would have had an untrained man spilling boxes everywhere. Not Hadley. Hadley had a talent for managing enormous amounts of crap. His all-time record was five hat boxes, one pair of jersey gloves, one Hudson seal wrap, and four pairs of shoes. "Why not just call her Diaper Rash?"

"I think she's called Vassie."

"And did you make whoopee with Mrs. Diaper Rash Jenkins after your dinner date?" Lucinda wanted to know.

"She isn't a *Mrs.* anymore."

"She's an ever-loving divorcee, for pity sake."

"I guess some people divorce their husbands when their marriage turns out to be a joke."

"What's that supposed to mean?"

"Are you jealous?" he asked from behind a striped hat box.

"Jealous of a black-skinned soup jockey with five brats? Are you out of your mind?"

He'd followed her through shop after shop while she tried on hats and slipped on shoes yet she didn't say a single word to him until they left Warson's. "This is supposed to bother Nina, not you," Hadley reminded her.

"Oh, it bothers me, all right. What did she say about your . . . thing, I wonder?" Lucinda waved a hand at the round silk box pressed against his stomach.

"My thing ain't none of your concern these days, remember? Your husband's got his eye on me."

Lucinda started for the car. "I know her type, dear. I bet you didn't even have to buy her dinner."

"Vaseline is a nice lady," Hadley said. "I didn't so much as kiss her good night. Happy?"

"You can do better." She waited for him to fit her packages into the trunk. "Anymore love notes from our girl?"

"Three since Monday."

Lucinda frowned at the reflection of her old hat in the car window, ripped it off her head, and threw it in the back seat. "Okay then, Diaper Rash it is."

Hadley and Mama had been having their Sunday lunch at the *Dinner Bell* for more than a year now, and Vaseline Jenkins had served them every slice of buttermilk pie they'd ever eaten there. The place served the best food in blackie town, if you asked Hadley, and that was saying a lot because Greasy Jim's was damned good, and Roadside did a hambone and butter beans that swept Mama off her feet.

Hadley had never paid Vaseline much attention, but one day she leaned in to pour coffee, and he got mesmerized by an unpinned lock of hair on her forehead. Most colored girls went for short finger curls, or else they wore something Mama called *made hair*. Made hair was straightened flat hair. Vaseline had a thousand long, wild corkscrews covering her head. She rolled the front ones back from her face and confined the rest in a yellow hairnet that matched her apron stripes. It was part Harlem/part Andrew Sisters/part Medusa. He didn't know why that one black ringlet made him swallow his whole bit of catfish in an un-godly lump, but he promptly fell into a daydream that featured him breathlessly watching as she set free all those wonderful shiny corkscrews. In twenty years, Vaseline Jenkins' twisty hair was the closest he'd come to fantasizing about anything other than Lucinda.

Of course, he and Mama talked to Vassie here and there while having their lunch, but then they talked to Willie Semple at the counter, too, and every other week, Mama brought a new batch of her melted mutton and turpentine cure for Chefee's peptic ulcer. The Dinner Bell was a chatty place where people leaned over the back of their booths to ask after ailing grandparents and broken automobiles.

Every time Willie came through the door, instead of saying hello, he said corny things like, "What's your story, Morning glory?" and the regulars that knew him always answered in perfect unison: "How's it shakin', Bacon?"

Like it or not, you absorbed a general sense of knowledge about the other patrons purely by eating there once a week. You knew about Chefee and the rest of the help, too. A person's chronic heartburn, pregnant dog, or noisy neighbor just naturally worked its way into your body along with the scrambled eggs.

Anyone who'd ever said two words to Vaseline knew that she was raising five rambunctious boys on her own. Five fire-setting, back-talking, bone-breaking, mess-making "A" boys. Hadley didn't know all their names, but he knew they all started with A. You couldn't talk to Vaseline without hearing the latest high jynx involving her A-named boys.

Vaseline made and sold cologne water when she wasn't waiting tables She gave Mama a sample once in a little violet bottle, and when Mama took off the cap and sniffed it, it didn't smell like anything at all.

"Thank you Vassie," Mama said, because she was too polite to mention that the perfume had no smell to speak of.

Vassie winked at Mama. "That's potent stuff you got there, Miz Crump. Just dab you some on your wrists and neck next time you go to church, I guarantee every man in the joint will wind up following you home."

Mama believed this whole-heartedly and locked that bottle in a drawer the first minute she got home.

Vaseline had little mushroom-shaped ears which meant that she had a way with hypnotic herbs and the like. Mama said mushroom ears revealed an earthy soul.

"How about Vassie?" Mama whispered on the Sunday after Dickie promised to keep his eye on things. This was not because Mama knew of Hadley's plans to find a woman. This was because Mama was always trying to interest him in Vaseline Jenkins. Mama had done this with so many women over the years that Hadley never listened to anything she suggested. He just smiled and shook his head and politely ignored any arguments she tried to start. But on this Sunday, for the first time ever, he gave the question some real thought. How about Vassie?

"She likes you, in case you haven't noticed."

Hadley hadn't noticed anything of the sort. "If she likes me so much, why doesn't she dabble some of that magic cologne on her wrists and make me follow her home?"

"Well now, that's a good point," Mama said. "Maybe she ain't so magical after all."

That's when Hadley remembered about the little black ringlet. "What do you think I should do about her, Mama?"

"Ask her to have ham and beans with you tonight over at the *Roadside.*"

241

When Vaseline came back with the coffee pot, Hadley didn't let himself think. "Vaseline, would you want to have ham and beans with me tonight over at the *Roadside*?"

Mama looked like she might faint dead on the floor. Vaseline, too. "Okay," she said, and darned if that black ringlet didn't' pop loose the same second in the middle of her forehead.

They'd had a swell time at the Roadside, which came as a nice surprise. The place wasn't anything fancy, yet Vaseline wore a red camellia pinned to her corkscrews, and she wore her corkscrews in a camellia-colored hairnet. "Why'd you ask me here?" she asked him as soon as they set down at the table. "After all this time, I figured you were taken."

Hadley laughed. "That's a good word for it."

"You work at that house with all the wisteria, don't you?"

"I do."

"What's that beautiful Mrs. Worther-Holmes like? I hear all sorts of crazy stuff about her."

Hadley often worried that people knew about him and Lucinda, but Vassie fixed her eyes on him in such a sweet way, he decided it was an honest question. "She has her good points and her bad points," he said. "What about the Dinner Bell?"

"It puts bread on the table, I guess, and man-oh-man can my boys eat bread."

Hadley touched the flower in her hair. "Flames," he whispered.

"Huh?"

"Red camellias. They symbolize flames." Hadley could feel the scar on his neck beginning to do some flaming of its own. "I read a lot of gardening books."

"I just wore it 'cause I thought it was pretty," she said. She straightened her flower with a sheepish grin.

"Prettiness aside, every flower has its own special meaning. Honeysuckle, for instance, means *bonds of love*. Heather means *protection*. It might sound dumb, but I choose where I plant flowers based on what they mean. Heather works out real nice by a front door."

"My favorite flowers are hyacinths," Vaseline said.

"Hyacinths mean *sporting*."

"Oh." She wrinkled her nose. "That ain't very romantic, is it?" Vaseline didn't look the least bit happy about the meaning of hyacinths. "What's wisteria mean?"

"*I cling to thee.*"

"That's a nice one," she said. "Flowers are my business, too, you know? I wouldn't be able to mix up Darratu without them." Darratu was the odorless perfume Vaseline gave to Mama.

"What's in your perfume?' Hadley asked. "Or is it a secret recipe?"

"It is a secret, but if you're interested, I'll show you sometime. Or maybe you'd like to guess?" She stretched her arm out toward him, but, luckily for Hadley, the ham came right then and saved him from being swept away.

Much to his surprise, he enjoyed the date with Vaseline more than he thought he would. In fact, he invited her to *Laughing Larry's Traveling Funfair* the following weekend. *Laughing Larry's* was the talk of Beattie's Bluff, and Hadley intended to show up the first minute the fair rolled into town and help put up bleachers and tents so he could get a free pass. Carnivals would do that if you came willing to work. A lot of funfairs wouldn't let coloreds ride the rides, but Laughing Larry's made a point of putting up different signs on their wagons meant especially for the South whenever they came through. EVERY SUNDAY IS NEGRO DAY! RIDES ARE OPEN TO ALL. There wasn't a negro alive that didn't know about Laughing Larry's Negro Days.

The fair was a calculated move on Hadley's part, and he felt a little bit bad about that. He knew Nina and her cousins were planning to attend on NEGRO DAY because NEGRO DAY was also FREE COTTON CANDY DAY. He hoped Nina would see him with Vassie. "Bring your boys too, if you'd like," Hadley told her. Even though it would take every last penny in his Jolly Nigger to afford her big brood, it wouldn't be right for boys to miss a carnival.

"My brother Joe is taking them on Sunday night after he gets offa work," Vassie said. "If you don't mind, I think I'd like to keep you to myself for now."

Hadley smiled when she said that; not because of all the candy floss and popcorn she was saving him from buying, but because of the way her eyes twinkled when she said *keep you.*

They strolled down the midway hand-in-hand, and he told himself he would be holding her hand even if Nina wasn't possibly there to see it. But later, when he won the biggest coconut in the *Coconut Shy,* he made a big show of giving it to Vassie, and his eyes darted all around, hoping to spot Nina. Where was the girl? They moved on to *The Swooper* next. Vaseline had giggled when she told him how much she loved to ride roller coasters. The line looked half a mile long.

"We don't have to wait in that big line," she said.

Hadley was glad for the big line. Maybe Nina was somewhere in the mob? Of course, giving Vaseline a ride on a roller coaster was the most important thing.

"We can't miss the swoopiest ride we'll ever take," he said, pointing to the faded sign that read: "Most Swoopiest Ride You'll Ever Take!"

As a result, they stood in the hot sun for an hour and a half with every black-skinned Beattie's Bluffer and his brother and, even though they never saw Nina and the boys, Vaseline laughed like a child at every swoop, and that made it all worth while.

The day rolled on without any sign of Nina, and Hadley grew more desperate. There were white kids zipping through the crowds, pepped up on cotton candy, but Nina and the boys were not among them. He paid for three shots at the *Coon Dip*, thinking that if he could just send the nigger boy for a splash in the tank, it was guaranteed to raise a ruckus of cheering and congratulations. It took all three shots, but Hadley won, and when the boy stood up in the water with his big bushy hair dripping like a fat sponge, dozens of on-lookers laughed and patted Hadley on the back. Three strangers shook his hand. Vaseline must of noticed him searching the crowd because she asked if he was looking for someone. Suddenly, everything he did felt contrived, even the stuff he was glad to do. Worse still, for reasons he couldn't fathom, the *Coon Dip* made Vassie mad.

"Why would you wanna knock that poor kid in the water? You ought to know better."

"I'm just helping him earn a living," Hadley said. "If people don't play, he's out of a job."

"It's degrading is what it is," Vaseline said.

"Why?"

"What do you mean *why*? It's called the *Coon Dip,* for pitysake."

"What else are they gonna call it?" Hadley asked.

Alas, two more hours passed without any sign of the kids. Hadley was disappointed, but the good part was, when he kissed Vaseline on the *Tumble Bug*, he didn't have to feel like it was all for show. Closed up in that hot metal ladybug car there was nobody to see. It was just Hadley and Vaseline.

It felt different kissing someone else. Hadley had been kissing the same woman for so long, he didn't know if he would mess it up if he tried to do it with someone else.

"You kiss nice," Vassie said, so that much was encouraging.

By the time he took her home, the kissing was getting easier. "The boys won't be back until the fair closes," she said. "Do you want to come inside?"

Vaseline Jenkins was far and away the most fun he'd had in years, and Hadley didn't want to stop kissing her. She had a startling way of talking, though, that made him twitchy. When she called her boss Mr. Slimstead, *Mr. Shithead*, it was almost as cute as it was surprising. Lucinda was known to curse a blue streak, but it wasn't never cute.

"Ain't you ever called anyone a shithead before?" Vassie asked.

"Not out loud."

"That figures. You look like a bottled-upper if ever there was one. Well, in case you ain't noticed, I don't believe in bottling up anything but my perfume. I think it's unhealthy."

Hadley wanted to go inside with Vaseline, and then again, he didn't. Lucinda had striped him like a zebra, and he was scared he wouldn't know the first thing about what a nice woman might like from him.

"I have to get back to work," he lied.

"Maybe another time then?"

"Sure," he said, even though he couldn't see himself ever having the courage to go in her house. *Shoot,* Hadley thought. *I am a bottled-upper.*

When Hadley got home, there was a note under his front door.

Who's the Negro lady?

Hadley smiled and sat down to write his first note to Nina Worther-Holmes. He no longer favored recipe cards for such work. Instead, he used the pad of paper Tilly had given him that advertised for Omo Washing Powder. Underneath the words *OMO ADDS BRIGHTNESS TO WHITENESS*, Hadley wrote: *Just a friend.*

"Friend?!" Nina screeched the next morning after Hadley had been summoned from the wild flower patch to drive Nina into Hartsville. No sooner had he slid behind the driver's wheel when the girl started railing at him. "You don't have any *friends*, Hadley. In all the years you've been with us, I've never known you to have a single friend."

She sat in the backseat, stiff as a china doll, twisting a pair of gloves in her hand. Every time she said the word *friend*, she slapped the gloves against her palm.

Hadley planned to get through the tirade by staying professional. He steered the Phantom toward Hartsville, even though it was obvious that their destination was of no real consequence.

"If you'll excuse me for saying so, Miss Nina, what I do on my day off is my own business."

"There's just one thing I'd like to know, Mr. Crump: What does this new *friend* of yours have that I don't have?" Her glove cracked extra loud again against the cup of her hand.

Hadley kept his eyes on the road. "For one thing, she's a woman. A divorcee, if you catch my meaning?"

"Being course will not dissuade me from the subject at hand."

"What will?" he asked.

"Nothing. You ought to know that by now. Anyway, I don't believe for one second that you actually care about this so-called *friend* of yours."

"You like to think you know me, Miss Nina, but you don't. You don't know anything about me."

They locked eyes in the rectangle of the rear view mirror. Nina smiled. "I know you peek in my room at night. I've seen you do it a million times."

Hadley was always careful to use his Negro Servant voice when speaking to Nina and the boys. A Negro Servant voice, as every Negro servant knows, has a distinctly chipper ring that requires a small spurious smile to be effective. Gone were the days when a servant must remain silent around family and guests, but a cheery unschooled way of speaking was always appreciated and practically a tool of the trade. When it came to Nina, Hadley sometimes found himself straying from his side of the species. This would never do.

He strapped on his best lackey grin. "It's my job to check the house before I go to bed."

"You're the gardener, Hadley. What are you checking for? Grub worms?"

"I like to make sure the house is secure, that's all."

"Why can't you admit that you care for me?" she said. "Is it because I'm white? I think of you as white, you know. You look white."

A tiger-colored cat sprung in front of the car, and Hadley swerved a little more than necessary to miss it. Nina sat so rigid, she barely moved.

"Is it because I'm younger?" Nina asked. "My friend Ludie Waits is married to a man older than you and everyone says they're a perfect match. Why do you fight it, Hadley? Every time you look at me, I see something extra in your eyes."

Hadley made the mistake of looking at her in the mirror again.

"There!" she said. "There it is now!"

He pulled off the road and twisted in his seat to face her. "I'm gonna have to quit working for your family if you keep this up, Miss Nina. Is that what you want?"

"Would you love me then?"

There was no more glove-slapping by this point. Only big fat glistening tears. In that awful moment, those teary eyes were worse than the eyes of Flora Gibbs, and Flora Gibbs' eyes haunted him like indigestion.

Hadley wanted to take Nina by the shoulders and scream, *But I do love you! I love you more than anything!*

"No," he said. "No matter how old you are or who I work for, I can't never be what you want me to be."

Nina covered her face with her hands. "You are the worst thing to ever happen to me, Hadley Crump."

Every word was a knife in his heart, a pain that took him back to Flora Gibbs.

The last time he'd seen Flora, it was three in the morning in a middle of a rainstorm.

"What are you doing?" she asked when she found him on her porch.

It was the same night he'd taken her to the Salamander Club to celebrate her birthday. The same night Lucinda told him about the baby.

"Your swing needs a new chain," he said. He was already half-way through the job.

Flora came out in Mr. Gibb's bathrobe, holding her hands tucked up under her armpits. "It's the middle of the night. Can't this wait?"

He ripped the old chain down with a clatter. "No."

Rain poured off the gutters, forming a cage around the porch.

"I see."

Hadley hooked the new chain in place and tried not to look at her. "I brought that, too," he said, motioning to the leather mail organizer he'd got as a Phoetus gift the year before. "It's for your mail."

Tears pooled in Flora's eyes, and even though he tried not to see them, he saw them. He would see them forever and ever. "I've got something for you, too," she whispered. "Wait here."

A minute later, she returned with the spoon.

Taking back Alabama was the hardest thing he'd ever lived through, until Nina asked him for his love.

CR

"I don't know about you, Hadley, but I ain't had a good roll in the hay in quite some time." Vassie nudged him with her knee and blew a smoke ring at the moon. "We've had a lot of laughs, you and me, and I like all the funny stuff you know about flowers. Mama's keeping the ziggaboos til noon tomorrow. I ain't gonna expect an engagement ring if you stay the night with me."

It was their fifth date, and Hadley had gone out on a limb and taken Vaseline to see *Devil's Island* at the Starlite Negrotorium. In the six years the picture palace had been open, he'd kept away for fear he might run into a certain painful person from his past. In fact, he'd given up quite a few modernities for this reason, but Vassie had a way of making him want to do things he would never ordinarily want to do. When she said she'd like to see a movie, Hadley was sure he'd be looking over his shoulder all night long for Flora, but once they settled on the bench and the lights went down and the picture came up, he completely forgot all his cares. It was a wonderful evening and, like most of their dates, he walked her back to the big lilac foursquare on Mayhew Lane where a wooden sign painted by her oldest son advertised Darratu in the front window.

Seeing how it was a house of boys, the lilac had surprised him the first time he saw it. Vassie told him that she and the kids had painted it a week after she gave her husband the boot. She wanted her cologne water business to take off, and she figured a *lady color* would stir up attention. And it had. The place stood out on Mayhew like a pearl button in a bed of slag. Vassie's husband, Peach, had inherited money when they were first married, and they'd use it to purchase a home. The judge in Divorce Court awarded the lilac house to Vassie after hearing all she'd suffered at the hands of Peach Jenkins, which was just as well since she hadn't seen or heard from him since. Sitting on the front stoop under the stars, you couldn't hardly see the busted window young Armstrong had cracked with his slingshot when he was hunting birds, or even spot the eggplant-colored dormer that came to be after the lilac paint ran out. In the dark, it was pretty as a dollhouse.

This evening when they sat on the stoop, Vassie put her head on his shoulder, started humming *Mood Indigo*, and lit up a reefer.

Mr. Shithead sometimes ran low on cash, she said, so he gave her a lumpy envelope of cigarettes instead. He always came through with the money in a day or so. Vassie stashed her "bonuses" in a Saltine box and smoked them sparingly. Hadley didn't even do cigars and almost never touched a drop of hooch, but when she passed him the cigarette, he was curious to see what it would be like.

249

Smoking on Vassie's front steps, he couldn't help but wonder if she'd spelled him with her magic cologne water. Smoking hop surely wasn't his thing, and he didn't go to movies in blackie town, either, yet here he was, his heart pounding, his bones knocked loose, and his head floating like a helium balloon. For some reason, his helium head greatly tickled him. When she asked if he wanted to stay the night, he opened his mouth, fully expecting a lie to pop out about how he had to get home and fix something.

"Okay," popped out instead.

"Okay?" she said. "Okay what?"

"Okay, what you said about staying the night."

Vassie shrugged her shoulders. "Only if you want to."

"Are you chickening out?"

"I'm not too good at this. I was married to the same man for ten years, and I almost never go anyplace with anyone older than this here pair of shoes."

Smoking made Hadley laugh louder than normal. "So you *do* want an engagement ring?"

"Hell no. I ain't too keen on marriage right now, thank you very much."

It was a relief to realize that Vassie was uncomfortable, too.

"I mean, I've been with some men in my time, Hadley. Maybe even ten or twelve."

"Oh."

She slid her fingers through his hair. "In any case, I think I might know how to handle a school boy like you."

Hadley dropped the cigarette and crushed it with his shoe. "Show me."

Ten minutes later, they were in bed inside the lilac house, and Hadley reached over and turned off the bedroom lamp.

Vassie turned on the lamp. "I want to see you," she said. "You been real fun to look at so far."

That'll change, Hadley thought. Vassie was down to her birthday suit, and he still had on everything except his shirt. When she made a move for his trousers, he covered her fingers with his own to stop her.

"You timid, Hadley? I bet you've gotten a lot a tail in your time, a sweet 'ole sugar lump like you?"

"Nope."

It felt strange being in her bed. Strange but also nice. Hadley almost never got a chance to make love in a bed. The room was filled with the rosey scent of her *Queen for an Hour* bath salts, and she sat on his legs looking at him like he was Jesus come to save her soul. Hadley reached up and loosened the pins in her hair and slid the hairnet off. A thousand corkscrew curls sprung free and trembled past her shoulders.

"Beautiful," he sighed.

"I know one thing," she said. "You can't be half as sweet as you look." With those words, she unbuttoned the top of his trousers.

"Lord have mercy!"

Hadley switched off the lamp.

Vaseline switched on the lamp.

There was a bottle of Thunderbird on the nightstand, and she poured herself a shot. She poured him one, too. "What is *that?*" she asked, waving at his tattoo.

"A souvenir," Hadley said.

"Yeah? I got a few of them, too, only mine are called stretch marks. Mary, Jesus and Joseph! That's weird."

Hadley sat up and pulled on his shirt. "This was a bad idea."

"Aw, now. Don't be so skittish, honey. We all got our quirks."

Hadley buttoned up his shirt. "I got a lot of quirks, Vassie."

Vassie unbuttoned his shirt. "Show me."

☙

Six hours later, he was in bed, and Hadley reached over and turned on the lamp.

The clock read 4 a.m. "Are you nuts?" he asked.

"I miss you badly. Do you miss me?"

He pulled Lucinda's hand out of his pants. He hadn't been home but an hour or so, and he wasn't expecting to see

Lucinda. "Dickie is gonna blow my brains out if he catches you in here."

In the seventeen years since Hadley had moved into his own house, Lucinda had never visited him in the middle of the night. They'd agreed to play it safe before the first brick was ever laid. It was one thing to sneak off to a room they both had business in. Lucinda had no business in Hadley's house. Steering clear of his bed was the one and only rule they'd come up with in a relationship that thrived on breaking rules.

"Has Diaper Rash Jenkins been touching you? Is that why you're not interested?"

"Your husband is asleep next door," he snapped. "How's that for a reason?"

"I don't care about that fat pig," she said. She pulled the sorriest face Hadley had ever seen, sticking her lip out like she was twelve years old. "I'm jealous, Hadley. I can't stand the thought of you being with another woman."

Hadley closed the bedroom window for fear someone might hear her snivling. Honesty from Lucinda was harder to take than scheming and conniving. "What do you expect me to do, Lucinda? Nina has made it all but impossible for me to stay here."

She put his hand on her cheek and pressed it into her skin with the fan of her fingers. If Hadley didn't know better, he would have thought she looked like a woman with a broken heart. "Do you have feelings for Vaseline Jenkins?"

He loathed when she called Vassie *Diaper Rash,* yet he wished she would call her Diaper Rash now. He knew how to fight with Lucinda. He didn't think he liked fighting with her, but seeing her tender made his stomach sick. "Come on, Lucinda. Get out of here before you get us both killed."

"I can't." A tear trailed down the back of his hand, followed by another. "Hold me, Hadley. Please, just hold me."

He tore his hand away from her face and balled it in a fist. It was wrong of her to come in his house and try to ruin the first chance he'd had in years of finding something good in his life. He wanted to throttle her for being so selfish. There were dark, seething moments when he hated her more than he loved her, and this was one of those dark, seething moments.

"Please, Hadley." She pulled his arms around her and sobbed against his chest.

Hadley grit his teeth and held her like a bag of feed. He wished he was a boa constrictor so he could squeeze the life out of her. He wished Dickie would break through the front door and shoot her full of holes.

"That was a memorable day to me," she whispered.

"What day?" he growled, but when she began to speak again, he recognized the words of Dickens. He recognized Pip.

"*That was a memorable day to me, for it made great changes in me . . .* " Lucinda stopped. She was not one to quote things well or accurately. "How does it go, Hadley?"

Hadley ground his teeth. He remembered quotes like Mama remembered the Bible. He had an especially good memory for all things Pip.

"*But, it is the same with any life. Imagine one selected day struck out of it, and think how different its course would have been. Pause you who read this, and think for a moment of the long chain of iron or gold, of thorns or flowers, that would never have bound you, but for the formation of the first link on one memorable day.*"

"You know it well."

"You made me say it twenty or more times until I got it exactly right, as I recall."

"And you got it exactly right. You always did."

"Don't do this to me, Lucinda."

"Hold me," she said.

And so, of course, he did.

൙

Note to the wise gardener: Early pruning is essential. Without training, wisteria has the capacity to fill every available space.

Hadley looked at the clock.

4:55 a.m.

What am I doing? he asked himself. Lucinda had just slipped out of the house. At eight o'clock, he'd been in bed with Vassie, convinced he was on his way to a new and better life. Vaseline was a good lady, and she didn't kick him out of bed when she saw his tattoo. Instead, she tried to be playful about it.

"I've had my share of surprises when I've unbuttoned a man's pants, but you, sir, take the prize."

He prayed she wouldn't ask what the "M" stood for.

"What happened to you?" was what she asked.

"I've made a few mistakes, is all."

Vassie nodded, like she understood, and Hadley was grateful she was such an understanding woman.

How could it be that by four a.m. he had his arms around Lucinda?

"Hadley, do you remember when we used to play Great Expectations?" By that point, Lucinda was holding on for dear life. "You sat at my little tea table with your curls all combed down, and we put you in Daddy's brown tie. You looked so darned cute. And in your Pip-iest voice, you said: *It was impossible for me to separate her, in the past or in the present, from the innermost life of my life.*"

"I probably didn't even understand what those words meant, Lucinda."

"But you did. You memorized all the good Pip parts, and you always said them with such feeling. Don't you remember?"

Hadley remembered. "*I, trembling in spirit and worshipping the very hem of her dress,*" he quoted. "*She, quite composed and most decidedly not worshipping the hem of mine.*"

"Oh Hadley," she said, and there was a genuine look of regret in her eyes. "What wonderful days those were."

CR

To make up for all the hugging he'd done with Lucinda, the following Friday Hadley took Vassie for a T-bone steak at *Big Harry's Steak and Spaghetti House.*

"How can you afford Big Harry's?" Vassie asked. *Big Harry's* was known for two things: T-bones and high prices.

"Are you kidding? Before you came along, I hadn't had a proper date in twenty years. I've got enough for Tahiti if you want to go."

Vassie laughed. "The boys would burn the house to the ground if I did. I'm afraid we'd have to take them with us."

He pictured himself playing on the beach with a big, rambunctious family. "That'd be nice," Hadley said. Of course, he didn't have the money to buy her family dinner at *Big Harry's,* much less take them to Tahiti, but judging by the way Vassie looked at him, he figured it was the thought that counts.

The A boys had taken a liking to him after he helped them put a *Radio Ace* together. Vaseline liked him better after that too. "In all their days, I've never known them to sit still for five minutes at a stretch, and that includes their time in the womb. I wish their father would take a minute out of his lazy, drunkard life and teach them how to build something."

Hadley didn't know a thing about raising boys, but it seemed to him that Vassie's bunch could use some male influence.

"I wonder if Andrew, Atticus, Anthone, Amber, and Armstrong would like to go to a stunt show instead of Tahiti?" he asked. "I heard Skip Fordyce is coming through next month."

Vassie clapped a hand over her mouth and promptly declared Hadley the man of her dreams. No one had ever remembered all her boys' names before, she said. "If you say 'em three times fast, I'll ball your brains out in the Lady's Room right now."

"Gosh," Hadley said. "It doesn't take much to please you, does it?"

"Shoot. My own mother can't even remember all their names." She toasted him with her gin sour. "Speaking of my mother, she's keeping the boys until tomorrow."

Hadley had already made up his mind to get a T-bone, yet he stared at his menu as if the Spaghetti was tempting him, too. "I have to work in the morning, Vassie."

"What time?"

"Six sharp."

"So you'll stay until five."

He put down his menu. "I don't know, Vassie." It struck him that she wouldn't be calling him the man of her dreams if she knew how wrapped up he still was with Lucinda.

"Do you like me?"

"Very much."

"Then stay until five. I want to show you my laboratory."

❧

The lilac house smelled of flowers and dirty socks. Sock sweat hit one's nose first. Honeysuckle followed. The front room had been girled up with lace doilies and a butter-colored love seat with pink fringy pillows. This was Vassie's "shop". Hadley had learned that the kitchen, bathroom, and bedrooms were fair game for anything, and thus the lot of were hopelessly littered with cap guns, crayons, hammers, and busted tire rims. But the shop was off limits. The boys had to come and go through the backdoor to keep down on the dirt.

Vassie had covered a gate-leg table with her mother's needlepoint, and she displayed her soaps and perfumes in a pretty row on top. What made the place shine though were all the delicate little fineries she'd added. Fake pearls bumped against bottles of lemon yellow and baby pink glass. Vassie had snipped the pearls off a necklace her husband gave her on their first anniversary and put them to a better use. Likewise, she rescued bows off old shoes and lace trim from worn-out slips. Once, she'd come across a dress in a trashcan that had cigarette burns on the sleeves, and she salvaged three jewel buttons that later got glued on the lid of a hand cream jar. That same hand cream jar sold the next day for three pennies more than what she usually asked, and this was in no small part thanks to the buttons.

"There's three of us in blackie town that put up perfume," she told Hadley. "But I'm the only one to offer real jewel buttons on her lids."

The front room was where Vassie conducted business. The cologne water was made elsewhere. She pulled a wooden ladder down from the second floor ceiling and led him up to the attic. Attics, as a rule, made Hadley nervous.

Up top, they stepped into a large room with a pyramid roof and an unfinished floor. A wall of boxes divided broken lamps, a crib, and Christmas lights from the heady heart of the *Darratu* operation.

No stench of socks prevailed here. It was pure verbena and lavender oil. On a sawhorse table, cardamom seeds and cloves soaked in saucers of rum. Tuberrose bathed in vodka. There were orris root for sashets and cinnamon sticks for smelling salts. *Bacon Shampoo* filled old syrup bottles. And along the windowsill, a line of colored jars lit up in the moonlight like stained glass, giving the place a strangely sacred feel.

"Most people don't realize this, but making perfume is an art," Vassie explained. "There's some that think you just drop a few petals in some booze and away you go. Well, I've got news for those people: making perfume is every bit as complex as painting a picture of a meadow, only with perfume, scent is your paint brush. If you're aiming to make a masterpiece, it's real delicate work. Perfume is not about smelling like a rose. Just like a canvas ain't never gonna be a meadow, a rose is always gonna do a better job of smelling like a rose than a person's skin. Perfume is about the feeling a man gets when he touches his lips to a girl's wrist."

"It's the same with gardening," Hadley said. "No living person can touch what God does with flowers in the wild. If a man's garden doesn't stir up anything different when you look at it, then what's it for?"

"It's the language of flowers," Vassie said.

Hadley nodded. This kind of talk was filling him with uncomfortable excitement. This was that moment, sometimes longed for, sometimes not, that happens every once in a great while between two people, like with Lucinda and books. Or Flora and everything. It was the sort of moment that can make even the most practical of men throw their lot in with fate, whole-heartedly accepting that there is something bigger at work than just the convenient happanstance of a waitress appearing with a pot of coffee when you're in desperate need of a date.

Then again, maybe it was nothing special at all. Maybe everybody was the same, living one life on the outside of their skin, and a whole other life on the inside? *The inner-most life of a life.* Hadley was perfectly capable of sweating buckets and working his outside parts to blisters, while his inner book-obsesssed-self locked fingers with Fitzgerald's Daisy and kissed her fickled lips. Whenever he mixed paint, there was a part of him scientifically tuned into measuring and stirring up the perfect shade of lavender, while another part set sail while dreaming of the dreams that might be dreamt up within those lavender walls. Maybe anytime you got close enough to scratch down to a person's insides, there was always a special feeling for lavender going on in there? *Don't give her too much credit for liking flowers,* he warned himself. *Every girl likes flowers.*

"Colors can work a spell on emotions, too," Vassie said. Her fingers moved like dark magic wands over a row of mismatched china bowls. "I use tumeric for making yellow and dogwood for blue. Pokeweed makes a smokin' shade of red. See all these sticks of weeping willow? They're the secret behind my salmon-pink *Kiss Behind the Earlobes.*"

"I like colors," Hadley said.

She handed him a little pillow made of softest leather. "Smell this."

Hadley's head went dizzy with the spicy scent of jasmine.

"A white woman from Long Street is paying me four dollars to make her a pair of pillows for the soles of her dancing shoes."

"I never smelled jasmine-flavored feet before."

She picked up a cotton handerchief. "I sell a shitload of these, too." She waved the cheap fabric under his nose, and bergmot and lemon ran wild through his sinuses.

Hadley could hardly contain himself. "This is wonderful, Vassie."

"But you still haven't had a sniff of Darratu yet."

"Maybe I have, and maybe I haven't. How would I know?"

Vassie's eyes twinkled. "You wouldn't. But I never wear the stuff to get a man. Wearing Darratu when you're courting would be like telling someone you have a million bucks saved under your mattress: how would you ever know if a person liked you for yourself or for your riches?"

"Then why do you make it?"

"Because there are plenty of woman out there who don't give a damn why a man likes them. They just wanna be liked."

There were times in his own life when he might have been tempted to sprinkle the stuff all over himself. Had he owned a bottle of Darratu when Nina was a baby, he'd have bathed in cologne water every day. Maybe Lucinda would have left Dickie, and they could have been a real family. "What does Darratu mean?"

"*Blooming flower.* It's Ethiopian. If you want to make something bloom, it'll cost you seventy-five cents."

"What's in it?"

She shook her finger. "That is a secret I've never told anyone." The violet bottle of Darratu went back in its place. "Let's move along, shall we?" She uncapped a jar of tiny crystals and poured some in his hand. "Until you've taken a bath in Vassie's *Sugar Soak,* you haven't taken a bath."

"I haven't?"

"Tastes good, too."

Hadley clapped the sparkles off his palm. "I think it's time for dessert."

It was dawn by the time he walked up Treebourne Street, and the pastel rays of early light made the nipple-pink wisteria look pinker and nipplier than they'd ever looked before. He thought he saw a bedroom curtain tremble behind the reflection of pink blossoms, and he got a sudden urge to wave. He hoped that Nina was hiding up there behind the lace, watching him through a lattice of diamond-shaped holes. He tugged at a vine and plunged his face into the cool, wet petals, confirming his theory that wisteria smelled softer and less intense before the heat of the day. Like a fresh pillowcase. Or a woman after a bath.

When he looked up from the flowers, Nina's curtains were still. But the red drapes in another bedroom slowly opened down the middle.

ॐ

Andrew, Atticus, Anthone, Amber, and Armstrong had become obsessed with winning the Bloody Lime after Hadley made the mistake of showing it to them during a wicked game of ring taw. The A boys were vicious when it came to all games, and marbles was no exception. By now, Hadley had seen them in action and knew to be afraid. Vassie's brood were known to take skin off the way they played tops, their goal being more to wound rather than out-spin an opponent. Similarly, football was just a good excuse to get the other players in a headlock. The twins, Anthone and Amber, seemed especially keen on murdering one another. Their method of choice was hockey. Apparently no one had ever told Anthone and Amber that you needed a puck to play. They preferred slapping around roller skates, food, or their father's old tools, and it was just tough luck if you were the goalie. When the A boys made up their mind to go after the Bloody Lime, Hadley knew his goose was cooked. The only thing remotely in question was which A would win the marble.

"It'll be me, I bet," said Armstrong, the youngest of the boys. "I want it so bad, I can practically taste it."

"It won't be you," sniggered Andrew, who was the oldest of the A's. "You can catch a ball like Spud Davis, but when it comes to fulking marbles, you ain't worth cow shit."

"What's that marble taste like when you think about it, Armie?" Atticus asked.

"Limes," Armstrong said. "And blood of course."

The contest to win the Bloody Lime was set for a Sunday afternoon in the dirt lot behind Vassie's house. Time was when Hadley could knuckle down with the best of the best, but Vassie's sons paid him little respect with regard to experience. In fact, age was of no advantage at all in any game involving the A boys. For one, Andrew and Atticus were taller than Hadley by a head. For two, even the younger, shorter ones were brutes to be bargained with. If Hadley were to hold a bag of grass seed in each arm, they'd out-weigh him all the same. Of course, marbles was a game where size didn't normally count, but this was not the case with these boys. Whereas Hadley and Loomis had rarely played any game that came to shoving or punching, Andrew had gleefully explained to Hadley that shoving and punching were a part of the family rules.

"Shoot, if you can't knock somebody's block off, why play?"

After a rigorous hour of marbles in the dirt lot, Hadley felt good just to come away with his life, much less his old marble. But come away, he did. He rubbed his bruises and headed for home, even as the boys hurled insults at him, and a broken bottle or two.

"Prepare to die next week, old fart!" they shouted, which was their way of saying that Hadley would not hold onto the Bloody Lime for long.

By some miracle, Hadley managed to go home with his own marble the following week, too, along with Anthone's root beer cat's eye and a minor nosebleed, courtesy of Andrew's elbow. Afterward, Hadley tossed the cat's eye in the air and held it up to the sun, feeling no less pleased with himself than he did after winning a marble as a boy. Maybe he was even more pleased.

"You taking toys away from my kids?" Vassie asked after he took the cat's eye out of his pocket for the fifth time to admire its beery sparkle.

All of Hadley's blushing parts heated up at once. "I guess I am."

"Well, ain't that something!" Vassie said. "I hope you steal every last one of them marbles. I'm sick of tripping over the stupid things."

Hadley was scared of Vassie's family, but he liked them, too. They were savage Indians until bedtime, and then they trampled over one another to kiss their mother goodnight. They hardly left a room without telling her how much they loved her, never mind that they might be chasing someone with a shovel two minutes later. It was quite a spectacle. Rich and Guido were not nearly so physical when it came to tormenting others. To see the goodness in Vassie's boys, a person had to look beyond the bruised knuckles and black eyes. Every Saturday they hawked perfume on the corner of 5th and Carson. Perfume! If that wasn't goodness and love, Hadley didn't know what was.

Vaseline was worried about the violence she saw in her sons. "I've tried everything under the sun to get the meanness worked out of them. Hell, we played dolls once for a whole week, and everyone had to hold their babies all day long, and if anyone kilt one or hit somebody over the head with one, I promised we'd play dolls for a month. Would you believe it, all the babies lived. I thought we'd turn some sort of corner, but the minute I let the little monsters put the dolls up, out came the boxing gloves again." She shook her head in disgust. "I chalked it up to one more lesson that didn't stick, but I'll tell you this:

last Christmas my sister-in-law's boy, Alvin, come across one of the dolls in the closet and decided to take it down to the tracks and tie it to the rails and wait for a train to run it over. It was Amber's baby, as I recall. Poopyhead, he'd named her. Well, when Armie saw what Alvin was up to, he charged into the house screaming his head off, and I was sure someone was dead. When the boys got wind of Poopyhead's plight, they mounted a rescue party such as you have never seen. The baby was saved, but to this day, Alvin's got an ear that won't stand up normal. Looks like somebody taped a banana peel to the side of his head."

Hadley winced. Mama would say that an ear damaged due to foolishness was a righteous punishment, seeing how ears said so much about a man. "Well, they're protective, at least," Hadley said of her boys.

"I'm not sure that's good enough."

ॐ

It was that same night that Vassie noticed the scars on Hadley's back for the first time.

"Turn over," she said after she touched one.

Hadley rolled on his stomach and Vassie ran her fingers up and down each one as though she were counting something much harder to figure than the number of marks on his skin. He buried his face in the pillowcase, wondering if he'd be able to lie when she asked him where the scars came from. But she didn't ask. She curled up next to him instead and took his finger and pressed it to the curve behind her knee.

"I got this one the day Peach lost his job at the Do Rite Hardware Store. He swiped me with a daisy grubber while I was drying the dishes."

Hadley fingered the bumpy dent in her skin. He'd never noticed it before.

"Feel this," she said, and she put his hand on her ribcage.

"I thought you said you got that from Andrew's racing top"

"I did. Peach threw it at me. He was a mean man, Hadley. More than that, he was a frustrated man, and frustration leaves some pretty bad scars, by my experience. I don't like the things it does to a man."

℈

Nina had taken to sulking like she was terminal. There were more notes than ever being pushed under Hadley's front door. The bulk of them were made up of only one or two lines, as though the depth of her anger prevented her from steadying a pencil long enough to write more. Some were so sweet, they shredded his heart into a million pieces. *I miss talking to you, Hadley.* Others were nothing but sour. *You have ruined my life!* Without wanting or meaning to do it, Hadley found himself avoiding her for the first time in his life.

One afternoon, Vassie's boys insisted on walking Hadley home, and when they spotted Nina in the front yard, all five were simultaneously struck dumb by her glum expression.

Nina was smoking on the front steps, and every time she inhaled, it looked like she was being forced to drink urine, her face was just that pinched.

"She sure do look like a pill," Atticus said. "I bet she's mean as all get out, ain't she, Mr. Crump?"

"Yeah," Anthone said. "She musta ate something rotten to make her face go like that."

Andrew rubbed his chin thoughtfully. "I dunno. I wouldn't kick her out of bed for eating crackers."

Hadley looked from boy to boy, unable to decide which one he wanted to strangle most.

"Can we meet her?" Andrew asked.

"No!" Hadley said.

At fourteen, Andrew had the eyes of a wolf. In addition to breaking windows and Indian burns, he had a God-given gift for making rude remarks. "What about that one then?" he asked, nodding toward the other side of the yard.

"Who that?!" Atticus asked.

"That the boss lady, ain't it?" Andrew asked.

"I thought she'd be older," Atticus said.

"She is older," Hadley said.

Lucinda was sunning herself in a chair, wearing a bathing suit the color of a blush. She pressed a glass of lemonade against her forehead and waved at Hadley.

"Damn!" Anthone said. "You get to be that lady's gardener?"

"I'd like to plant my seed in her," Andrew said.

Hadley ordered the boys to go home.

Usually, Hadley made the trip alone. The problem with making the trip alone was that Mayhew Lane, where Vassie lived, was one block over from Dixon Street, where Flora Gibbs lived. Hadley had not set foot in the colored branch since the night Flora made him take home his spoon. He'd avoided Dixon Street as well. While the walk home from Vassie's house did not require a trip down Dixon, Hadley had let himself be tempted once to take a more heartbreaking route.

It was the day he heard from Anthone that Mr. Gibbs was dead. A neighbor boy had told Anthone that the old man that lived in the yellow house had slipped off a step stool and hit his head on the kitchen stove. The neighbor and Anthone had spent the afternoon throwing a ball to each other across the street, hoping to get a look at the body when it was carried out of the house.

"I knew Mr. Gibbs," Hadley told Anthone in an attempt to shame the boy. "He was a good man. There are people who will miss him." Hadley remembered Flora's father as happy and green. He wondered how she was handling such a terrible loss.

"He had a hole in his sock," Anthone said, clearly unshamed. "That was the only thing you could see on account they put a sheet over him."

When you come from a family that believes in collecting regrets in a jar so they can be saved forever, you aren't going to have the luxury of forgetting a girl like Flora Gibbs. Hadley had given up a life with Flora so that he could be near his child, otherwise Mr. Gibbs wouldn't have slipped off that stool because Hadley would have been there to get stuff down for him. When he broke off with Flora, it didn't feel like a choice. But it was. He tried to remind himself of why he made that choice whenever he got to daydreaming about what might have been. He tried to remember how lucky he was to be a part of his daughter's world.

Hadley had watched Nina take her first step, and he'd been there at her fifth birthday party and on the night of her first school dance. Whether or not Lucinda would have banned him from Nina's life, he was sure he wouldn't have seen the things he'd seen had he not been the gardener in Nina Worther-Holmes's house. He was grateful for the things he'd seen. Vassie had once asked him if he was black or white, and he'd told her he was neither. The sad truth was, he didn't appear to have too much say-so in either world. In light of this, Hadley knew better than to ask God for anything more than the mercies he'd been given.

Outside of the dozen or so snide remarks that Lucinda had made over the years, he knew nothing of Flora's life now, and that was on purpose. He'd tried to tune out Lucinda's gossip, too, but she had a knack for catching him unawares, and sometimes things snuck in.

"I hear she's fat as a Chevy." "I hear she's in love with a parrot." "I hear she caused a big fuss at the alderman meeting when they voted to take down that old merry-go-round."

Mostly, he made a point of shutting Flora out of his mind. Then again, there were occasions when his willpower failed him, and he would find himself drifting back. The smell of good pie could do it. Or the words of Jack London. And anytime someone mentioned that damned singer Helen Humes. Hadley didn't think about *Garlic Blues* like everyone else did; he thought about a word scratched on a wooden door in a little stone house. Full minutes might be lost to thoughts of her then. Or even an entire night. Mainly, he thought about Flora when he was low. He couldn't live properly with Nina or Lucinda, but there was a time when he could have happily lived with Flora. Very happily. And so, like a souvenir spoon that's too shiny to throw out, Hadley had long-since found a place to keep Flora. A Whoops Jar inside his head, or something like that anyhow, and when he was in the right mood for it, he filled it with what might have been.

He couldn't open the lid too often, of course, enticing as it was. It was too hard to face the porch swing where they might have sat in old age, or the wall with its message under coats of blue paint. Everything he put into this special place—birdsong and chess pie and lemon-scented azaleas—all of it was as painful as his coffin nails, because they *were* coffin nails. But when

THE READING LESSONS BY CAROLE LANHAM

Albert Gibbs died, Hadley ignored the pain and went home by way of Dixon Street.

He pulled his hat down over his eyes and kept to the opposite side of the road and waited to see if the walk past her house would kill him. He didn't know what he expected to see, but the sight of Flora's front door made his heart thump like a flat tire. The house was shabbier than he remembered and in bad need of work. There was one light on inside, and Hadley knew that this was the room where Mr. Gibbs had bashed his skull on the stove. As he weighed the risk of getting closer, a small slender figure moved across the window.

"Flora," he whispered.

ॐ

The first time Nina curled her little fingers around his big finger, Hadley got overwhelmed. He forgot who he was. He forgot who Lucinda was. He asked Lucinda to run away with him. "I don't care if she's mine or not; I want her, and I want you."

Lucinda cared.

Lucinda cared about her big new house and having a husband who could dance like George Raft. Lucinda had assured him that she loved Dickie, and Hadley had believed her when she said it because he was young and had yet to see how she deceived and acted selfishly toward her husband.

Hadley didn't believe it anymore, though. To be loved by someone like Lucinda would take something special. Truth be told, Dickie wasn't that special.

Dickie was, however, a decent man. For the most part, Lady Luck had shined on him in every way, and this didn't seem fair to Hadley. But luck was like that. When everyone in the country was losing their shirt, the New Deal came along and started the Home Owners' Loan Corporation, making it possible for people to get thirty year loans so they could buy Worther-Holmes Homes. Daddy Dick took a big hit in the market and had to get shocked by electricity a full three times in a loony bin in order to get happy again, but not Dickie. Daddy Dick had called Dickie a horse's ass for staying out of the market, but Dickie had no interest in stocks and had always found banking a bother. He preferred to keep large amounts of cash at home. As a result, while other men suffered mightily to keep their families fed, Lucky Dickie hung onto his job, his money, and about fifty percent of his unnaturally luxurious hair. He got to be Nina's daddy, too, and this made him the luckiest man alive. It wasn't right that one fellow should have so much, but still, he didn't deserve what Hadley and Lucinda had been doing to him all these years. Even so, Hadley would have taken Lucinda from him if he could have. Nina, too.

"Don't fool yourself, Hadley," Lucinda said when he asked her to run away with him. "The only reason I like you is because you *aren't* my husband."

He knew this was the truth. He was handyman Hadley, and that was all.

A week after the A boys walked him home, Lucinda snuck into his house again and crawled into his bed. Hadley was enjoying himself with Vassie, so it was easy to push her away.

"I can't be with you, Lucinda," he said.

It was more than Vassie, really. It was seeing that swing on Flora's front porch hanging there on a rusted chain. It was Nina and the A boys and Dickie's promise to keep an eye on him. It was something else, too . . .

"Don't you miss me, Hadley?"

Hadley thought about this. "No. I don't."

Lucinda was next to him under the covers, but she bolted upright like a shot. With a sad and terrible screech, she clawed his face.

Hadley grabbed her wrist to stop her doing it again, but she fought. They growled at each other as she struggled to get free, and he struggled to keep her from getting his face. It was the Hadley/Lucinda Tango all over again and, somehow, before he knew it, he had her arms pinned behind her head, and he was kissing her, and even the kiss was a fight. She tried to bite his lips, and he avoided her teeth by kissing her harder.

Finally, he shoved her away. "Shit."

"Don't stop."

He looked at her swollen lips and shook his head. "What's wrong with us, Lucinda?"

"Nothing," she said.

But Hadley knew there was.

CR

The next day was Sunday, and Hadley had promised to watch Armstrong's baseball team, The Whips, take on the undefeated Mud Hens in the baseball park, but when he looked in the mirror, he strongly considered missing the game. Going would mean lying to Vassie about the red scratches on his face. Not going would mean disappointing Armstrong, and Hadley couldn't stand to be the cause of that. Anyway, today was the day that someone was going to win the Bloody Lime, or so the boys had vowed. "Atticus dreamt it," Anthone told Hadley. "And when Atticus dreams something, it either comes true on its own or Atticus makes it come true."

So Hadley went. And Hadley lied. "I was playing with the neighbor's new dog, and it scratched me," he told them.

The game was fun even though The Whips lost. The A boys liked Hadley, or at least they liked having someone new to pick on. As Hadley cheered for The Whips, he thought of all the dance recitals he'd missed over the years. There just never seemed a good way to show up without it looking strange. He cheered extra hard for Armie. For Nina.

Afterward they all had ice cream in the park, and the boys asked Hadley a million questions about his face. "What kind of dog was it?" "Did you cry?" "Do you have rabies?"

When they exhausted of that, they started hitting each other with sticks, and this left Hadley alone with Vassie for the first time all afternoon.

She ran her fingers down his damaged face. "Poor dear," she said, which instantly made him feel worse than worse.

"It wasn't a dog," he said.

"I know that, Hadley."

He touched the delicate yellow net she wore over her hair. There wasn't a damned thing he could say for himself that would make any sense at all.

"How long have you been with this woman, Hadley?"

"All my life." He pressed his lips against her forehead, but Vassie stepped away.

"Would you like to know the secret of Darratu?"

Hadley was too caught off guard to answer.

"It's water. That's all it is, just plain old water. Don't be thinking I'm cheating my customers though because water will work if you believe it'll work. It's all about what's going on in here." She tapped on her temple. "Ain't nothing more powerful than what's in a person's head."

"I reckon that's true."

"And she's still in there, am I right?"

Hadley nodded.

"Do you think that's fair to me?"

"No."

"I want to help you, honey. I just don't think I can."

It felt like losing Flora all over again, and he grabbed her hand and kissed it, fully intending to beg for a second chance.

But Vassie was a battle-wearied woman long before Hadley came into her life. She cupped her hand over his mouth. "Don't, Hadley. Don't talk me into something that neither of us will know how to make work. I've had a good time with you. Why don't we leave it at that?" She started gathering up her herd. "Tell Mr. Crump thank you for the ice cream," she said. The A boys thanked Hadley by sailing sticks past his head.

Hadley had known it would come to this the night she showed him that scar behind her knee. Vaseline Jenkins had enough frustrated men in her life without adding Hadley in there, too. She deserved to find someone who didn't mix love with something that was her worst nightmare. Much as it hurt to let her go, he wasn't the right man to replace a beast like Peach Jenkins.

"Hey Armie," he called to the youngest of the As. Hadley lobbed the Bloody Lime at the boy, and Armstrong, who could catch like Spud Davis, caught it in his fist.

The boy left in a hail of blows, but he was smiling ear to ear. Vassie left with a wave.

Hadley left alone.

As further punishment, he took a trip down Dixon on his way home from the park. This time it was broad daylight and his hat felt too small to conceal him. He wanted to see Flora. Then again, he didn't. What he saw instead was a panel delivery vehicle parked in the drive. The letters printed on the side of the truck hit him like a kick in the stomach.

A moving van would have been bad enough. Hadley liked knowing his daydream was alive and well on the other side of Beatties Bluff. But Flora hadn't hired a mover. She'd hired the *Fast & Cheap Rafferty Brothers ~ Home-Painters Extraordinaire.* While he stood there hiding under his hat, the Rafferty brothers went into the house with a ladder and several gallons of white paint.

⟡

Finding a woman was just about the worst idea Hadley had ever come up with. Nina was no less ardent in her pursuit of him and he hadn't managed to free himself from Lucinda in any real way. Vassie was merely a painful reminder of why he'd never bothered to seek out anything more than a weekly tumble on The Reading Room floor.

And then there was Dickie. "You want to tell me what happened to your face?" he asked.

It was breakfast time and Dickie's head was behind the newspaper, but Hadley could read the man's knuckles clear as a bell. They looked mean and taut, like they could smash a hole through a man's head.

There was irony to be found in the fact that, in spite of his deceitful existence, Hadley could never come up with a convincing lie when he needed one. The words that came out of his mouth surprised him. "It was the Gilbert's new puppy, Jeb," he lied. "Jeb's a little scratcher."

Holy cow, Hadley thought. *I'm a USDA Certified Liar!*

Dickie's blood-shot eyes peeked over the paper, drawing Hadley to the headline of the day: *MERIDIAN MAN FOUND DANGLING FROM A TELEPHONE POLE AFTER WHISTLING AT A WHITE WOMAN.*

Dickie snapped the pages and said, "If you have any sense at all, boy, you'll keep away from that little *scratcher* in the future." His eyes retreated behind the dangling man headline. "I'd like you to see to that loose shutter today. My wife can't seem to sleep a wink for all the banging going on."

Hadley couldn't stop staring at the word *dangling* no matter how hard he tried. "I'll take care of it first thing tomorrow."

"Today, Crump. Put an end to it today or I'll fix it myself."
He folded the newspaper and tossed it at Hadley, which seemed
to Hadley an eerie coincidence.

Of course, Mama would have said that there is no such thing
as a coincidence. Hadley didn't normally read newspapers, so
this was the suspicious part. He tried to leave it alone, but that
headline about the hanging was like a big glass of milk that you
know has turned sour, but you have to taste anyway, simply
because it's yours for the taking. He picked up the paper and
started to read.

*The body of thirty-seven year old, Loomis Sackett, was
discovered early Sunday morning suspended from a utility pole
near the Central Street hooverville where he was believed to
reside. Bystanders had observed the Negro late Saturday
evening "lurking about" and whistling at hostess Ella Mae Clark
as she was attempting to lock up after her shift at Brassy's
Barbeque. Concerned patrons asked the nigger to move along
and that was the last anyone saw of Sackett alive. "This death
serves as a warning," Officer Luther Gates of the Meridian
Police Department told the Dispatch. "Meridians will not stand
for this kind of trouble in their town."*

Hadley imagined Loomis hanging in the kitchen before him,
only instead of seeing a grown man, he saw the frozen stare of a
young boy circling round and round as his limp body twirled on
the rope. He thought about that bad luck backscratcher with the
grasshopper painted on the handle. That scratcher had always
scared Hadley.

"What if you get an itch someday that's so big, you forget
yourself and scratch it by mistake?" he'd asked Loomis once
when Loomis was still Lucky Loomis and working as a hoeboy
for a man who couldn't fire him.

"The day I scratch is the day you're doomed," Loomis said.
"I resist temptation better than you."

Loomis Sackett hung from the ceiling all day long in every
room Hadley entered, that old backscratcher tightly clenched in
his cold dead hand.

☙

Hadley opened the back of the commode and started wiggling things around. "LOOKS LIKE THE TIME HAS COME FOR YOU TO FIND YOURSELF A NEW BALL," he said loud as he could, just in case anyone was listening. THE OLD ONE IS JUST ABOUT SHOT.

Lucinda stood in the bathroom door sawing on a fingernail with a metal file. "Very funny, Hadley. What's the matter with you? You're white as a ghost."

He flushed the flusher and waited to speak until the sucking sound of water all but covered up his words. "He knows about us, Lucinda. He practically said as much today, only instead of shooting me outright, he's got it in his head to scare the piss out of me first."

Hadley wished he had a dime for every whispered conversation he'd had over a toilet plunger. Contrary to popular belief, his best skill was not his ability to plumb but rather his ability to make it seem like he was plumbing when really he was talking about lust or murder.

"You worry too much." Lucinda scoffed. "I've been married to the man for nineteen years, and Dickie is dumber than horse doot. If he does know, he's always known, so why should he do anything about it now?"

"THE BACKFLOW PREVENTER IS GIVING OUT," Hadley announced to anyone who cared.

Lucinda rolled her eyes.

He spoke in a low whisper. "You've been coming to my house in the middle of the night, Lucinda. Honestly, I don't know why I'm still alive. Have you noticed how much he's been drinking lately? Tilly can't hardly keep the liquor stocked."

"Oh phoo. Dickie just hates the house-building business, that's all. If he didn't belt back a few every night, he'd have to blow his brains out."

"That's precisely my point, Lucinda. He's wound up pretty tight these days. IN ANY CASE, YOU'RE ASKING FOR TROUBLE IF YOU DON'T MAKE A CHANGE REAL SOON."

"I'll handle my husband, Hadley. With that divorcee out of the picture, you need me more than ever, I think." She shut the door and slid the plunger from his fingers. "I'LL NEED TO SEE THE PIPES BEFORE I MAKE UP MY MIND." She opened the top of his pants.

"Do you think this is some sort of joke?"

Using the tip of her filed fingernail, she followed the whorls of her initial on his skin. "It's a riot, dear. You always have to be Mr. Fix-It, don't you? Well some things can't be fixed. Some things are forever. No one can stop them."

"I've never seen him like this before. What if he asks you about me, Lucinda? What will you say?"

"I'll deny you to the bitter end, Hadley. I'd kill you myself before I admitted what you are to me."

"What am I to you? Do you even know?"

Her nail stopped short of finishing its journey. "You're my dirty little secret, Hadley. And it's gonna stay that way. Now are you actually gonna do some plunging, or are we through?"

Hadley closed his pants. "I got a shutter to fix."

Hadley was tightening the shutter when Nina appeared at the foot of his ladder. "Guess what. I've managed to *wheedle* two seats for the Plantation Festival this Saturday afternoon, and I'd like you to be my date. *Wheedle* is one of my Words of the Week, in case you're wondering. It means *to obtain through flattery.*"

"No thank you, Miss Nina," Hadley said. He said it politely and patiently, as if he hadn't played this same game with her a dozen or more times.

"Don't worry. The Plantation Festival is for white folks *and* colored folks. Have you ever seen mule racing? It's very exciting."

"We both know I can't go." It killed him to tell her no. He would have liked nothing more than to have her to himself for an entire afternoon.

"All righty then, I'll ask someone else; a young fellow I know called Pleasanton Nabb. If Father says yes, would you be willing to drive Mr. Nabb and myself to the festival?"

"Nabb? As in *Nabb's Luxury Autos*?"

"The very same."

"Yes, Miss Nina. I'd be happy to drive you and Mr. Nabb to the mule races if your father approves."

"Woohoo!" Nina said.

What Nina failed to mention was that Pleasanton Nabb lived in Rosedale where the festival was, and the festival was near Arkansas. Driving to Nabb's house meant they'd be spending more time alone than they ever had before.

Nail Number Eight:
Lily of the Valley

"You think you're pretty clever, don't you?" Hadley muttered as he tossed away the map.

Nina sat in the backseat, looking smug as sin. "Don't be so full of yourself. Pleasanton is a very good catch. I know plenty of girls who would drive weeks to see him."

"You like this boy?"

"Not as much as I like you, but he almost never fights me, and I find that highly refreshing."

There were times when Hadley wondered if it would be so terrible if Nina discovered the truth. Sure, she might be embarrassed after all the silliness, but wouldn't she like to know that Hadley loved her more than anything else in his whole entire life? Hadley thought she might.

"Father thinks I should marry Pleasanton. What do you think?"

Hadley started the engine. "I think that's a fine idea, but only if you love him." It occurred to him that he'd spent the majority of Nina's life sneaking peeks at her from the front seat of a car. He stole a peek now.

The mule races were a big social event in these parts, and Nina was wearing a black skirt with little white dots and a hat shaped like a plate. He noticed, with a pang of sorrow, that she looked more like a woman than a child.

"Do you think my mother loves my father?"

"She's told me so many times herself."

Nina sighed a Lucinda-sized sigh. "I don't think she does. I think Mother loves Mother and no one else. Not even you."

"Me?"

"Miriam Dewberry says that you and Mother are the worst kept secret in all of Madison County."

"You shouldn't listen to rumors, Miss Nina."

And there it was. Inevitable as death. Hadley couldn't spend five minutes with the girl without setting her off. "Quit treating me like I'm ten!" she shouted. "For Christ sake, do you think I'm stupid? I've know about the two of you for years."

It was a struggle to keep his eyes on the road. Hadley couldn't decide if she really knew anything, or if she was only fishing. He hit the curb and swerved back in the lane.

"How old were you the first time you made love to a woman?" she asked.

Hadley gripped the wheel so hard, he actually heard the stitches popping on his driving gloves.

"My first lover might be Pleasanton," she said. "Tonight."

Hadley ran the LaSalle into a Silverbell tree.

If there was one thing that was certain in all the world, it was the indisputable fact that Dickie loved his new LaSalle. "I love my new LaSalle!" he shouted when he first brought it home. He kissed the hood quite tenderly, that's how much he loved that car. Dickie was sure to kill Hadley now.

Hadley didn't care. As Silverbell pods rained on the roof, he whipped around to face her in the back seat. "I'll knock his lights out if he lays a finger on you."

Nina's lips curved with a smile.

When she was a little baby, he was constantly scared—scared that Lucinda would try and keep her from him, scared that clumsy Dickie would drop her on her head, but mostly scared that something bad was going to happen to her if he let her grow up at Wisteria Walk. One time, he actually ran in her room, grabbed her out of her scarlet red cradle, and started to leave with her. Luckily, the new nanny came in just then or Hadley might have had to add kidnapping to the list of nefarious things he'd done.

For the most part, his fears were irrational. Lucinda wasn't the most attentive mother, but she always made sure Nina was taken care of. Once he'd said goodbye to Flora forever, Lucinda never threatened to keep Nina from him again. More amazing than all this was Dickie. Nina was crazy about him. She actually shot guns with the man! Nina and Dickie were two peas in a pod. Yet Hadley had been tempted to steal her away for eighteen years, and he was already wishing that, instead of smashing Dickie's car, he'd taken off with Nina for good. He was of a mind to take her far away from Beatties Bluff and the slippery clutches of Pleasanton Nabb.

"You've broken Father's car," Nina said.

Hadley jabbed a finger in her face. "You need to be a good girl, Miss Nina. You deserve a wedding ring and a white dress before you start talking like you're talking."

"You're just jealous because Pleasanton might have the nerve to do what you won't."

There were tears prickling at the back of his eyes. He wanted to shake the life out of her. He wanted to hug her until he grew old. If she knew about his relationship with Lucinda, there seemed no reason not to tell her the rest. "Do things right, Nina. I wish I had."

"You called me Nina again. I like that."

Hadley squeezed her face so tight, he pinched off her words. "Stop it! Stop it right now!"

Nina's eyes simmered with anger and confusion, and Hadley couldn't take one more minute of it. He got out of the car and tried to clear his head by focusing on a different sort of damage. "Damn it to hell."

The back door opened, but Hadley was checking under the hood, and it took him a while to notice that Nina had taken off down the road.

She's as big a pain as her mother, he thought as he started after her. "Come back here, Nina," he pleaded. "Please don't run away."

Nina started running the minute he said *don't,* but she had on platform shoes and a narrow skirt, and she wobbled as she went.

"I'm sorry," Hadley called after her. "Slow down."

Nina looked back over her shoulder. "You're a coward, Hadley. A coward and a fraud!" Her eyes were glassy with tears.

Hadley saw the tears first. Then he saw the Ford flatbed that was barreling around the same bend that had spelled trouble for the LaSalle.

The driver was a stupid kid, you could tell that much even at a speeding glance. He had rotten reflexes, too. For instance, Hadley made out the kid's mouth taking the Lord's name in vain long before the truck jerked away.

"Nina!" Hadley screamed as the tires screeched, and Nina's eyes grew big and round, and the boy said *Lordy Lorrrrrrrrrrrrrrrd!*

Hadley and Nina tumbled on the shoulder of the road and the Ford whizzed past, tearing off a piece of polka-dotted skirt along with a piece of skin.

"Oh God. Oh God. Oh God," Hadley said, grabbing Nina and checking her face, her elbows, her knees.

The driver came to a screeching halt in the middle of the road and sprang out of the truck. "Are you okay?"

The kid was stupid all right, he had to be. He'd come around the bend way too fast for a fellow who wasn't even in the middle of a fight with a girl who thought she was in love with him because she didn't know she was his daughter. He was stupid, but he took one look at Dickie's smashed-up car and the way Hadley was gripping Nina, and he flexed his stringy muscles and said, "You giving this girl a hard time, Mister?"

Nina ignored the boy. She put her hands on Hadley's cheeks. "Tears?"

"Just say the word, Miss," the kid said. "I'll knock his block right off fer you."

"I don't want you to knock his block off," Nina growled. "Look at the man. Can't you see he loves me?"

Hadley was shaking like a seizure. What if she'd been killed? He could have lost her forever, quick as that. It was just like the day she fell through that stupid wooden stage. Hadley still had nightmares about that stage.

"Oh, I get it!" the kid said. "You're her daddy, ain't you? I should have knowed it right off. Anyone can see you got the same eyes."

Nina laughed at that. People always said she had Grandma Browning's eyes, but Hadley knew that wasn't right. Nina Worther-Holmes had the gardener's eyes.

Sadly, Nina failed to see any resemblance between their eyes or anything else. "You really do love me, don't you?"

Hadley took a deep breath. *Tell her the truth, you idiot.* He pictured Dickie aiming a pistol between his eyeballs after Nina went into hysterics and told the whole world she was his daughter. He didn't want to die, but this particular outcome might have offered some minimal form of relief after all the years of lies if not for the fact that he pictured something else too: He pictured the orange leather chairs Nina sat in every day after school with her friends at Ruffio's coffee shop. He pictured the Colored Counter where Mr. Ruffio let the black teenagers sit. If Hadley were suddenly to become her father, the orange chairs wouldn't want her. The Colored Counter, neither.

He opened his mouth. Nothing came out.

"It's Mother, isn't it?" Nina said. "She's what's keeping us apart."

It was there on the tip of his tongue. Like salvation. Like damnation. "I can't," he finally said.

"Can't what?" Nina asked.

Spit it out, man!

"Can't what?" she snarled.

"Can't help how I feel about her."

There it was, the only truth he could give her. After all these years, Hadley still loved Lucinda too much to destroy the phony existence that was so important to her.

There were other truths, too, and maybe they were even more important truths. He didn't want Dickie to murder him. That was a biggie. And he hated like hell to let his Mama down. The Crump Curse was no small thing to her. A full five lives stood to be ruined if Nina found out he was her daddy. Even so, he might have been willing to risk them all if only he hadn't lived the life he'd lived. To unburden his soul and set things straight, he'd have to turn Nina's skin from white to black and white, the distinction of which could best be determined through the use of an ordinary grocery sack.

Nina swatted at her tears. "To hell with you."

These were the last words Hadley heard before a black DeSoto came along, spotted the flatbed parked in the middle of the road and, veering sharply, ran him over instead.

ℭ

279

When Hadley woke up, he was in a ward in Saint Jo hospital, and he was all alone.

"Hello?" he yelled.

He yelled several times before anyone heard him, the ward being utterly empty and dark. It was the middle of the night, he was soon to learn. Miss Casey, the hefty colored woman who was the night nurse for the empty ward, informed him that his family had left two hours earlier.

"Family?"

"The negro lady and the white people."

The memory of the black DeSoto came screeching back to him. "There was a girl with me when I was hurt," Hadley said. "I need to know what happened to her."

"Don't choo wanna know what happened to you, honey?"

"Nina first," he said.

"Oh she jest fine. A lil banged up is all. You the one with skid marks acrost your belly."

His belly did hurt, now that she mentioned it. He touched his hospital gown and felt lumpy layers of gauze wrapped around his ribs.

"Partial splenectomy," Miss Casey said. She shrugged her big shoulders. "There's worser things. Better things, too."

"They took out my spleen?" Hadley said. "Don't I need that?'

"They took out part of it. A spleen helps keep a body well so it's a good thing to have, but you kin live without it if you take care not to go around sick people. Recovering is no picnic. Good thing you got so many peoples looking after you."

Hadley was lucky to be alive, everyone said so. Number One, he'd gotten pretty torn up on the inside after the De Soto ran him over. The doctors had seen a lot of bleeding going on in there and they were worried he would catch an infection. Number Two, Dickie was still cussing and weeping over his car. If ever there was a sign that a man ought to be making big changes in his life, it seemed as though this were it.

Because Mama had been such a faithful servant to Mr. Browning and had never even taken a day off sick, he gave her two weeks leave so she could nurse Hadley after he got out of the hospital. This was a lucky thing. Lucinda was terrible when people were sick and tended to make things worse. Nina had been nothing but hostile and distant since their fight. When it was all said and done, Mama and Dickie were the only *peoples* Hadley really had. And, while it was true that Dickie read the funny paper to Hadley every morning before he left for work, it was also true that the man never could seem to take his leave without saying, "I can't believe you wrecked it."

It took a long time for Hadley to see any improvement and, even after he was better, the doctors cautioned that he would get sick a lot easier with part of his spleen gone. It would be more dangerous if he got sick, too. They said he might want to take on a less rigorous career for a while. In the weeks it took for him to recover, Hadley had a lot of time to think, and he started toying with the idea of leaving Wisteria Walk. Much as he loved gardening, he was in a lot of pain if he bent over. If he was down on the ground doing something, he wanted to stay there for a while. It was the getting up and down that made him hurt so bad.

One morning, he was kneeling down pulling weeds in the petunia bed when Lucinda dropped a book on the ground in front of him. *As I Lay Dying*, the cover said. "I need your eyes, dear."

Hadley looked up from the petunias. "Are you out of your mind?"

They had managed to steer clear of each other while Hadley was healing, and Dickie seemed as though he was finally getting over his suspicions. It even looked as if he might get over his car.

Lucinda nudged the book with her toe. "I want to read this. Come up after lunch so we can look at it together."

Hadley wiped his hands on his pants. "Forget it, Lucinda. 'Reading' with you is the last thing I need."

"Oh fiddle. First you go and tear up your insides and almost croak, and now you won't even read with me. I hate Dickie for playing these stupid games. If he was a real man, he'd just go on and shoot you and have his daddy hire him a good attorney."

"Maybe you ought to suggest that to him, Lucinda."

"Do you know what he said the other night? Nina was waltzing around in the other room singing *It's a Sin to Tell a Lie*, and Dickie looked me square in the eye and told me that sometimes he'd swear that girl was part nigger."

Hadley swallowed. "Is it true you fired Narcissa yesterday?"

"Narcissa?" Lucinda said, like she didn't know who Narcissa was. "Why are you asking about her?"

"Because I had burrs in my pants this morning."

"No idea what that has to do with the price of tea in China, but I did fire her. Did you ever notice that her right eye is bigger than her left? Of course you did. I saw you gazing into that wonky old thing just the other day."

"She got Dreft in it when she was washing your slips. I was helping her get it out."

"Yeah, well I never did like the looks of that big ugly eye. I couldn't eat my breakfast with that big ugly eye always looking at me."

Hadley nodded. "I'm gonna get a new job, Lucinda. It's time. I need to leave before anyone else gets hurt."

"Then you best read with me while you can."

But Hadley didn't. Hadley couldn't.

◌

The next day, he went over to talk to Mr. Shel Boyd of Sunset Lane about a driving job. Mr. Boyd was a wary looking fellow. He stepped out the front door with his hands clutched behind his back and a frown that made his whole face squash up like a sock doll that'd been stitched together too tight. "The job would be a step down for you, son," he said when Hadley told him that he was interested in the driving position. "I can't think why you'd want to take care of automobiles when you've got such a grand reputation for gardening. Unless you're in some sort of trouble over there at the Worther-Holmes place?"

Hadley didn't want to mention his halved spleen. "I just like automobiles, Mr. Boyd. Honest. I always have."

Mr. Boyd shot a look at his upstairs window where a woman stood in the curtain crack, looking down at them. "My wife's twelve years younger than me, Mr. Crump, but perhaps you already know that? My ears work just fine though, if you catch my meaning? I believe I'll say good day to you now."

Hadley did not catch Mr. Boyd's meaning. "What about Mr. Farley or Mr. Stumps? I heard they might be hiring."

He turned his squashed face up to that curtain crack again. "They got wives, too, don't they?"

Hadley was thunderstruck. He'd thought Nina was making up about the rumors just to bother him, but was it true? Was there really talk going around town about him and Lucinda?

Mama confirmed his suspicions later when he told her about Mr. Boyd. "Oh honey," she said, giving his arm a little pity-pat. "People like to talk, you know that. Mrs. Worther-Holmes fires more maids than anyone in town. Of course nobody knows a thing. They just gossip like they do."

They were eating lunch at the *Sunny Side Café*, the *Dinner Bell* no longer being an option. "I don't get it, Mama. I mind my own business. I do a good job. Why should anyone care about that sort of stuff?" But even as he said the words, Hadley knew how naive they sounded. It was a known fact that people liked nothing so much as sex. They even sold soap with it. Hadley knew because he'd been building radios for years, and he was fond of listening to them. "Oh hell. I wonder what Dickie is waiting for?"

"You could try Forest Green," Mama suggested. "That's fifty miles from here."

Hadley reached across the table and took her hand. "Are you ashamed of me, Mama?"

Mama squeezed his finger. "Got no right to feel ashamed. I only wish you were a happier man for it all."

Mama hadn't brought up Lucinda Worther-Holmes since Hadley was a kid. After Flora, she seemed to give up. He rubbed his thumb over the back of her hand, surprised to note how thin it was. "I'll leave the state if I have to."

"Maybe that's for the best."

A man had to be crazy to give up a good job these days. People weren't hiring domestic help like they used to. A lot of folks didn't have much money anymore. "Times are awfully tough," he said. "And I got me this bum spleen now."

"There's plenty of work you could do. You know how to do so many things."

"I reckon that's true."

"Sure it is. Maybe you could get assembly work? *Armstrong Tire and Rubber* just opened up over in Natchez, I heard. Or you could try the Magnolia Mill. You just need a fresh start, that's all."

"A fresh start. I like the sound of that."

Hadley knew he was fortunate. He could paint and plant and hammer things together and anyway, he wasn't a kid anymore. He had a whole big box of things to show for himself now. Thanks to Phoetus Day, he owned one Tiffany shoehorn, a Huddie Ledbetter record, a special deck of forty-eight playing cards for pinochle, a tortoise shell traveler's comb, a Borsalino fedora, and a good pocket watch that had never even been wound. He could pawn his box and live off it for a year, if he had to. By the time they left the café, he'd decided to use his box to fund a fresh start.

ॐ

"You'd leave me, Hadley Crump? After all we've been through together?"

Hadley and Lucinda were alone in the Reading Room, but he went into the hall to make sure no one was listening to them. He was not there to read. "People speculate about us, Lucinda. Did you know that?"

"So what? People speculate about Babe and her gardener, too."

Hadley gave her a pointed look.

"But Forest Green is so far away. What about our daughter? Don't you care about her anymore?"

"So now she's *ours,* is she? Well, let's go break the good news, shall we?"

"What is this? Just because you aren't getting a little something on the side, you don't care about her anymore?"

Lucinda's words hurt worse than a slap. Hadley closed his eyes and took a deep breath and thought about the life he might have had with Flora. He did that sometimes. He pictured their kids and their house. He even gave them a dog sometimes because dogs were a sign of stability and roots.

"Wake up, you fool," Lucinda snapped. "Don't you care about us?"

"You'll never know how much," he whispered. The children and the dog dissolved from his brain.

"Then don't go to Forest Green."

"You don't know what's it's like with Nina. It's killing me, Lucinda."

Lucinda brightened suddenly. "But she's leaving for Sophie Newcomb in August, Hadley. Didn't you hear the news?"

"Who is Sophie Newcomb?"

"It's a women's college in Tulane."

Hadley sat on the window seat. "Louisiana?"

"It'll be good for her. It'll be good for us all."

"What about Dickie?"

"Dickie is a mess right now," she said, and she actually looked sorry for her husband. "He doesn't want Nina living two hundred miles away. It's tearing him up."

"Well, I can understand that, Lucinda."

"If you left us, Hadley, we'd have to hire three people to do all the things you do around here. Maybe four. It would cause Dickie more chest pain right now if you go than if you stay."

"I'll think about it," Hadley said.

His baby was going to college. In Tulane!

☙

A couple of days later, Lucinda called him upstairs. "I need your help packing these things," she said. She was sitting on the floor in Nina's old nursery, folding up a pink blanket.

"No," he mouthed when he saw the blanket with its embroidered sweet peas and white eyelet trim.

"Remember this?" she said, as if he might actually have forgotten. Mama had made the sweet pea quilt as a christening present for Nina. "It was always one of my favorites," Lucinda said.

"You packed that away a long time ago, Lucinda."

"Nina gave me a list of items that she wants to bring with her."

"Why does she want a baby blanket?"

"Girls like to have their favorite things around them when they leave home, dear. I would have thought you'd know that by now." She patted the floor beside her. "I can't do this on my own."

"This might surprise you, Lucinda, but I've got real work to do today."

"This is real work. Now get in here."

There was a big cardboard box marked with Nina's name, and Hadley sat down by it.

"Hand me something else," she said.

"She'll be needing this at college, I suppose?" Hadley grumbled. He handed her an Uncle Wiggly rattle from a mountainous pile of old stuff. It was cruel, really. Every bootie, diaper pin, and tangled bow stirred a different memory. He picked up a well-played-with doll by the foot, dangling it like a dead mouse. He and Lucinda had had one of their biggest arguments over this faded, little rag-baby.

Hadley had tried to buy it for Nina the day he went with Lucinda and the kids to the *Hoxie Bros. Gigantic 3 Ring Circus.* Because something came up at the last minute, Dickie had asked Hadley to walk around with his family in his place, and it turned out to be Hadley's all time favorite day ever. Nina was seven at the time, and she had these brown eyes that no human heart could possibly say no to. Even Lucinda's heart was vulnerable. When Nina said she wanted the doll, Lucinda insisted on buying it herself. Hadley had already bought the boys popguns, but for some reason, Lucinda wouldn't let him get the doll.

"What would Dickie think if he heard you bought the kids toys?" she'd asked.

"He'll think I like the kids, which I do."

"No. I won't have it. Either I'm paying for the doll or we're putting it back."

"Don't put it back, Mother," Nina mewled.

Hadley was angry as hell, but there wasn't a thing he could do about it. "Besides," Lucinda said. "You can't afford a rag-baby."

Regardless of the incident with the doll, Hadley loved spending the day with them. For a few hours, it felt like he had a family of his own.

"Mimi," Hadley whispered. This was what Nina had named the doll.

Lucinda took it from him like it was a real baby. "That was a fun day, wasn't it?"

Even though Mimi played perfectly into her plans, Hadley didn't feel like Lucinda was trying to be mean anymore. She was remembering that day, too. "Do you recall how much that doll cost?"

"One dollar and ten cents," he said.

Lucinda patted its yarn curls. "I should have let you buy it for her."

"Yeah. That would have been nice."

"How much you got on you now?"

Hadley checked his pockets. "One dollar and ten cents."

Lucinda held out her hand, and Hadley gave her a dollar and two nickels. She added Mimi to the new box. "I'll send it with her," she said.

The next day, Lucinda asked him to paint the foyer, and when he went to put on his paint clothes, he found a package on his bed.

It was wrapped in cream-colored paper and tied with a pale blue bow. Hadley didn't trust it. When he finally got up the nerve to rip off the paper, it was just a book. *Anna Karenina*. It looked as deceptively boring as it had all those years ago.

He started to put it on the nightstand when he noticed another package. He opened this one with a bit more gusto. *The Adventures of Tom Sawyer*. It was musty and decrepit and warped with age, but when Hadley opened the cover, Tom and Huck were waiting inside, young and devious as ever.

Dracula was in the bathroom. It still had an old price tag taped to the cover that read *Pringles Second Hands*. It was the same book Spitbone had bought for him twenty years before. A blank piece of violet paper served as a bookmark. It marked the page where Jonathon is seduced by the brides.

When Hadley looked up from the brides, Lucinda was standing in the doorway. She handed him one final package.

Inside was Nina's first book. *Uncle Wiggly's Automobile*.

"Don't leave us," she said.

He stacked the chapters of his life in the cardboard suitcase he'd picked up at *Wendell's Pawn* when he sold his Phoetus Day gifts. Mister Wendell had given him one hundred and twenty dollars for his box of gifts and thrown the suitcase in for free. There was only one Phoetus Day gift that Hadley had elected to keep, and that was a Dictionary filled with dried flowers. Lucinda had pressed a marigold in the "M"s and a violet in the "V"s and a buttercup in the "D"s, because she thought it was a dandelion.

"I'll miss you if you leave, Hadley," Lucinda said. "I already miss you madly and badly."

Hadley dug his fingernails into the lid of the suitcase and tried to think of all the things he wasn't going to miss. Like watching Dickie kiss Lucinda.

Lucinda sighed a shaky sigh. "Sometimes I wish we were still ten years old so we could do it all over again. Do you ever wish that?"

"Never."

Lucinda looked surprised and hurt. "You don't?"

"I'd never wish for that, Lucinda. Not unless it could be different."

She squatted down by the suitcase. "Different how?"

"You know how."

Lucinda fingered her hair. "Tell me anyway."

Hadley didn't tell her about the parallel life he wished for with Flora. He took his wishing further back than that. "I'd change it at the attic part. I'd change it one of two ways."

"In what way?"

"You'd still come to the attic only instead of biting me, you'd give me a different birthday present. You'd say, "To hell with everything. I want to marry you and spend the rest of my life with you.'"

"I hope your other wish is more realistic."

"It is. You'd never show up. You'd leave me waiting around like a fool, and I'd be sad and disappointed, but you'd never come to the attic. You'd let me go on and live my life because deep down, you'd love me enough to know that I'd be better off without you."

"You'd really wish it all away?"

"Yes." He looked at the books that filled an otherwise empty suitcase. Would he really wish his whole life away? "Maybe." He touched the corner of Uncle Wiggly. "I don't know, Lucinda. I really don't know."

❦

The sign in the Gibb's front yard read: *P & W Reality Company ~ A better home for a better tomorrow.* The house had a clean coat of yellow paint and an abandoned look about it. Hadley stumbled up the front walk and peered through the kitchen window. The room was empty.

"Would you like to see it?" a voice asked from somewhere behind him.

Hadley jumped. He hadn't heard the black Cadillac pull up to the curb.

A young man wearing a three-piece suit and a felt fedora thrust his hand out to Hadley. "Delbert Wiggins, P & W Reality. What do you say, old man? Shall we have a look inside?"

"Yes," Hadley said. "I do believe I'd like to have a look inside."

"Thadda boy!" Mr. Wiggins clapped him on the back. "It's a real gem, I tell you. A real gem."

"I know," Hadley said.

Truth told, Hadley didn't remember how he'd come to be standing on Dixon Street at six o'clock on a Saturday evening. He was at the hardware store, last he knew. The sun was still bright. He was looking at paintbrushes. Now the sun was setting.

Mr. Wiggins flipped a light switch, and Hadley came face to face with the milk-white glow of four freshly painted walls. The previous spring, a newspaperman had taken Hadley's photograph next to the wisteria, and that's what those glowing walls reminded him of, that same eyeball-searing flash. He blinked now like he'd blinked then. He probably looked as boozy-eyed as he did in that picture in the Beatties Bluff Dispatch. He turned in a circle, disoriented. Where the birdcages and collectable spoons? Where were the magazines? Everything was gone.

"The kitchen's through here," Mr. Wiggins said. "It comes with a brand new Electric Buffet stove."

Hadley entered the kitchen as if entering a dream. Part of him could still see the mail and the feathers and the plates of chess pie. He could almost smell the pie. In reality, the table where Mr. Gibbs had once stuffed himself with peas was now gone. But for four thumbprint-size grooves in the linoleum, there wasn't a single sign that Hadley had not dreamed up that table. The room smelled like paint instead of pie.

"Where did she go?" he asked.

"I'm sorry? Where did who go?"

"The woman who lived in this house. Do you know where she went?"

Mr. Wiggins' enormous shoulder pads went rigid under his big square suit. "Are you interested in buying this house, Mister, or are you just snooping?"

"Just snooping," Hadley said. He headed for the sun porch.

He remembered it red. He remembered it blue. He thought of all that hogwash he'd given Flora about a room having emotions. He braced himself for the emptiness of the place.

"I hope you haven't been wasting my time," Wiggins said, but Hadley barely heard him.

Here it was, the place where he fell in love with her. Hadley pressed his hand against the wall and felt time fall away.

"Hmm. The painters must have missed this room," the realtor remarked.

"No they didn't," Hadley said. "She left it blue."

☙

Words. There were times when Hadley wished he'd never learned to read them. They came in dirty novels, on violet paper, under blue paint. They left their mark on his skin. Saying goodbye to Wisteria Walk would mean saying goodbye to twenty years' worth of words carved into the backs of china cabinets and the lips of windowsills. A tiny *nipple* had been carved into the window seat and there was a soup tureen in the kitchen with a *dong* hidden in its lid. Centuries from now, when they were all dead and buried, a man might bend over to tie his shoe one morning and see Hadley's *yearning* still clinging to the baseboard.

The fact that Nina was similarly stricken with an obsession for words, seemed like sure proof of his paternity. Her notebooks overflowed with *Words of the Week,* many of which she used against him. Recently, her notes had trickled to one or two every few days. *I don't give a darn about college, if you must know. I am fleeing under DURESS and it's all because of you . . .* He fed Nina's words to the stove because they were too dangerous and painful to save. If Hadley left Wisteria Walk, he'd be fleeing words as much as anything. They lifted him up, and they tore him down. He wondered where he'd be without them.

A Going Away party had been planned for Nina, and the staff from both Wisteria Walk and Browning House had been invited to attend. At Nina's request, it was a simple affair with cream cake and sparkle punch and white paper napkins, but Mister Rich and Mister Guido had put on suits, and the oldest boy was on punch-ladling duty, and the youngest agree to play the piano. Mama had been invited, too. She sat on a wooden folding chair and ate her cake with the rest of the female help, all of whom picked at their food and squeaked about in their seats, barely saying a word. It was upsetting to the staff to have their positions reversed, if only for an afternoon. Most of them were so worried that Mister Rich couldn't properly handle that ladle, they couldn't even enjoy the break.

Hadley looked around the Fireside Room and thought about how the place had looked when it was brand new. He'd been afraid of the house back then, with its complicated conveniences and its wisteria-less lawn. Now the yard flowered from stem to stern, and the icebox was out of date. The pristine walls had been scuffed by children. Empty bottles of *Berry's Best* sat atop the dusty radios in the Radio Room. Hadley had cleaned and hammered and fetched wayward rodents from every secret cranny. He knew which floorboards objected the loudest when you stepped on them and which ones could be counted on to keep silent. The place was as familiar to him as his own skin.

Nina had called him aside before the party to give him one final chance. "Just say the word, and I'll stay. We both know you're going to miss our anomalous love with every beat of your heart."

Anomalous? "The place won't be the same without you, Miss Nina, but we're all very excited for you."

She pounded her fist on a newly painted apple-green wall. "If you let me walk out of here tomorrow, I will walk out of your life forever. Do you understand?"

It was all he could do to hold himself together. Everyone was sad that Nina was going, but Hadley had not been able to eat. He hadn't had more than five hours of sleep in five days. He'd read *Uncle Wiggly's Automobile* two dozen times since Lucinda had given it to him. "What about Christmas?"

Her voice was low and trembling as she leaned close to his face. "I may be here for Christmas and a Sunday dinner or two. I might even say hello when I see you, but you will be dead to me in my heart. Are you prepared to live with that?"

Hadley couldn't answer because Hadley couldn't speak.

She handed him a lily of the valley. "Goodbye, Hadley."

When he joined Mama in the circle of folding chairs, he still had the flower in his sweaty hand. "It must be hard to see her go," Mama said.

He crushed the flower by mistake, and when he opened his fingers, the bells were limp and flat in the cradle of his palm. In eighteen years, Mama had never said one word about Nina. Some Sundays she would send Hadley home with *Silhouette Pudding* because *Silhouette Pudding* was Nina's favorite dessert. But other Sundays it would be bourbon balls instead because Mister Rich could wolf down a whole plate of anything that was chocolate in two minutes flat, especially if it had bourbon in it. Other weeks, it would be Mister Guidio's treat of choice, *Mystery Cake* with *Philly-Vanilly* – frosting—the the mystery ingredient (unbeknownst to Guido) being tomato soup. Mama never played favorites. She never asked if Nina could be her granddaughter.

They sipped their punch and watched Mister Guido hammer his way through *Goodnight Irene*. Dickie was standing by the piano with his arm slung over Nina's shoulder. Lucinda stood next to them, swaying to the music, her eyes half-closed.

"They're a complete family, aren't they, Hadley?" Mama said. "A mother. A father. A houseful of cousins. That's a good thing. A real gift."

Hadley took her slender hand in his. "It's what you always said was right."

"That's true. That's what I said."

He squeezed her fingers. "Our family ain't been so bad either, has it?"

Mama's reached into her carrying bag and pulled out her Bible. Pressed between the tissue-thin pages was a single four-leaf clover, the heart-shaped leaves brittle and clear with age. "Do you recognize it? You picked it from that clover patch many moons ago."

Hadley didn't dare touch the little thing, it was so frail after all these years. "I never knew you kept it."

"Well I did," Mama said. She closed the Bible and returned it to her bag. "I'm a lucky woman, Hadley. Having you was the best thing I ever done, and that's the USDA Certified Truth."

Hadley nodded. He thought about what it would be like to say *Merry Christmas, Miss Nina* every year and to hear her say *Merry Christmas, Hadley* and know that she didn't really mean it. Then he thought about what it would be like to never see her again.

"I don't think I can leave, Mama," he said. He began reshaping the little broken bells one bell at a time.

It would hurt like nothing had ever hurt before if Nina really shut him out of her life as promised. His heart would surely begin to match his spleen, only it would feel so much worse, and having his spleen cut in half had hurt like a son of a gun. But if he never saw his daughter again, that would be unbearable. Hadley had learned that it was rare to get everything you wanted in the world. You couldn't always control your circumstances, but you could make the best of them. "Everything I care about is here, Mama."

"Oh honey," Mama said. "I don't want you to leave either, but are you sure staying is a good idea?" It hurt to see how she worried about him. He wished he could have given her an easier time. "What about Mr. Worther-Holmes?"

"I don't want to leave you, Mama. It's as simple as that. Anyway, Dickie might not know it, but he needs me. I don't think he likes Lucinda any more than she likes him. Without me around, the place would go to rack and ruin." He nodded at the blonde woman dancing by herself to *Goodnight Irene*. "Don't want to leave her, neither."

Mama glared at Lucinda. "After all she's done to you?"

Lucinda pinched the hem of her dress and did a little twirl.

"I wish she could have loved me. It would have been so nice."

"You got black skin, and she's got white," Mama said. "What would it have changed?"

"Everything," Hadley said. Lucinda opened her eyes and smiled at him. "Every little thing."

Meg

Nail Number Nine: The Language of Flowers

The world changed suddenly and unexpectedly for Meg Baldwin the day Old Hadley took sick, a trick of fate that snuck up like a bad germ, which is really what it was. For Meg, that was a memorable day.

From far away, a person might take Grandma's gardener for a young kid, he was always so peppy. Up close he looked like any other old man, except he could bend and reach and lift like it was nothing. He fooled you like that. Meg realized there was something wrong when she drove up for one of her weekly visits and he looked like an old man from all the way up the street.

There were a sad few things to like about Meg's grandmother, but she had to admit, the woman had always treated her help surprisingly decent, Old Hadley and Patti Carol, the housekeeper, being the extent of her help. It was that single idiosyncrasy that kept Meg coming back. That, and Pinochle.

"It won't kill you to play cards with her for an hour or two," Mom would always say whenever Meg felt like blowing off a visit. "Now that Father's gone, we're all she's got."

So even though spending time with Grandma was about as appealing as flossing (another habit Meg submitted to with teeth-gritting disdain), she went every Thursday after she got off at the bank. The habit was such that her car could not be made to drive anywhere on Thursday evening that did not involve Grandma.

Every Thursday, she picked up two Big Macs, a large fry, and a couple of small Cokes, the entire bag of which she and her grandmother would politely consume at the dining room table on a lace tablecloth, the French fries divided equally between two Nippon plates with blue butterflies hand-painted around the rim. Grandma ate Big Macs like they were filet mignon, actually cutting her hamburger into dainty little bites and spearing them with a silver fork. Sometimes she ate her Big Mac wearing a hat, if she happened to have a Library Committee meeting that day. Meg knew she only ever wore a hat in the house when she'd forgotten to take it off, yet she never reminded her grandmother that she was still wearing it. You had to save that for special occasions. Should their conversation become particularly annoying, Meg would pick a feather or a wooden cherry and fix her gaze on it until Grandma finally noticed and took the hat off in a huff. It was the only way to shame the woman. Once, Grandma had left her gloves on and not even noticed. That really threw her for a loop.

After this fancy meal, Old Hadley would come in from the yard and they'd have a game of cards. Sometimes Patti Carol played, too, but usually not. Patti Carol was such a poor sport at Pinochle, she made Grandma look like Little Mary Sunshine.

"What's wrong with Old Hadley?" Meg asked on the day she saw him looking like an old man from all the way up the street.

"Wrong?" Grandma said. She sprang from her chair with uncommon sprite and flew to the dining room window to squint at him through the blinds. "Why, there's not a thing wrong with that old fool. What makes you think there's something wrong?"

"He was sitting on the steps when I got here. I've never seen him sit."

"He's just being lazy," Grandma said.

"I've never seen him lazy," Meg said. She buried her nose in the sweet pink flower he'd plucked off the princess tree. "He gave me this."

"Why?" Grandma said. "Is it your birthday?"

"No."

"Hmm," Grandma said.

The funny thing about Old Hadley and birthdays was that he had been at every single one of Meg's birthday parties for her entire life. Grandma was so formal, she drank pop from a champagne flute, but her gardener got a piece of cake every year on Meg's birthday. And on Stephen and Henry's birthdays, too. He was even there when they all got baptized. Grandma threw lavish birthday parties. She had that much going for her. It seemed ordinary to Meg that Old Hadley should attend them until the year she was allowed to invite Nancy Youngerman to her Sleeping Beauty birthday party, and Nancy wondered why the dark-skinned man in the gardening clothes was eating an Maleficent cupcake at the table with the white grownups.

"Who is that guy?" Nancy asked.

"Old Hadley," Meg said.

"What's an Old Hadley?" Nancy asked.

"He cuts the grass and plants the flowers," Meg said, as though this made him good as an uncle.

When you went to Grandma's house for a party, there was always Grandma, Grandpa, and Old Hadley, and after Grandpa had the heart attack—Grandma and Old Hadley. Patti Carol didn't come to birthday parties unless they were during the week. Weekends were for Patti Carol's own kids.

The week after he gave her the pink flower, Meg drove up the driveway and Old Hadley was nowhere to be seen.

"Shhh . . . " Grandma said when Meg walked in the door. "Hadley's feeling poorly."

"Has he got that bad bronchitis Stephen is just getting over?" Meg asked.

Bronchitis was going around, and Old Hadley had long suffered from a poor immune system. It didn't normally slow the man down.

This being the second Thursday of the month, it was Library Committee day, but Grandma wasn't wearing one of her Jacques Fath designer dresses, much less her fruit hat. Grandma never missed a committee meeting.

"The doctor came this morning, and he isn't sure what it is. I'm supposed to take him for tests tomorrow."

Meg held up the McDonalds bag. "Hungry?"

"Christ, Meg. How can you even think of eating at a time like this?" Grandma scolded.

That was the last day Meg brought Big Macs because, after that, Old Hadley was always worse. "Go and sit with him for awhile, will you, Meg?" Grandma said the fourth week he was in bed. Grandma never looked so tired.

It had been a month since the man was up and around, and Meg was worried what she would see when she went in his bedroom. Before he'd taken sick, she'd never even set foot inside his house. Now she spent every visit there.

Grandma's house was an old house and everything in it was old-fashioned and smelled like yellowed books. The oldness of the place made Meg sneeze every time she walked through the front door. Old Hadley's house was worse, a peculiar blend of bleach and stale air. There had been a cold snap recently so you couldn't open a window. Thankfully, on this particular visit, it was a beautiful day, and the first thing Meg did was crank open the window above his bed. Old Hadley opened his eyes and took a great breath. "The lilacs are blooming."

"Yes they are," Meg said, even though the only thing she smelled was sickness and Borateem.

There was a chair pulled up to the bed with a blanket and pillow on it, and this surprised Meg. Grandma was the last person you wanted around when you were sick. She got put out if you asked for an aspirin. She was deathly afraid of "germies".

"Your wisteria is looking a little wild these days," Meg told Old Hadley. "When do you think you'll get back to it?"

There was sunshine lighting up his face now, and Meg was amazed how much he'd shriveled. He'd always been a bony geezer, but his poor little head looked like a raisin on a toothpick now, and his thick dark hair was going gray.

"I wonder if you could water them until I'm back on my feet?" he said. "I'm worried about my wild flowers, too. Fairy spuds need lots of moisture."

Worry about your own moisture! Meg thought. He was looking more dried up than the dried up fairy spuds she'd passed on her way in. "I'll water everything before I go."

He seemed to rest easier after that. "I'd ask Lucinda to do it, but she's got her hands full with me."

"What does the doctor say?" Meg asked. It surprised her to realize how much his diminished state upset her. She'd always liked Old Hadley, of course. She liked him more than Grandma, actually.

He waved a skeletal hand. "He charged me twenty-five dollars to tell me I'm old. I should rest, he said, as though that'll make me young again."

Meg laughed. Was Old Hadley ever young? This seemed doubtful. "Do you want anything? Are you thirsty? I could read you a book?"

Old Hadley's room was full of books. That was practically all there was. He had a nice large walnut shelf for books, but the contents had long since spilled down into piles on the floor. The dresser and nightstand were stacked with books, too. One dresser drawer was half-open, and the red corner of a book poked out. He was like one of those crazy old lady's with too many cat only his cats were all books.

She picked up the book next to his bed. "You're quite a reader, aren't you?"

"I reckon I am."

Meg opened to the beginning of the book and started to read:

He was an old man who fished alone in a skiff in the Gulf Stream and he had gone eighty-four days now without taking a fish...

"What do you think you're doing?" Grandma barked. She stood in the doorway with her hands on her hips, looking fit to be tied.

"I was just reading," Meg said.

"Give me that," Grandma said, and she snatched the book away. "Go home, Meg. I can take it from here."

Meg shrugged and climbed to her feet. "I'll run the hose before I go," she told Old Hadley.

꿍

Outside, the pansies looked up at her with sad little purple faces. Meg couldn't shake the feeling that the flowers missed Old Hadley as much as he missed them. She got a whiff of something tasty and sweet and knew it must be the moth orchids. Moth orchids smelled like vanilla ice cream. You could smell Lily of the Valley, too, because there were a lot of those around. They looked as lonely as the pansies.

Thanks to Old Hadley, Grandma's wisteria was the envy of the county. It had been featured once in Southern Living magazine. Every year, during the first week of April, the Dispatch came out and took pictures of it. The front page would be spread corner to corner with pearly clusters of Grandma's wisteria. SPRING IS HERE! If you ordered a pizza from Pizza Hut, you didn't even have to give an address. You just had to say it was for the house with the wisteria. And when relatives visited Beattie's Bluff, seeing the sites almost always included a ride out to the Beattie's Bluff bluff, one complimentary game at Turner's Mini Golf, and a long, slow coast past Wisteria Walk. It broke Meg's heart to realize that Old Hadley was missing the blooming season this year. She thought of him tucked in that dark stuffy room.

"This will never do," she told the orchids.

Grandma all but slammed into Meg as she rushed past with the first armful. "What on earth are you doing?" Grandma asked.

Meg took the tin pitcher off the windowsill. "I'm going to need as many of these as you can find, Grandma."

Grandma watched her fill the pitcher and dump the orchids in. "Smells like ice cream," Grandma said. She went over to her own kitchen after that and returned with a silver platter loaded with hoity toity vases. The hoity toity vases were used up before they made it through the orchids.

The crystal supply having been exhausted, Grandma started pouring pickles down the drain. "Get the ketchup, Meg."

Bottles and jars were working out nicely for the flowers until the sink backed up. They switched to drinking glasses then. Wisteria tumbled across the kitchen table like lavender caterpillars. Poppy petals trailed the floor. Meg carried in magnolias, pink bush honeysuckle, and orhids. Grandma seemed especially partial to the orchids. She even rattled off a peculiar little poem about them: "A rose will prick my finger, and a bluebell makes me blue, but the soft mouth of an orchid makes me dream of kissing you."

Meg stared at her grandmother.

"Hand me a juice cup," Grandma said.

It took them nearly half an hour to carry all the flowers into Old Hadley's room and find a place to put them. Stacks of books became pedestals, and lamps were unplugged and cleared out of the way. Old Hadley watched blue stars and bead lilies cross the room and never said a word. By the time they were done, the outside gardens were choppy and bald, and Old Hadley's room was a messy explosion of purples, oranges, and reds. Even Meg could smell the lilacs now.

"But your Garden Girls are coming tomorrow," he finally said.

Grandma had been named Queen of the Roses more years than not and never tired of reminding you that she was royalty. "Don't worry about that. It's still prettier out there than Mercy Levine's pathetic little excuse for a flower bed." Grandma sniffed. Mercy Levine was usually crowned Queen of the Roses during the *not* years.

In truth, the garden was all stems now, yet Grandma was actually humming as she rearranged a bucket full of snowball lobelias.

"Stephen and Henry are going to stop by tomorrow," Meg told Old Hadley. He was happy about the flowers and even happier to hear about the boys coming for a visit, but she could read the unspoken question in his eyes. "Mom still has a cold and says she better stay away."

Mom and Grandma didn't get along. They probably hadn't spoken two words to each other in all Meg's years. Mom felt responsible for the old woman, certainly, but that didn't mean they were friendly. At family gatherings, they ignored one another with the exception of what Meg and her brothers called *The Nod.* "Mother," Mom would say, and then she would do this quick stiff nod. "Nina," Grandma would say, and she'd give a quick stiff nod, too. Then they'd be so busy taking lids off Jell-O molds or setting the table that they couldn't be bothered to look at each other again. It was creepy.

One of the things they disagreed about the most was Old Hadley. Mom had a housekeeper, too, and she gave Tilda an extra twenty-five dollars at Christmas, and that was that. Tilda did not come to birthday parties and baby christenings. Mom said it would have been stupid to even ask her.

"Do you want to spend five minutes more at the bank than you absolutely have to?" she asked Meg.

Mom wasn't as snooty as Grandma when it came to most stuff, but she did not like to see Old Hadley eating birthday cake next to her at the dining room table. "Father should never have let that get started," she complained.

When Meg suggested that her mother ought to go visit Old Hadley, Mom had asked, "Why would I visit the gardener?"

Mom visited orphans and brought tater tot casseroles to shut-ins, but she would not visit Old Hadley. Dad had dropped by with the boys twice, and Mom had ridiculed him for it.

"Mother has always given that man too much attention and now you're doing it, too. What next? Shall we offer him a kidney?"

"That's pretty heartless, Nina," Dad said, so Mom threw a piece of buttered toast at him, and he had to go change his pants before work.

Mom acted furious whenever the subject of Old Hadley came up, yet she asked after him one day completely out of the blue. "Any improvement?" she asked.

"Maybe you should go and see for yourself?"

"No thank you," Mom said, and she wrinkled her nose like Meg had just asked her to root through the trash. "I was simply wondering how much longer we can expect to be waiting on him."

Meg clenched her fists. "Oh, probably just another month or so, and then we can bury him and be done with it."

Mom was doing Jane Fonda at the moment, but she stopped mid-lunge, and all the blood drained from her face. "You really think he's dying?"

This was the first time Meg had actually admitted the truth to herself. "He's worse every week, Mom. He can't get out of bed anymore."

"Well," she mumbled. She gave her falling legwarmer a tug and straightened the sweatband on her left wrist. "I had no idea this was so serious."

"That's because you're too high and mighty to pay him a visit," Meg said. She hurried and left before the woman could throw a barbell at her.

The most startling thing about Old Hadley's decline was the way Grandma declined along with him. She was not a small woman by any stretch, and yet she shriveled up, too, matching his pathetic portions at mealtime as if to show support for his poor appetite. Grandma was busy with her committees normally and the hours of sitting in a chair beside Old Hadley were robbing her of zest. Every hour she spent in that chair next to him looked to age her another year. Her poofy hair drooped and fell out of place after so many missed beauty parlor appointments. Her clothes got too big. She creaked when she walked.

"We need to get you out of the house, Grandma," Meg said. "You're as pasty as Old Hadley." But Grandma was not easily budged from his house.

"Will you help me get these dead carnations out of here?" Grandma asked.

The carnations were done, that much was true, and so was the vase of daisies with bright blue baby's breath. Grandma slid the kitchen wastebasket around behind her, tossing in soggy clumps as she moved around the room. Meg did the same with the bathroom can.

"These gardenias sure lasted long, didn't they?" Meg whispered, so as not to wake the snoring man.

And then it hit her.

Old Hadley grew dahlias and daffodils and delphinium. He had every kind of wildflower a Mississippian could hope to coax from the earth, and there was a rose garden and a lily garden to boot. But Old Hadley did not grow carnations. She stared at the gardenia in her hand. Old Hadley didn't grow gardenias either. "Grandma?"

Grandma motioned her into the hall. "It turns out that Orville Brix from the Good Samaritans is having a slow time with his flower shop. I used Hadley as an excuse to help him out. Don't let that get around, dear. Orv Brix might be a Samaritan, but he won't have anyone pitying him."

Meg hadn't thought to question the fact that all the flowers in Old Hadley's room had stayed fresh for weeks. They seemed as commonplace as the books now, and she had begun to take them for granted.

Before Meg could say anything else on the subject, the doorbell rang. No one ever rang the bell at Old Hadley's house, and she thought it might be her mother. She didn't give a crap if Mom was a cold-hearted snob, but for some silly reason, she could tell Old Hadley was hoping to see her. Maybe he didn't realize that Mom didn't like him? She ran to the window and pushed the curtain aside. A pale pink van painted with the words *Brix Florist* was parked in Grandma's driveway.

Ten minutes later, they were back at the sink refilling cans and ketchup bottles from the tap. Brix had delivered twenty-five fat bouquets wrapped in green paper. Grandma extracted a white rose from the rose bouquet and a blue iris from the iris bouquet. She snipped off ends with her kitchen sheers to make the flowers stand right in the etched Lalique water pitcher that she normally took from the china cabinet once a year only for the Beattie's Bluff Theatre Guilde's Victorian Christmas Tea. Meg had once asked to have lemonade in it for her own Victorian tea party and was promptly tossed a pair of Dixie cups and directed to the garden hose.

When Old Hadley woke up an hour later, Meg and Grandma pretended that nothing was different, as if an old gardener wouldn't notice new flowers. His eyes moved from blossom to blossom until there wasn't a one they had not touched. He closed his eyes and smiled.

ॐ

"What we're seeing on your x-rays is something called pnuemocystis pnuemonia," Dr. Buckerfield said, his pale eyes entirely sorry and grim behind a pair of large wire-rimmed glasses. He sat in a chair next to Old Hadley's bed, hugging a metal chart to his chest. "That's a lung infection, Mr. Crump."

Grandma stood in the doorway rubbing her palms up and down on her skirt. Meg perched on the edge of the bed.

"How do you fix it?" Old Hadley asked.

The doctor looked to be giving the matter some serious thought. "There's a real effective medicine for treating normal cases of pnuemocystis. I'm afraid this isn't a normal case."

"Leave it to Hadley to be abnormal," Grandma said, but she sounded like she might cry.

Dr. Buckerfield licked his lips. "Have you read anything about Gay Compromise Syndrome, Mr. Crump?"

"What's that?"

"An alarming number of people have been coming down with this new strain of pneumonia in the last year or so," the doctor said. "It's mostly homosexuals becoming infected."

It was a question, of sorts. A question that made Meg squirm. Suddenly, she knew exactly what Dr. Buckerfield was talking about. The bank had let a man go last month at the Biloxy branch. He was sick with homosexual cancer, and there was concern he'd infect the costumers. She seemed to recall that a fight had broken out at the Saint Jude's Food Pantry not long ago over something similar. A young priest was charged with hitting a sick homeless man. He claimed the man was endangering others at the shelter.

Poor Old Hadley. No wonder he never married.

It was Grandma's cackle that answered the doctor's dangling question. "Hadley's not a homosexual, Dr. Buckerfield."

"Thank you, Mrs. Worth-Holmes, but maybe we'd best let Mr. Crump speak for himself," Dr. Buckerfield said. He gave Old Hadley's arm a soothing pat. "It's a private matter, of course." Initially, the doctor had tried to persuade Old Hadley to speak with him alone. "Is there some chance it could be this new disease?"

Old Hadley's eyes lit up for the first time. "Nope. No chance at all. Guess you better look for a different diagnosis, Dr. Buckerfield." Old Hadley rubbed his wrinkly brow. "Whew. You scared me for a minute there."

Dr. Buckerfield didn't look convinced. "I'm sorry. I guess I made a false assumption." He was a new doctor, and Old Hadley had not been to see him until his recent troubles. Dr. Buckerfield opened the chart and started flipping through the pages. "What about this splenectomy you had some years back?" he said as he flipped. "There's some recent information suggesting that some bad blood might have worked it's way into the blood banks. Did you have any transfusions with your surgery, do you recall?"

The color dropped from Old Hadley's face. Grandma's hands fell to her sides.

"Ah, here it is!" Dr. Buckerfield cried, looking almost pleased. "I see here that you had a partial removal of your spleen about fifty years ago, and they had to take the rest in October 1977. Three transfusions were done. If it's true that you caught this from one of your transfusions, your case could be very important in understanding more about Gay Compromise." He looked up from the paperwork. "For one thing, we might need to find a new name for this thing, eh?"

"Can you make me better?" Old Hadley said.

The doctor closed the chart. "At this point, no. But scientists are learning more everyday. I realize you're very weak right now, Mr. Crump, but I'd like you to come down to the Hermosa Avenue Clinic tomorrow if you think you might be able. I volunteer there on Wednesday afternoons with a researcher named Dr. Simon. We've been working with patients with similar health concerns. I'd like to have Dr. Simon look at you."

Grandma cackled again. "You expect us to carry him there, I guess?"

Meg had one vacation day she'd been saving for a long weekend in Vegas with her friend Annie. "I could take off tomorrow and help you get him there, Grandma."

Dr. Buckerfield nodded at Meg. "Thank you for that. This is important."

The next day, Meg and her grandmother spruced Old Hadley up and put him in some clean clothes. "I don't see why they think he has this gay sickness," Grandma kept muttering. "Waste of time, is all it is."

"We're lucky Dr. Buckerfield knows someone who might be able to help," Meg reminded her grandmother. Old Hadley was tired, feverish, and in some pain, but he didn't make a peep until after Grandma complained for the tenth or twelfth time.

"Wouldn't it be funny, Lucinda, if it turned out I was a homosexual fellow and didn't never know it?"

He was steadier on his feet than Meg might have hoped, but he took to snoring on the drive to the clinic, and it wasn't but fifteen minutes away.

"Looks awful crowded," Grandma said as they pulled up to the little brick building. Indeed, there were a lot of people at the Hermosa Avenue Clinic on this bright and beautiful afternoon. Meg wondered just how many people had come down with this new 'condition'.

"Must be giving away free china," Grandma joked.

Meg parked on the front curb, intending to pull around back after she helped Old Hadley walk through the front door. She'd barely gotten him out of the passenger seat when grandma said, "Here comes Dr. Buckerfield."

Meg heard him shouting something across the parking lot, but the crowd of people in front of the clinic was so thick it was hard to hear. She looked up just in time to see the man with the brick. Meg saw the brick, and then she saw Dr. Buckerfield waving his arms. He was mouthing the words: "Go back!"

But it was too late. Old Hadley stood on his shaky legs, looking frailer than ever in the full light of day. "Look!" Someone shouted. "It's one of them!"

The brick sailed past Meg's cheek close enough to graze her skin. It hit the car mirror, and glass flew. One piece opened a cut on Old Hadley's forehead. Blood gushed down his face and dripped off his chin onto his shirt.

There was a lot of screaming and shouting after this. "Queer blood!" someone hollared. The crowd began to scatter, running for cars or taking off down the street on foot.

Dr. Buckerfield took hold of Old Hadley's elbow and began steering him toward the clinic. "Let's get him inside."

Grandma was out of the car by now, and she planted herself in their path. "Put him back in the car, Meg. This was a terrible mistake."

Everyone started talking all at once then. " . . . might need a stitch." "He's bleeding, Grandma!" "There's entirely too much danger."

Old Hadley held his tongue while they all fought to be heard. He must have been waiting for them to shut-up. When this didn't happen, he raised a shaky hand in the air like a student wishing to be called upon. Meg stopped mid-sentence. So did Dr. Buckerfield. Even Grandma got quiet. "I want to see Dr. Simon," Old Hadley said.

"But you're bleeding all over the place," Grandma protested.

Old Hadley shook his bleeding head. "Move out of the way, Lucinda. The doctor here said this was important, remember?"

Grandma sneered. "And you do so love feeling important, don't you?"

Meg wanted to smack her grandmother for being so cruel. The man's face was covered with blood. He could hardly even see.

"We drove down here to talk to Dr. Simon, and I mean to go in there right now." He pointed a long old finger at the clinic.

For a moment or two, Old Hadley and Grandma glared at one another, and then a rare thing happened. Grandma stepped aside.

℘

The forehead needed six stitches so they worked on that first. Dr. Buckerfield apologized half a dozen times. "There was a report in the newspaper this morning from the CDC saying there's been four hundred and fifty-two cases now in twenty-three different states," he explained. "We've never had trouble like this before but the paper called it a gay epidemic, and I guess people are scared."

"Me too," said Old Hadley.

Dr. Simon had an owlish sort of look which made him seem wise. He had a nice plain way of speaking, too. They did x-rays, stained sputum, and took Hadley's blood. The official results would not be available for a few days, but Dr. Simon was convinced that Old Hadley had Pneumocystis carinii Pneumonia and that the infection was the result of a bad blood transfusion.

"But Hadley got that blood transfusion five years ago," Grandma said.

Dr. Simon said it was possible that Old Hadley could have gotten it from a transfusion even it was ten years ago. "We just don't know much about this right now. It's only in the last few months that we've begun to understand that you don't have to be a gay men to be infected."

He told Old Hadley that he could temporarily relieve some of his symptoms, but he could not cure him.

"You mean I'm going to die from this?" Old Hadley asked.

Dr. Simon looked him straight in the eye. "I'm afraid so, Mr. Crump."

Meg had been expecting something bad, but still, it was a hard thing to hear. Grandma sniffled in a handkerchief and shook her head.

"Is it contagious?" Old Hadley asked.

"The wisest thing I can suggest at this point is that we get some x-rays and bloodwork done on these two ladies. I don't want to sound any false alarms, but we consider partners, spouses, and caregivers to be at risk."

Meg felt her heart grind momentarily to a stop. She'd been exposed to a deadly disease! She was at risk. She was only twenty years old. Old Hadley looked mortified. "We must find out right away!"

"I think that's for the best," Dr. Simon agreed.

Grandma cried harder.

"Even though I can't offer you any real hope of survival, Mr. Crump, I would like you to think about undergoing some more extensive testing. It could be a tremendous help to others. The only way to stop this illness from spreading is to learn all we can from those who have contracted it."

"Are you off your rocker?" Grandma snapped. "Someone threw a brick at him today. How can you expect any more of the man?"

"It's a lot to ask, I understand that. Some of the tests will be more invasive than the ones we did today. But if people are becoming infected from this killer blood, and I really believe they are, it's vital we find out what' going on as soon as possible."

"Can you gaurentee his safety, Dr. Simon?" Grandma wanted to know.

"We'll take better precautions next time, I can promise you that much."

"But you can't promise that there won't be more imbiciles throwing things at us when we get out of the car next time, can you? And you can't guarentee that Meg and me won't get our skulls cracked either."

Dr. Simon made the mistake of looking unsure.

"Forget it," Grandma said. "Come on you two, we're going home."

"I'll do the tests," Old Hadley said.

Grandma looked ready to choke the life out of him. Surely she would have given into the urge if he wasn't all bandaged and pathetic.

Old Hadley sat up tall in his chair. "Maybe they can't save me, Lucinda, but if there's some small chance we can make it walk, I want to do it."

"Make it *walk*?" Dr. Simon said.

"It's a pinochle term," Old Haldey said. "It's a way for a low card to win a trick. We're a couple of old pinochle players, you see."

"This isn't a card game," Grandma said. "The only thing I want to make walk is you, now come on." She picked up her purse, put on her hat, and stomped to the door, expecting Meg and Old Hadley to follow.

"I'm going to do the tests, Lucinda." Old Hadley rubbed his taped head. "In all my years, I don't guess I've ever done much to change anything. I've taken the world as I found it, and I do believe I've made the best of it. I reckon I thought that's what I was supposed to do. But I'm old now and I've lived a long time. These tests are a small thing and I mean to have them. You and Meg must get some tests done, too."

Grandma's eyes were teary red and sparking with fury. When she slammed out of the office, Dr. Simon visibly sighed a sigh of relief. "I know this is very hard on everyone involved, but now that your wife has stepped out of the room, I wonder if I could ask a different favor of you, Mr. Crump? I was a little afraid to bring it up before."

Meg whispered a silent thank you to the Lord that her grandmother didn't hear Dr. Simon mistake her for Old Hadley's wife. She was upset enough as it was.

"If I could arrange for your safety, how would you feel about making a trip to a medical center in Birmingham, Alabama?" the doctor asked.

"Alabama?" For some reason this made Old Hadley's face light up bright as a Christmas tree. "Well now, isn't that something."

❧

For Meg, waiting for her test results was an excruitating experience. Panic took hold of every spare second of her life that wasn't suitably mired in distraction. In vivid detail, she recalled every balled up Kleenex she'd retrieved from under Old Hadley's bed in the last few weeks. She'd washed her hands over and over again, she reminded herself. But did she wash well enough? Sometimes she was in a hurry.

Laying in bed at night, she wondered about the temperture of the dishwater she used to clean Old Hadley's drinking glasses. Was it hot enough to kill his deadly germs? And what about that half empty bag of peanut M&Ms she'd found in the cabinet and dipped into one night when she hadn't gotten a chance to eat dinner. It seemed impossible that she could have avoided catching his terminal illness.

Whenever there was a lull in customers at the bank, she'd find herself standing frozen behind the counter, listening to Dr. Simon with his kindly owl eyes speaking to her inside her head, informing her that there was no hope.

It terrified her that she could not daydream him saying, "The tests have come back, and everything is fine."

She sat in her car on her lunchbreak and practiced giving her parents the bad news. She rehearsed what to say when her friends learned that she was dying. She wept on her tuna sandwiches.

Grandma was cranky so no change there. Whether this was due to a fear of dying or rage over Old Hadley's intentions to put himself in harm's way for tests that could not possibly beneifit him in any way or simply just her usual unpleasant funk, who could say? She refused to discuss anything relating to Old Hadley's illness. She refused to say much of anything at all.

Old Hadley looked placid enough, but he jumped everytime Meg or Grandma wallked through the bedroom door. "Anything?"

Meg didn't like having to put on a happy face for him when she was worried sick inside, but acting like everything would be okay had the unexpected effect of helping her believe that it might. Truth be told, their shared case of nerves about the test results provided a temporary excuse to worry about something besides his own very real, very much confirmed diognoisis.

"Do you want to talk about it?" she asked him one afternoon.

He shook his head. "My prayers are tied up with other business right now."

The call finally came at 3 o'clock on a Thursday afternoon at the bank. Meg was not supposed to receive personal phone calls, but she'd requested to be notified about her test results the first minute they were available. When prune-faced Miss Dutton motioned her over to her desk and held out the phone, Meg gave no thought to the evil look she got.

"Yes?" she gasped into the receiver.

"I'm pleased to tell you, Margaret, that your test revealed nothing suspicious or out of the ordinary in the least," Dr. Simon said. Meg's knees gave out, and she let out a sharp cry. Dutton was so shocked, the wrinkles on her face fell away, and she looked half-way human for half a second. A teenage boy signing up for a savings account gawked at her. "Carry on with good hand-washing and follow all the precautions on the form we gave you . . . " the doctor was saying, and Meg solemnly vowed that she would.

Dr. Simon could not share Grandma's results, and when Meg risked losing her job to ring the old woman at home, she got no answer. Waiting out the rest of her shift until five was second only in agony to waiting for her test results. The drive to Grandma's had never seemed longer. When she reached Wisteria Walk, she found a note scotch-taped to the front door.

Meg,
Please tell Hadley that I am not going to die. I hope as much for you. I am off to bed now.
Grandma

⊂ℛ

The University of Alabama sent a special medical team to travel with Old Hadley. They were springing for the airfare, too, and Old Hadley was tickled pink. He'd never been on an airplane before. Since the incident at the Hemrosa Avenue Clinic and her own misable experience with testing, Meg had noticed a lot of news stories about the general state of unrest going on. There were doctors who feared treating the disease. An infected college student had not been allowed to return to class. No one could promise Old Hadley that there would not be another angry mob on hand when they got to the medical center in Alabama, but this time they would be on the lookout for trouble.

With three full weeks of medication in him, Old Hadley was feeling improved and excited. He'd never been to Alabama before, and he got a dreamy look in his eyes anytime the word Alabama came up.

Grandma, on the other hand, was still treating them both decidedly cool. Her anger (or was it sorrow?) was turning her into a crazy old woman, and Meg was worried about her state of mind. The day before old Hadley was to leave for his trip, she gave Meg a musty old snow muff made of white fur and asked her to pack it in Hadley's suitcase. "Don't look at me like that, girl. Just put in there with his shirts. He's going to need it."

"In Alabama?" Meg said.

"Yes, in Alabama. You don't know everything, missy."

On the appointed day, Meg drove her grandma to the airport so they could see him off. They stood at a window and waved as his plane taxied down the runway. Well, Meg waved. Grandma was still too bent out of shape about the trip to do anything but scowl at him through the glass. He was to be gone two weeks.

Poor Patti Carol. She had no choice but to play pinochle in Old Hadley's place every afternoon. The clock in the hall ticked extra loud and extra slow as they shuffled their cards. It was so loud, one could barely hear Meg's feeble attempt at small talk under the tick tick tick. The only thing to cover the sound was the sporadic fits of fury that erupted whenever Patti Carol lost.

Meg was back to bringing Big Macs. At first, every bite stuck in her throat, refusing to go down, but she learned to combat this by pretending that Old Hadley was out digging in the garden. The strategy worked well until the third day when Grandma dipped a French fry in a pool of ketchup on her china plate and said, "Hadley's going to die."

No one had mentioned this out loud since Dr. Simon had spelled it all out in his office. Old Hadley went home that day, took his medicine, and asked for a map and a red Magic Marker so he could trace the way to Birmingham. No one mentioned dying.

"Maybe it will take years," Meg said. This was the only thing she could think to hope for. He was already an old man. Two or three more years would be about ordinary, wouldn't it? "He's had a long life."

"You only say that because you're not sitting where I am, Meg. Doesn't seem long to me at all. I want longer." She pushed her half-eaten burger away.

"Not to worry, Grandma. You're so stubborn, I don't guess you'll die a minute sooner than you choose to."

"Damned right I won't," Grandma said.

Meg's mother was still too busy to visit, even with Old Hadley out of the way, but she did send Tilda over with a crock pot of beanies and weenies one night. She paid the boy who cut their grass to cut Grandma's grass, too. And the second week that Old Hadley was gone, she made an applesauce cake and wrapped up three pieces for Meg to take to Grandma.

"I like chocolate better," Grandma said when Meg gave her the cake.

It was a long two weeks.

On the day Hadley flew home, Meg skipped her lunch break so she could leave an hour early and take Grandma to the airport to meet him. Grandma was furious that he had not called home even once.

"I have half a mind to ring the little cheapskate's neck when I see him," she said as she waited for him to deplane at the gate. She tapped her foot and called him ten bad names for every minute that passed. Ungrateful son of a bitch. Thoughtless fool. Worthless no good shifty-eyed skinny-ass ugly old Negro with gay disease . . .

"Hi," he said, as his medical team rolled him off the plane in a wheelchair. He looked well enough, in spite of the wheelchair. He handed Grandma a bouquet of flowers.

"What's this?" she asked.

"Azaleas. I carried them all the way from Alabama."

The woman who was pushing his chair confirmed this. "He held them in one hand and ate with the other."

"Smell 'em," Old Hadley said. "They smell just like lemons."

Grandma took a tentative sniff.

"Don't get too attached to them though," he said. "You have to share them with Meg. I picked them for the both of you."

☙

God sure did know how to throw a mean curve ball. Meg's friends wondered what had happened to her since she'd all but disappeared off the planet. Some thought it sweet when they found out she'd been spending her evenings with her grandma. Some thought she was weird. "But you don't even like your grandma," Brenda James said. Brenda was the sub on Meg's bowling team, and she felt put out because she'd been promised she'd only need to fill in here and there, not every week.

"Oh, she's completely awful," Meg said. "But I'm all she has right now."

After Old Hadley got back from Alabama, her time was more her own. He was tired after the trip, but whatever they were giving him, he was not as sick as he was before. A few days after his return, he rubbed Grandma's stinky old snow muff against his cheek and passed it back to the old woman.

"Thanks for letting me borrow this, Lucinda," he said, like he'd walked around Alabama wearing her silly fur muff. Either he was humoring Grandma or they were both a little nuts. It was hard to tell with old people.

In any case, Grandma seemed less angry. Things felt more stable. Meg went back to visiting once a week. Old Hadley went back to his garden. He said he well might be the first person to survive Gay-related Immune Deficiency, which is what they were calling the disease in Alabama.

For a while, it seemed like this might be true. Even Buckerfield and Simon were amazed by how well their old patient was faring. But the newspapers didn't have anything promising at all to say about GRID. It crossed Meg's mind a time or two to worry whether or not she could become infected. Buckerfield said no and Simon referred again and again to the Good Handwashing sheet. She washed her hands sore most days even so, a fact that caused her a good bit of shame even as she felt helpless to stop herself. One day she realized that, if they were to suddenly announce that the disease was catching through casual contact, she was hopelessly screwed.

Somehow this freed her of the hand-washing compulsion. It also gave her a new appreciation for the fear that was griping the country. It was terrifying to think that this disease could slip into your blood and sleep there for years, waiting to reveal itself.

"Aren't you scared?' she asked Old Hadley once.

"Sure I am." He was putting away the pinochle cards at the time. "No one wants to be sick."

"You don't seem to be letting it bother you," she observed.

"Oh, I've always been good at looking unbothered," Old Hadley said.

His health remained decent through Meg's birthday the following March, which seemed a minor miracle. He'd taken sick the previous spring, recovered by June, and had been feeling well for almost a full year. Between this and the fact that it was Meg's twenty-first birthday, there was a lot to celebrate.

She had plans to go to a bar with some girls from work so Grandma was organizing an afternoon party for the family, a luncheon catered by her favorite restaurant. The dining room had been set up for fourteen guests, and Meg was excited.

A week earlier, her mom had asked what she wanted for her birthday. It was clear by the way the woman clapped her hands that she expected Meg to say she wanted a new tape deck or the fringy black dress they'd seen at the mall. "Name it, honey. This is a special birthday, and I want you to be happy."

"Good," Meg said. "Because what I really want more than anything in the world is for you to patch things up with Grandma."

God! She might as well have asked her mom to cut off her own head and fork it over on a platter. "You can't ask for that, Meg. That has nothing to do with you. It's private."

Meg was determined that things were going to change. Life was too short for this kind of nonesense. "And I want you to say hi to Old Hadley at my birthday luncheon, too. I'm tired of watching you ignore him every year like he doesn't count."

Mom gave their cat, Ichabod, a little kick with her foot. She knew Old Hadley might not have long to live, but she hated to give up a fight. "Its just so quixotic of you to even ask for such a thing," she snapped. Mom was fond of using bizarre words that nobody understood. "Oh all right. I'll do it. But only because it's your birthday."

On the day of her party, Meg arrived early because Grandma said she had something special to give her before everyone else arrived. It was a book called *The Meaning of Flowers*, and it looked very old. "Hadley gave me this years ago, and I thought you might find it interesting."

Meg was too stunned to speak. Grandma was known for giving meaningless gifts. Meg had more monogramed fingertip towels than the law allows. Too touched to do anything else, she gave her grandmother the first real hug she'd ever given her.

"It's just a crumbling old book," Grandma said.

Before the doorbell started ringing, Meg went into the dining room and rearranged the place cards. She put her mother across from Old Hadley and next to Grandma, even though Grandma originally had Mom at the other end between the two boys. She reminded herself to be happy if her grandma and her mother would simply drop The Nod and actually say a few real words to each other. She had especially high hopes when it came to Old Hadley.

Ever since Mom had heard he was terminal, she'd been better about asking after him. She even looked a little worried on occasion. Old Hadley was the main reason Meg had asked her mother for this particular gift this year. The old man had watched Meg's mom grow up and for some unfathomable reason, he still seemed to care how she treated him, even though it was never good. If Mom would just say hello to him, it would make his day, Meg was sure of it. He perked right up when Meg told him that Mom was looking forward to seeing for herself how he was doing today. She wondered if the new blue shirt he was wearing was for Mom. The color somehow made him look more robust than normal. Then again, maybe he was just in a good mood.

Meg's cousin Joanie was the first to arrive, then her brother Henry who had come from work. Old Hadley and Grandma each had a tray of Mimosas, and they were cirulating the room. At twenty minutes past twelve, Grandma had everyone sit down to eat. Mom, Dad, and Stephen had yet to arrive, but the stew was starting to congeal. "Leave it to Nina to ruin my oxtails," Grandma said.

Meg was angry too. This was no way to make peace. When the doorbell finally rang at 12:35, she and Old Hadley both jumped up expectedly. "You eat your soup," Meg said. "I'll let them in."

Meg opened the door and Stephen and her father and both pushed past into the dining room, the former carrying a plate of brownies covered with clingwrap, the latter bearing a bottle of champagne. Dad went directly to Grandma and gave her his customary kiss on the cheek. "Sorry to be so late, Lucinda. Nina came down with the flu at that last moment, and we got held up."

"The flu?" Meg said. "But she was fine when I left this morning."

Dad shrugged. "Came on out of the blue, honey. What can I say?"

Grandma, of course, looked like she could care less. Meg glanced at Old Hadley, but his eyes were on his soup.

The next day, her mother handed her a stripped box with a big purple bow.

It was the fringy black dress.

Meg smiled in spite of her hangover and gave her mother a good long hug. "Thanks Mom. It'll be just the thing for the funeral."

ᘓ

The pnuemocystis was back by the first of April, and Old Hadley was sent to bed with fevers, shakes, and bonebreaking coughs. In point of fact, he broke a rib from all the coughing.

Like before, he missed the best of the blooming season, but this time Meg was prepared. She'd gone to the Dollar Store for cheap vases so as to save on ketchup and pickles. Everyone thought Grandma was crazy for tearing up her beautiful gardens again when Mr. Brix might easily have delivered all the flowers they needed.

Grandma scoffed. "As if anyone else's flowers are half as beautiful as these."

It was true. There was something about Grandma's gardens that, try as they might, no other green thumb in town could ever seem to match. Berries were juicier, roses more luminous. The wisteria crept and curled and cascaded as precisely as a symphony. And you'd never tasted pawpaws until you tasted the rich, custardy pawpaws that grew at Wiseria Walk. The air around Old Hadley's flowers had a distinctive flavor that verged on sweet cream and almonds. And the smell!

People habitually stopped on the sidewalk, placed a hand over their heart, and closed their eyes. The mailman unwrapped his sandwich in front of the house every day and sat down with a smile on the curb to polish off his bologna. Even after Meg and her grandma cut down all the flowers last year, people still stopped on the sidewalk, and the mailman still opened his lunch on the curb. It was like the air around the house was so used to smelling like Lily of the Valley, it forgot to stop even after the tiny white bells were gone.

Unquestionably, Old Hadley must have his own flowers. The difference this time was that Meg couldn't help but wonder what would happen to the community if Old Hadley never got back on his feet again. For instance, how would people ever know that Spring is Here if the wisteria went to ruin? To those that counted on such things, Old Hadley's garden was the only clock of it's kind. What would Beatie's Bluff do if that tender clock were to break?

It was sad watching Old Hadley wither to bone, but Meg felt a tender feeling for the flower-arranging. So much about this awful disease left her feeling helpless. The flowers were something concrete they could do to make him feel better. And it worked.

"Smells like Lily of the Valley in here," Old Hadley said when he woke up to his inside garden. There was coughing, sure, but there was Lily of the Valley, too.

It kept them busy, anyway. Meg would clear a space for a vase of tulips and spend several minutes turning it in different directions, adjusting the angle of each flower until it was in the most pleasing of positions when viewed from the bed. Grandma would come in and do the same with her pot or vase, then she would head straight to Meg's perfectly centered tulips, pick them up, and move them to a stack of books or a dresser top and fiddle with the arrangement. "There now. It won't do to have the red tulips clashing with the hyacinths."

If she was honest enough to admit it, there were more than a few peevish moments when Meg felt resentful of how much time Grandma and Old Hadley took from her. Most of her friends were out dancing every night at Wingdings, and Meg made a point of doing this, too, when she wasn't busy running in the Dollar Store for vases or picking up her grandma's gardener for a doctor appointment. Even before Old Hadley started to slip again, it sometimes felt like they had become her whole world. On the day they brought the flowers inside, she could easily have made it home in time for a shower and grabbed a bite before meeting her friends at eight. She called to cancel though. Not because she had to, but rather because she wanted to sit with Grandma and Old Hadley and enjoy what they had created.

"Sure is pretty," someone would say, and they would all agree and marvel at the flowers in silence for a while.

The illness seemed worse this time around, or maybe it was just that they all knew how deadly it was. Grandma kept saying he'd recover the same as he did before, but Dr. Buckerfield always said goodbye when he left like he was saying goodbye forever and Meg often found herself checking for a heartbeat whenever he slept. Once the first batch of blooms were done, Meg was the one to arrange for deliveries. Grandma started slipping away with Old Hadley and the flowers, and the only way Meg could keep them all going was to pull out the dead roses and tulips and bring in fresh ones. It became necessary to stop in every day after work to make sure nothing was drooping.

"What do you make of all this business, Meg?" Old Hadley asked one day.

"If you mean your illness, I'd have to say, I think it's horribly unfair."

Old Hadley was propped up against a big pile of bedpillows, and he looked horribly small. He had one finger in *The Hotel New Hampshire* to hold his spot. "How do you figure?"

"Most people are getting this from sleeping around. You got it in a hopsital from a medical procedure."

Old Hadley rubbed his chin. "I see what you're saying. All the fuss and none of the fun. I never have been good at doing things the right way," he chuckled. "At least you're here, I got that much going for me. And soon I'll be seeing my mama. She's going to hit me up with a whole lot of *I told you so's*, and I'm just thankful God gave me a little time to prepare."

Meg touched his cheek, pretending to check for fever. "I liked what you said in Dr. Simon's office about making it walk. It was very brave of you to go to Birmingham."

He shook his head. "I had a handful of reasons for going to Birmingham, and I don't think being brave was one of them. I'm just doing what anyone would do in my shoes—looking for a way to win."

"A lot of people in your shoes would be too busy thinking about what they're losing to realize there might be anything at all to win."

"Maybe they need to take up pinocle," he said.

After that, Meg didn't feel so peevish anymore. She told Brenda James to go on and finish off the bowling league. She told her friends to count her out at Wingdings. She raided the old toyroom at home for board games and carted them over to Old Hadley's house. Grandma was quite taken with Hi Ho Cherry-O.

She also made up a schedule, of sorts, to help pass the evenings. Mondays were *Make Grandma Eat a Big Mac Night.* Tuesdays were *Change the Sheets & Take a Shower Night.* Wednesday's were *Stay Up Late and Watch Dynasty Night.* And every night was *Game Night.* When Old Hadley couldn't manage *Drink Your Water Night* due to the painful sores in his throat, Meg considered taking him to the hospital.

He wanted to stay in his home, he said. The medicine wasn't working so well this time, and there was nothing much they could do for him. "If I'm going to get better, I stand the best chance of it here in my own house. If I'm not, well, I'll not get better here best in my own house, too. Either way, I don't mean to miss out on *Dynasty* or losing to your grandmother at *Clue.*"

Old Hadley didn't even like *Dynasty,* but he sure did enjoy ribbing Grandma about it. Sometimes the only spark he got all week long was the spark he got when he pretended they were going to watch *The Facts of Life* instead, and Grandma had to beg and plead and fluff his pillows until he'd agree to let them switch the channel.

Some days it seemed like these little tifs were the only thing to keep them going. Grandma was exhausted trying to help him. Patti Carol had left six months ago when she overheard Dr.

Buckerfield mention GRID. They hired a nurse named Shaniqua Brown to come for eight hours during the day, and this helped. Shaniqua was a big bossy black gal, though, and Grandma didn't care for her one little bit.

"Got no use for bossy people," Grandma said.

This set Meg and Old Hadley to laughing until they both could hardly catch their breath. Still, it wasn't like people were lining up for the job so Grandma was stuck with bossy Shaniqua.

℞

Eventually, Old Hadley got too weak to even move Colonal Mustard around or put little plastic cherries on a tree. About the only thing he opened his eyes for was the news story Meg read him about a group in San Fransisco that had banded together to promote awareness of the disease.

"I hope they kick its ass," Old Hadley croaked in a voice so raspy, the words sounded more like coughs than speech.

Buckerfield told Meg that he didn't have long. Many a night, she'd stood over his bed with her hand pressed to his heart, whispering, "Please oh please oh please." It was always such a relief to feel his heart still beating in there. Then, a funny thing happened one Saturday morning when she went to check on him. She peeked in the bedroom and discovered Old Hadley out of bed and wearing his old coveralls.

Grandma was holding a pair of carpenter's pants pinched between two fingers, sneering at a brown splotch across the seat. "And what about this one? Are you sure it's paint?"

"What else would it be?" Old Hadley asked.

Grandma snorted. "You're an old man. Lord knows."

"Hello, Meg," Old Hadley said when he saw her standing in the doorway. "Your grandma and I are going to paint my bedroom."

Meg almost fell over. "You've been laying in bed for weeks."

Drop cloths had been spread over the furniture and floor. The containers of flowers formed an explosive garden off in one corner. "What's your hurry all of a sudden?"

He shrugged his bony shoulders. "I'm tired of the color."

Meg glanced at the bedroom walls. "They don't have a color."

"Precisely," he said.

She didn't know how he managed to stand when he couldn't even managed to sit the day before. Still, his face looked more brown than gray at the moment, and he was stirring a can of paint with some of his former vigor.

"Well, this is quite a change," Meg said.

Grandma leaned on Meg and stepped into the carpenter's pants with the brown stain. "He could have painted this room a thousand times over yet he waits until today."

"Couldn't do it until today," he said.

"Why the hell not, you doddering old fool?" Grandma said.

"Didn't know what color to make it."

Grandma gave Meg a pointed look and made the cuckoo sign.

"What color did you pick, Old Hadley?" Meg asked, twisting to look over Grandma's shoulder as the woman fought to work her highheel through the pants.

"Magenta," he said.

"That seems an odd color for a man," Meg said.

"It is an odd color for a man," he agreed. "Did you know that Newton didn't even put magenta on his color wheel? He believed that only the spectral colors counted." Old Hadley smiled and stirred his magenta paint. "Now Goethe, on the other hand, he argued that magenta was the natural result of mixing violet with red in the dark spectrum, just the same as mixing blue and yellow in the light spectrum will give you green. You see, I was reading *Theory of Colors* last night. Goethe thought magenta was an essential color."

"Blah blah blah. What does that have to do with the price of tea in China?" Grandma asked.

Old Hadley quoted a poem for her:

Should your glance on mornings lovely,
  Lift to drink the heaven's blue
Or when sun, veiled by sirocco,
  Royal red sinks out of view -
Give to Nature praise and honor.

Blithe of heart and sound of eye,
Knowing for the world of colour
Where its broad foundations lie.

He stood up with a wince and a creak. "Goethe said that." He picked out a paintbrush from a pile on the floor. "Would you like to help, Meg?"

The three of them stood before the first dingy wall, contemplating where to begin. "I knew a woman once who painted her walls the most God-awful shade of red," Old Hadley said.

"And how is this different?" Grandma asked.

"It isn't. What you got to understand is that it's about how the color makes you feel. That woman, she needed to make her walls red at the time."

Meg couldn't stop looking at them both. How could he be well enough to paint a wall? And Grandma! It would have been funny enough to see her in pants, but carpenter's pants?

"I always start with a message when I paint," Old Hadley said. "Some little thing that will secretly live on underneath the color."

"You do?" Grandma asked. "Do all my walls have secret messages hidden under their colors?"

"Every single one of them. Now what sort of message shall we put on this wall?"

"If no one knows it's there, what good is it?" Grandma wondered.

"We'll know it's there."

Meg dipped her brush in the magenta paint. "I don't mean to get all corny with this, but Old Hadley has taught me something that I hope I never forget. Maybe we could paint that on the wall, just to be on the safe side?"

"What is it?" Grandma said. "Never sit in poop-colored paint?"

"No, Grandma. He's taught me that you don't have to just lay down and die just because you're going to die. I've played a lot of pinochle with you both, yet I never understood until now that there is more than one way to win. I propose we paint one word each. Grandma, you get MAKE. I'll go in the middle with IT. Old Hadley can do WALK.

"That is corny," Grandma said, but she went up to the wall and painted her word in curly, pink letters. Meg made her letters big and wide. Old Hadley finished like a pro, his lettering beautiful and strong. They all stood back to admire their work.

MAKE IT WALK

"Needs an exclamation point," Meg said.

Somehow, all signs of illness seemed to evaporate as they slapped on coat after coat of bright paint. They opened the windows, and the sun came in, and when magenta splattered on Grandma's shoes, she didn't even stop to wipe them off.

Old Hadley knew grandma when she was a child, and Meg asked him what she was like back then. "Was she as sassy as she is now?"

There was a time when Meg would have never voiced such a thing out loud for fear of the repercussions, but the strokes of noisy pink paint made her feel bold.

"She was terrifying," Old Hadley said as he meticulously cut in around the door. "Some things never change."

"He always thought he was so special. I had to knock him down a peg or two," Grandma said.

"Her hair wasn't that phony color of yellow that it is now," Old Hadley continued.

Grandma looked like she might kick over the paint bucket.

"It was the color of butter," he said.

Grandma shook her paintbrush at Hadley. "He pretended he couldn't read so I would have to give him lessons."

"She liked giving lessons."

Meg wished now that she had never brought up their childhood. She hadn't meant to ruin the moment. It was always ticklish with Grandma.

"We read some wonderful books," Old Hadley said.

Grandma nodded. "We had a book club, believe it or not."

"We made up our own holiday."

Grandma looked down at the trail of little pink footprints she'd made across the drop cloth. "He was my closest friend." She slapped a few sloppy strokes over their message. "Pathetic, isn't it?"

The room was hot now, thanks to the sun. It smelled of paint and flowers, and everyone's skin was the color of a rose. The paint pinked everything. "It's like a sunset in here," Meg said.

"Or a sunrise," Old Hadley said.

Because he was beginning to look tired and there wasn't a good place to move the vases, they decided to paint around the flowers. White shadows in the shape of Ballerina roses remained on the magenta walls. "We can go back and get those later," Meg said. "Let's put you on the couch tonight."

A bed was made up in the other room, and Old Hadley looked sleepy but happy when she tucked him in. "Thank you," he said, and he squeezed her paint-stained fingers.

Meg cleaned the brushes under the hose outside and the grass and mud turned the color of Old Hadley's bedroom. She hammered the lid down on the paint can and left it by the front door so they could finish up another time. She hung the carpenter's pants next to Old Hadley's coveralls and took her grandmother back to her house. "We can move Old Hadley into his magenta bedroom tomorrow," Meg said.

❧

Meg stopped at the market for some milk and doughnuts the next morning, and when she paid Mr. Bing, she noticed there were dark crescents of magenta still clinging under her fingernails. The color made her smile.

When she opened Old Hadley's door, it was clear he'd already moved back into his bedroom. The house smelled of the work they'd done, and Meg pondered his other white walls, wondering what wild color they might make them. She put the doughnuts on a white china plate she found in the kitchen, poured three glasses of milk, and carried them on a tray into the magenta bedroom.

Grandma was back and sitting in a chair beside his bed with a book in her lap and a drop cloth bunched around her paint-dribbled shoes. She was fast asleep, and something about her looked different to Meg. She suspected it was all that lovely pink light. It softened her. Old Hadley was in bed, just as she'd guessed, and she tiptoed in, quiet as a mouse.

A jar on the nightstand caught her eye when she made room for the tray. Every vase, cup, bottle, and jar to be found had been confiscated for the indoor garden except for three glasses they'd saved for drinking. The jar stood out like a sore thumb. The word WHOOPS had been handpainted on one side, and there was nothing in it. *Now why did they empty this one?* Meg thought.

She glanced around at the mess they'd left behind, dropcloths splattered with multicolored drips from other walls and other secret messages, magenta-tipped paintsticks, the occasional loose nail scattered here and there on the floor, and the snow-white silouette of ballerina roses growing up one wall. *Perhaps we should leave that wall alone,* she thought? The white of the roses somehow made the magenta all the more special and beautiful.

With a little searching, she was able to spot the brushmarks that hid the message they made. As she patted the spot, it occurred to her that she'd not heard any coughing since she came into the room. Maybe Old Hadley really was going to make another amazing recovery?

He looked awfully still. She rested her magenta stained fingers on his chest and softly chanted, "Please oh please oh please."

Nothing.

She kept her hand on his quiet heart and whispered her prayer for a long time. Long enough for tears to fall on the tops of her fingers and slide away between them. "Grandma," she said. "He's gone."

At that same moment, she realized what was different about Grandma. She was wearing glasses! Grandma didn't own glasses. Grandma was like Mrs. Leaf across the street who could only hear half the words anyone ever spoke to her yet refused to be fitted for a hearing aid. She placed her hand on Grandma's chest, but this time she knew there was no point.

Just like that, on the same sunny morning, both of them were gone.

For the longest time, she stared at the glass full of purple-pink orhids that Grandma had arranged two days before. The flowers they'd shoved into the corner were crowded and mashing into each other, and Meg set about returning them to their appointed locations around the room, taking care to remember where Grandma had originally placed them, positioning flowers for optimum viewing. "There," she whispered.

Curious to know what the last book was that Lucinda Worth-Homes and Hadley Crump read together, Meg slid the worn volumn from her grandmother's grasp. It was a shabby, well-read thing and tucked between two pages near the very end was a yellowed recipe card printed in childish handwriting.

From the kitchen of . . .
Great Expectations
By Charles Dickens.

But, it is the same with any life. Imagine one selected day struck out of it, and think how different its course would have been. Pause you who read this, and think for a moment of the long chain of iron or gold, of thorns or flowers, that would never have bound you, but for the formation of the first link on one memorable day . . .

BONUS MATERIAL

V.I.L.E. Reading Selections

Rating System . . .

Juicy Swears !
Lots of Kissing x
Pain and Suffering +
Could Make You Go Blind *

Books

Anna Karenina x+

Age of Innocence x+

Tom Jones x+*

Romeo and Juliet x+

Portrait of the Artist as a Young Man +x

Great Expectations +x

Hunchback by Victor Hugo +

Adventures of Tom Sawyer !

Pit and the Pendulum by Edgar Allen Poe *

The Postman Always Rings Twice +x!*

Dracula by Bram Stoker +x

Ulysses x*

Venus Wears Furs x*+

Of Mice and Men !!

Lady Chatterley's Lover x+*

The Language of Flowers

Absinth: Torment of Love

Amaranth: Fidelity

Apple Blossoms: Good Fortune

Asparagus Fern: Fascination

Aster: Daintiness

Azalea: Ephemeral Passion

Begonia: Beware! I am fanciful

Bindweed: Busybody

Blue Bell: Delicacy

Buttercup: Childishness

Camellia – Red: You're a flame in my heart

Chrysanthemum, white: Truth

Clover: Fertility

Cockscomb: Silliness or foppery

Daffodil: Unrequited love

Dahlia: Good taste

Forsythia: Anticipation

Gardenia: I love you in secret

Heather: Protection from danger

Hollyhock: Fecundity

Hydrangea:
Thank you for understanding

Lavender: Constancy

Lily, day: Coquetry

Lily of the Valley: You've made my life complete

Monkey flowers:
One who performs
behind a mask

Phlox; Sweet dreams

Pecan: Hard to crack

Peony: Healing

Rose, dark pink: Thank you

Spider Flower: Elope with me

Tuberose: Dangerous pleasures

Wisteria: I cling to thee

Witch Hazel: A spell

Zinnia, pink: Lasting affection

Secret Names

Secret names for flowers arose long ago from a need to conceal the identity of certain herbs.

Lupine: Blood from a head

Tuberose: Mistress of the Night

Clover: Semen of Ares

Burdock: Love Leaves

Great Mullein: Peter's Staff

Vervain Sage: Christ's Eye

Wild Geranium: Shameface

Southernwood: Maiden's Ruin

Yarrow: Devil's Plaything

Goosegrass: Sweethearts

Meadowsweet: Queen of the Meadow

Blackberry: Scaldhead

Earflapology

A Sure Fire Method for Identifying Blessings and Peculiarities Through the Reading of Ears

1.) Large with loose lobes: Ambitious, gossipy, given to tell lies. Little ears with loose lobes, however, should be treated with even greater suspicion. Trust not a man whose lobes are disproportionate to his God-given ear size.

2.) Spotted or hairy when combined with a bald head: Gift for cobbling. Ought to make shoes or bricks.

3.) Feminine ears on a man: Gentle but foxy. A nice-dresser. Likes to dance.

4.) Small "c"-shaped: Expect complete candor. May prove disagreeable in bed. Likley to be bad with money.

5.) Pointy and wolfish: Of vital temperament. God-fearing but selfish. Will fix your plumbing when pressed.

6.) Small hemmed ears: Generous in nature. Deeply kind. Given to insanity.

7.) Curvy or vivacious: Untrustworthy. Mean-spirited. Covets jewels.

8.) Young ears on an old person: A good listener. Enjoys cake. Easily pleased. Soon to die.

9.) Flat: Knows their Bible. Slow to smile. Smells like fruit.

10.) Purplish around the edges: Subject to bouts of indecision and lower back fat.

11.) Square as a box: Noble, maternal, blows a lot of smoke but knows how to keep an open mind. Watch out if you forget to put your toys away.

12.) Resembling of a mushroom: Earthy. Savvy with herbs.

Reading Guide Questions

1. In The Reading Lessons, books serve as a form of communication, as an excuse for spending time together, and as a symbol of frustration. Taken as a whole, they are life changing for Hadley and Lucinda. Is there a book that changed your life?

2. Rather than writing a story about people fighting for racial equality, the author tried to point up the ridiculous nature of bigotry through the use of characters that are forced to go to desperate and tragic lengths in order to reinvent the world for themselves. Which of the following was most shocking to you: The unusual reading habits of V.I.L.E. Hadley's decision to give up a life with Flora and silently watch Nina grow-up from the sidelines. Or the fact that Hadley and Lucinda carried on a secret relationship that lasted a lifetime.

3. Many things have changed since the 1920s. Do you think Lucinda would marry Hadley if they met today?

4. While Hadley clearly longs to feel like he's someone special, he also accepts his lot in life without a great deal of thought or complaint. Keeping his coins in something called a Jolly Niger Bank or playing a game called the Coon Dip, for instance, are things that don't appear to phase him. At the end of the book, he sums up his "philosophy" fairly well when he says: "In all my years, I don't guess I've ever done much to change anything. I've taken the world as I found it, and I do believe I've made the best of it. I reckon I thought that's what I was supposed to do. " Do you find this outlook admirable at all, or does it make you angry?

5. Do you think Dickie knew his wife was having an affair with their gardener? If so, why do you think he tolerated it?

6. Hadley doesn't tell Nina that he might be her father, even when she vows to hate him forever. His life surely would have been in danger if the truth came out, but he also makes the choice to hold onto the secret so that Nina can continue to have a "proper" life with a mother and father who are married, and so that Nina will never become caught in the middle between being black and white. Did you find yourself wishing that he would spill the beans anyway? Does the fact that he becomes close to Meg at the end of the book make up for what he loses with Nina?

7. Lucinda, Flora, or Vaseline: Who do you think was the best fit for Hadley?

8. Being biracial, Hadley has the feeling that he's always stuck in the middle. Was there ever a situation in your life when fitting in proved impossible for reasons that were beyond your control?

9. If you had a WHOOPS Jar, would it be empty or full of nails?

10. Hadley experiences a great deal of pressure from his mama when it comes to having children. Mama's greatest wish is that Hadley's children will have both a mother and a father. In a very real sense, Hadley gives up both Flora and Nina because of this. Did your parents ever put pressure on you to do something that ended up altering the course of your life? As a parent, do you ever feel like you've pushed one of your kids to do something for reasons that have more to with your own personal issues than your child's best interest?

11. There is some irony to be found in the fact that the accident Hadley has as a result of an argument with Nina eventually leads to AIDS, which, in turn, leads to an unexpected bond with Meg. The two share something special in the end. Does it matter that Meg never finds out that Old Hadley might be her grandfather?

12. How is the fear and prejudice that Hadley experiences due to skin color the same as the fear and prejudice he experiences due to his illness in the 1980s?

13. Did you find Lucinda's treatment of Hadley unusual? Do you believe her behavior toward him stems from an evil flaw in her nature, or is it an attempt to protect her heart? Is it possible she's trying to protect Hadley's heart as well? If you removed the constraints placed on them by society, do you think their relationship would be less violent?

14. Some people have described the ending of The Reading Lessons as bittersweet. While Hadley is never able to marry Lucinda or publically acknowledge their relationship, they are together to the very end. Do you think the sacrifices they were forced to make in order to be together were in any way worthwhile?

About the Author

Carole Lanham has published twenty-four short stories and is the author of *The Whisper Jar*. She lives in the St. Louis area with her family and a large collection of aprons. Please drop in and say hello at carolelanham.com or horrorhomemaker.com.

Made in the USA
San Bernardino, CA
13 January 2014